Y0-DKO-217

Legacy
of the Priest

Deb
Good Reading
Stephe P Mulanee

Legacy
of the Priest

Stephen P. Matava

1075-MATA

Copyright © 2000 by Stephen P. Matava.

Library of Congress Number:		00-190300
ISBN #:	Hardcover	0-7388-1721-X
	Softcover	0-7388-1722-8

All rights reserved. No part of this book may be reproduced or transmitted in any form or by any means, electronic or mechanical, including photocopying, recording, or by any information storage and retrieval system, without permission in writing from the copyright owner.

This is a work of fiction. Names, characters, places and incidents either are the product of the author's imagination or are used fictitiously, and any resemblance to any actual persons, living or dead, events, or locales is entirely coincidental.

This book was printed in the United States of America.

To order additional copies of this book, contact:
Xlibris Corporation
1-888-7-XLIBRIS
www.Xlibris.com
Orders@Xlibris.com

Contents

1075-MATA

My wife, Helen
whose faith, understanding and support
made this work possible

1075-MATA

1

The Carpathian Mountains are a crescent shaped chain that runs from Bratislava, in the south of Slovakia, to Orsova in Rumania. The highest peaks are in north of Slovakia where the range is called the High Tatras. Although missionaries came to the small hamlets at the foot of the mountains, in the ninth century, to convert the Slovaks to Christianity, they failed their efforts. It was not until the Jesuits came from Italy to introduce the Christian faith that it finally took hold and work began on the Abbey of St. Francis in the small town of Ruzbachy in 1561. The town was founded on a level plain, next to the great forest that went up the slopes to the peaks of the High Tatras. It was divided into two actual towns, nizne (lower) Ruzbachy and vishnu (upper) Ruzbachy while the Poprad River separated the two. In the lower end of town lived the working class, the shop keepers, artisans and day laborers. There were little cottages with garden plots in back and flower gardens in front. In the upper section, large estates featured horse and dairy farms and acres and acres of land required to support them. Some of the people who lived in the lower end of town worked for those living in the upper end.

The bridge spanning the Poprad River was old and in need of repair. It was made of oak and constructed by forgotten artisans of past generations. It was narrow and meant for only one cart at a time but traffic moved steadily if the carts, going in different directions, alternated going over the bridge. The river was normally about ten yards wide, but each April, when snows melted in the High Tatras, the river overflowed its banks and was milky white as it moved rapidly to the Danube.

By the end of the eighteenth century, there was still was no formal church and there were no priests, but one came from Polodencz, every once in a while. An old wooden building served as a church, very few children were baptized. Couples lived in sin until a priest came to marry them and sometimes, a marriage and a baptism were performed on the same day. A group of townspeople finally rode down to Bratislava to petition the bishop for a church and a full time priest and the first Mass was said in the Abbey of St. Francis, six years later. A small stone church and a priest came along with three friars. The priest and the friars were housed in private homes in vishnu Ruzbachy until their quarters could be built and they moved into their new home two years later. Most of the townspeople donated work, time and money when they could, and some money came out of Bratislava with the understanding that it had to be repaid. It took three generations of hard work to pay back the money from private donations and the sale of commodities from the abbey. The Catholic church in Bratislava never forgave or forgot the money that it sent to Ruzbachy to build the church. A wall was built around the Abbey with room for many other buildings. Next came the barns, a stable, a pig sty and chicken coops, and it took many years to reach this point but the people finally had their church.

The Abbey of St. Francis sat on a grassy knoll overlooking nizne Ruzbachy and it became wealthy with the richest land and the largest herds of sheep, horses, swine and cows in the region. The friars did their own work, except for the planting and harvest times when they employed extra help from the men in nizne Ruzbachy. The townspeople, anxiously awaited the seasons when the fields had to be plowed and crops put in because of the wages to be earned. They worked during the harvest season, but the spring was the most difficult time, for with the end of lent, the cupboards were bare. The time before Easter was a time of sacrifice for the people of Ruzbachy because spring, in the shadow of the mountains, came a little later. With the wages earned at planting time, the people were able to buy food at a discount from the friars. When the friar's own supplies ran out, they went to the large landowners, who always had food to spare, it was this food that was sold to the people of the town. Other landowners competed with the abbey for workers, but the workers usually made out better with the friars.

Having fertile lands at the base of the mountains, the small town of Ruzbachy grew and the people recognized the abbey as the center of activity. Once it started to grow, new people moved into town. They came from Hungary with their brown skin, brown hair and dark eyes. The Poles, with their fair skin, blond hair and blue eyes, came through the passes of the High Tatras mountains to settle in the fertile lands on the other side. The Germans came from the west, with their own language, eager to work and earn a better living. Hard work caused the abbey and Ruzbachy to prosper. The bridge across the Poprad River, was repaired using the oak trees found in the forest on the side of the mountains. While the Germans provided the technical expertise to build the bridge, they also started and ran the small shops as tailors, weavers, shoemakers, pottery makers and blacksmiths. The people began to intermarry and formed the nucleus of a proud and determined people.

In the beginning of the nineteenth century, the Napoleonic wars came and the economy took a turn downward. Crops were burned, cattle taken for food, people were left without seeds or stock to replenish their food supplies. With the downturn in the economy, the abbey fell to disrepair as the people put their energies into the gathering of food for survival. Many left the area to seek a better living elsewhere, revenues fell off at the church. The church in the abbey could not support itself and when the Abbott died, the Jesuits were on the verge of closing it.

In 1849 the Bishop of Bratislava, Josef Messinek, sent a young priest named Damian Benarek to the abbey to rebuild it. A Slovak by birth, whose last assignment was saying mass at St. Martins Cathedral in Bratislavia. Although ordained only three years earlier, he had shown some promise as an administrator and was forever volunteering for tasks that no one else wanted. The bishop decided to use this zeal and, although he had not taken the vows of the Jesuit order, Father Damian was sent to the abbey with instructions to recruit new friars from the town people, since only nine friars were there at that time. He was to repair the structures in the abbey and to build additional structures to satisfy at least one hundred friars. The priest was to build up the herds and farm the lands to provide food for the friars yet to come. He would provide work for the people of Ruzbachy and make the abbey the center of the economy for the area. As a missionary, he was to educate the people in the fundamentals of reading, writing and numbers, and lastly, but most importantly, he would attend to all of their spiritual needs and convert all who were not catholic into the faith.

On August 18, 1849, Father Damian rode into Ruzbachy on a horse pulling a pack mule with all the books, papers, materials and clothing he could gather. He walked around his new domain and shook his head in dismay at everything he saw. No one was in sight, the doors were open and the place was filthy, except for the grounds which were full of color from the flowers. It was clear that there was no leadership as he went to the church and rang the bell so it could be heard over the High Tatras. Father Damian pulled the bell rope and rang it for a few minutes until friars came running from all directions. They held up their robes so as not to trip and when they reached the church, they saw the tall, slender priest with a bush of dark hair and piercing eyes. The priest made eye contact with all eight of the friars in attendance, and each friar broke off contact as if he were ashamed. Father Damian waited for someone to speak, but feet shuffled and no one wanted to be first. Finally, he invited them all into the church and had them sit in the front row.

He spoke softly, but with a great deal of authority, "Who is in charge?"

They all looked at a friar who appeared to be in his late 40's. The friar stood up and said, "I am Brother Albert and I handle the financial matters of the Abbey."

The priest handed Brother Albert a letter of introduction from the bishop and asked the friar to show him around the following day. "I am going to tell you what you know. This monastery has been neglected for a long time, but that will change." He looked at brother Albert, "I need a list of all the brothers and what their duties are. I assume that there is a room for the head of the abbey and I will occupy it. I want to meet with each one of you individually, starting with Brother Albert. There will be morning prayers at five and Brother Albert will ring the bell three times. The morning meal will follow the prayers and I will talk to all of you tomorrow."

The priest dismissed them to their labors and walked with Brother Albert. Father Damian went to his room, found it dirty and packed with discarded materials, as it had, obviously, been used as a storeroom. He and Brother Albert cleaned it and once that was finished, Brother Albert excused himself to find his assistant, Brother Josef to clean the priest's bedroom. It was almost time for the evening meal and after he washed, the priest went to the evening meal only to find only eight Friars there. They ate in silence and after washing their plates, went directly to vespers. After the evening prayers, everyone retired to their cells to await the coming of the next day. The following morning, Father Damian went to the morning prayers and again there were only eight friars present.

After the prayers, he addressed the friars once more and looking at each one said, "This is how the abbey will function as of this day. After the morning meal, you will return to your cells for cleaning and meditation. Work will begin at 6:30 a.m. and end at 5:30, when you will get yourselves washed for the evening meal at 6:30. Vespers would be at 7:30 and then you will retire for a good night's sleep. This routine will be followed for six days and on the seventh day, Sunday, the Lord's day, there shall be a day of rest. On that day, the morning meal will be at six with a two-hour Mass at eight and you will be free to do as you want until six. The evening meal would be at that time and then vespers at seven-thirty."

He looked at them for a reaction. The brothers were looking at each another in disbelief as they were expecting a tirade, possibly some dismissals, but this was more then fair. He dismissed them and had Brother Albert give him a tour of the abbey. The priest wanted to see the facility the day before, but there was just too much that had to be done so he postponed it for a day. The tour took an hour with Brother Albert's sincere apologies. They went to the priest's study where Father Damian sat in his chair, crossed his hands in his lap and asked Brother Albert to sit in a chair across from him. Father Damian made it a practice to look directly into the eyes of the person he addressed.

He had trouble making eye contact and when he did, he asked, "Please tell me what your duties are at the Abbey of St. Francis?" The friar explained, "I keep track of the day-to-day activities of the abbey."

"May I see the records showing the tallies?," asked the priest?

Brother Albert went over in his mind how he was going to explain and finally answered, "I cannot produce a tally because there has not been any activity."

The priest smiled and asked, "I want to see all the records that you have since you assumed the duties and I want them on my desk by 6:00 tomorrow morning. I now want you to compile a list of all the brothers and their duties."

He waited while Brother Albert composed the list and since the friar was not the most educated man, this task took some time. The priest waited patiently. Once the list was finished, the priest asked to see the friars one at a time.

The first to come in was Brother Theo. He was dark complexionted with short black hair and soft dark eyes, his teeth were even and white and his smile was contagious as anyone seeing his smile had to smile back. His face was as round as his mid-section and when he smiled, there was a glitter in his eyes. He gave the impression that he told the truth and could be trusted. This friar was a simple man and Father Damian took a liking to him at once and asked, "Do you like your work in the kitchen."

Brother Theo smiled and said, "I love cooking for the brothers and I do not mind working seven days a week when the others work six days."

"Do you keep any records as what food is brought in, how much was consumed and how much was sold to buy other provisions?"

The cook replied, "I do not have an inventory of what there is in the stores but I do know that it will not feed all of our brothers during the winter. No one had ever asked me to keep records and there are very little stores to inventory."

The priest said, "I know that you are doing the best that you can with what is available, but you have to keep records. I have to know what is grown, what is consumed and how much we are going to need to get us through the winter."

Brother Theo told his superior, "When we run out of food, the townspeople will donate some, but we have gone hungry waiting for someone to donate."

The priest leaned across his desk, folded his hands and said, "It is important that you keep records so plans can be made and if you have trouble, I will set some time aside to help you, but I want to see a report on my desk the first of each month. I will see to it that the days of hunger for the brothers are over."

The friar said, "I enjoy serving my brothers a good meal. If there was enough food, I will gladly cook seven days a week and I would thank the Lord for letting me do it."

The priest dismissed the friar with a soft smile. He felt that he had made a friend of this man and he asked him to send in the next man.

The next friar, a young man who helped in the kitchen and baked the bread, was Brother Josef. The priest looked up from his papers and told the nervous young man to sit.

He asked the friar, "How long has it been since you said your final vows."

The friar answered, "Only a year and a half."

"Can you read and write?"

The young man said proudly, "I have had 10 years of schooling in Polodencz and was going to be a teacher until I received the calling from God."

The priest leaned over his desk to hear the young man better and asked, "How did this calling from God come about?"

"I was an altar boy when I was young," he answered, "I had observed the satisfaction the priests received when they helped someone with a problem. I wanted to experience this feeling, so I volunteered for some charitable projects of the church. I would decline any payment and gained satisfaction from the people that I helped and I could see God thanking me through their eyes. It was especially good to help people who were old and sick and if I could help the suffering, then I was happy. My parents felt that the best chance to further my education and help other people would be to come to the abbey. We had no money for me to obtain an education as my family was very poor, so I became a friar. I enjoy my work with Brother Theo and I have learned much from him. I want to keep working with him and request that I be allowed to stay."

The priest was impressed with this young man and said, "I want to assure you that I have no intention of sending you anywhere. I want you here with us. Would you be willing to tutor anyone at the abbey who has trouble with his writing or ciphers? This would be in addition to your regular duties."

Brother Josef eagerly agreed, "I would look forward to helping my brothers."

When Brother Josef left, the priest leaned back in his chair. He was rather pleased with himself, things were not as bad as they seemed. The first two friars were willing and able and they wanted to help. If the rest of the brothers were like this, then he could make the abbey profitable and fulfill the conditions set forth by the bishop. As he was smiling to himself, he looked up to see a tall, gaunt, giant of a man standing before him. He blocked out the sunlight and cast a shadow over the priest. His cheeks were hollow, his eyes receded into his head and his lips seemed to be in a perpetual frown. He identified himself as Brother Klaus and he handled all the animals except for the sheep. Brother Klaus was born in the west, in an area that had alternated between the Czechs and the Germans in history. The friar really did not know what nationality he was, but he spoke German, Czech and Slovak. The priest looked him over and asked the friar to sit but when he sat in the chair, his knees rose to hide his face. The friar had to open his legs in order to see the priest.

He asked the friar, "Do you know how many animals you have?"

The friar produced a list and handed it to the priest. His big hand came across the desk and when the priest was slow to take it, he deposited it in front of him.

His next question was, "Does the abbey have more or fewer animals than it had the previous year?"

When the answer was less and when no explanation came from the friar, the priest asked, "Why is this so?"

The reply was, "Our only stallion is old, and the bull can no longer accommodate the cows. I know every stallion and bull in the area and whether they could be bought but we have no money to buy them."

The priest said, "You and I will work together to obtain a new stallion and bull within the next two months so that animals will be animals born in the abbey next spring. I want you to compile a report on the animals that the abbey has owned since you arrived. A record will have to be kept on each animal, the sire and the dame and the production so the herd could be built. With God's help, and careful breeding, the abbey will be the envy of all the farms in the area."

As an afterthought, the priest asked, "Brother Klaus, can you read and write and tally numbers?"

The friar lowered his eyes and said, "I can tally some and, although I know animals, I have difficulty putting my thoughts on paper."

The priest sent him to Brother Josef to teach him how to compose his report.

He told the friar, "You will do well. The most important part of your work is that you love animals. We will work on the rest."

The friar stood up, thanked the priest and for the first time, in a very long time, he smiled.

A young slender man next came through the door. He was not too tall with a flock of golden hair. He had deep blue eyes that got brighter when he smiled, and he smiled often. Father Damian guessed that this was the shepherd, Brother Igor. The friar looked like he came from Poland and his speech confirmed it for he pronounced some words the way the Poles pronounced theirs.

Father Damian asked, "You must be Brother Igor. How old are you?"

The friar said, "Father, do not let this boyish demeanor confuse you. I am thirty-two years old and have been a shepherd all of my life. I started herding sheep in the Ukraine, but I was educated in Poland."

Brother Igor anticipated the priest's questions and answered them before they were asked.

"The abbey has thirty-eight sheep, four rams and thirty-four ewes and I know them all by name. Most of the wool buyers visited the farms in the area, but that was not the best price. I take my wool to the farmer's market in Podolencz because my wool is a better grade. I take my sheep to the pasture land in the High Tatras during the summer where it was cooler and when the weather turns colder, I bring them down to the abbey. The sheep are always in colder weather and their wool is thicker. I stay with my sheep in the higher pastures and live off the land. Some years ago, I built some crude shelters where I could be close to my sheep and even though there are wolves up there, I enjoy my time alone in the High Tatras for I am closer to God. I have time to meditate and reflect on the joys of the life I have chosen. When I came to the Abbey, there were twelve ewes and two rams but I have further plans to build up the flock."

He presented the priest with accurate records of what had transpired with the flock and his plans for the future. Father Damian dismissed the friar and as he left, asked him to tell the remaining friars to give him an hour to reflect on what he had seen and heard.

Once Brother Igor had gone, Father Damian knew that this young man would not be a shepherd much longer.

Father Damian rose from his chair and stretched out his arms. He bent at the waist and touched the floor and he felt good that he could still do that. This had been an interesting day and he noted that what, the abbey needed was leadership and a little discipline for he was impressed with the people that he had met. He sat and made some notes on the list that Brother Albert had given him. He put his head on his desk, slept for fifteen minutes. When he awoke, he felt refreshed, but thirsty. The priest went into the kitchen where Brother Josef was just taking some bread out of the oven. The bread smelled good and he would have to come into the kitchen more often. He asked Brother Josef for a drink of water. The friar went out to the well, drew up a fresh bucket of water and poured it into a pail. He brought it to the priest who dipped the ladle into the cold water and drank. Brother Josef said, "God had indeed blessed us with good water." Father Damian walked around the well-kept grounds with flowers around the trees and along the pathways. He thought that the gardener has a gift for growing beautiful flowers and he would speak to Brother Gregor, who would be the last one to come in. He hurried back to the office because the hour was up and when he returned, he found Brother Isaac sitting in the chair waiting for him. Brother Isaac was a short, squat man and his legs were bowed and the priest could see that, even with his robe coming to the ground. The friar looked like a raging bull, his eyes darted back and forth and he was nervous for he thought that this would be his last day at the abbey. There were not many animals at the abbey and his duty was to provide food for them. His work was not too demanding and possibly could be handled by one of the brothers along with his other duties. Father Damian watched the man before him with his harsh features and he judged him to be very difficult to reason with or to persuade to try new ideas.

Brother Isaac spoke first, " Father, I have no records to show you because I keep every thing in my head."

Father Damian looked into the dark eyes in front of him and asked the friar, "What would happen if the Lord was to call you to your great reward? You would leave your brothers with a huge problem which might take years to unravel. We have to know what is happening in the abbey. We have to know how many acres you have under cultivation, what crops you have planted and the amount of the harvest. Certain questions arise such as, will your harvest feed the animals through the winter? Do you plant the same crops in the same fields? Do you have any idea of what the yield is per acre? What use do you make of the manure from the animals for fertilizer? We need to know all of these things if we are to increase our herds."

The friar did not answer and the priest thought that there might be another problem. He asked the friar, "Can you read and write?"

It was inconceivable that a Jesuit friar had come this far without learning to read and write, Father thought, but the question had to be asked. By the time that it took Brother Isaac to reply, Father Damian knew it to be a good question. The friar became humble; the priest had hit upon the problem very quickly.

He said, "I know very little about reading, writing, figures or measurement."

The priest understood and said, "We will work together to solve the problem. You know what seed to put into the ground so that the proper plant comes up, and we are going to work on better seeds so they can yield more. For your education, I will schedule two hours every afternoon with brother Josef who will teach you everything you will need to know. I will check from time to time with brother Josef to monitor your progress. Some time next week, you and I will walk around church property and measure it. Then, we will draw maps giving each section a name so we can identify the section."

The priest and his friar shook hands and agreed that they would work together for the good of the abbey. Brother Isaac went right to the kitchen to talk to Brother Josef.

Brother Benjamin was next to see the priest. He came into the room slowly, which gave him time to study the priest before he was asked to sit.

The priest asked, "I have some good news to convey, but first, I want to know what crops are grown at the abbey for the good of the brothers."

Brother Benjamin replied, "Father, I am in charge of the garden which provides the food for the brothers. I grow beets, potatoes, cabbages, onions, carrots, wheat and barley. The wheat is ground for flour and the barley is dried to preserve for later use. It was used by Brother Theo to make the soup that we ate at the evening meal."

The priest asked, "Do you produce enough to last until the next harvest?"

The friar shook his head, from side to side, indicating a negative answer, the priest already knew that.

Brother Benjamin said, "When we run short of food, the townspeople would donate some. Word gets out to them that the friars had little food and the townspeople have never let us down. The next step is to either use the animals or barter them for food, but we never had to resort to that."

The priest told him the good news, "I have managed to get some seeds in Bratislava that would give us a better yield. I have also found some seed from a plant called maize which was successfully grown in America. The maize could be eaten by livestock and the brothers. The crop was grown in America in the same climate that we enjoy in Ruzbachy. If it is as successful here and we have a surplus, we could use it as a cash crop and barter for other food. I will teach you how to grow and harvest maize and I will work with you so both of us will plan the crops next year. With the new seeds and the help of God, we will prosper very well."

He dismissed Brother Benjamin and asked that he send the next friar to visit him. The priest waited a few minutes but he could smell the man before he came into the room. He knew that it had to be Brother Henrik, the keeper of the barns. The animals were kept in the barns from fall until spring so that manure could be collected and used as fertilizer. The excess was sold to the people of Ruzbachy to be used on their garden plots. The manure was put on by hand by shoveling it out of a wagon as soon as the first frost came down from the mountains. Brother Benjamin would bring it out and spread it around. Just before the friar came to the door, the priest caught him. If the friar entered, the priest would have to live with the smell for weeks, both real or imagined. He led the friar outside and suggested that they speak outdoors for he had been shut in on such a beautiful day and he needed to be outdoors. Brother Henrik was a rather short man, with a large chest and head, he had bushy eyebrows with little eyes that rested on either side of a crooked nose. His hair was unkempt, his robe was soiled and under the hem of the robe, the priest could see boots covered with manure. The friar spoke slowly and thought some time before he spoke. He had rehearsed his talk for two days, and now was his chance to speak to his superior.

He came right to the point: "Father, there is something that I must tell you. I do not like working in the barns. I would like to be relieved of my duties and I want to leave. I receive no respect from the other brothers. They call me "Brother Manure" and they will not have anything to do with me, they will not let me sleep in my cell and I have to eat my meals in the barn."

This was the reason that Father Damian saw only eight brothers at each gathering and he said, "I want you to continue with your duties, but there will be some changes made. I want you to continue for the good of the abbey, and after our talk, if you still want to be relieved of your duties, then I will do so. I will ask the bishop to send someone to take over for you and you will be assigned somewhere else where no one will know you."

The friar listened eagerly for he really did not want to leave the abbey. He just wanted to be accepted.

The priest went on, "I will give you new robes. The robe you have on now will be used only in the barns and stables. You will also be given a new pair of boots. At the end of each day, you are to remove your robe and boots and leave them in the barn. There will be a large metal tub put in the barn and at the end of each day you are to bathe in the tub. You will put on a fresh robe and the new boots and go to the evening meal with the rest of the brothers. Every Sunday you will wash the robe that you have been wearing in the barn and hang it up to dry outside. You will wear the robe that you wore to the meals all week in the barns for the next week. This way you will not bring the odor with you. I have the feeling that you consider yourself an outsider and not a part of the Brotherhood."

That seemed to be the problem and the solution to the problem. The friar said, "Brother Albert would not let me come to the meals or prayers and I miss the prayers very much."

The priest said, "I feel that you should be included in all activities of the abbey as you are one of the brothers and you have committed your soul to God. You have provided money from the sale of manure which brought food to the other brothers. I will find a robe and a pair of boots and you are to come to the evening meal tonight. Brother Henrik kept his eyes on the pathway. He did not look up because he did not want the priest to see his tears. Brother Henrik had been sent to the abbey because his mother and father decided that he showed less promise than his four brothers and four sisters and he was just one more mouth to feed at home. Now this priest was helping him rejoin the brotherhood and he would seize the opportunity to prove to his brothers that he could belong. Father Damian made a friend and Brother Henrik was to continue his duties at the abbey. He realized that acceptance would take time, but it was a start.

On the way back, Father Damian could not help but see the flowers on the grounds. The buildings needed repair but the grounds were well kept and he was soon to find out why. As he went around a corner in the path, he noticed a frail looking older brother bent over in a flock of red, orange and purple flowers. He was pulling weeds and throwing them into a cart. Father Damian could not see the man's face, but it had to be someone who loved his work.

He stopped and said, "Good afternoon, brother what are the purple flowers called?"

Brother Gregor stood up, put his fist on his hips and bent backward. He looked up into the face of the Priest and said, "they are a variety of heather, I found them on a hillside, dug them up and planted them here and they are doing much better than they were doing on the hillside. The red and orange flowers are wild marigolds and they too were doing well. I need them to keep the insects away. I go into the forest and the fields and gather the wild flowers, fertilize them and prune them and make them grow. I try to plant the flowers so that some would always be blooming and we have continuous blooms from April to November."

The priest asked, "Where did you receive your training?"

The friar answered, "I learn by watching others and I keep looking for new flowers. The townspeople come to learn from me, but I actually learn more from them."

Brother Gregor smiled as he spoke of his work and Father Damian could not help but smile at this simple, gentle and caring man and he marveled at the man's gift.

He asked, "How old are you?"

Brother Gregor answered, "I was sixty-three years old on my last birthday. My work in the gardens keeps me young for I have to wait for April to see what I had planted the previous October. God has allowed me to do this for many years and for that I am grateful."

Father Damian asked, "Do want some help?"

The friar answered, "I do not need any help but if you wanted to bring someone for me to train, then I would be happy to do so. When the Lord calls me, I will be ready and I would like to leave His work here on earth in good hands."

Father Damian walked away and he could still smell his encounter with Brother Henrik. He thought of the events of the day as he slowly walked to the kitchen for it was getting close to the time for the evening meal. He was not hungry for he was too excited to eat, but he had to be at the evening meal and vespers afterward. The priest was used to moving about freely and not having to be at certain places at certain times in the day. This would take some getting used to, but there was much work to do at the abbey to make it improve and this would keep him occupied. This was a good opportunity and he would have to make the best of it. All that was needed was someone at the helm to steer the course,he wondered why the bishop had picked him for this mission. He was a priest who he did not even belong to the Jesuit order. There were older priests with more experience and wisdom, but he was chosen. The good father would have a long time to contemplate this as he spent his days in the abbey.

As he went by the kitchen, he saw Brother Josef and asked him to bring a new robe and boots to Brother Henrik at the barns. The young friar looked at him in disbelief and the priest added that he should knock on the door of the barn and leave the clothing outside. Once Brother Josef disappeared, he told Brother Theo to set an extra place at the table. He would sit at the head of the table and Brother Albert would sit on the other end. There would be four places on each side of the table with the one to his right remaining vacant. The cook nodded his acknowledgment and left to go into the dining room to carry out his instructions. Father Damian went to the wash basin when he heard the bell ringing to call the brothers to the evening meal. They lined up at the wash basin, washed their hands and dried them on the cloth placed next to it. They then went into the dining room to stand behind the chairs as directed by Brother Theo. The brothers waited for the priest to say grace and they noticed the vacant chair. The priest seemed to be waiting for something else to happen. The dining-room was larger than they now needed since it had room for ten tables with ten friars at each table. One end of the room had tables that were stacked, some had legs missing to make other tables whole and the entire room needed work. The priest made a mental

note to see if he could get someone from town to donate time to
do some work in the room.

The brothers were still standing behind their chairs with the
one on the right side nearest to the priest, being vacant. They were
looking down at the pot of soup and bread on the table when,
suddenly the kitchen door opened. All eyes turned to see who was
coming into the room. In the doorway stood Brother Henrik. All
eyes watched him as he tentatively made his way to the only vacant spot on the right side of the table. He had on a new robe, was
clean shaven, his hair was combed, and his hands scrubbed until
they were red. He walked across the stone floor in his bare feet. No
odor came from his body or his clothes. Father Damian looked at
Brother Albert and nodded while the brother nodded back, smiling. The message was sent and acknowledged.

"Let us say Grace,"said Father Damian, "In the name of the
Father, Son and Holy Ghost."

He blessed himself, the brothers followed and they said as in
one voice, "Amen."

The blessing began,"Dear Lord, thank you for allowing your
servant to be at this place with these dedicated and talented people.
Please make us more tolerant of each other and let us not shut out
those whose failings are evident. Teach us to show our brethren
how to conquer these failings so we can all benefit from these lessons. Keep us well and show us how we can help the less fortunate
to achieve a better life here so we may go into everlasting happiness when we are called to our reward. Bless this food on the table
that you have provided for us. Bless Brothers Theo and Josef who
prepared it with love. In the Name of the Father, Son and Holy
Ghost. Amen."

Nine voices said, "Amen."

Father Damian pulled out his chair and sat and the rest followed. Brother Theo took the ladle and filled each bowl with
"Krupi," a soup made from beans, barley and small bits of smoked
ham. The brothers passed the soup down to the priest who waited
until all had a full bowl and a piece of bread in front of them

before he picked up his wooden spoon and began to eat. He wanted conversation at the meal so he would know what was happening but none of the brothers knew if they were allowed to speak. The priest looked up and, in a matter a fact manner, said "you are allowed to speak as I want the meal time to be a happy time."

The soup that they were eating came from an old recipe used to make the smoked ham go as far as possible. The ham bone was placed in a pot and boiled until all of the flavor of the bones had been extracted. The bones were taken out and the rest of the ingredients were put in, all the vegetables were grown at the abbey. Brother Theo put in beans, barley, carrots, celery and onions. He went to his herb garden outside of the kitchen door and added various herbs that were on hand. He grew his herb garden every year and dried those that remained until the frost, for winter use. The fat had not been taken out of the soup as this was a source of energy and was needed by the brothers especially those who did heavy work.

The meal turned out to be a pleasant time since no one had previously spoken while they were eating, thinking that they were not allowed to speak at the meals. They would eat their food in silence, when all were finished, they would get and carry their bowl and spoon to the kitchen. Each washed his own utensils, put them in his own spot and then left the kitchen. As soon as Brother Igor asked Brother Klaus how the herd was faring, everyone began to speak at once. They were all speaking and no one was listening. Soon the conversation slowed and some of the brothers listened and gentle murmur seemed to flow around the table.

Brother Benjamin told Brother Henrik how well he looked and he was included in the conversation. As they got up to leave, Brother Henrik's eyes met with the eyes of his priest's. They were moist and red. The friar said, "Panbuk zaplaz" (God thanks you) and the priest answered "Nema zaso." (He has nothing to thank me for.) After the meal, Brother Igor sought out the priest and asked permission to take his sheep back to the high country. He asked to be excused from vespers as he had three hours to travel this night. He wanted his sheep to go to the high country to be sure that their coats remained thick for the coming winter. Permission was granted and the rest of the brothers went to vespers. This was a quiet time of the day when each friar thanked his God, in his own way, for the blessing he gave during the day. They chanted and prayed together, and then went to their cells where they took their own quiet time.

It had been a tiring day for everyone and they were all happy when they returned to their cells. They had expected the worst, but now they looked forward to tomorrow and each welcomed his own cot. Brother Josef had prepared a cot for Brother Henrik without being told and led his brother to his cell. There were two cots in each cell but Brother Josef had only one cot in his cell. Since he arose so early, he did not want to disturb a roommate. Brother Henrik was to share his room, however and Brother Josef would be able to help him with his ciphers and social graces. He did not want to see Brother Henrik spend another night in the barn and he told Brother Henrik that he could sleep in his cell from now on. He led him in and there were two cots made up and on one of the cots there was a pair of new sandals made for someone with large feet.

Brother Josef said, "I have been meaning to give the sandals to you for some time but I never got the opportunity, I made them myself because I had never seen you wearing sandals."

Father Damian finally retired to his bedroom at about nine o'clock. It had been a very long day. He did not unpack all of his clothing as he had one more task to perform that night. He took off his vestments, put on a pair of trousers that he had worn at the seminary, a shirt and a jacket. The door to his room opened without a sound. He listened and, everything being quiet, he thought to himself that he must have worn the brothers out. He found a long corridor that led to one of Brother Gregor's gardens and walked down a path that ran along a side of the wall until he found a strand of spruce trees. As he reached into the branches, he found a door latch. He opened the door, hoping that it did not creak,it was well oiled.

The priest smiled as he made a note to find out who was using this door as he slipped outside the wall and once outside, he walked around the wall until he found the path leading into town. As he crossed over the bridge, he knew that he was in nizne Ruzbachy. He knew that the abbey would be in competition with other farmers in the area, and his main support would come from this side of town. It seemed that the richer the people, the more they expected from the church, the less they gave to it while the poorer people were more generous with donations, even though they had less to give. There were a few candles glowing in a house now and then, but the majority of the homes were dark. He walked along the street past the shops and businesses until he came to what he was looking for, a tavern. If one wanted to find out what was happening in town, he should go to a tavern.

He entered the tavern, looked around and saw that only a few men in it. They gave him a glance, but they did not know that he was a priest and went back to their discussions. He wanted to talk to people before they knew who he was so they would tell him what they thought of the abbey. From the looks of the men it appeared that there must not be much money in the town and this would mean that collections would be sparse. There were three men at one table and two at another and from their dress, they appeared to be working men. There were two empty tables, he picked one and sat. Because it was rather late, most of the other patrons had gone home earlier. There was a woman standing behind the bar which was made up of a board resting on two upright barrels. Behind her was a barrel of beer on its side with a spigot pounded into one end. Still no one in the tavern took any notice of him and except for the casual glance when he first came in.

The woman came over to his table and asked, "What can I get you?"

"I will have a beer, please," he said.

She smiled and answered, "I am glad that you ordered a beer because that is all we serve."

The five men smiled at her little joke. She came back with a mug of dark beer and asked him if he was going to have more than one. He shook his head and she brought back change.

The beer tasted good and it brought back memories of his time in the seminary when they smuggled a few bottles in once in a while. He waited for a lull in the conversation so he might join in with the men.

The woman went back behind the bar and never took her eyes from him. She asked, "Are you a stranger in town? I have never seen you in here before."

He spoke loudly so everyone could hear, "This is the first time that I have visited your town"

One of the men spoke up, "Are you staying a while or are you just passing through?"

He answered, "I might stay a while. Do you have a Catholic Church in the town?"

Another man spoke, "We do not have one in town but if you wanted to go to one, you would have to go to the abbey on the hill. I do not go to the abbey because it is such a depressing place."

He took a sip of his beer and said a prayer of forgiveness since he enjoyed it so much.

A third man said, "We really do not know what they do at the abbey. There were about ten friars, but no priest or an Abbott to lead them. The land was good and it could be profitable if the church knew what it was doing. No one knew how much land the church owned, but other people were farming church land for free while the abbey was struggling to make ends meet."

The priest asked, "Do you know if there are wood workers, carpenters, and masons in town who could help restore it?"

One of the men said, "There was no one in charge since the Abbott died, no one had coordinated the restoring of the abbey. There is a priest who comes only on Sundays to say Mass, but he leaves right after Mass to go back to his parish in Polodencz. The priests are usually different ones who come out and the people never got close to them."

Father Damian asked, "Who performs the baptisms, marriages and funerals?"

Another man replied. "If one is fast enough to catch the priest, he would do a baptism, but the townspeople usually say a few words before the burials and marriages were usually held when they could make arrangements with the visiting priest."

One of the men asked "Are you looking for a farm to buy. There is one for sale on the other side of the river that could be purchased very cheaply. It has good rich land that has not been farmed out. The rain storms move north up against the mountains and stop to deposit the rain there."

The priest said, "No, I am not in the market for a farm at this time."

He had finished one-half of his beer and it was getting late, but he could not disengage himself from the conversation. Besides, he was receiving valuable information that could be stored for future use. He decided to press on a little further when one of the men offered to buy the priest another beer. He declined saying that one was his limit. Now everyone in the tavern was speaking to Father Damian. They told him who the good carpenters and masons were and where to buy the best building materials at the best cost. He found out where to get the grain milled into flour, and who the most influential people were in Vishnu Ruzbachy. The Priest discovered that the economy was stable, but it could stand improvement.

He finally excused himself saying that he had a difficult day coming up, and he left. He got to his room the same way that he had left and as soon as he undressed, he collapsed on his bed. It was one a.m. and the bell for the morning prayer would be rung in a few hours. He lay on his bed with facts, figures and ideas swimming in his head. The biggest problem was to make the abbey profitable and this would give him money to make improvements. He had to bring the abbey back into the community, to earn the trust and make it the central point of the community. He had to change the image from that strange entity on the hill to a place where people who came to the abbey would be comfortable. With these thoughts, he dozed off, and soon was awakened by the sound of the bell.

2

The following days went by so quickly that Father Damian had to be reminded that it was Saturday and he had to make time to hear confessions. He also had to prepare his sermon for the Mass on Sunday. Word had spread around town that the abbey had a permanent priest who was also going to run the abbey and people began to drop in, unannounced, to make arrangements for baptisms and marriages. The funeral home sent people to him to make arrangement for burials and even some of the landowners came with offers of help. No one who offered to help was turned away. Father Damian made it a point to go into the town every few days, as a priest should, to talk to the people. He also stopped at the tavern with his collar on, just to show the people in the tavern that he was not trying to deceive them. The woman behind the bar told him that she thought him to be too good to be true.

Father Damian made himself visible in town, stopping to talk to people that he passed by on the roadway. His investigation revealed that there was a Lutheran Church in town with a very small congregation and he visited the pastor to gain some new insights into the make-up of the town. He wanted to be accepted by everyone in the community and, sometimes, the owners of the little shops would see him browsing through their inventory. He had no money to buy anything, but he wanted to show an interest in their businesses. Men appeared at the abbey looking for work with the harvests and they were showed an interest in working for the abbey in the spring. As he walked through town, people would wave, stop and talk and bring him up to date with the latest gossip. He always listened and paid attention to what they had to say. He noticed more people coming into confession and Mass on Sunday so he scheduled another Mass. And, while the collections were steadily increasing, the abbey could buy food so it did not have to rely on donations from individuals. This also helped the economy because the people had more money to give back to the abbey.

He found that helping people with their problems gave him the most satisfaction so, no matter how busy he was or how pressing the matter was before him, he put it aside and helped with some parishioner's problem. He earned the reputation as a "People's Priest" and soon people were telling others to see Father Damian with their problems. Once he helped someone, or showed him how to help himself, the reward came back in the form of volunteer help. Women came to clean the church and do the laundry, and he even got recipes to give to Brother Theo to help stretch what food there was. Some of the carpenters and masons came and helped on the buildings and furniture until materials ran out. His door was always open and he spoke to everyone. The brothers thought that he was sent from heaven and did their best on any task assigned to them.

On one of his trips into town, he stopped into the records section of the Town Hall and spoke to the notary. The notary handled all the records, collection of taxes and the payment of town bills. Father Damian asked and received a map of the churchowned property; the holdings were considerable. The church owned 1623 acres with some forest but the largest portion was tillable land. The notary would not allow the map to leave his office, but if one of the brothers came down, he would allow him to copy it. Brother Albert went down the next day to trace the map. He was given materials by the notary and that evening Father Damian had a copy of the map.

Armed with the map, the priest and Brother Isaac mounted horses and rode the perimeter of the property. They marked the tillable land on the map and drove stakes into the ground to identify the boundaries. They noted that crops were being grown on church property and, while some were entire fields, some were small garden plots. The friar noted these on the maps and when they returned to the abbey, the priest and Brother Isaac discussed their findings. Brother Isaac was instructed to find out who planted the crops and once one person was identified, Father Damian would help to identify the rest. The priest was not so concerned with the small plots as people needed the food to survive, he was determined to stop the rich landowners use of the church land. If he could not identify the trespassers, he would harvest the crops and bring them back as belonging to the abbey. If he could identify the people, then he would ask for one quarter of the crop as rental and the trespasser would have to petition the church for its future use. Brother Isaac would collect the crops due to the church and if any tenant was caught cheating the church, he would be barred from using the church property for life.

Father Damian was calm but adamant as he said, "These people have been making a profit by using the church land without paying rent and this has to stop. Tell the people that either the abbey farms the land or the abbey collects the rent."

Within three weeks, Brother Isaac handed the priest a list of names of people using the church's property. There were names of only three large land owners from vysni Ruzbachy and fourteen names of people from nizne Ruzbachy who used the small garden plots. The priest agreed to see the large landowners and Brother Isaac would visit the others. His instructions were to see how well off the people were and if they looked like they would need the food to get by the winter, he should allow them to keep the food. He did not want to take food from their children's mouths. He was to use his own judgment, but, above all, he was not to make any hardship for these people. The priest would see the three landowners on the following day.

After the morning meal, Father Damian took the list and the map and set off on his rounds. The first two on the list agreed to the terms at once because they did not want it known that they were cheating the church. Each one felt that next year they would plant a quarter more to make up the rent, and Father Damian agreed as long as the abbey was not using the land. Father Damian had already made up his mind to increase the planting acreage next year.

The third man made it difficult. His name was Pavel Dombrowski. The priest introduced himself when he found the man in the stable grooming a handsome stallion. Pan Dombrowski owned fifty acres which was being used in its entirety and he planted crops on thirty acres of church land because he needed those crops grown on church land to feed his herd of horses for the winter. Without the church land, he would have to go through the expense of clearing land of trees to till more of his own land, but he had been using church land so long that he considered it his own. The man looked up from his work and eyed the priest up and down.

He said, "I do not go to church and I have nothing to discuss with you."

Father Damian smiled as he said, "There is something that I must discuss with you. It has come to my attention that you have hay on thirty acres of church land. You have been using the land for some time now without paying rent and the rent is now due. The church wants one quarter of the hay for rent."

He watched as Pan Dombrowski's face became red with rage.

When he could finally talk, he said, "I know that the abbey is not using the land. I have improved it by fertilizing it and I am not going to pay any rent."

Father Damian said, "I suppose that I will have to talk to the notary and a charge of trespassing will be brought against you. You will be barred from coming on the property and the church will harvest the entire thirty acres."

Pan Dombrowski asked, "What about the other two land-owners?"

" They agreed to terms," answered the priest.

The farmer thought for a while and said. "Harvest one quarter of the land since I am not going to do your work for you."

The priest left saying. "Also, prior to next year's planting, please contact the abbey because the thirty acres might not be available next year."

As he left, the priest thought to himself that this man would never use church land again. He then realized that he was acting toward this farmer exactly the way that the brothers were reacting with Brother Henrik. He would have to give this situation some further thought since it would be better to bring this man into the fold. The church would be making a profit by having him come into the church and putting something into the collection basket. The brothers shunned Brother Henrik because of his odor and he was shunning Pan Dombrowski because of his attitude. There was no difference in his mind.

The next day Brother Isaac came to see him with his report on the use of church land. He said, "None of the people owned land on which to plant gardens and while there were children running around each home, most of the men were out of work. Some worked for the abbey when they could and they were all living from hand to mouth. The women took in laundry, sewing or anything else just to make ends meet. I remember seeing some of the women cleaning the church and some of the men working at the abbey. I could not ask them for even a token rent. Since they only used two acres in total, I told them, if they could, they could donate part of the food back to the church. If they could not, they should pray for the brothers and I asked them to talk to you before they planted next year."

Brother Isaac did not know how his superior would react to this news, but Father Damian was delighted. He said, "Brother Isaac, you are a good Christian man and I would have done the same because you have shown compassion. I am proud of you."

When Father Damian sat, he felt tired. It had been one month since he had ridden into the abbey and he could see changes already. Brother Igor would be coming down from the hills soon, and tomorrow he had to spend some time with Brother Albert on the ledgers. He thought that he should have heard from the bishop by now, but there was no word forthcoming.

Soon, two months had gone by and he still had not heard from the bishop. The priest thought about sending a message to him, but then thought it wiser to let the bishop summon him.

Christmas was coming and he had to prepare for the celebration at the abbey and with Advent being now only six weeks away, surely the bishop knew what time of the year it was. The brothers, along with the help of the townspeople had the harvest in. The barn was full of hay, enough to last for the winter. The hay from the land-owners had made the difference. The wheat had been ground into flour, but he had to give part of the flour to the millers, Father Damian vowed that some day the church would own its own grist mill. The root cellar was almost filled with vegetables but they still had cabbages, onions and potatoes to harvest. He was anxious to tell the bishop how well things were going.

The next step would be to harvest the cabbages and this would begin next week. The cabbages would be shredded and placed into barrels. A cover being made too small was placed inside the barrel and a large clean rock was placed on top of the cover. The weight of the rock would compress the cabbage causing it to fer-ment and the liquid produced, called "uha," rose to the top. A little salt was poured into the cabbage as a preservative. The liquid was extremely bitter and was used as a medicine for colds and some stomach ailments. The reasoning behind the medicinal use of the liquid was that anything that tasted so bad had to be good for you. The result of the cabbage became "Skoshna Kapusta" or sour cabbage known in Germany as sauerkraut.

Brother Benjamin had devised a contraption to aid him in the shredding of the cabbages. He took a board about six feet in length and eight inches wide and fastened sides on it, about two inches high along the length of the board. In the center of the long board, he cut out a two-inch slit on the diagonal and, to this he fastened a sharp blade slightly raised above the board. He sat on a stool and put one end of the board on his lap while the other end rested on the floor. Under the opening he placed a clean cloth and as he pulled the cabbage toward him, the shredded cabbage would fall on the cloth. When the cloth was filled, he would dump it into his cabbage barrel. When the barrel became four-fifths full, he would put in a hand full of salt, mix it up, put the cover on the cabbage, then place the stone, and store it in the root cellar.

Brother Benjamin would harvest the onions and potatoes and place them into the root cellar. He would separate the potatoes and those with many "eyes" were put into the darkest part of the root cellar. By spring these potatoes would sprout "legs" and he would deftly cut them up so each piece had a leg, for these were used as seeds for next year's crop. The priest often came into the root cellar to see Brother Benjamin work and he helped out when he could find the time. He handed the cabbages to Brother Benjamin so he would not have to get up, but actually, the friar liked to get up and stretch because sitting there for hours was hard on his back. He did not complain, however, because the priest was only trying to help. Father Damian marveled at how efficiently the friar worked. There was no motion wasted and he seemed to do his work automatically. He also marveled at how Brother Benjamin was able to stretch the food supply to cover so many meals. The friar processed the food to be used with the many recipes that he and Brother Theo had worked out and the meals were varied with the same food day after day. The priest could tell by the way the brothers devoured the food that he was doing a good job.

On November 1, a messenger came from the bishop and the priest was being summoned to the cathedral to report on his progress. He knew that the bishop was under fire by sending him to the Abbey of St. Francis and he would have to make an excellent presentation to justify his choice. He got all of his records together and left on a Tuesday morning. In his message, the bishop had asked him to stay a few days, but the bishop knew that Father Damian had to be back by Friday to prepare for the confessions on Saturday and the Mass on Sunday.

Father Damian rode to the Cathedral of St. Martin on horseback. He liked the time and solitude to better prepare his report. The priest left right after morning prayers, leaving Brother Albert in charge with a list of instructions. The potatoes had to be stored while the rest of the root vegetables had to be brought in as well.

Brother Albert was to supervise the operation, expecting it to be completed when he returned. The trip was uneventful and he arrived at the cathedral at six pm on the same day. It was a good thing that Brother Theo packed him some food for his trip as he went directly to the bishop's office to announce his arrival. This left him only Wednesday and Thursday to confer with his superior but the bishop's receptionist was waiting for him and ushered the priest in to see the bishop at once. The bishop was a jolly man and was genuinely happy to see him. Father Damian kissed the bishop's ring as was customary, but the bishop did not want to stand on ceremony and embraced the priest instead. The bishop knew that the priest was tired, but the evening meal would be served in half an hour so he told the priest to freshen up and he would meet him in the dining room. He was led to a small room with a bed, chair, dresser and a lamp. On the dresser was a vase with flowers, a pitcher of water and a bowl. He unpacked his clothes, took off his dirty clothes and hung them up as he could wear them on the return trip. He was going to sit when a knock came at the door and a young priest entered and told him that he would escort Father Damian to the meal. The young priest said that his name was Father Jon and he was assigned to look after the guest until he left. He washed his hands and face and dried them on the clean white cloth placed there for that purpose, then followed the young priest to the dining room. The bishop had not arrived but twelve priests were standing around, talking. Actually the bishop had been waiting for Father Damian to arrive because he did not want to place the priest in the position of being late. Father Jon led him to his chair on the right side, at the head of the table.

The bishop arrived a few minutes later followed by the young priest and once the bishop was seated, all of the others sat in their places at the oval table. The bishop introduced his guest as Father Damian from the Abbey of St. Francis in Ruzbachy. Many of the priests knew him and the bishop asked all who did not know Father Damian to meet him after the meal.

The bishop looked at each face at the table and stopped at his guest and asked, "Father Damian, would you honor us by saying a prayer of Thanksgiving for what we are about to receive?"

Everyone looked at Father Damian who rose and blessed himself. Everyone, including the bishop, stood up to hear the grace.

The blessing began, "As I look around me, I thank you, Lord for bringing these fine men into the priesthood. May the work they do on earth, bring honor to your holy name. Help us to be more tolerant of each other. Help us to make each other better priests to honor your name. Bless this bounty that you have placed before us and may it give us the energy to serve you. Amen."

The other priests echoed the amen and they all sat. The bishop leaned over to Father Damian and whispered to him that he could always count on the priest to say the correct words. This did not go unnoticed around the table. Each priest knew that Father Damian had the bishop's ear and that it would be wise to get to know him. The meal was made up of beef stew, potatoes, carrots and a number of herbs. It was well prepared and well served. The bread was tasty but not as good as brother Josef's bread. After the meal, Father Damian met the priests for a short time, then excused himself to go to his room. He took out his papers and went over his presentation because he did not want to forget anything. At ten o'clock he went to bed and as he looked around the room, a soft light illuminated the room just enough so that he could see the walls. There were paintings of various members of the clergy, and the last thing he remembered was thinking that he was indeed safe with all these eyes looking over him. He slept all night, woke up at his usual time, washed and dressed. About ten minutes later a rap came on the door, he opened it and there stood Father Jon to take him to the morning meal.

Father Damian met with the bishop at nine am. The bishop was a large man and had been bishop for so long that, unless there was a special problem, the Cathedral ran itself. His main duty was to entertain priests or other visitors when they arrived.

He began by telling the bishop about the poor condition of the abbey when he arrived. He spoke about each brother and his talents and gave his opinion of each brother. The records were brought out and discussed in detail. Father Damian apologized for the lack of records before he arrived.

The bishop was not pleased and said, "I am sorry that you were not able to find more material because we do not know what went on before your arrival."

The priest said, "That is regrettable but we should be looking into the future."

Their discussion took the whole morning and at about noon. Father Jon stepped in and asked if he could prepare something to eat and drink. The bishop asked for some hard-boiled eggs, bread, cheese, fruit and a decanter of red wine. The wine came from the Bishop of the Cathedral of St. Stefan in Vienna which he retrieved from his private stock. The bishops of eastern Europe lived very well. Once the meal was completed and the dishes cleared, they resumed their discussions.

The bishop asked, "What measures are you taking to put the abbey on the correct path?"

The priest answered, "I have had a private discussion with each friar and with some leadership, they will be able to do their tasks in an excellent manner. I do not feel that anyone has to be replaced and I want to work with the brothers who are already there. They are now working well over what would be expected of them, but I would like additional friars to train since some of the brothers are getting older."

He told the bishop of his late night intelligence gathering mission into town and the information he had received. He had done this only once since the townspeople had quickly found out who he was.

The bishop liked the idea and said, "You are only human and a little refreshment every once in a while might be what was needed. You know that you were my personal choice to go to the abbey and make it profitable, but I have received some misgivings from my advisors for sending a non-Jesuit priest to a Jesuit Abbey. The Jesuit order wanted to send a Jesuit priest but I finally won out when I picked you. The Jesuits had left the abbey leaderless for a long time as they tried to find someone of their own order capable of turning it around. I am sure that you will make me proud of my decision."

At about four pm. the bishop said that he wanted to rest, so the priest excused himself and left. He had some time so he took a walk around the grounds. He had not gone far when he found that Father Jon was walking next to him. They walked and talked for an hour and he was surprised to learn that Father Jon had only been ordained for nine months. He liked the cathedral but he wanted a parish of his own some day. Father Damian felt that the young priest was sending a message that he would be willing to be transferred to Ruzbachy. After a respectable time, he excused himself and went back to his room. This was certainly a trying day and he was exhausted from his talk with the bishop. He had thought it went very well, but he would be happy when he returned to the abbey.

The next morning at nine o'clock, Father Damian again met with the bishop, but this time, there were not so many questions and the talk was confined to the priest's plans for the future.

Father Damian told the bishop, "With the aid of the skilled people from town, it would take two years for the abbey to begin to look better. I am experimenting with new crops such as maize and turnips that would feed both man and beast, I want to expand the acreage and I am planning to increase the planting. The herd should be building up and I have to expand the grazing and increase the yield of the animal crops to hold them through the winter. I want to buy some seedlings to plant so I might start an orchard but I do not know which fruit would be most profitable. I have some long range plans that I will present to you. I want to either build or buy a grist mill which will be a highly profitable enterprise for we are paying too much for the grain to be ground into flour. The town of Ruzbachy needs a church, in town, which will be not connected with the abbey. It should be made of cut stone, not wood and I know that the people of Ruzbachy could support a new church. It should be found in Nizne Ruzbachy where people could walk to church. If the church was built, then the abbey could convert the existing church into a chapel and use the extra space. The abbey would have to expand anyway some-time in the near future because, with more animals, the barns would have to be expanded to accommodate the animals and the winter feed for them. The stables would have to be expanded for the same reason and I will be needing more cells for the friars. The dining room and kitchen would have to be remodeled and ex-panded."

Father Damian noticed that the bishop was taking notes and when he finished this segment of his talk, he looked at the bishop who appeared to be pleased.

The bishop said, "Father, your plans are very ambitious and I am now sure that I picked the right man."

The bishop felt that this was the end of the presentation, but Father Damian persisted and before the bishop could dismiss him, he went on.

"I need, at least, two more priests and I suggest that the priests should come from the brothers at the abbey."

The bishop said, "The Jesuits would not like this because the brothers took their vows in the Jesuit Order and the Jesuits should be the ones to designate who would be priests."

"Yes, Your Excellency," he agreed, "But in this case, the broth-ers were already known in the area and they would be the logical choices."

The bishop wanted to hear what the priest had to say before he made a decision, so he said. "Go on, Father."

The priest said, "I have two friars in mind. One is Brother Josef Martinek. He is a bright, eager to learn and is very intelligent and I feel that if he was picked, then he should be educated be-yond that of the seminary. He has a compassion for people and he should be trained in medicine. Ruzbachy does not have a doctor and if we had a doctor who was also a priest, the position of the church would be much improved."

The bishop smiled and said, "Father, you may drop the other boot. I want to know who the other candidate is."

The Priest went on, "I have a friar by the name of Brother Igor Sokoff. He is intelligent also but he has a gift with animals and he is building the flock of sheep for the abbey. Rather than destroy an animal who is ill, this friar would make every attempt to cure the animal and he would be able to crossbreed animals to give us a stock that would be more healthy. We could breed a stock that would resist some of the diseases. Brother Igor would be the only one in the region who will be trained in animal husbandry and anyone who wanted to use his services would have to deal with a priest. He could help us to bring in some of the landowners who are not going to church now and by getting the area to grow, then the church would also grow."

The bishop cupped his chin into the palms of his hand for a full ten minutes and when he finally looked up, he told the priest, "I believe that I can handle the Jesuits. I want you to prepare your people to enter the seminary on January first. The time required to train them would be ten years. I want to postpone the discussion on the church until a later date. We cannot progress too rapidly or we will lose everything. One thing at a time, Father."

Father Damian took this statement to mean that he was really dismissed. He kissed the bishop's ring and left the room and he spent most of the afternoon walking the grounds, talking to his fellow priests before he went back to his room to retire early.

Father Damian left the cathedral before dawn. He pulled a pack mule with some supplies that Father Jon had packed. The bishop left orders with Father Jon that Father Damian was to come back to the Catheral, in six months to report on the progress. The way back to the abbey would be slower since he was pulling a stubborn mule but it gave him time to think.

After Father Damian left, the bishop reflected on his visit with the priest. The bishop and Jesuits were always at odds as to how the abbey should be run. He had gained a victory by sending this priest to the abbey because he knew that the Jesuits had no one to run the abbey. He would use the report Father Damian had given him to convince the Jesuits to allow the two brothers to enter the seminary. The Jesuits would add two more priests to their order but the bishop also understood that the Jesuits were a very close order and they did not like to be upstaged by anyone outside the order. He would have to warn Father Damian to protect himself when he dealt with the order and once the Jesuits trained an Abbott, then Father Damian would be a target.

In riding home, Father Damian collected his thoughts. He knew that a church and the abbey would have to be separate entities when the church was built. He would have to be either the pastor of the church or the Abbott of the abbey, as he could not handle both. Since the bishop postponed the building of the church, he would not have to think about it for the time being and it was a decision he could postpone. As he rode along, he formulated plans in his head. There was not too much to do at this time of the year for the cold wind was already blowing down from the High Tatras. In another month there would be snow on the ground and the weather would turn bitter cold. He would have to have Brother Theo set up a table in the kitchen as the dining room would be more difficult to heat and he prayed that his first winter in Ruzbachy would be a mild one.

His immediate problem was to convince the two brothers to enter the seminary. He could command them to go since they took a vow of obedience, but he wanted the choice to be theirs. They should be able to see that they could accomplish more good for the people of the area by being trained in a profession rather than by baking bread and herding sheep. He felt that he could talk Brother Josef into it, but Brother Igor loved his flock. He rejoiced when a lamb was born and sobbed when a ewe had grown too old and had to be used for food. Since he had built it up, and knew each one by name, It will take an act of the Almighty to convince this young dedicated friar to leave his flock, so he decided to postpone telling the friars about his plans for further study unless they brought it up somehow. The fact that they were going to the seminary was news enough for now, for he knew that his decision to send them was a correct one.

Father Damian arrived at the abbey about midnight on Saturday, after stopping only once to rest at a very inexpensive inn and was on the road again after a brief morning meal. Father Damian was a little hungry and went into the kitchen after he had unloaded the mule and put the animals away for the night. He thought that he must remember to return the mule to the bishop and thank him for the use of the animal. As he entered the kitchen, he found Brother Theo asleep with his head on the table. The fire was still burning brightly so the friar had not been asleep very long. A bowl with a cover was placed just far enough from the fire to keep it warm and Father Damian was pleased that the cook had tried to stay awake so he would be fed.

He took the bowl and placed it on the table so as not to wake Brother Theo but the friar woke up, anyway, when he felt a presence in the kitchen. It was his kitchen and he seemed to know everything that was going on. Since Brother Theo had tried to stay awake, the priest was going to eat the food and he was going to show Brother Theo that he enjoyed it. He was glad that the friar had awakened so he could go to sleep in his cot. He had to get up in a few hours to start his day.

When he saw the priest, Brother Theo said. "I feel like St. Peter did when he fell asleep and did not hear a cock crow."

The soup was lentil and Brother Theo had saved a piece of bread to have with it. The priest ate hungrily and watched the smile on Brother Theo's face, this was the only reward that the friar wanted.

Brother Theo asked, "How did the meeting with the bishop go? I had hoped that everything went well. The brothers had been discussing nothing else for each was speculating as to what news you would bring back."

This was the friars' only contact with the outside world and the priest wanted to keep them informed. He said, "I will give all the details at the evening meal on Monday. However, there was no criticism of the way things are progressing at the abbey and I told the bishop that I was proud of each of my friars. The bishop had no recommendations and gave instructions to continue with our plans."

The priest finished his soup and wiped the bowl clean with his bread. He looked up and saw Brother Theo's broad grin. He would go to sleep with that delightful vision in his head. He thanked the friar and went to his room. He did not unpack. He went directly to bed and he fell asleep immediately.

When Father Damian had arrived at the abbey, he promised the brothers that Sunday would be a day of rest but the talks with Brothers Igor and Josef could not waits, he decided to talk to Brother Josef first. The friar entered the room and Father Damian could see that he was nervous. Brother Josef felt that he had done something wrong and he could not think of what it might have been. Father Damian stood up, asked him to close the door and to sit. When the friar sat, the priest sat and leaned across his desk to be sure that Brother Josef could hear him. The friar was puzzled and asked what he did that was wrong, but the priest assured him that he had no complaints with his work and he was pleased with the manner in which he was helping the other friars with their schooling.

He thanked him for his help and said, "You have been the subject of a discussion with the bishop. You have been selected to study at the seminary in Bratislava for the beginning of the year and we both wanted you to be ordained."

The friar was worried, "But who would take over my duties at the abbey because I do not want to leave Brother Theo without help. He is getting older and needs more help as the months pass."

"We will manage and I want you to understand that once you have finished your studies, you will return to the Abbey of St. Francis. Your place is at the abbey and I told the bishop that I wanted you to return."

There was silence in the room and finally the priest had to ask for an answer.

The friar nodded his head and said, "I will go if you feel that I am capable of finishing my studies and becoming a priest. I have heard that the studies are very difficult and I do not want to disappoint you."

The priest rose from his chair and he put his hand on the young man's head. He looked hin in the eye and said, "Brother Josef, I have all the confidence that you will make the abbey, your brothers, the bishop and especially me, proud of you. May God go with you and guide you. You should prepare to leave on St. Stefan's Day, the day after Christmas. There will be two events to celebrate this year, the birth of our Lord and your embarking on a new career."

Brother Igor had just come down from the high country with his flock of sheep. They had their winter coats on already and it looked as if the wool would fetch a good price at the market in the spring. He entered the priest's office looking tanned and healthy, but a little thin. He looked confident, as he always did and he handed the priest his records but was surprised that he did not look at them. He brushed them aside to go over later.

The priest asked, "How are you feeling?"

The friar answered, "I am a little tired but other than that I am in excellent health as the upper pastures seem to agree with me."

Father Damian said, "I have some good news that I want to share with you. You have been the object of a discussion between myself and the bishop. We both feel that you should enter the seminary on January first of next year and we both feel that you will make an excellent priest."

Brother Igor looked stunned. "You know that I love my work at the abbey," he said, "I could not leave my flock because the flock is too much to add to the duties of Brother Klaus. He has barely enough time to handle his own animals."

The fact that the friar was concerned about one of his brothers brought a smile to Father Damian for this man was definitely priest material and he must convince him to go.

He asked the friar to listen to him, "Your work at the abbey is excellent and you still have time to train someone to take your place. Once you are ordained, I want you to return so you can share your knowledge with the others and I also want you to return so you can train the townspeople in the production of wool. The bishop promised me that I will receive more help or I could hire someone from town to help. Pavel Dombrowski had expressed an interest in starting a flock of sheep and he has some pasture land that he was not going to cultivate."

Brother Igor quickly replied, "I refuse to allow Pan Dombrowski to handle my flock. He does not have the temperament to raise sheep. He knows horses but not sheep and I cannot turn over my flock to that man to raise. Pan Dombrowski does not treat his animals very well. Sheep are creatures of God and they require gentle handling. Shepherds even watched over the birth of Christ. To have Pan Dombrowski handle my flock is unthinkable."

Father Damian realized that he had struck a raw nerve and he changed the subject quickly "I should receive a replacement and one with experience to handle your flock but you will have time to spend with the replacement. You have the intelligence and patience to become a priest and it is a gift from God not to waste. You would leave for Bratislava on December 26 with Brother Josef so you could ride mules back to Bratislava and leave them with the bishop."

Brother Igor was silent for a while and said, "I will go if you want me to and I will do my best to justify the confidence that you have placed in me. I have thought about the priesthood for some time but I am so happy at the abbey with my sheep that I never asked to go. If God wants me to become ordained, then there must be a reason so I could do His work better."

After the evening meal on Monday, Father Damian gave an account of his meeting with the bishop and all the brothers were pleased that their work was being appreciated. He explained, "Brothers Igor and Josef will be leaving the day after Christmas to enroll in the seminary at Bratislava and they would come back to visit from time to time. Their duties will be divided so that each of the brothers will be doing a portion of them. I have not decided how to accomplish this, as yet, because I have requested additional brothers to replace the ones who are leaving, but it is up to the Jesuits to send the help. The bishop had promised to use his influence with the Jesuits to obtain the much needed help. The Jesuits have technical jurisdiction over the Abbey of St. Francis, but they are allowing me to run it until further notice."

The next six weeks were devoted to the preparation for the two events that were to take place. One was the most Holy time of the year, the Birth of Christ, and the other was a show of support for the brothers who would be embarking on new careers as priests in the Holy Roman Catholic Church. He explained that the two meals of the day would be taken at a table to be set up in the kitchen near the fireplace. It would be unwise to light a fire in the dining room for so few people. The time spent there would be so brief and the wood could be put to better use in the kitchen. The dining room would not be heated or used until the spring.

He announced, "I have thought of a new way to heat the cells. Since the journey from Bratislava was so long, I had plenty of time to think and I had given this matter some deep thought. I will ask the blacksmith in the village to make cast iron bowls about a foot wide and a foot deep with a cast iron cover. The cover will have slits in it and will be about four inches at the top of the dome. After the evening meal, the bowls will be placed into the fire to heat up and once heated, ashes will be put into them. They will be placed in each room for heat. Each of you will be responsible for your own bowl so, at least, this will take the chill out of the cells."

He looked around and saw that the friars were nodding their heads. They were pleased that their superior was thinking about their comfort.

Father Damian put Brother Albert in charge of the Christmas decorations. There would have to be an evergreen tree cut and dragged from the forest at the foot of the mountains. The brothers would have to make the time to string evergreen vines into garlands to hang over the doors and archways. Holly had to be gathered to be used on the walls and the altar of the church. Brother Benjamin was to make many small candles that would be fixed to the branches of the yule tree. The tree will stand in the courtyard, in front of the entrance of the church where the townspeople could gather on Christmas Eve to sing Christmas carols. There would be an additional Mass said for the Holiday and that would be at midnight on Christmas morning.

The townspeople would be asked for donations to be placed under the tree. They would be in the form of toys carved out of wood, pastries, knitted articles of clothing, scarves, babushka, hats and gloves made by the women. Any other crafts donated by either the brothers or the townspeople would be accepted. Brother Klaus would dress as Father Christmas and after the Christmas morning Mass he would pass out all of the donated articles to the children. Christmas was usually celebrated by the adults and the children on the night before Christmas. After Mass on Christmas day, they spent the day visiting friends and relatives, exchanging food, telling stories, arranging marriages and remembering friends and relatives who passed from this life. The time of Christmas was a joyous time with much singing and dancing. It was the one time of the year when the poor people of Ruzbachy did not go hungry, when everyone was friendly and old grievances were forgotten.

Once the plans were made, Father Damian dismissed the brothers and went to his room to retire. No one else left the table. This would be the first Christmas that many of the brothers had celebrated with the people of Ruzbachy. They were all speaking at once, exchanging ideas and customs that came from their own childhood. Brother Gregor knew where all the evergreens grew and where the greenest holly bushes were. He offered to show the brothers where they were and offered to plant some in his gardens so that next year they would not have to gather so many in the forest. Everyone was eager to help and this would be the first happy holiday that some of the brothers had celebrated at the Abbey of St. Francis.

This was a busy time for the abbey for everyone was moving around with their own tasks and no one came to see the priest with any problems. Things were running so smoothly that no one even noticed that a cart was driven into the courtyard with five friars sitting in it. There was some food for Christmas, new robes, boots, sandals and tree seedlings. The first thought that crossed Father Damian's mind was that the bishop had, indeed, been listening. He had committed himself when he had chosen him to lead the Abbey, instead of a Jesuit Abbott, and he now was committed to support the abbey. Father Damian had the provisions unloaded and stored and then asked the new friars to report to him, one at a time. They all looked young and probably had not taken their vows too long ago. It seemed that the Jesuits were sending their youngest friars to the abbey for a reason. This suited Father Damian just fine; it would be easier to train these young men rather than change the habits of the older ones and retrain them.

He was happy that they were here because now he could replace the two friars that were leaving and have three more to assign as aides to some of the brothers who were growing older. He would assign one to Brother Gregor who should have retired some time ago and he would have to find a place for the other two. The priest set out to look for Brother Albert because he wanted him to make some suggestions in the assignment of the young brothers. He found him in the kitchen counting the stores that were just brought in.

The first friar to come in was a short thin youth, with short blond hair and the bluest eyes that he had ever seen. He came from Nove Mesto, a town about the size of Ruzbachy, about 60 miles to the east. It was a farming village and he had worked on a farm all of his life prior to joining the order. He knew animals, but had never worked with sheep so he was assigned to Brother Klaus. Father Damian expected the herd to grow and this would be a good time to train someone new in the abbey's methods. Brother Albert assigned him a cell and gave him the routine of the abbey.

The young man said that he was happy to come to the Abbey of St. Francis because he had heard of Father Damian's visit to the cathedral. The young friar had also heard that the abbey was a good place to work and serve God. He wanted to be assigned to an abbey where one could express his own ideas and try out new methods to help his new home prosper.

Once he had left, Brother Albert turned to the priest and said, "Your fame is spreading far and wide."

Father Damian and Brother Albert interviewed the remaining four friars. Each expressed happiness at being assigned to this abbey because each had heard of the Abbey of St. Francis. Brother Karol was assigned to the kitchen to take the place of Brother Josef. Brother Jan was assigned to Brother Gregor since he had some experience in the planting of flowers. Brother Pavel went to Brother Isaac because this position needed someone who was large and strong. The work was hard and this young friar was ideally suited for it. He would also get along with Brother Isaac since they were of the same temperament. Brother Stefan would help Brother Benjamin because he had some experience in planting orchards. The last youth, Brother Simon, was assigned to the flock of sheep and Brother Igor. He had a temperament similar to that of Brother Igor as he appeared to be shy and the type of person who would be happy if he was left alone. It took a special type of person to be able to spend all that time in the high pastures without companionship. The shepherd would be relieved of all responsibilities for the next two weeks so he could concentrate on training Brother Simon. The only problem would be in the spring when the lambs would come, and it would be time to harvest the wool but he could get Brother Isaac to help or hire someone from town.

Father Damian reflected on the events that he had brought to pass. He wondered if he had made an error in sending Brother Igor to the seminary and leaving the most profitable area of the abbey in the hands of a novice. The choice was between the immediate profit and the long term impact on the profitability of the abbey. He doubted that Brother Igor would have enough time to train the young friar to make him capable of handling the flock of sheep. Christmas was coming and he would be busy at the abbey but he would have to watch the young man carefully, and hope that God and time would help him. Father Damian prayed a long time that night.

075-MATA

3

In the latter part of the winter and the first part of the spring, the abbey had to buy food from the people in the upper part of town. Father Damian vowed that this would be the last time that food would have to be purchased for the abbey. Brother Simon was surprisingly good at his work, but the priest had to hire an experienced sheep shearer the first spring. Brother Simon learned quickly and he would be able to do the work next year. He handled the lambs very well and, in time, he would prove to be as good a shepherd as Brother Igor.

On his next six-month trip to see the bishop, Father Damian learned that both Brother Josef and Brother Igor were doing very well at the seminary. They still had five and one-half years to spend there, plus the four years of their specialized training. The priest gave his report to the bishop and left as soon as he could without being disrespectful. It was planting time and he wanted to be sure that all the crops were being planted in the correct fields. He also wanted to make contact with his tenants to be sure there was no misunderstanding on the use of church property.

On the day of his return, Brother Henrik met him as he was putting up his horse. "I have more than enough manure to spread on the fields and in the gardens and I want permission to sell some in town for the villagers to use in their gardens. Most homes have a garden plot and I could deliver it and collect something. I want to know what I should charge for it."

Father Damian smiled, "You are to use your own judgment. You should charge what you consider reasonable and the family's ability to pay, those who cannot pay now, should donate food to the abbey at harvest time. I want you to keep records as to who paid and who did not. Let me see these records when you are finished selling your wares." And thus the abbey went into the manure business.

The fields were planted with barley, wheat, hay, cabbage, sugar beets, maize and various garden vegetable such as cucumbers, kale, peppers, tomatoes and potatoes. Brother Theo planted his herb garden with the help of his new assistant, and the orchard was in, although it would not bear fruit for many years. The seedlings sent by the bishop were apples, peaches, plums and pears and everyone was excited to put new plants into the ground. Each year seed was thrown into the ground and eventually they would grow into plants which provided food. This was a miracle that happened every year and it amazed the brothers that this could happen. God was good to them and it came as a sign that they were doing His will. Brother Isaac kept track of who was using church land for their crops and he visited all those who had gardens, even the large land owners. He told the small plot gardeners that the abbey would expect a donation of food at harvest time and he told the others to leave one-quarter of their harvest in the fields and the friars would harvest it. Everyone agreed and the next year's harvest would provide enough food for the entire year. The spring produced six calves, two colts, eight goats, five lambs and twenty-four piglets. The abbey was growing.

When the time for harvest came, villagers who were using the church's land brought in vegetables to church on Sunday morning and left them at the kitchen door. Brother Theo and Brother Karol would play guessing games as to what would be at the door when they arrived from Mass. Apparently, the villagers talked among themselves because there was a variety and no one vegetable was in an abundance. If it were not for the rent of the large land owners and the produce supplied by the townspeople, the winter would have brought hunger. The cords around the middle of their robes would have hung longer than usual. Brother Theo and Brother Karol were able to preserve more food than they had ever done in the past. The cupboards were stacked and the root cellar was full. Five pigs were slaughtered and were curing in the smoke house and Brother Albert was keeping excellent records. However, he had nothing to compare since the records of the previous years were non-exsistent.

By the end of the third harvest, the abbey was not dependent on the townspeople or the landowners for food. The abbey had added four new brothers and had a population of sixteen friars plus Father Damian. The land used by the landowners had been cut in half and the abbey took all of the harvest from the land not used by the landowners. This was not well received as some of the landowners had to clear land for planting of their crops, adding to the cost of production.

On his last visit to Bratislava, Father Damian asked the bishop for some grapevines as one of his brothers had some knowledge in the growing of grapes and the making of wine. The bishop took some interest in this and searched for some fine vines to be sent to the abbey. The vines arrived and Brother Mikel, the brother in charge of the vines and the wine, went to work making the casks, barrels, wine press and storage facilities for the new venture. If it proved profitable, then the town folk would be encouraged to try to grow grapes for wine and they could sell the grapes to the abbey creating new capital for the town of Ruzbachy. The economy of the little town was bound to improve.

At first glance, the climate appeared to be too cold to grow grapes of a quality to make wine, but the ground was fertile. They were in the plains between the High Tatras and the Low Tatras where the average temperature was 70 degrees in the summer and the average rainfall in July and August was four inches per month. The vines were planted next to the river where water could be diverted to the vines in the event of less rainfall. The Poprad river that divided the town came from Poland through the low passes of the High Tatras, through the city of Stara Lubovna and then into Ruzbachy. The church land was northwest of the river and on a bend in the river. A trench could be dug with a gate installed so water could be diverted when needed. Because the field ran down a hill slightly, it was a perfect spot for the grapevines. The bishop had requested that Father Damian keep him advised of the progress of this daring venture. Father Damian was most anxious to start so he helped Brother Mikel plant the vines. Together they designed the slough and gate.

4

During the winter of the fifth harvest two events saddened the priest. The first was that Brother Gregor passed away in his sleep. Father Damian rode to Polodencz and used a new device to send the news to the bishop. He sent a telegraph over the wire and he received a reply that afternoon. The bishop was coming to Ruzbachy, to arrive in two days. He wanted to say the funeral Mass for Brother Gregor. The bishop took a train from Bratislava to Podolencz and came the rest of the way by carriage. Father Damian had known of the railroad but he did not like to spend the money for the fare and, besides, he enjoyed the ride down through the countryside. This gave him a time to reflect without the constant interruptions that occurred while he was in the abbey and this was the only time that he got to enjoy his solitude.

The other event, was that the owner of the grist mill passed away. He was a widower with three grown daughters who were not married. They lived to take care of their father who provided for them. Father Damian presided at the funeral Mass and asked the daughters to meet with him in his office after the funeral. At this meeting, the priest presented a proposition to the heirs of the grist mill since the mill was next to church property on the river which powered the wheel. The abbey would take over the running of the mill and would give the heirs one-half of the gross receipts, except for the church grain. The arrangement would be in force for 10 years after which the ownership of the mill would be taken over by the church. This would give the heirs an income for the next 10 years, enough time for them to find husbands to take care of them. Two of the women planned to move away from Ruzbachy while the youngest one was seeing a young man who had no interest in the hard work associated with the mill. A deal was struck and everyone shook hands. Father Damian invited them back so he could compose a contract that would legalize the arrangement.

The women were delighted. They did not want the mill and had no idea how to sell it and besides, no one in Ruzbachy had the money to buy it. If they entered into an arrangement with someone else, they could be cheated and if they could not trust the priest, then who could they trust.

Father Damian was taking a risk because he would have to obtain authorization from the bishop. Technically, he would have to obtain authorization from the Jesuit order, but the bishop could do that. It was all one church and the Jesuits should be pleased to add the property to the abbey at no cost to the order. The bishop was due to arrive the next day and Father Damian had a great deal to do. He would have to assign one of the brothers to run the mill, draw up the contract, and prepare a place for the bishop to sleep. He would let him sleep in his room while he took his rest in one of the cells, which meant moving clothes and cleaning both rooms. He stopped by the kitchen to talk to Brother Theo who had a menu planned and everything there was under control. He made arrangements to have his room cleaned, fresh bed clothes provided and an empty cell cleaned. The tired priest went back to his study and worked on the contract for the grist mill. This took him well into the night.

The next day at three o'clock, the bishop arrived, cold and tired, for he was not used to the travel. Father Damian took him to his room where he had two of his heating pots placed. The room was warm and the bishop commented on the heating. Father Damian had arranged to have the pots replaced so that the room was warm all the time. Since they were first used with wood, he had substituted red-hot coals which lasted longer. There was a basin of warm water, and a clean white cloth for the bishop to use after washing. His luggage was already in the room and the bishop commented that the priest lived fairly well for the head of a small Abbey. Father Damian bowed his head so the bishop could not see his smile and said, "we do our best."

The bishop wanted to rest and then he wanted a tour of the abbey, but the priest suggested that they wait until morning since it would be dark in an hour for it got dark earlier in the shadow of the High Tatra mountains. As Father Damian was preparing to leave, he heard a knock on the door. He opened it to see Brother Karol standing in the doorway with a tray of three flat cakes and a mug of warmed cider.

The bishop said "Thank you, young friar. What is your name?"

The young friar answered, "I am Brother Karol. Brother Theo and I thought that you would like a little refreshment after your long journey."

The young friar looked at Father Damian who was smiling, apparently pleased with the gesture. He put the tray on the dresser and left.

As Father Damian opened the door to leave, the bishop said, "Father, please close the door and stay for a few minutes. I want to tell you something that you should know."

The bishop was having a difficult time getting the words out and Father Damian expected the worst. After all, he thought. A bishop does not travel this distance because a friar had passed away. Something, more important was bothering the bishop and he wished that he would just tell him.

The bishop finally told the priest why he had come. He started to speak slowly, "You are unaware that Brother Gregor was my brother. I did not tell you because my Brother asked me not to. He did not want any special treatment. One of the considerations in selecting you to come to the Abbey of St. Francis was because I knew that you would make my brother's last days pleasant and peaceful. My brother spoke highly of you when he wrote to me when he managed to slip me a note once in a while through various routes. He loved the abbey and he had also learned to love his superior very much. I had asked my brother to come to Bratislava, but he loved the gardens at St. Francis too much to leave."

Father Damian settled back in his chair and heaved a sigh. He was relieved to know that he did not travel all that distance because of a problem with the abbey and he felt that the Jesuits might be causing some problems with his being stationed at the abbey. Father Damian looked at his superior, noticed a tear in the bishop's eye while his voice kept getting softer and softer.

Father Damian said, "Brother Gregor did receive special treatment because he was a special person. He will now be tending the Lord's garden and the Lord will be pleased."

The bishop sighed and softly told the priest that he really did need some rest. As he left, Father Damian suspected that the bishop knew what was going on all along, since he never seemed surprised at what Father Damian was doing. He had better tell the bishop everything as he might have another brother at the abbey.

The funeral Mass was the following morning, and the funeral services were held directly after the Mass. After the funeral Father Damian took the bishop on a tour of the abbey. They took the wagon into town and went to the grist mill. When the priest explained the agreement that he had made with the heirs to the property, he told the bishop that there would be no outlay of money. Father Damian continued to explain the advantages of the enterprise as he had to give one-half of the gross receipts to the heirs for ten years and after that, the mill belonged to the church. He now had to give one-quarter of the flour to the mill for grinding his grain and it would require only one friar to run the operation, so there would be no expenses in hiring someone to run it. The grist mill was closest to the abbey; the next closest one is in Podolencz ten miles away, down the river. All of the farmers in Ruzbachy were expanding their fields just as the abbey had plans to expand the production of wheat and rye so if the mill should fail then, the church would simply walk away and the only thing it would cost would be the labor of one friar. They looked over the condition of the gears, stone and water wheel which appeared to be fine; they would last a long time. The bishop did not hesitate, and told the priest to proceed. Father Damian was pleased, he thanked the bishop and took him back to the abbey where they sat in the garden to have a glass of wine and some fruit that Brother Karol had prepared.

Everything seemed in order. The bishop wanted to leave the next day and since there was a train leaving Podolencz at one in the afternoon, he wanted to take it. He was quite anxious to get back to the cathedral and enjoy the luxuries that he was used to having.

5

The next five years saw the Abbey grow to forty-one friars. Plans were being made to increase the size of the barns, stables and pens. Hay was being stored outdoors or under a make shift lean-to made from the oak and beech trees from the forest. The further up one went into the High Tatras, the more conifers were found, but they were difficult to get out. Brother Klaus had passed away a year before when a horse that he had been training kicked him in the back—he had bled to death internally. The brothers still mourned him and spoke about him fondly. Brother Josef took over the handling of the animals but he needed two brothers to help him as he was not the administrator that Brother Klaus had turned out to be. Father Damian was watching this situation very closely.

Work at the grist mill now required two brothers to handle the grain and the stone wheel was continuously moving. They had to work in shifts to keep up with the work for there was grain coming in even in the slow season. The grain was ground only when needed and the two bothers barely had time for repairs and maintenance of the mill. Father Damian was considering assigning a third Friar to the mill.

The vines produced average grapes two years before and an attempt was made to produce a wine. The wine was fed to the pigs, however, because it was bitter. The second crop was better but still not good enough to make wine. The wine had to be of a quality that would compete with the wines made further south; it would take a few more years to produce a wine with that quality. Father Damian heard of a wine maker in Podolencz and sent Brother Mikel to talk to him. The man promised to visit the abbey in the fall to see if he could help.

Things had been going so well that Father Damian had been going into town once or twice a week after the evening meal. He kept his collar on since everyone knew him anyway and he often stopped into the tavern for a beer. At first he could not talk to anyone except for the woman behind the bar; she was not pleased that he stopped in because she said that she lost business. Gradually, the other patrons began to talk to him because Slovaks can stay silent for only so long. Then they will even talk to a priest. Slowly, he became a regular and the other men talked to him freely. He would come in on irregular days, not wishing to establish a pattern because he wanted to talk to as many different people as possible. He learned that his grist mill was gaining a good reputation and people were coming from as far as Podolencz to get their grain ground into flour because it was worth the trip to get the cheaper price.

The men told him that there was a rumor that the Poles were going to charge more for their salt. The salt was mined in Poland and had to be trucked through the High Tatra by mule pack and although the region in Slovakia had copper, gold, silver, lead and coal mines, salt had to be bought in. One of the people of Ruzbachy had to travel to Poland periodically to barter for salt. The abbey had always gotten its salt from this man in town who brought it from Poland and traded it for food, leather and meat. It was essential in the preservation of food for the winter because Brother Benjamin used a good quantity of salt for his kapusta alone. The priest asked if there was another source for salt besides Poland. He was told that at the foot of the Carpathian Mountains in Hungary there were salt mines but they did not know what was charged for the salt. It was a good distance away with a three-day trip to get there and a three-day trip back, possibly longer if a large wagon was used.

Father Damian had an idea, "What if a group of men formed a cooperative and took a caravan of large wagons to travel the distance and buy all the salt that was needed for the whole town. Salt does not go bad and it would be sold to the townspeople all year long. The trip could be made in the late summer or early fall when most of the salt would be used and then a lesser amount would have to be stored. They could buy either the salt in Poland or Hungary depending on the price that would have to be negotiated, with a guarantee to the seller that they would buy all of their salt from them. If the seller knew that he had a market and did not have to store it, then he might be willing to give a cheaper price. It would only be two more days travel to Hungary and if the price was right, then it would be worth it. Since the Poles were convinced that there was no other source for the salt, they could keep going up on their price."

The more they talked, the more men joined in the conversation and there were five men in the room who had wagons that could make the trip.

Father Damian went on, "You should buy the salt in August and as it was now June, you would have two months to prepare for the trip. I would suggest that you send advance men to both Hungary and Poland to see if they could buy that amount and at what price, but they should negotiate the price. After all we should tell the mine owners that a half of a loaf of bread was better then no loaf at all."

The priest had one more comment to make and that pertained to the salt mines in Poland, "If you choose the mines in Hungary, then your market in Poland could dry up and one of two things would happen. The Poles would have to find other markets to sell their salt and there could be no salt left to sell to Ruzbachy so you would have to travel to either Hungary or Salzburg, Austria. The second thing that could happen would be that the Poles would not find another market for the salt and would be left with a surplus so next year they would be willing to lower the price."

It never occurred to the Slovaks that they could band together and negotiate a better price for the salt or anything else that they had to buy from outside of their resources. The priest suggested that they send envoys to both places and explain, as honestly as possible, their position. Once they returned, a meeting would be called and they would then decide what to do.

Two weeks later, Jan Bzrenski came to the abbey to see Father

Damian and he was brought into the priest's study. Both envoys had returned from their trips and they found that the Poles were willing to give them a better price if they bought all of their salt from them. The quantity would suit them because salt was corrosive and they did not want to store it. The mines in Hungary had their markets all lined up and they were so large that the quantity needed by the people of Ruzbachy was not a large quantity to them. They would not lower the price since the other buyers were paying the same price. The price charged by the Poles was less than they would have to pay for it in Hungary, so in August the wagons would go through the pass and buy their salt. They had a place to store it so the decisions were made.

Pan Bzrenski told the priest that the men of the town were impressed with his reasoning and business sense.

He said, "We want to include you in any other discussions that we might have involving the prosperity of the people of Ruzbachy."

Father Damian smiled and said, "I would be willing to consult with you at anytime and I will give the best advice that I can. My work, in this life, is to help the people of Ruzbachy both spiritually and any other way that I can. My door was open when I arrived and it is always open to the brothers or anyone else who comes to see me."

Father Damian was pleased with the outcome but he would now have to negotiate a better price for the purchase of salt for the abbey because salt was so essential that it was worth its weight in gold. When Pan Bzrenski went back to the village he reported his conversation with Father Damian and the people of Ruzbachy nodded their heads; the good father's reputation was spreading.

The abbey was established as the central activity in the life of the residents of Ruzbachy and Father Damian found that the people coming to confession had increased as did the weekly collections at Mass. The Church was not in competition with the landowners and other residents of the town, but was an equal member. Townspeople of Ruzbachy finally felt comfortable in going to the church, not just on Sunday, but at any other time; this was now the time to build a church in town.

Father Damian took nine months to prepare his presentation for a new church to the bishop. Brother Josef and Brother Igor were now Father Josef and Father Igor and would be returning to the abbey of St. Francis within a year and a half. The new church must be ready and it would be proper for them to move in. He drew up plans, enlisted the aid of stone masons, carpenters, the local government and all the influential people he could muster. In March of the following year he made his trip to Brataslava to see the bishop, armed with charts, plans, costs and letters from the people of Ruzbachy.

He found the bishop feeling poorly; he was up in years and he should have resigned at least five years ago. The bishop's argument was that his churches needed him, especially the Abbey of St. Francis. Father Damian got right down to business and the bishop arranged a meeting for the following day with his advisors. The meeting was held at 10 am. in the conference hall of the cathedral. Six people were present besides the priest. The bishop was too ill to attend. The presentation was made and Father Damian answered questions for the next two hours. At one o'clock lunch, consisting of bread, cheese, fruit and wine was brought in and the meeting continued.

Finally a priest, Father Mikel Zokofski, in his seventies, who apparently had been with the bishop asked the final question, "What do the people of Ruzbachy want from the bishop."

Father Damian answered, "We would like authorization to build this church in the center of town and have it independent from the abbey. I would like Father Igor Sokoff and Father Josef Martinek to be co-pastors. We would like to obtain as much money from the Holy Church as needed to build this church. As you are aware, the Abbey of St. Francis has been profitable for the last six years and I have been bringing the profit to the bishop during that time. I feel that once the church is built, it could sustain itself and within a few years it could send its fair share as other parishes do to support the cathedral. There are many good Catholics in Ruzbachy. The church in the abbey is just too small and with three Masses every Sunday, the church is filled to overflowing. They can and must support a parish church in Ruzbachy."

Father Mikel smiled and said, "You have made an excellent presentation and stated your case very well. Please allow the plans and cost estimates to remain with us while we confer with the bishop and you will have his answer within two weeks. He will send the answer back by a messenger along with your plans and estimates. The bishop will have them copied so he can retain a set for his own use."

Father Mikel polled the rest of the priests at the table and, since there were no further questions, he closed the meeting.

As they were leaving the hall, Father Mikel stopped Father Damian when they were alone. He said, "The bishop has asked me to receive the report on the abbey from you tomorrow and I want an opportunity to go over it before I see him. We can meet in my study at nine o'clock. The bishop would like to see you before you leave and asked me to end our discussions early so he might talk to you."

Father Damian wanted to leave for home as soon as possible but since the bishop was expecting him, Father Damian visited him at his bedside. The bishop had rested well and he appeared to be in good spirits.

Father Damian asked, "How are you feeling, your Excellency?"

The bishop replied, "I have chills at one time and fever the next and my right foot hurts from the gout so I cannot get out of bed. The doctors come in at odd times and it seems like they are here every minute. I am happy to see you because you are one of my favorite people. I want to thank you for all that you have done for your community, and I am proud of you. Without you, my association with the Jesuits would not have gone well."

Father Damian did not want to prolong his visit, but the bishop did not want him to leave and he wanted to prolong the priest's visit as long as possible.

The bishop asked, "How do the grounds look now that my brother is gone?"

Father Damian answered, "Your brother taught Brother Jan well as the grounds are beautiful. Your brother in Heaven must be us smiling down on us."

Father Damian suddenly looked serious and said, "Your Excellency, I have not been to confession in ten years and I would like you to hear it now."

The bishop also turned serious, "Please get my vestments from that drawer and close the door."

Once the vestment was put on Father Damian started, "Bless me, bishop for I have sinned. It has been ten years since my last confession."

He had moved the chair close to the bed so he could whisper his sins, "And these are my sins. . . ."

The confession took fifteen minutes and when the priest had finished, the bishop spoke; "I absolve you of all your sins both spoken or otherwise in the name of the Father, the Son and the Holy Ghost. You have no penance as you have been doing your penance for the last ten years and will continue to do so until the day you die. Now go, my son and keep your faith in God and all men."

Father Damian thanked him and left. He had a supper of stew and bread in the kitchen and went to bed. He must rise early the next morning for a meeting with Father Mikel.

The meeting went smoothly, Father Mikel asked a few questions and he gave Father Mikel the papers that Brother Albert had prepared along with the sack of money. Father Mikel asked him to stop in the kitchen as he asked the cook to prepare some food for his journey. He left the cathedral and was on the road, traveling at a brisk pace towards Ruzbachy. The priest arrived at the abbey late at night and went directly to his study and worked on the endless paperwork until he heard the bell ring for the morning prayers. He went to his room, changed his clothes, washed and shaved and then went to the church for prayers.

A week after he returned to the abbey, Father Damian was working on the planting schedule when a knock came on the open door. He looked up to see Brother Theo carrying a basket which he had found at the kitchen door when he went out to get some herbs. The friar told the priest that it was not food and he had better look for himself. He got up and walked over to the basket, pulled aside the cloth and saw a tiny round face looking back at him. It was a baby not two or three weeks old. He asked who the baby belonged to, but Brother Theo said that there was no note. He looked into the basket and saw that it was a little boy who looked well fed and dry. He must have been put there while the friars were at the morning meal because there was no activity in the abbey at that time. The priest looked around and saw Brother Albert standing behind the cook and asked him to send someone down to fetch Pani Benerik. She had eight children of her own and she was the one and only midwife in town. He wanted to have her check the boy over as soon as possible while Brother Theo, relieved, ran from the room wiping his hands on his apron.

Father Damian tried to get back to work, but his thoughts kept going back to the little boy whose basket was sitting on a chair next to his desk. He knew that there was no sense trying to work with two brown eyes looking at him. He sat back in his chair and waited for Pani Benerik to arrive. He did not have long to wait, as she burst into his room and when she entered a room she commanded everyone's attention. She was a short, stout woman with a large bun of hair on the back of her head. She had fat cheeks that actually glowed red and there was a twinkle in her blue eyes that matched the color of the dress that she was wearing. Over her peasant dress, she had on a white apron, and she was never seen without her apron except in church. Her eyes darted around the room until she saw the basket. She lifted the boy out, put him on the priest's desk and took all of his clothes off. The midwife looked him over, from top to bottom, she felt his arms and legs, poked him in the stomach, turned him over and checked his back. As he lay on his back, she moved her hands back and forth in front of the wide brown eyes while the eyes followed her hand. She clapped her hands loudly and startled the baby and as tears began filling his eyes, she picked him up and pressed him to her bosom.

She looked at the priest and said, "You have a beautiful, healthy baby boy. Where did he come from?"

Father Damian answered, "Brother Theo found him on the doorstep. Do you know of anyone in town who was in a family way and had delivered a baby recently?"

She shook her head; for even if she knew, she was not going to tell the priest.

He asked her to keep the boy for a few days until he could decide what to do with him. She gathered up the child, put him in the basket and left the room. Brother Theo followed her out and left the priest to contemplate the fate of the innocent young soul.

After evening prayers, he asked the brothers if anyone had any opinions as to what should be done with the child and everyone voiced an opinion that the abbey should keep him and raise him. Brother Karol stood up and said that he was raised with six brothers and sisters and he knew how to take care of a baby. If they have any problems, they can ask Pani Benerik to help because most of the women used her as a midwife and she was very knowledgeable about children. All the other brothers nodded their heads in agreement. They had already made up their minds and wanted to keep the baby. They had elected Karol as their spokesman.

Father Damian looked around and stated in a loud voice, "We will probably live to regret this, but I have to agree. He will be a diversion for all of us and we can raise him in God's light. Brother Karol, please go to Pani Benerik and tell her to put baptism clothes on our little boy and bring him to the church at one o'clock the day after tomorrow so we may baptize the young man. Brother Karol will be a godfather and we will ask Pani Benerik to be the godmother. We will all be, in effect, godfathers to our charge. Work will be excused for that afternoon and I expect you all to be there."

At one o'clock on the appointed day, all the friars sat in the first two rows of the church. A small bowl of holy water was placed on a stand and Pani Benerik came in carrying the baby along side Brother Karol. When they reached the stand they stopped and Father Damian appeared in front of them. The baby had a white gown on with a little white cap tied under his chin. Pani Benerik took off the cap as Father Damian wet his finger, dipped it into the small bowl of salt and placed some on the baby's forehead, lips and chest, while speaking Latin. Once the salt struck the baby's lips a scream was heard and all the brothers smiled, "good lungs," they whispered. The priest took a small pitcher of holy water and poured it over the baby's forehead.

In Slovak he said, "I baptize thee, Johan Janek, in the Name of The Father, The Son, and The Holy Ghost" and under his breath, he said "May the Lord have mercy on your soul."

All the brothers stood and clapped and on that day Johan Janek became a resident of the Abbey of St. Francis.

6

Pani Benerik had brought some used clothes and other baby articles for Brother Karol to use but the big problem was how to feed him. Brother Karol went to see Brother Simon who tended the sheep and asked how the newborn lambs were fed when either something happened to the ewe or she would not allow the lamb to nurse. Brother Simon gave him some options to solve the problem. He could get a substitute mother to nurse the child or he could use a device that he made out of a thin piece of leather. He had fashioned the leather into a cone and poked three holes into the narrow end. He would put some milk into the cone and allow the lamb to suckle on the small end until it did not want any more.

Brother Simon said, "Mother's milk is best and I have noticed that those lambs fed with the cone did not grow as rapidly as those with mothers' milk."

Brother Karol took the leather bag with him and left. He tried to feed Johan and managed to get some warm milk into him. Soon Johan started to grimace and then he started to cry and nothing Brother Karol could do would stop the crying. He then put the baby down into the basket on his stomach and Johan let some gas out of his mouth. His face turned from bright red to its natural color and he fell asleep. Brother Karol went to get a bigger basket, one with a rounded bottom so he could rock the child because he now knew what the problem was.

Another problem presented itself because there was a constant stream of brothers coming by to check on the infant. They checked to see if he was breathing and whether he was dry or not. There was nothing that the baby could do that was not noticed by at least one or two of the brothers. When they were told to leave, they answered that they had a right to check on the infant since they were his godfathers. Brother Karol just shrugged his shoulders and walked away.

Toward the middle of the third day, Pani Benerik came to see the baby. She brought two women with her and they checked to see how the infant was being cared for. They nodded their approval and produced some more clothes and some bottles with nipples on them for feeding. The two women had just delivered babies and they had an abundance of milk. They were both large women with large heavy breasts which they were willing to share with Johan. A schedule was set up and the women would give Johan at least one good feeding of mothers' milk per day. Brother Karol offered to keep the women well fed, but all they wanted was milk. One had three children and the other five and as they were leaving, Brother Karol thanked Mrs. Benerik for her help.

She smiled and replied, "We could not allow a good strong Slovak boy to go hungry and there was no one at the Abbey of St. Francis equipped to feed him. Besides the women were happy to help since they both have garden plots on church property."

Brother Karol reported the good fortune to Father Damian, who marveled at the methods that God used to get his work done. At the time the priest had allowed the people in town to use church land for food, he did not know that it would come back in so many ways. The food had come and was left at the kitchen with no one taking credit for the donation. The money in the collection plate was rising and he attributed that to the use of church land. The church was receiving back much more than the one-quarter of the harvest and that was not counting the good will of the people.

The good brother asked if the priest had any knowledge about who the parents of the child were because he feared that someone might show up one day, claim the child and take him away from them. Father Damian had made some inquires in town, but he had nothing definite to report except rumors. The father could be anyone who happened to be in town on the day of conception and the man might not even know that he had sired a child. Even if he knew, he would deny it since it would contain certain responsibilities which he felt could be avoided.

There was a rumor that the barmaid at the tavern could be the mother. She, supposedly, became ill about six months ago, left her job at the tavern and suddenly went north to Poland as she had a better job up there. No one had seen her since she left the tavern and she had no money. No one knew how she supported herself and how she got money to go to Poland. The speculation was that a wealthy landowner sired the child, supported the woman until she had the child and then paid to have her taken to Poland where there was less likelihood of her revealing who he was. He might have even paid for her silence. There might have been a threat that if it became known who he was, no one would believe her and she might place herself in physical peril.

Brother Karol felt relieved for he was beginning to love this child and his being in the abbey had seemed to bring the brothers closer together. They had a common bond besides the working of the abbey and they were more attentive at the prayers as if each was thanking God for their good fortune.

*　　*　　*

Father Damian was awaiting a reply from the bishop on the new church. He knew that the bishop was ill and the answer would be late but he was counting the days. It was now four weeks since his visit to Bratislava and he still had not replied. He had considered making a trip to Polodencz to send a telegram to see if he could provide any additional information since he had left in such a hurry, but that would be too obvious. He would have to be patient and wait. There might be someone with objections about putting a church in Rusbachy, but he could not see who that could be since they were all so receptive to the project.

In the middle of the sixth week, a messenger came from the cathedral, carrying a package that could only be presented to Father Damian. Brother Albert had received the messenger while the priest was inspecting the grist mill and he sent a young friar to fetch him. Father Damian came running into his office all out of breath, signed for the package and dismissed everyone from the room.

He opened the package and found an envelope, a bottle of brandy and a bottle of red wine. A note said that it was with the compliments of the bishop. He opened the envelope and started to read. Father Damian realized that he was perspiring and it was not warm in the room. He took the cover letter from the bishop and scanned it to the most important part.

The bishop wrote, "I have considered your proposal to build a church in Ruzbachy with my advisors and we agree with your proposal with certain conditions:

1. We have budgeted the amount of 250,000 crowns to build this church.
2. The Diocese will provide one half of the money, but only after you have pledges from the people of Ruzbachy for the other half.
3. We agree with your choice of co-pastors, but if the church is not built, then the priests will be assigned elsewhere.
4. Suitable land must be found which is either donated or cheap enough, in our judgment, on which to build this church. The diocese will pay for the land.
5. There will be no funds from the abbey to be included in your share of the pledges.
6. We will accept pledges in the form of labor and materials to be included in your half of the pledges, but we reserve the right to pass judgment on whether the pledges are fair in their content.

This latter condition is not mine, but was insisted upon by my advisors. They do not know you as well as I, but they were impressed by your zeal in establishing a church in Ruzbachy. I have included a bottle of fine brandy and wine, as an apology for this condition.

7. We have set a time frame to start this project. The pledges must be in and acknowledged by the end of six months with construction begun within one year. I will send an envoy from time to time, unannounced, to assess your progress. May the grace of our Lord shine upon you in this endeavor."

The priest sat back in his chair, put the letter down and asked out loud, "Where will I get 125,000 crowns in pledges within six months."

He raised his eyes to heaven and prayed for help. "Why did I undertake this project? The people in town have a church to go to on Sunday, and the abbey is performing very well. Why did I ask for this? The dam has been breached and there is no way to stop the water from coming through and I will just have to do my best to follow through."

What bothered him the most was the fact that he had put the return of Father Josef and Father Igor in jeopardy. The bishop was a wise and shrewd man and he knew that by adding this condition, Father Damian would not allow the project to fail. He would have to learn from this because he had a long way to go to raise the child, Johan. He would use this tactic as often as necessary to prepare this young man for the rigors of the world. He had been taught from his first recollections that Slovaks are survivors. They had been invaded by the Magyars, Tartars, Turks and Avars. They have been part of many empires under the rule of many monarchs and the boundaries have shifted north, south, east and west, but they had survived. The Slovaks have been forced to speak Hungarian, Latin, Czech and German, but they preserved their own language and they survived. They paid in blood, sweat and tears, but here they are, being fed, clothed and housed. Why is it so difficult to build a little church in a little mountain town? The stubbornness of the Slovak was beginning to come through. He would build this church one way or another, with help or without, even if he had to build it with his bare hands. Time to get to work.

He put on his coat and left by the front gate and went directly to nizne Ruzbachy. He did not find a big enough parcel within the town limits for they were all small parcels with homes built on them. There were only two ways to solve the problem. One, was to get the town officials to change the limit of the town's boundaries and the other way would be to buy three or four homes and move the people to another part of town. This solution was discarded at once since it would be difficult to raise money by displacing its citizens. There was, however, a parcel of land in the center of town and it was used as a park, but it was not used very much. The people in town did not have the time to sit and contemplate for there was too much to do. When the weather permitted, there were the gardens that needed attention, some had animals that they had to handle and in the winter, it was too cold with the wind coming down from High Tatras. It might even be advantageous to have a building in which to sit and it would be a holy place, with priests to talk to and the presence of God would be there. This avenue must be explored and it might be a solution to his problem.

As Ruzbachy was too small to have a full time starosta (mayor), a part time mayor ran the affairs of the town. He did not have much to do except to collect a tax, settle disputes, marry people in civil ceremonies. He had a committee of four residents to help him on the more important matters, two large land owners and two members from the other side of the river.

The mayor's name was Alexander Kopec. He had been in office since his father retired and he had done a reasonably good job. No one challenged him, he had the position as long as he was fair and did not create many enemies. The mayor was the only shoemaker in town, so his business did not suffer because of any decisions that he made as the mayor. It seemed to bring in more business than he could handle. Father Damian sought him out at his shop. He found the cobbler seated at his bench putting a sole on a pair of boots. He had his mouth full of nails and had to take them out in order to speak. Alexander was a man in his early fifties, broad about the middle with a large upper body and his cool brown eyes seemed to sparkle when he spoke. The cobbler rather liked the good priest, remembering the episode with the salt that had helped many of his people.

The cobbler got up to greet his visitor and the leather apron, he was wearing spilled leather shavings over the floor. His voice was warm and he came right to the point, "To what do I owe the pleasure of this visit?" he asked.

The priest replied, "I need to talk to you about a business proposition. Do you have time to talk for a few minutes?"

The cobbler replied, "I will always have time for you. It is a pleasure to see you."

After the pleasantries were over, the priest outlined his plan, "The church wants to buy some land and erect a church on the spot that is now used as a park. There are many catholics in town who do not make the trip to the abbey to go to church every Sunday so this would make it more convenient for them to attend church. Every town needs a church and since most of the residents were reared catholic, this would be the logical solution to satisfy the town's spiritual needs."

The mayor listened, and said, "I need to call a meeting of the committee on a matter of such importance. I cannot make such a decision on my own."

The priest asked, "May I be invited to attend the meeting to make a presentation?"

The mayor said, "I will contact you in about three days."

The first link of the chain of events had been forged and the priest left the shop to walk over to the plot of land to pace it off. It would be enough on which to build his church and to add a rectory someday.

Father Damian went back to the abbey to check on the infant. In the month since his birth, the young boy had gotten a beautiful pink complexion. He was content in his basket crib because Brother Karol had made some toys that made a noise when he moved them. He did this to test the child's hearing which was perfect. He could not find a thing wrong with this child while he looked him over from top to bottom.

"This child is going to grow up to be a large man. Look at the hands and feet," said Father Damian with a smile. Brother Karol agreed. He said, "The child is going to be intelligent, his facial features are perfect and he will be a handsome man. We are all praying for him. We must be careful and build his character and we do not want to spoil him."

The priest went back to his office to contemplate other matters. He worked on his presentation to the mayor and his committee but he did not know the names of the members, and this worried him. He had enough material to convince them to donate the land for the Church but he did not know when they would meet. He had to prepare as soon as possible, because preparation was the key to obtaining the land.

Brother Albert came into his office and asked if he needed any help, as he could spare some time to give him a hand. The priest thanked him and told him that he could use all the help he could obtain.

The friar went to his tiny office with papers piled on every surface, and pulled papers out of various piles. He knew where everything was and he returned to the priest's study with a pile of papers in his arms. He looked at his superior and asked if he was growing a beard. The priest answered that he was and he was hoping that it would give him a more distinguished look. They worked on the presentation for hours, refining it, changing the emphasis from one topic to another and, at Brother Albert's suggestion, they moved the agreement of bringing the two priests into town until the very last. This was the climax to the whole argument and if nothing else would convince the representatives of the town of Rusbachy to donate the land to the church, this might do it.

The priest asked Brother Albert to make any suggestions on how to raise the 125,000 crowns to complete the bargain with the bishop. He suggested that Father Damian visit all the landowners personally and try to obtain written pledges for either money, materials or labor to build the church. Each friar would be questioned on the people in town that he knew personally and the friar would visit each family to obtain a pledge. The whole town would be divided up among the rest of the friars and each family visited. A second collection would be installed at all the Masses so the people would know what was happening with the new church. They would know soon if it was a realistic goal.

The hour was growing late so they concluded the meeting and went to the evening meal. At vespers, Father Damian would announce the plans for the new church. His estimate was that 70 percent of the town was Roman Catholic and 30 percent were Lutheran. He felt that if the Lutherans built a church first, then the church would lose some of its parishioners so he had to build a church as soon as possible. He was now anxious to get started and so were the brothers. The priest received an enthusiastic response to his proposal to build a new church and the brothers clapped their hands and when the priest had finished, they stayed and talked among themselves. They decided to write to their relatives in an attempt to have each one organize a small fund drive through them and their friends to help Father Damian raise the quota.

When Brother Albert told the priest what had happened, he turned his eyes to Heaven and said, "Thank you, Lord, for helping us sinners. We will build your church."

He was pleased with the brothers and he thought that if his life ended on this earth at this time, he would happy. The next Wednesday he received a visit from the mayor who told him that the meeting would take place the next afternoon in the back room of his shoemaker's shop and he should be there about three o'clock. Father Damian asked who the members of the committee were. The two townspeople were Jan Kafoski, the blacksmith, and Volek Benerik, the husband of the woman who was helping with Johan. The two landowners were Jozef Jasworek from whom the priest extracted rent, was not using church land now and Pavel Dombroswki, who had given Father Damian a difficult time when he had spoke to him about the use of the land. This is going to be more difficult than he thought.

The meeting was held at the appointed hour and the committee had met with the mayor an hour earlier to decide what questions to ask. No one had reached a decision as to whether to donate the property.

As Father Damian sat, Mayor Kopec started the meeting. "You have always been fair with us as a member of this community and you have helped us with our problems, but we have a church in the abbey and why would we need a separate church?"

It was obvious that none of the five men before him had been to Mass for a long time.

The priest started his presentation and he decided to begin it just as he had rehearsed it. "If there are any questions you wish to ask, please ask them right away so we do not forget to answer them. Unfortunately, the Lord has not made us perfect and I wish to answer all questions to the best of my ability. The church in the abbey is too small, we have three Masses and they are all filled. We would like to use some of the space at the abbey since we are also growing and we need the space for our own use. The town should have a separate church with a priest who could devote his full energies to the people of Ruzbachy."

The mayor spoke up, "If we sell the land to the church, how will the money be raised to build the church? Will the bishop give you enough money to build it?"

"I have spoken to the bishop," came the reply. "He and I have reached an agreement. If we can raise 125,000 crowns, the diocese will match that amount and 250,000 crowns would be enough to build the church."

Pavel Dombrowski asked, "How do you know that 250,000 crowns will be the correct amount?"

At that point, the priest brought out his facts and figures that he and Brother Albert had compiled and they were set up in logical form, showing material cost for each section along with the labor costs.

"The church will be built from stone which would be transported from the quarry twelve miles away. The twenty eight windows will be of stained glass. The roof would be constructed of slate which will not need maintenance for a long time and the doors and other wood will be of oak from our own forests, sawed and planed here in town.

"We will try to use the masons and other craftsmen from our town which should help the economy. It should cost 250,000 crowns but if the cost is more than that, then we will have to cross that bridge when we come to it. Once we have the building up and it goes over our costs then we will either try to get the extra money from Bratislava or we will have to go into debt and pay it as we can. That is the most honest answer I can give you at this time."

Since there were no further questions coming, he went on, "The location here is perfect and there is enough land. It is within walking distance from Nisne Ruzbachy and the people without carts could walk while the people from Vishne Ruzbachy who have carts could drive them to church."

Volek Benerik asked, "Why do we need a church so big? Is it because you priests could say fewer Masses?"

Father Damian smiled, his white teeth shown through his dark stubble of a beard. "No, Pan Benerik. In the time that I have been in Ruzbachy, the town has grown and it is my projection that it will grow even more because a fine church will make it grow. This would mean more customers to buy produce to eat, and more people to hire to grow the produce. It will mean more people to have articles made at the blacksmith, more cloth to buy, more wool will be needed to weave into cloth. When a crown is spent in town, it is used ten times. For instance, Mayor Kopec makes a pair of shoes for a crown. He then deducts his profit and pays part of it to Pan Kafoski for a new anvil. Pan Kafoski deducts his profit and buys some cloth from Pan Benerik who deducts his profit and buys his cloth from the weaver who buys his wool from Pan Dombrowski or from Pan Martinek. Now, if someone lives in

Ruzbachy buys his shoes in Podolencz, that money is never seen here in Ruzbachy and it is gone forever."

He looked up and saw all five men looking at him sitting on the edge of their seats.

He let this sink in for a moment or two before he spoke again. "That, my friends, is how that system works. The more people we have the more money is brought into town. The church will be built so that it can accommodate people who move to town in the future. It will be built in such a way that it can be expanded to satisfy the people of the future."

Pan Benerik said, "I understand what you are saying, but how do we know if people will move into our town?"

"If you make it attractive enough, if you make a better life for yourself, if you have a fine place to raise children then people will come to share them with you. Times are changing. Towns are growing and people move more than they used to. We have rail travel, wagons are being built better, thanks to men like Pan Kafoski."

He saw the smile across the table. Father Damian was getting the feeling that he was winning them over, but he let them think about his comments a little longer.

Jozef Jasworek spoke, "How do you expect to raise 125,000 crowns in this little village? Do you expect us from vysne Ruzbachy to pay for a church to be placed across the river?"

"Good question," said the priest. "No, I expect the entire community of Ruzbachy to contribute to the church. The ideal situation would be to have half come from each side of the river but I do not consider each side of the river as being separate. This is one community and we would have to pull together like two horses hitched to one wagon. When one horse pulls more than the other, the wagon tends to go in that direction. I want this wagon to continue on a straight path and not to veer from side to side. We are all going to benefit from this venture. The town, the church, the people and the abbey. Do you know what my brothers are doing? Well, they are going to write to their relatives and friends, whether they are in Slovakia, Hungary or wherever. They will ask for contributions to build a church in your town. They believe in you and they want a better way of life for you, to see your children grow in the eyes of God, to grow strong and to give their children a better life than you had. Isn't that what we all want?"

Father Damian felt as if he had them won over when Mayor Kopec asked, "How much will the church pay for the land?"

The priest answered, "I'm not authorized to make an offer, but if you will tell me how much you are willing to take for it, I will convey it to the bishop."

The mayor said, "We had a meeting and we came to an agreement that we should ask 25,000 crowns for the land. It is a rather large parcel in the center of town and with some cleaning we could make it into a nice park. It is a valuable piece of property."

Clearly, the committee did not expect to receive this amount. It was a starting point for negotiating and Father Damian thought that these Slovaks were a tough and hardy people. They knew value and how to be paid for it.

He replied, "I know that the bishop will not agree to that so I had hoped that, in light of the contribution the church will make on our town, you would donate the land."

He looked into five pairs of determined eyes. He had said the only thing that the committee did not want to hear.

The mayor spoke up first, "We cannot do that because the land belongs to all of the people in our town."

"So would the church, Mayor Kopec," replied the priest. "Before we go any further, let me explain what I have done. I have had two brothers at the abbey, Brother Josef Martinek, who worked in the kitchen and who was meant for better things and Brother Igor Sokoff from the Ukraine. He started our flock of sheep and I believe he has spoken to you, Pan Dombrowski, and he may have helped you. Brother Josef had an aptitude for helping people for he is bright, intelligent and he was working well below his abilities. His education was not neglected by his parents who wanted him to be a medical doctor. Brother Igor understands animals. He has the ability to see what the problem is and how to fix it. I spoke to the bishop about the brothers ten years ago. I asked him to put both of them into the seminary and they have said their final vows and became priests. Instead of placing them into a small parish, I asked the bishop to further their education. Father Josef went into training as a medical doctor and Father Igor went into training as a medical doctor of animals. He will be called a doctor of veterinary medicine. The only arrangement that I could make with the bishop, to bring them to Ruzbachy, was to have a church. They would be co-pastors of our church and if we have no church then they will be assigned elsewhere and we will have lost them forever. Gentlemen, we cannot afford to lose them.

As far as I know we have no doctor in Ruzbachy so we have to use the women who have a knowledge of herbs and minerals. We have no one to treat our children and we have to go to Podolencz for medical treatment. We need a doctor badly."

"Pan Dombrowski, what do you do when an animal becomes ill? You destroy it. With Father Igor, you could save the animal. He could show you how to cross-breed to get the biggest, strongest and hardiest animals. If we intend to see this town grow, then we will have to progress with it. That is all I have to say to you at this time. Please consider what I have told you and let me know what you decide."

With those words, he folded up all of his papers, put them in a leather sheaf and left the room with five confused faces watching him exit. He went back to the abbey, closed the door to his study and locked it, the first time he had done that. He went to the cabinet and took out the bottle of brandy. His coffee cup was on his desk, he looked inside and finding it clean, poured himself a good amount and drank it. He now knew why the bishop had sent it to him. He would be drinking more before this was over.

Father Damian knelt on the floor for he knew that he had done the best that he could as he lifted his eyes to Heaven to pray. He stayed in this position for about an hour and finally rose. His muscles ached and it took them a while to loosen up. The evening meal and vespers could do without him for one night, he went to his room and lay on his bed for a little rest. There was work wait-ing for him to complete on his desk but his eyes became heavy and then fell shut. It might have been the fatigue, the brandy or a combination of both but the next thing he remembered was a knock on his door. He heard Brother Karol's voice asking, "Are you all right?

He awoke and answered, "I am fine. Please come in. What time is it?"

Brother Karol said, "Four thirty in the morning. We missed you at vespers the night before and we were worried about you. Will you come to morning prayers so the brothers can see that you are all right?"

Father Damian realized that he had slept through the night, he had not eaten since the morning meal, the day before and felt the hunger pangs in his stomach. The priest dismissed Brother Karol and washed up. His beard was coming in nicely but there was more gray then he remembered the last time he had looked, which seemed ages ago. He threw himself into his work for the next three days but he checked on Johan at every opportunity and tried to keep his mind off the church. He had to wait for a decision from the committee and he had worked himself up to such a state of anxiety over the church, that it frightened him. He was not getting any younger and he would have to slow down his pace.

Sunday came and the priest was relaxed and looked forward to saying Mass. This always relaxed him as he was, foremost, a priest. At the nine o'clock Mass, he looked into the people of the parish and saw the mayor sitting in the fourth row with his family. He looked even bigger with his finest clothes on. His wife was very large and the children, all dressed well, appeared well fed and he assumed that all six children sitting between him and his wife were his.

He changed his mind about the sermon that he was going to give and substituted a sermon about the value of the new church, the benefits of teaching Catholicism to the children so as to bring them up as Christians. He spoke about the Sacrament of Holy

Communion, Confirmation and Marriage which only a parish priest could provide. After all, he was only one man who was serving as a parish priest and the Abbott of the abbey. He watched the faces of parishioners as they listened to his words and he had them listening. No one was staring into space. This was a good sign!

After Mass, he positioned himself outside the church to greet the people as they came out and he heard some comments on the church, Good comments were about three to one in favor of the church. When he met His Honor Mayor Kupek, he shook his hand and the mayor said that a decision had been reached and they should meet as soon as possible. Father Damian told him that he would stop by at his shop first thing in the morning. At nine the next morning the priest walked through the door of the cobbler's shop and the cobbler jumped off his bench to greet the priest as he closed the door.

"I suppose that you want to get down right to the matter at hand," the mayor said with a smile.

"Yes sir, I do," replied the priest.

They both sat opposite one another and the mayor spoke. "We have had considerable discussion over your visit the other day. The committee has spoken to many of the citizens of Ruzbachy and we found that the general opinion of the people in this village is that we do have to ask the church for a nominal amount. We have lowered our price to 5,000 crowns and this seemed to satisfy almost everyone. There will be people who will criticize us no matter what we do but they are in the minority. We should have an answer as soon as possible as people tend to be fickle and we want to strike while the iron is, hot as Pan Kafoski would say."

"Thank you, sir," he replied. "I will have to confirm it with the bishop, but I'm sure he will accept it. I have another favor to ask of you. If I can persuade the Bishop to send 25,000 crowns, can you accept it and return 20,000 crowns to the church fund as a donation? I agree with the committee that the sum of 125,000 crowns is going to be difficult to raise and this will go a long way in getting us started."

The mayor put his hand to his beard and went deep into thought, "If it will be just between the two of us only and nothing is recorded on paper, then I will arrange it. By the way, if we need a negtoiator for the town, would you consider doing that for us?"

"Yes," said the priest. "You know that I would do anything that I can to help Ruzbachy and I have proven that. I have one question to ask you Alexander, and I feel that under the circumstances we should be on a first name basis."

"I agree, but what is your question?"

"How did Pan Dombroski vote?"

"He was for you from the beginning. He said that you were an astute business man and if you felt that a church should be built, then it should be. He likes the idea of a doctor and a veterinarian residing within easy reach and he helped convince many people to support you. I do not know if you had any dealings with him in the past, but you have an ally in Pan Dombroski."

When Father Damian arrived at the Abbey, he took his horse and rode to Podolencz. He sent a telegram to the bishop which said, "Agreed, please send 25,000 crowns to buy the land."

No sense in wasting words thought the priest and within five days he had the money delivered with a note from Father Mikel saying that the bishop was very ill and would most likely leave this world and enter the next one very shortly. The bishop wanted to start the church while he was still able to authorize it. There was no reason for him to come to Bratislava at this time but he might be getting a cable any time now and the decision to come to St. Martin's Cathedral would be his to make.

At vespers that evening, he addressed the brothers, "I have secured a 20,000 crown cash donation. I ask Brother Albert for a weekly report and will give the brothers a report on the progress of raising the money for the church. You are to turn in any money, or pledges of money, labor or materials to Brother Albert. In the event that someone wants to donate a stained glass window, either in the memory of someone dear to them or in the name of his family, it would cost 2,000 crowns. If he wants the name on the oak front door, it will cost 10,000 crowns. Statues would cost 5,000 crowns and the donor's name would be displayed by a permanent plaque. Duties will have to be shared by everyone until the fund drive is completed. A list of the cost of the doors, windows and statues is available from Brother Albert."

The fund-raising effort had begun in earnest and Father Damian would not get much work done in the next six months for he would have to throw all his energy into funding the new church.

Two months after he had received the money from the bishop, he received a telegram from Father Mikel, "Our good friend and mentor has passed away in his sleep. I am waiting for confirmation of a new Bishop for the Cathedral of St. Martin. I was nominated, but my chances of being appointed bishop are very scant."

Three months later he received a letter by messenger from Father Mikel Zakafski, "I want you to attend my coronation as bishop of Bratislava. You are expected to attend and give a full report on the result of your fund-raising efforts."

The results of the fund raising had been disappointing to Father Damian. In addition to the 20,000 crowns donated by the town, he had only 26,000 crowns in pledges for cash, labor and materials. All 14 windows were taken for 28,000 crowns. The front door was taken by Pan Pavel Dombrowski, two statues had been purchased and the grand total to date was 94,000 crowns. The Brothers reported that no more money could be extracted from the townspeople because the people were postponing repairs on their homes to pledge the money for the new church.

The landowners had the money, but were reluctant to pledge any more to the church. Word had gotten to them that Father Damian was running out of donations and time. He had two weeks before he had to make the trip to Bratislava, time was running out and, once again, he prayed for guidance. What could he do to bring in extra money? The brother's friends and relatives had been generous but he could not ask them for any more since the brothers were mostly from poor families who had many children to support. Their estates that were divided did not go very far, so the youngest ones were sent to the seminary and those who could not get accepted into the seminary became friars. Their friends and families just did not have the resources to send more.

The priest buried himself in his work. He was checking the work schedules for he wanted to be sure that he had the best suited people for their jobs when Brother Albert burst into the room.

"I have wonderful news," he exclaimed. "All the brothers have been writing to their friends and relatives to ask for donations for our fine church and one of the newer brothers, Andrej Baranowski has received a reply from America."

He was speaking so fast that Father Damian had to concentrate to understand him. The brother went on, "Brother Andrej is one of eleven children and is the youngest. He comes from Presov and it seems that his oldest brother, Michel, went to America many years ago. He settled in a little town in New York, next to a river just like ours. Its name is Cohoes and there is a Slovak community living there that works in the clothing mills. Michel went to his parish priest and told him of our need for money to build a new church. The priest, Father John Stepsik, is a Slovak whose parents came from Stara Lubovna. He went to the Bishop in Albany, New York who agreed to hold a special collection in all the churches in the Albany Diocese to help us raise the money."

Father Damian asked the friar to sit as his face was becoming flushed from the excitement.

Brother Albert sat still waving some papers over his head, "May I go on?" and without waiting for a reply, he continued. "Father John held a special collection in his church for six weeks and when they had gotten all the money together, they have raised in excess of 15,000 dollars which will be 22,800 crowns in our money. He wants to deliver it in person and he also wants us to be a sister city with Cohoes, New York. I do not know what they mean, but it can only be good for Ruzbachy."

The priest rose from his chair, went around his desk and embraced the old friar. "I want to see Brother Andrej as soon as possible," he stated. "As soon as possible."

The friar hurried out of the room to find Brother Andrej who was working in the fields. The priest spent the time pacing back and forth waiting for the young friar to come and when Brother Albert and Brother Andrej finally came into his office, Father Damian eagerly embraced the young monk. "Thank God you had written to your brother about our church. You have saved our church."

"Thank you, father," said the friar. "But I only wrote the letter. My brother deserves the thanks. You can thank him yourself as he will leave by boat from the Port of Boston tomorrow. He should arrive here in 10 days and I know that you leave for Bratislava soon after that but I hope that you will meet him and thank him yourself."

"I hope to do more than that," answered the priest. "I want him to go to Bratislava with me and to receive the thanks of the new bishop. I want him to deliver a letter of thanks from our bishop to his bishop when he returns to New York and I hope that he brings a map of his country so we will know where the town is. What is the name of that town again, Brother Albert? Ah, yes, Cohoes, New York. America is a big country and we want to know where it is."

7

On the appointed day, Father Damian and Brother Andrej were at the railway station at Podolencz waiting for the train to arrive. As the schedules were almost never followed in the European rail system, the train was three hours late. It was a splendid day and in speaking with Brother Andrej the priest learned of Brother Andrej's family, the hardships that they had endured, the lack of food, and other necessities. With thirteen mouths to feed, his brother went to America when he was sixteen years old and Andrej was very young. He did not remember his brother, but the money and the packages he sent from America helped to pull them through many a winter. Andrej's father was a miller but he had trouble finding work. When he did find it at harvest time, they had plenty to eat but if they did not put away enough for the winter, he had to go into the forest to hunt game so that the children could survive. When Andrej became old enough, his father tried to enroll him in a seminary but, with his lack of education, the only thing he was suited for was the brotherhood. Father Damian made a mental note of this conversation for future use. He liked this young man, who was intelligent, although not educated and with proper training would prove to be more useful than working in the fields.

The train finally arrived. Only one person, a large man, well over six feet tall and dressed in a suit with a jacket that had three buttons down the front, got off. The buttons were straining to stay attached to the material and he wore a brown hat with a narrow brim. The top of the hat was shaped like a bowl upside down.

Andrej ran to him and asked "Michel?"

"You must be Andy," he answered. "Please call me Mike. That is what everyone calls me in America."

They embraced and stared at each other but both felt the presence of a third person.

Brother Andrej spoke, "Mike, this is Father Damian, the priest who is in charge of building our church."

"Nice to know you," he said. "I have something for you in my suitcase." He put out his hand to shake the hand of the priest but Father Damian ignored it and tried to embrace the man.

With his protruding mid section, he was only able to grab him by the shoulders and pull him forward.

"Thank you, my son," he said. "You have done us an invaluable service."

"Don't thank me," he answered. "We have a lot of Slovaks in Cohoes who wanted to help. We know what things are like here and the least we could do was to help you build a church."

They had gathered Michel's luggage and were walking to the cart when Father Damian asked, "Were you frightened carrying all that money with you all this distance?"

"No," Michel replied. "I have my friend here with me." He unbuttoned his coat, pulled it back and showed the little pistol that he had strapped to him under his arm. "Everyone in America has one of these little friends." He smiled as they got into the horse cart.

Father Damian was trying to bring up the subject of money as delicately as possible and so far he had failed. They rode in silence for most of the trip back but once back at the abbey they took Michel on a tour of the monastery. Then they went to the priest's room where Michel would be staying.

"I would like to visit my family while I am here," said Michel. "I thought that I could do that tomorrow if you will lend me a horse and cart."

Father Damian explained, "I would like you to accompany me to Bratislava to see the new bishop installed so you should rest for a day and we could take the train down the next day. We will only stay a few days and when we return, I would be happy to loan you the horse and carriage so you could spend as much time there as you wanted. I will give Brother Andrej some time off and you could go together."

Michel said, "I have a letter to be delivered to the new bishop from the Bishop of Albany. Now, what do you want me to do with the money?"

"I will take if off your hands and deposit it into the bank in Podolencz where we have the other funds. We do not have a bank in Ruzbachy."

Michel put his suitcase on the bed and took out all of his clothes. He reached for a secret clasp and the bottom panel became loose. He lifted it up to reveal the money neatly stacked in the false bottom. While he took the money out, he kept talking, "We had the dollars converted into crowns in Albany. From the time I sent my letter to Andy until I left, we were able to add some more money to the total. We had collected 15,000 dollars and that came to 22,800 crowns in your money and then we were able to collect 3,000 dollars more. I had 1,000 dollars in the bank which I added to it and the total came to 19,000 dollars or almost 28,800 crowns. The priest of our parish rounded it to 29,000 crowns and I am pleased to give you this money for your new church. I would like to come back with my family when the new church is dedicated."

"You are certainly invited, Michel," said the priest. "It will be my personal pleasure."

He tried to embrace the man, but failed again. Michel looked a little embarrassed and stepped back. "I will personally take this to the bank tomorrow. I will give you a receipt so you can show your bishop that I received the money. I want to give you a letter of thanks to the people of the Diocese of Albany for the generous aid in the building of our church."

"I want to discuss our plan for being sister cities, but we can do that on the train," said Michel. "Right now, I am tired and would like to know if I can lie down for a while?"

"Certainly, my son," replied the priest, "but first let me give you a receipt and take the money off your hands. I will put it away for safe keeping because we do not have any of your little friends to keep it safe for us. I will have someone come and collect you in time for our evening meal." He gave Michel a handwritten receipt for 29,000 crowns, took the money and left.

He hid the money behind a loose stone in the wall of his office. The cavity behind the loose stone was made for this purpose and he used it to store the entire collection of valuables belonging to the abbey. He went to Brother Theo and Brother Karol in the kitchen who had been cooking all day. They had slaughtered a pig and had cooked it over an open pit for most of the day. They were told to prepare a feast for the guest and they had done so. All the brothers were looking forward to the meal this evening. The brothers were told to leave work early, get cleaned up and to put on their best robes for the occasion.

On the train down to Bratislava, the priest and visitor discussed the two towns in which they lived and they found many similarities. They were about the same size, both were on a river, and both had the same form of government. The majority of both of the communities were Catholic and both were destined to grow.

Michel said, "Sister cities meant that they would keep in touch with each other and they would send people to visit from time to time. We would keep track of each other's progress and help each other in time of need. Cohoes is a much wealthier town, but it was susceptible to the flooding of the Mohawk and Hudson rivers. The people of the town want to develop a kinship and since there was a large Slovak community in Cohoes, there would be no problem expressing ourselves to each other."

Father Damian said, "This seems like a good idea and possibly next year, we could send a visitor to America."

At the installation of the bishop, Michel was seated in the area reserved for dignitaries. It took four hours for the ceremony to be completed. Priests came from all over the area, from as far as Poland, Austria, France and Belgium. The reception was lavish and Michel ate enough for three men. He never did get enough to eat in Ruzbachy and to eat only two meals a day was living on a starvation diet for him. He would probably get less to eat once he visited his family so he might as well eat well now. They spent the night in the quarters prepared by the bishop's staff and they were comfortable but they had to share one room with two beds.

The following day the bishop received them, Michel exchanged letters and was taken on a tour of the Cathedral. This was done so that the bishop and Father Damian could talk and conduct their business. The bishop opened his letter from America and asked the priest if he had received 29,000 crowns from the Bishop of Albany for the new church. Father Damian nodded his head.

"I suspect," he said, "that my colleague in America did not quite trust the messenger."

"The money was in cash and I put it in the bank yesterday. The people in America saved the day," said Father Damian.

"How much did you raise?" asked the bishop. "Are we going to have a church in Ruzbachy?"

"I hope so, your excellency," answered the priest as he handed over his list of contributors. "We have raised 123,000 crowns and once the land owners know we are going to have a church then they will want their names on the list of contributors to be preserved in the history of the church. I suspect that they did not believe that we could raise the money. There is still money out there to be donated."

"I had my doubts when you started, but Bishop Messinek, my predecessor had all the faith in the world. He told me many times to believe in you as he did and I must confess that he was correct. With God's help, build your church and I will be pleased to dedicate it when you are ready. I will deposit 125,000 crowns in the bank in Podolencz within a month and all I ask is that you keep good records and spend the money wisely. Understand, I have superiors to whom I must report concerning our church."

"Thank you for your confidence. I will do the best that I can. We still have not chosen a name for the church and I have a suggestion. Your predecessor was Bishop Stefan Messinek. I would like our church to be known at St. Stefan."

"My thoughts exactly," came the reply without hesitation.

Father Damian then sighed and said, "Well, I had better go and entertain my visitor."

The rail trip to Polodencz was uneventful and they chatted on about life in Ruzbachy and in America. Michel told the priest, "Life is good in America. We work long hours but the pay is such that we eat well, can buy what we need and are able to save some money. I am able to send money to my family in Presov and I also brought some extra money so one of my brothers could come back with me. I have arranged work for him and he will stay with me until he saves enough to get his own place. My goal is to get all of my family except Andrej to America."

Michel spoke of the great unrest in his adopted country. The people of the north wanted an end to slavery in the south and the people in the south knew of no other way to conduct their lives. He prayed that there would be no bloodshed over this issue. Cotton and wool were still coming up from the south so their industry was thriving. Father Damian learned a great deal about the economics of America and how it could apply to his little corner of the world. He made mental notes to put some of his ideas into practice once he returned to the abbey to build his church.

Brother Andrej was waiting for them and very soon they were on their way back to the abbey. About three miles from the rail station, the road winded through a rather thick strand of forest of oak and beech trees that extended down from the foot hills of the High Tatras. Brother Andrej was telling his older brother how life existed at the family homestead. His parents had gotten old and could do very little work so his brothers ran the farm. There were still too many people there for the farm to support so some of the boys had hired out to the large farms to make extra money. With the money that Michel sent, they were just getting by.

"I will be able to help when I get there," said Michel, but he did not elaborate. As they came to a strand of underbrush, two men jumped out of the undergrowth and pulled the horse to a stop. They had kerchiefs over their faces and their caps were pulled down so only their eyes could be seen. They wore rough workers clothing and the soles of their boots were held together by twine tied around the front. The highwaymen looked desperate and unsure of themselves. The smaller one had a cap and ball pistol in his hand. The larger one had a knife, which looked to be an old rusty hunting knife.

The smaller man spoke, "Give us all your money or we will be forced to kill you!"

Father Damian answered, "We are only poor holy men. We do not have money. Take anything you want, my son. What we have, you are welcome to take. You do not need firearms."

The smaller of the two spoke again, "We know who you are. We do not look to you for anything. We want the American to give us all of his money. We have been watching him since he arrived and all Americans have money. Throw down your money pouch or it will be you that I will shoot."

Michel did not even know if the weapon he had pointed at him would fire, but he had to take a chance. His family needed the money he carried and he slowly unbuttoned his jacket as he slipped his right hand in as if to get his money pouch. He suddenly pulled out his pistol and before the bandit could realize it, he had been shot in the right shoulder. He discharged his gun into the air and it was now useless as a firearm. The man grabbed his shoulder with his left hand and screamed. This caught the bigger man by surprise and he lunged toward the horse cart, Michel fired again and caught the bandit in the upper right leg. As he fell to the ground Michel jumped from the cart, took the knife from the man and threw it away. Michel pulled the kerchief away.

"Why, they're just boys!" exclaimed the priest.

Michel said calmly, "The pistol does not know who pulls the trigger and the weapon was pointed at my heart. If he had pulled the trigger, I would be dead now. The larger youth could easily have overpowered me and could have harmed both of you. This happens in America all the time and I have learned to protect myself. Usually the highwaymen work in pairs, so I purchased a pistol with two shots. I took lessons to be sure that I could fire the weapon and I have become a good shot."

He looked at the bandits. They were both losing blood and in need of needed medical attention. The priest and Brother Andrej had gotten off the wagon and Father Damian was examining the smaller man.

He turned and said, "Help me to put him in the back of the cart. We have to go back to Podolencz and seek out the police. They will be able to find a doctor to help them." Brother Andrej turned the cart around and made room for the men in the back.

Michel reloaded his pistol, put it back in its place and did not say a word on the way back to Podolencz. They found the police station quickly and reported what had happened after a policeman came out. The priest told their story to the policeman who asked to see the weapon that Michel carried.

"We do not see many of these in this part of the world," he said. "Who makes this?"

Michel answered, "A man called Derringer. He usually makes a single shot, but he will also make this one with one barrel over the other so there would be two shots. I imagine that the thieves did not suspect that I had the pistol, so we surprised them."

The policeman said, "I too would have been surprised to see it. I'm happy that the three of you were not injured. We have been looking for these two and this is the third time that they have struck on that road. We have put up a sign to warn travelers to be careful, but they must have taken it down. We will take care of them now that we have them in custody."

He asked the trio to come into the station to give a written account of what had transpired so that they could give it to the magistrate. There was no doubt about their guilt, so they would go to prison for a long time. Two other policemen came out and helped the robbers into the police station. They did not appear to be in any hurry and they were not too gentle with the prisoners.

Father Damian said, "We do not have this problem in Ruzbachy.

All we have is a part time constable who handles any problems quite well."

The policeman explained, "Podolencz is a bit larger than Ruzbachy and everyone does not know everyone else. These crimes have been more frequent. Times are getting worse and we have noticed an increase in violence. If there were only the two of you from the abbey then they would not have attempted this, but they were after the American. Now he has to be careful."

Once they were on their way back to Ruzbachy, the priest spoke, "I do not approve of violence, even to combat violence but in this case I'm sure the Lord will forgive you. If you had killed either of them, then I would have been highly upset. When we arrive at the abbey, I will hear your confession."

"All it would have taken would have been to move my aim three inches to the right and I would have killed him." Michel said, "but I chose to keep them alive and to render them harmless and that's what I did."

The priest said, "You will be a hero to the people of Podolencz but not to any friends the thieves may have had. They now know that you are armed and will not be taken by surprise again. I suggest that you leave once we arrive at the abbey and you go see your family. Take Brother Andrej with you and he can drop you off at the railway station on your way back."

They arrived at the abbey just before the evening meal and after vespers. The priest heard Michel's confession and Michel went to pack as he was leaving at dawn. At dawn, Father Damian said his goodbyes to the visitor and put him into the charge of Brother Andrej. Michel left the abbey, never to return. Brother Andrej came back, alone, about a week later with many stories to entertain his brothers.

8

The priest turned his attention to the building of the church. The land had to be prepared and that would be as far as the actual building would progress for this year. By the time they finished that phase, the snow would be flying and winter would be a good time to cut trees for supports and planks. If the river freezes over, then the saw mill cannot cut the logs into beams, planks or boards but the logs could be moved over the snow easier and stockpiled until the ice breaks. The building of the church would provide work for the people of Ruzbachy and the surrounding area for a few years. Once the ground is prepared, they could start building in the spring.

The winter passed with but a few events to be mentioned. Brother Henrik passed away in January and Brother Albert became ill with a bad cough. He was in his bed for ten weeks, unable to perform his duties. His duties were taken over by Brother Voltek, who came to the abbey very well educated at the University at Bratislava. He did not want to become a priest but wanted the quiet life of a friar. He was assigned to the Abbey of St. Francis by the Jesuits, in hopes of having him became the Abbott when the time came to replace the priest now in charge.

Brother Voltek made some changes to Brother Albert's methods of accounting for the monies received and spent. It made it easier for Father Damian to understand should he need to check anything. The new keeper of the records also set up a ledger for the building of St. Stefan. He was helpful in providing the priest with a schedule of construction so as not to waste time and money waiting for materials. Stone was ordered from the quarry. The statues and windows were also ordered. On April first, the building of St. Stefan's church began and people began looking for work. The priest was able to negotiate good contracts with the various tradesmen. There were no guilds in this part of Slovakia, as yet, so Father Damian was in a good bargaining position.

By the end of the summer, the walls were up and there were enough beams to span the roof. They worked until the middle of November when the first snow storm struck, coming off the High Tatras with a vengeance. All work stopped and the workers went home to their families.

The long hard winter had passed and in the middle of the following April, the workers started on the roof. The windows were delivered, the oak doors were made, and the statues were coming in at the end of summer. Brother Voltek found two wood carvers to carve an altar and they promised to finish it by the end of the summer. The project was running in accordance with the budget and perhaps slightly below the projected budget thanks to the work of Father Damian and Brother Voltek. The priest had hoped that the church would be quite finished for the dedication at Christmas Mass. He pushed the workers and went to the construction site daily to check on the progress. Snows held off until the first of January that year. It was highly unusual to have snow that late but some said that what Father Damian asked for, Father Damian received.

The month of December was devoted to making preparations for the dedication of the church and there was to be a great celebration combined with the birth of Christ. Brother Theo asked for and received extra help in the kitchen. Animals were slaughtered and prepared while ingredients for the various traditional dishes were stored in the kitchen storeroom. The people in town were making the same preparations and even the Lutherns were going to take part in the celebration. There would be food, music, dancing, speeches and a special Mass offered by the bishop. The bishop would bring a group of priests, and place would be needed to house them. The bishop would stay at the abbey, and his priests would be quartered at various homes on both sides of the river. This would mean giving them a place to sleep, providing them with food and all their personal needs. The bishop left a skeleton crew at the Cathedral of St. Martin to handle all the duties there.

Father Damian received a telegraph message that Father Josef and Father Igor would be arriving two weeks before Christmas. The message showed that they were bringing an excess of baggage and were to be met at the train with a rather large wagon. Finally, the day came and the friars came together for the morning prayer. They spent an unusually long time at morning prayer this day, as there was much to be thankful for as God had indeed been good to them. The priest wanted this time with the Brothers because after this day, their lives would change. They could not expect the steady flow of people in and out of the abbey all the time and Sunday Mass would be only for them. They would go into seclusion, the abbey of St. Francis would be a separate entity, falling into the role of a traditional monastery. At some point in the future, Father Damian would be replaced by a Jesuit Abbott. Yes, their lives would change but the priest wanted them to know that he was still part of their lives and he would always be there for their needs, spiritual or otherwise. He loved them all and he wanted there to be no doubt that they knew this.

He would be able to spend more time with them as he could now concentrate on the abbey. This is what he wanted and this is what the brothers wanted so he could now start to train new brothers from this area and the abbey would grow. He could now spend more time with Johan, teach him, mold him into a man who could stand before any judge, even God.

On Christmas Eve, the traditional time for celebrating by the Slovaks, people came to the abbey early. By about two p.m. the people started to come in and they were dressed in their finest clothes, the women in their colorful folk dresses, the men in their three button wool suits. Even though it was cold, they carried their coats so everyone could see what they wore. The women made their own dresses. They were proud of them and the children were the exact replicas of their parents except for some of the younger men. They wore long sleeve shirts in many colors, trousers with a thick waist band and pant legs tucked into high black boots. The townspeople have been practicing the dancing in their homes for weeks and now they would perform.

They all came through the gates of the abbey, the women carrying dishes of galumki, pierogi, both sladka kapusta and skvasna kapusta. They brought all kinds of breads, babka bread with cheese baked inside, potato bread, sauerkraut bread, and sauces to put on the bread, some brought a dish made of kielbasa, sunka, jahna, and braucove.

When they entered the compound of the abbey, they found long tables set up for the food, a bandstand for the band that would play until the midnight mass at the church. Father Damian would say the midnight Mass while the bishop would say the high Mass at ten o'clock the next morning, when he would turn the church over to Father Igor and Father Josef. The celebration would go on for six days with people visiting their relatives and friends. Past differences were forgotten on this holy day for this was a time of peace. Enemies would embrace and wish each other "Happy Birth of our Lord Christ" then would have a drink together. The band began to play the waltzes, polkas, polkas in three-quarter time and women would check out the dresses worn by other women as they whirled by. The more athletic men would sit on their heels and kick their feet out, in tune to the music. There was much laughter and singing and the men would sing a song that they wrote for the occasion. There were men apologizing to each other for the time wasted being angry with each other.

And there was food, food, food. Everyone ate to make up for all the times that they went to bed hungry. They drank wine from the abbey which was getting better and better. It still was not good enough to sell, but the people of Ruzbachy loved it because it was produced at their abbey. They watered the wine down and gave it to the children, who agreed that it was good.

The party started to break up around 10 pm. and upon seeing this, the band packed up and left. Some would play for the midnight mass and some would provide music for the solemn high

Mass with the bishop. Some of the townspeople, under the direction of a new Brother by the name of Jacob, who had a booming
voice, formed a choir and had been practicing. They had never
practiced with music and they wanted to practice in the abbey
before the midnight mass.

The band had been well fed as the women brought them all
food and drink during the celebrations. They met with the choir
and Brother Jacob an hour before Mass and it appeared that they
all started together and ended together but the singing in between
needed much work. The people of Ruzbachy had never heard a
choir before so they really did not know what a choir would sound
like. All that they knew was that they had a new church, two
pastors and now a choir. This is a very nice place to live, they
thought, and it is no wonder that people are coming through the
High Tatras from Poland to settle here. There was but one man to
thank, Father Damian. They hoped that he would live forever to
enjoy what he had made for the people of Ruzbachy.

The people with small children had left the festivities early to
put the children to bed, for during the night, Father Christmas
would come and bring gifts for all the good children. Each home
smelled of pine as the oldest boy went into the forest and brought
back an evergreen to put into the house until after the new year.
The gift, for each child, would be placed inside the tree during the
night.

The midnight Mass went very well and Father Damian gave
the last sermon for the people in the abbey church. He talked of
all the good people of Ruzbachy. The brotherhood that was shown
that day did not go unnoticed for the priest knew who was feud-
ing with whom. He introduced the two priests who were to be
pastors and welcomed them back to Ruzbachy. The people of
Ruzbachy were fortunate to have these fine young educated priests
in their new parish. He thanked God for this fine church and he
hoped that God would give them the wisdom to appreciate
this gift.

The Solemn High Mass with the bishop was inspiring and all

the priests there marched up the aisle two by two and kissed the ring of the bishop. He blessed the entire church and parish by sprinkling holy water on the people and in every nook and cranny of the new church. The church was decorated with pine boughs, holly and mistletoe and the Mass lasted two hours. There were only a few children at mass because every adult in town wanted to attend and everyone in the church received communion. The sermon, by the bishop, lasted one-half hour and was delivered with force. The bishop promised to come back when the First Holy Communion class was to be received and when the Confirmation class was sufficiently trained to receive that sacrament. The people left the church impressed, there would be many more people coming to church in future weeks for this was a good start for the new church.

The bishop and his entourage left the following day, but the celebrations went on. People visited other people, ate their food, drank their beer and tea since some of the people of Ruzbachy did not have the money to buy anything stronger. The large land owners had hard liquor, as some made their apple juice into hard cider or bought a bottle in Podolencz but the people in nizne Ruzbachy did not taste it unless they were invited to vysni Ruzbachy.

After the new year, the town became quiet and the people went back to their routines. Father Damian decided to take a hand in the education of Johan, now three and a half years old. He was large for his age and since he was around adults all day, he had an excellent vocabulary. He knew all the brothers and how to get around each one, recognizing their weak points and using them to his advantage. The boy needed training and discipline because he had the run of the abbey since he was born. That had to stop and his training had to begin, so Father Damian called in Brother Karol.

"How is Johan doing?" asked the priest.

"Very well," answered the friar, "he is an intelligent young man, he knows how to count, recognizes his name when he sees it, but he cannot write it as yet. The young man knows about God and the birth of Christ and I feel that his formal education should be started soon. I do not know that I can qualify as an educator because it must be someone who is trained to educate."

"Do you know of someone like that?" the priest asked.

"The only one that I can think of is Brother Voltek. He has had a formal education at the University and he would be qualified to educate Johan."

"Thank you, brother. Do you have any feelings about giving up some of your duties with Johan?"

"No," he answered. "I will still be close to him as I will be taking care of him, I hope. I love the child and I am the only one that he will mind."

"Good, brother. Would you please ask Brother Voltek to stop in to see me when you leave?"

Brother Voltek came in soon after. "Is there a problem?"

"No," answered the priest "Please sit. I am looking for someone to take on the formal education of Johan. Can you assume that responsibility?"

The brother thought for a minute. "Do you really want me to handle that? It it is a great responsibility."

"Since the church is built, can you use half a day of your time to teach this youngster?"

"Well," answered Brother Voltec, "he does not mind me and I have not been very close to the child. I would not know how to discipline him."

The priest smiled. "I will handle the discipline. You just see me at the end of each week to report on his progress and I will take care of the discipline, I will be the only one to discipline him."

"Fine, then. I know that I can teach him," said the friar.

"Do you know anyone who excels at religious training? I do not want you to do both because you will have your hands full for the first few years as it is."

The friar thought for another minute. He usually thought over his answers very carefully. "Brother Andrej would be a good candidate because he studies all the time. I think that he wants to go to the seminary and he wants to educate himself. He has come to me with some profound questions and in his discussions I have found that he has the ability to find the answers."

The priest seemed pleased. "Maybe by educating young Johan in religion, he can also educate himself. Excellent suggestion. I'll set up a schedule."

His next talk was with Brother Andrej. The brother came in feeling that he was going to be talked to about the stories that he was telling the other brothers about Americans. Father Damian thought that he looked nervous when he entered the room.

"Sit," he said. "Have you heard from brother Michel?"

"Just received a letter from him. He has been made a foreman, whatever that means, in the mill. I know that it means more money and he can send more to my family."

"How is your family?" the priest asked.

"Fine,"was the answer. "Michel has made it possible for two of my older brothers to go to America. There is more work to do for those remaining, but there are two fewer mouths to feed. There are four boys and two girls left in Presov and Michel is planning to help two more to move to America."

"Do you want to go to America, Brother Andrej?" asked the priest.

"No, I want to stay here in Slovakia. I want to become a priest some day."

"I think you will," said the priest. "The reason I asked you to see me, Brother Andrej, is that I need you to handle a project for me. I would like you to train Johan in religion. Brother Voltek is going to handle his secular education and I feel that with your religious zeal, Johan would benefit from your teachings."

The friar looked relieved. "I would be honored, but Johan does not mind me. I do not know if I can handle him."

Johan must be a handful, thought the priest. "I will handle the discipline. You will report to me every Friday concerning his education and any problems that you may have with him. I will be the only one to discipline this child. At vespers tonight I will announce that you are going to handle the religious instruction and Brother Voltec will handle the secular instruction. If the child needs discipline then any one of the brothers should report to me and I will handle the problems. The first thing I want you to teach him is the rosary. Take this one and it will be his." He handed a large bead rosary to Brother Andrej. "I will set up a schedule and let you know when you will teach religion to the boy."

The priest took a few hours off and walked down to St. Stefan to visit with the pastors. He found them in the rear of the church where a room had been built to adapt to the priests. They shared the room and there was no furniture except for two beds and a desk. They were setting up a record book so that they could keep track of the income and expenses and Father Damian saw that all was not going well.

He said, "If you have any problems with that, Brother Albert can help you. He does not have much to do these days. He can also help you in scheduling the Masses, ordering supplies and any other problems that you may have. Brother Albert ran the Abbey of St. Francis for many years before I came and he has learned a great deal since I have been here."

Father Josef spoke, "That is an excellent idea, I'm sure he will help. We will contact him tomorrow."

Father Damian added, "May I make a suggestion? You will probably want to define the duties each of you will have so that your duties will not overlap and some duties go undone. Besides this, how are things going? How do you like the church? If there is anything we can do to help you at the abbey, all you have to do is ask."

"We know that," replied Father Igor, "but we have been so busy that we could not stop up to see the brothers. We will go to visit at the first opportunity."

Father Josef smiled and said, "We hear that you have a new addition to the abbey. Do you know who the parents are? Can we help with the religious instruction? We have plans to start a Catechist for the young people so we can start Holy Communion and Confirmation classes."

Father Damian explained that he had put a new brother, Brother Andrej, in charge of Johan's religious instruction but if Brother Andrej had any problems he would seek out either of the priests for help.

The priests at St. Stefan were getting organized, the church began to look like a real parish and the two priests were having an impact on the community. They rented a small store in the town to be used by the priests while they were practicing their other professions. Father Igor would occupy the store in the morning and consult with the people who came to him with problems about their animals. Sometimes he went to a farm if the problem could not be solved in town. Brother Josef stayed at the store in the afternoon and treated the townspeople for their various illnesses. They both charged a nominal amount for their services, just enough to cover the rent. The church and abbey were run independently of each other, Father Damian did not offer advice unless he was asked, and then he referred the priests to one of the brothers who had more knowledge about the problem. Father Damian felt that the two young priests were too proud to ask for help, so he made a point of stopping in two or three times a week and usually found that he could help solve some minor problem.

The education of Johan had begun but it started very slowly, at first, with Brother Voltek seeing Johan every morning for six days a week and Brother Andrej seeing him in the afternoons. Father Damian obtained a list of supplies needed by the teachers and went to Podolencz to buy them. When he visited the school in Podolencz, he was told by the senior instructor that he would have to obtain special permission to teach Johan in the abbey rather than have him attend a public school. Father Damian spent the morning going from one public official to another to obtain the permission but no one had ever heard of the church teaching a child. The officials felt that the schools were better equipped to teach. Finally, he found the notary who gave Father Damian the forms to fill out so he could apply for authorization to teach the child. He was told that usually the state taught the child in secular matters and the church could teach in religous matters. It turned out to be a frustrating morning for the priest, but at least now, he knew what to do. He went back to the abbey and filled out the forms but there was much he could not fill out since he did not know the father or mother. He could estimate the date of birth and where the boy was born from the baptismal certificate that he kept on file in the abbey.

The forms asked for the qualifications of the instructor and Brother Voltek was called in to be questioned about his education. The priest was impressed with how far Brother Voltek had progressed in his education and he could be qualified to be an instructor at the University so his qualifications were not to be disputed. He took the forms to Mayor Alexander Kopec's cobbler shop and the mayor promised to take the matter up with the committee. Two days later, he had the signed form in his possession. Little did Father Damian understand, that he was starting the first Parochial school in Slovakia.

The education of Johan was difficult. As it would with any three and a half year old, for all he wanted to do was play. The first two years were devoted to playing games with a shift to the learning process slowly interwoven into the games. The religious instruction was little more than acting out the roles in the new testament but Johan had learned to say the rosary and that was said at the start of each new class.

Both of the brothers exhibited more patience than the priest could find in the relationship with the boy. Father Damian thought that the boy should be learning at a faster rate than he was progressing but his teachers calmed him down. The teaching fell into a routine and there was not enough to report at the end of each week, so Father Damian sat with each instructor once a month. The classes were held in the dining room which now had five large tables with a head table, two on each side and a fifth one on the end. The instructors tried to take the classes outside when the weather would allow, but there were too many distractions. Each time a brother walked by he would wave to Johan who would wave back and the train of thought was broken. They spoke to the brothers, but they all loved the child and once they saw him, the wave was a reaction.

The classes were progressing well enough at this time, so Father Damian turned his attention to other projects. The two priests had established a routine at St. Stefan and he had not been down there in almost a month. The parishioners were now going to the church instead of the abbey for Mass and both priests were well liked by the people in town.

*   *   *

In his walks around the farm land, he noticed a strand of about twenty large straight oak trees. He had also noticed that people in larger numbers were coming from Poland on the road through the High Tatras, settling in Ruzbachy. He had always had the idea of creating a shrine on the side of the road where it leveled off. Since he had more time now, he drew up some plans for twelve crosses to be built in a bowed line on the site he had chosen. The crosses would be twenty feet high and eight feet across. The beams would have to be at least thirty feet long and they would have to be placed eight to ten feet into the ground. Each cross would have a plaque with the name of an apostle fixed on it and a little wooden area set before each one so that two people could kneel at one time for prayer.

He went down to the saw mill and found that Jan, the owner of the mill, would cut the eight-inch square beams if the priest would mill his grain for him at the next harvest. A deal was struck with a hand shake and Father Damian went to St. Stefan to talk to Father Igor who promised to mention it in church the following Sunday.

The brothers, with the help of a few volunteers from town, went out and the project was started. The trees were cut down, then cut into twenty eight-foot lengths and hauled into the saw mill. It took two weeks to saw the timbers and it was decided that the crosses would be affixed to the beams at the site so they would be easier to transport. It took a whole month to dig the holes, finally, the crosses were built. A month later, the stations were erected and the project was completed. It took six months from the time the plans were drawn up until the time the shrine was in place so that it could be used.

One of the brothers remarked "I hope that the Jews had this much trouble in building a cross when they crucified Christ."

Father Damian smiled and said, "Everyone worked hard and they have done an excellent job ont his project."

The crosses would have to be maintained and he would have to work on that at some future date but right now, the shrine was impressive. He instructed Brother Theo to have his cooks, now there were four of them, prepare a special meal for the brothers, the volunteers and their families for the work they had done and he gave each volunteer a bible. He never had trouble getting volunteers to help him and this practice continued for each project.

*   *   *

Father Damian turned his attention to the education of Johan once again. He spoke to the two brothers who were having a difficult time in holding his attention. Johan missed his carefree days when all he did was meet the brothers and play games and he did not like the learning process at all. Father Damian began visiting the dining hall when school was in session and while he was there, the boy paid attention. But when he left, Johan reverted to his day dreaming and it was difficult for the instructors to reach him. When both brothers reported this to the priest, he had to devise some method of reaching the boy without punishing him. After all, he was dealing with a six-year-old boy. Finally, he asked to see the boy in his office.

"Johan," he said, "It has come to my attention that you are not interested in your studies."

"Why do I need these studies? The brothers will teach me

everything I need to know in the abbey," he answered.

"What if you did not want to stay in the abbey but wanted to go out into the world? How do you think that you would fare in the outside world? Do you feel that you are now equipped to find work to support yourself?"

"Well, I like working with animals and Brother Josef can teach me all that I need to know to do that type of work."

"All right then, I will give you two weeks off from your studies and you can work with Brother Josef as a test to see if you want to do that type of work for the rest of your life. Starting Monday you will report to Brother Josef at seven o'clock and you will work until you are finished for the day. You realize that the animals do not know that it is Sunday, so they have to be cared for seven days a week. I will not talk to you until the two weeks have gone by. I will talk to you two weeks from next Monday at seven in the morning. We will decide then which path you will follow." With that he dismissed the boy.

Once Johan had left, the priest sought out Brother Josef in the barns and told him what the arrangements were. Brother Josef knew what to do. He would work the six-year-old from seven in the morning until it was time for the evening meal and vespers. If the boy wanted the morning meal, then he would have to rise at the same time as all the Brothers did and work their hours.

Brother Josef had between three and five helpers depending on whether the friars were needed elsewhere and he had plenty of work that had to be completed each day. He was to treat Johan exactly the way he treated the friars who worked with him and Johan would be back in school in two weeks. Brother Voltek and Brother Andrej were delighted, neither realized how devious Father Damian was when it came to convincing someone he wanted to bring over to his side. They left his office with just a little more respect than they had before and they also knew that they need to be a little more wary of their dealings with the priest.

Once the two weeks had gone by, the priest asked Johan, "What have you decided?"

Before he answered, Johan asked a question of his own. "Is the work done by the other brothers in the abbey as hard?"

Father Damian answered, "No, some are harder. Would you like to work two weeks with Brother Simon or possibly Brother Henrik in the barns? I would like your answer now, Johan."

"I will stay in school," said Johan. "I would like the kind of work that Brother Voltek does."

The priest looked at him and said, "Then you will need training, but even before the training you will need to know how to read, you will need to know how to write and you will need to know your numbers. Once you have mastered all of these subjects, then I will assign you to each of the brothers to learn their trade. When you finish, you will know more than I do about the work that has to be done to handle an abbey of this size. Trust me, Johan, I have your best interest at heart. As long as you stay in the abbey, you are under my care and I owe it to you and our Lord to make you the best that you can be for the rest of your life. Do you understand what I am telling you, Johan?"

"Yes, I do," he answered. "And I will try my very best."

Johan returned to his studies a little wiser and his teachers gave good reports in the months that followed.

9

It was time for Father Damian to visit the bishop again, but the bishop had asked that he need not make the trip as often. The bishop was confident that the abbey was being run properly and he was being pressed for time with trouble in the other parishes. Father Damian had not seen the bishop for a year. The longer time between visits was fine with Father Damian, because the larger the abbey had become, the busier he became. He visited St. Stefan before he went to Bratislava to give the pastors time to prepare a report on their progress and he would pick it up a few days prior to his leaving. He had many things to attend to before journeying down to Bratislava. He had to prepare his own report with brothers Albert and Voltek; he had to prepare the finances with them to justify the amount of money he was sending to the Cathedral and he had to prepare a report about the education of Johan.

He had received authorization to educate Johan instead of sending him to school and the next step would be to set up a school for local children. The school would naturally progress from the secondary education to a higher education so he could get local boys into the brotherhood of St. Francis. Once he had all of his material in order, he left for his trip to Bratislava. He decided to take the train down from Polodencz so he would have time to work on his presentation. He arrived at the cathedral late in the evening and was shown right to his room. Brother Theo had made him some food which he ate on the train, so he was not hungry and went directly to bed and slept through the night.

The next morning he met with the bishop. He had heard of the shrine that the priest had installed on the pass though the High Tatras and he was pleased.

Father Damian explained, "The cost of the wood for the crosses was nothing as we went into the forest and cut them down ourselves. The saw mill cut them into poles and we ground the miller's grain for him. The first thing that I the want the travelers to see when they entered our country is that Slovaks are people who take their religion seriously. It had cost nothing but labor, a good meal and a few bibles."

The bishop changed the subject, "Why do you keep Johan in the abbey? You have not transferred him to a family who would take care of him and relieve you of the burden of care."

The priest stated that it was no burden. It gave him an opportunity to bring up the matter of the school. He explained, "I have plans to begin a new school in the abbey, but would have to receive authorization from your Excellency and the Jesuits. It is an excellent method of giving a good catholic education."

The bishop looked puzzled, "Why has no one in Slovakia thought of this before? I will take it up with the Jesuits at the first opportunity. I will try to obtain some instructors because, after all, the Jesuits are a teaching order and they do have people who would qualify as instructors."

Father Damian brought up a new subject, "I want to send another friar to the seminary. His name is Andrej Baranowski and he should be ready to go by the first of the year. I will need a replacement since he is the religious instructor for Johan and I want to keep up his education."

The bishop made a note and said, "I will give this my most serious consideration and will look for a replacement. How is the church doing? Are there any problems?"

Father Damian had his opening, "The church population is growing and so is the outside work of the pastors. Father Josef's store is now more of a clinic and he is seeing more patients every day so there will come a time when he will have to devote all his time to his medical practice. Father Igor is gone from the church every afternoon taking care of the animals of the farmers around Ruzbachy and the church needs a full time pastor. I would recommend Brother Andrej when he returns from the seminary."

The bishop smiled and said, "Somehow, I knew that was coming but the church will need one sooner and I have just the man for you and he can serve as an interim pastor until Brother Andrej would become a priest. He plans to retire in a few years and he has had a parish before."

After they discussed all the other matters, the bishop had supper sent in with a bottle of wine. He asked about the Ruzbachy wine and Father Damian told him that he was disappointed and felt that the grapes would never be of the quality to produce good wine. The bishop suggested that they try a new strain of grapes and to use the other grapes for something else, but Father Damian smiled and said that it might make a good vinegar. He doubted even that.

The meal ended and they were both relaxing before a fire with a glass of brandy when the bishop brought up another subject. He said, "I have been getting some pressure from the Jesuits to replace you with an abbott from the Jesuit Order but you could still be the pastor of St. Stefan and someone else could run the abbey. You could even have Brother Andrej as an assistant pastor once he becomes a priest, or, I can find you a nice parish where you can relax for a while without the problems you have now. What are your thoughts?"

Without hesitation the priest replied, "I do not want to leave St. Francis as I have much to do there. The townspeople have confidence in my abilities and it took me sixteen years to accomplish this. To send in an abbott now would set the agenda back ten years. I have long range plans such as clearing more land for animals and expanding the orchard. I am helping my two young priests to expand the parish and to make the Holy Catholic Church a power in the region. If you want to see the influence of the Church grow in the area, then please do not replace me. Please pardon me, your excellency, but it would be a mistake."

"Thank you for helping me make up my mind," he replied. "I will leave things alone for now. How old are you?"

"Forty-two years old, your excellency, and I have at least ten more years of work to put in. When I am too tired to continue, I will tell you, but please do not make me leave now before I can complete my work."

The bishop changed the subject and they talked for a few more minutes. The bishop excused himself, embraced the priest, and since he would not see him in the morning, said goodbye and left.

Father Damian sat by himself for an hour and prayed to God that he had made the correct choice. He did not even think about it when he gave his answer but he thought of how life would be in a small parish without the constant problem solving at St. Francis.

He asked God to guide him on the correct path and suddenly he thought, "I thrive on problems and being able to solve them. I would not be able to survive in an environment without problems. We Slovaks are survivors. We have kept our language, customs and our toughness, if only we were not obsessed with procreation. When God said, GO FORTH AND MULTIPLY! we took him literally."

He left St. Martins very early and took the train to Podolencz to find Brother Mikel waiting for him. On the ride back he spoke to Brother Mikel, "Do you feel that we should abandon our plan to make wine?"

Brother Mikel shook his head back and forth and said, "It takes sometimes twenty years to make a fine wine. I want to graft our vines with other vines until we can make a wine that we can put on the market. Since we have all the equipment in place, we should continue."

Father Damian replied, "The land could be put to other use such as expanding the orchard. I will, however, agree to give you some more time to develop your wine."

The friar was relieved and relaxed for the rest of the trip.

10

When the priest returned to the abbey he found everything in order; even Johan was behaving himself. As he was about to get to work on some paper work, Pani Benerik came through the door. She was flushed from running up to the abbey.

Out of breath, she gasped, "We need you now!"

"What is it?" he asked

"Please come and send someone for Father Josef. We have a sick woman on our hands and she cannot be moved."

He met Brother Karol in the kitchen and told him to saddle a horse and fetch Father Josef as quickly as he could. When he arrived in the kitchen, he found a woman, obviously in labor lying on the table. She was moaning, crying and asking to be helped and her accent told him that she was Polish.

Suddenly, Mrs. Benerik exclaimed, "The baby is coming! . . . boil water, get me clean cloths, thread and scissors."

Everyone in the room moved except the priest who was holding the woman's hand and talking to her in a low, soothing voice. Her breathing was labored and she felt greatly over heated. The husband was in the dining room. He would hear the commotion, but knew enough to stay out of the way. The woman lying on the table helped with the delivery and once she heard the baby cry she sighed her last breath. Father Damian gave her the last rites and thought to himself that he did not know this woman, or whether she was Catholic or not.

Soon after Father Josef burst into the room with a small leather satchel. He checked the woman over quickly, told Father Damian that she was gone and turned his attention to the baby. It was a little girl and she was very plump. Father Josef estimated her weight at 12 pounds. She was red in color with a full head of black hair.

As he was tying the cord Father Josef said, "If this woman

walked the pass carrying this baby, it is no wonder that she died. Her heart just could not handle the strain and she must have survived on pure will power to make it this far. She sacrificed herself for her baby. As soon as I have finished with the baby, I'll go in and speak with the husband."

He worked quickly washing the baby and clearing the air channel. He wrapped the child in a clean cloth and handed her to Mrs. Benerik and examined the dead woman next.

Father Damian, with tears in his eyes, said, "I felt so helpless when she died. I did not know what to do."

"There was nothing you could have done," said the doctor. "There was nothing I could have done. Her death was a certainty when they laid her on this table. Do not feel sad. She has gone to a better life for something had driven her out of Poland. Now, I had better go and talk to her husband."

He left the room and entered the dining room.

After a few minutes, Father Damian heard shouting from the dining room. "Why did you not save her? Do you call yourself a doctor?"

Father Damian entered the room and saw the heavy set man with his fists in the air ready to strike at anything in their way.

He said quietly, "This is the Abbey of St. Francis. It is a house of God and we do not tolerate violence here."

The man looked at Father Damian. "I do not care where I am. I have just lost my wife. I have no need for your God. Where was He when Anna breathed her last breath? Why did He not save her? Give me my child. I will come back for my wife when I can," he said.

He went into the kitchen, took the baby and left; he did not look at the covered body of his wife lying on the table.

Father Damian looked over at the doorway and saw Johan looking at him in bewilderment. He told the boy to go to his room and closed the door and then turned to Pani Benerik and said, "Tell me everything that you know about these people."

She said, "I was home alone. My family was visiting elsewhere, and it was just getting dusk when there was a banging at the kitchen door. This man said that his wife was having a child on the side of the road and she needed help. I hitched up the wagon and rode out there where she lay by the side of the road. She looked extremely ill and I feared for both her and her unborn child. Since the abbey was closer than my home, I brought them here. We lifted her on the table, sent the husband into the dining room and that is when I came to get you.

The priest asked, "Did you talk to the man? Tell me anything that the man may have said, no matter how trivial."

She told him, "The man and woman had gone through the pass from Nowy Targ, Poland and had followed the river until they came to the High Tatras. They had been walking for seven days and she was getting weaker and weaker. Her name was Anna and she was going to deliver her baby anytime. He said that his name was Pavel Valigursky and he was trying to reach his cousin, Pavel Dombrowski who had come over from Poland fifteen years ago and had settled here. He said that he had to leave Poland but he did not tell me why."

"Well," said the priest, "at least we know where he was going. I will ride out to the Dombrowski's home first thing in the morning. Do you want someone to accompany you home? Your family must be worried."

She declined and she went out the kitchen door. He had the wagon brought to the kitchen door and they put Anna Valigursky in the back, drove it into the barn and locked the door. The following morning, Father Damian had the body taken to the village undertaker to arrange for the funeral. The undertaker was a solemn man, who first questioned who was going to pay for his services. The two brothers referred him to Father Damian. The priest rode out to Pavel Dombrowski's home through its vast acreage. The priest found Eva Dombrowski in the kitchen with a young girl who he assumed to be a hired girl to help in the kitchen. They were washing dishes, drying them and putting them on the shelf over the sink.

Eva came to the door. "Bless this house,"she said as she opened the door to let him in. He entered a spotless kitchen with everything in its place.

"Hello, Eva,"said the priest. "Is Pavel Valigursky staying with you? I would like to see him."

Just them Pavel Dombrowski came through the door and into the kitchen. "I expected you," Pavel said. "How did you find us so quickly?

"He happened to go to Pani Benerik and you know how she is," said the priest. "She found out that you were cousins so I came here to speak with him. I had Anna's body sent to the undertaker."

"Good," said Pavel. "I'll take care of the expenses. I suppose that you would like to talk to my cousin."

"Yes, I would,"came the reply. "I would like to make arrangements to baptize the little girl. Father Josef needs to get information from Pavel so he can fill out the death certificate and birth certificate. He needs to file these documents with the clerk of the records. I'm afraid that the undertaker will be reluctant to bury her in the cemetery unless he has those records.

"I'll take care of it," said Pavel. "We will see Father Josef sometime tomorrow. In the meantime, my cousin is resting. He has been through a tiring experience. He was exhausted when he came here last night and I still do not know how he found us. The baby is doing fine, Eva has been through this a few times, as you know, so she can handle it." He looked at his wife who had a broad smile on her face as she nodded her head.

Pavel Valigursky was not seen very much after that. Father Damian heard from Father Igor, who had visited the Dombrowski farm a few weeks later, that Pavel Valigursky had felt guilty for pushing his wife through the pass in her condition. She had wanted to stop at the shrine of the twelve crosses to pray but he said that it would do no good and he did not want to waste the time. She had cried for sometime after they left the shrine. Pavel was staying in the guest room and came only for his meals. Father Igor felt that he would have problems for a long time and he wished that he could talk to the man and try to bring him out of it. He would have to make more trips to see the animals so he might get a chance to talk to him. The baby was growing older and still had not been baptized and Father Damian was getting worried. He should have baptized the child when he had the chance. Finally, he took his materials and rode to the Dombrowski farm.

He went directly to the barn and found Pavel brushing down a beautiful horse. "Is that an Arabian?" the priest asked.

"Yes," answered Pavel, proudly. "This is the stallion that is going to build my herd."

"You will have a herd with good blood lines," said the priest. "I have come to baptize the little girl. It is not good to have the child go unbaptized and we want her to go into the Kingdom of Heaven. Will you and Pavel allow me to baptize her?"

"I will go and talk to my cousin," said Pavel, "Please come into the house and Eva will make you a cup of tea." They both went into the house, in the parlor, the priest was led to a blue overstuffed chair. Soon Eva brought in a tray ladened with cups and saucers, the teapot and a dish of little cakes. She did not get many visitors and, when she did, she wanted to show him that she could entertain.

Pavel entered the room as they were talking and said, "I have spoken to Pavel. He said to do what you wanted, so long as he did not have to see you."

They took the baby into the parlor with a bowl of cold water. The priest blessed the water and was about to start the ceremony when he asked, "What is her name?"

Eva said, "Pavel had decided on Olga Anna Valigursky."

"Who are the Godparents?"

"We are," Pavel and Eva said at once. They looked at each other and smiled.

"'I baptize you, Olga Anna Valigurski, in the Name of the Father, Son and Holy Ghost. There, I feel better now. I was able to give Anna the last rites so my work is done." With that, he left the farm to go home.

As Father Damian was sitting at his desk, Johan was suddenly and quietly in front of him. "What happens when you die?" he asked.

Father Damian thought for a minute and then he spoke. "Your body is not needed any longer, but your soul goes up to Heaven to be with God. This is, of course, if you are good. If you are not good, then your soul goes to the devil and he takes it to Hell, where you suffer for all eternity."

"What is eternity?" asked the boy.

"Eternity is forever and ever. You have the choice of being with God or being with Satan. It depends on what you do on earth and when you are not good then you have to confess what you did wrong to the priest. He will give you a penance and then forgive your sins in the name of God."

The next question by the boy was, "Can he do this?"

"Yes, he can if he is a priest. Brothers cannot do this because they are not priests."

Johan pondered the next question, debating whether to ask it or not. Finally, he decided to ask, "Is that how babies are born? Is that how I was born?"

"Yes, it is and yes, it was."

Johan was burning with curiosity. "How does this happen? Something has to happen or all women would be having babies."

The priest thought it best to be honest. "Do you remember what the ram does to the ewe? He mounts her from the back and deposits his seed into her which combines with her seed forming a lamb, which is born sometime in the spring."

"Oh," said Johan.

That's how it happens with people, too?"

"Yes, Johan, that is how it happens."

Johan left thinking about what he had just heard. The priest sighed a sigh of relief. He had dreaded this day, but the episode with Olga had brought it about much sooner than he had expected. He was happy that it was over and it was better that he heard it at this age rather than later. If he heard it later, he would have more questions and that would be more difficult to answer. He heard no more from Johan about the subject.

*   *   *

About two months later he had heard that Pavel Valigursky and his cousin Pavel Dombrowski were seen in the tavern. At least he was now getting out and seeing people and the priest made a mental note to stop in for a visit when he was close to the Dombrowski Farm. As chance would have it, he met the two of them in the cobbler's shop when he went in to ask the mayor about getting a permit to open a school at the abbey. The two men seemed happy enough but Pavel Valigursky had very little to say. When asked how Olga was getting along, Pavel Dombrowski answered that she was growing and was going to be a big girl, she was a happy child, well fed and dry. Father Damian told the mayor that he would return another time. The other two had come in to see if there was a farm for sale that was not advertised as Pavel Dombrowski was going to loan his cousin the money to buy a farm and stay in Ruzbachy.

Two new faces appeared in Ruzbachy when they arrived by train from Bratislava without advance notice. One was a priest in his early fifties by the name of Father Edvard Nadovny. He had a small parish in the southern end of Slovakia about fifty miles due west of Bratislava and he was now assigned to St.Stefan. The bishop felt that the church should buy a small house near the church to be used as a rectory and all three priests would live there to serve as pastors to St. Stefan church. Father Igor and Father Josef would pursue full time duties in their secular professions and act as assistant pastors for St. Stefan. There were now four priests in Ruzbachy where sixteen years ago there were none.

The second new face belonged to Brother Jerome who showed excellent abilities as a teacher of young children. He was patient, innovative and well educated in both the secular subjects and those of religion. He would be the teacher to take Brother Andrej's place when he went to the seminary on January first of the following year.

Father Damian saw nothing but problems when there were three priests living in one house. He had to define the scope of authority of each when he had met with all three at the abbey. He found Father Edvard a little set in his ways, head strong. He told all three that, although the church and the abbey were separate entities, Ruzbachy was still the town where he was perceived as the priest. He told them that he still had the ear of the bishop. If there were problems, he would not hesitate to contact the bishop to see that the person not getting along with the other two priests would be transfered and he would assume the role as pastor of the church. He made sure that they understood him before he dismissed them to look for a house to buy for the rectory.

There were many homes around the church, but none was for sale. No one wanted to move out of a home in the middle of all the activities and then have to walk from the outer limits of town. There was enough room on the land behind the church to build a rectory. Father Damian, with Father Edvard's input, designed a house, drew up the plans, included a cost estimate and sent the package to the bishop for approval. Father Damian sent a postscript with the package telling the bishop that since the church already owned the land, they would not have to purchase another plot. They could get away cheaper by building the rectory on the existing site and they could also build it with the idea of expansion at a future date.

A month later, authorization came from the bishop. The bills for the construction were to be sent to the Cathedral for payment. With Father Edvard supervising the building of the rectory, and Father Damian acting a consultant, the building came along smoothly and it was built under the budget recommended by the two priests.

Father Damian had little to do with the education of Johan since he had three instructors and Johan was getting much attention. On January first, Brother Andrej went to the seminary and he would be gone for six years. By that time, Father Edvard would be about 60 years old and it would be time for Father Andrej to become pastor of St. Stefan. Father Damian had nothing to do but to keep peace among all of the clergy in the area.

Pavel Valigursky had been successful in buying the farm that he wanted and his cousin loaned him the money. The cousins were close and Eva took care of Olga until she was ready to go to school, her father picked her up, each evening and she spent the night in her own home. When Olga was not with her father, Eva took care of her.

11

The trouble began with Johan, when he was eleven years old. He started to test his teachers and Father Damian as to how far he could push them before he reached a limit. Each day he would try to do a little less and he would always have an excuse as to why he did something or failed in what he was supposed to do. At first, there were insignificant chores and someone always did what Johan was supposed to do without telling anyone. Johan thought to himself that this was easy and if he kept doing this, soon he would have everyone doing his work. When he failed to do one of his outside assignments, his teacher would put it off until the next day so it got to the point when both of his teachers finally reported it to Father Damian. The priest decided to watch the boy more closely, in school and in his daily work outside of school. He saw a pattern forming and, before he decided what to do, the boy went too far.

Brother Voltek told Johan that he must study his lesson for the next day because he was going to be tested to see how much he was learning. Johan decided that night that he was going to take the day off and hike through the forest. He would do so without telling anyone and would see what the reaction would be when he returned. To take it one step further, he would pretend that he was lost and when he was found, they would be so happy to see him that there would be no punishment. The weather had been sunny and warm that early summer day and he felt that he needed a day off from his school and work. The children in town received time off at planting time in the spring and harvest time in the fall but he had to go to school every day. (When he had pretended that he was ill, Father Josef would come and give him some foul tasting concoctions made with sauerkraut juice, castor oil and fruit juice and that really made him ill.)

On the next day while everyone was at morning prayers, he went to the kitchen and took some rolls, butter, fruit and a small piece of meat that was in the cold storage. He had planned to be "found" by the evening meal. He left the abbey through the front door and went around the wall to the rear of the wall. He followed the road that ran along a side of the hill to the road that became the pass through the mountains. The road was scenic and he passed an area where wild flowers grew. He would have to remember to tell Brother Jan about them so that he could use them around the abbey. He finally decided to leave the road and go into the forest. The boy was worried that he might meet someone on the road and he did not want to meet anyone just yet. He came across a small brook, found himself a log to sit on and ate his rolls and butter. Better to carry them inside than outside, he thought as he left very few crumbs for the animals. He was tired from his long walk. The sun was getting high in the sky and as he sat on the ground with his back on the log, he fell asleep for more than two hours.

* * *

Meanwhile, back at the abbey, Brother Voltek went to see Father Damian to tell him that Johan did not come to school and he could not find him anywhere. The priest went looking for him and his first stop was the kitchen. No one remembered seeing the boy, but Brother Theo said that he had noticed something unusual. He had prepared the baskets of rolls and butter for the morning meal and he put the same amount in each basket. The friar noticed that one of the baskets was three rolls short and he had to replace them. He had thought that he had miscounted, but he had not done that in many years. There was also some fruit missing from one of the fruit baskets, and he had to replace that also.

The priest thought that the boy might be hiding somewhere in the abbey, he had Brothers Voltek and Jerome go to the different parts of the abbey where the boy might be hiding. They were to report to his office at eleven o'clock. He went back to his study to contemplate the punishment that he would give to the boy. He had an idea as to what he was going to do to him, but he would wait until he was found.

At eleven o'clock the teachers reported that the boy was no-where to be found in the abbey. They felt that he must have gone outside. Father Damian went to the bell and rang it until all the brothers that could hear it were gathered in the courtyard. He had brought his maps and sent the brothers to comb certain areas and if he was found, he would be brought back and the bell would be rung three times. Everyone would then come back to the abbey. As he was giving out the assignments, a group of people came from town. They heard the bell being rung at such an odd hour and they knew something was wrong. Soon the entire search party went into the forest. More towns people joined the mission.

*   *   *

Johan woke up from his nap, and looking around, found nothing that looked familiar. He did not remember which way he had come so he started to walk away from the sun, which should take him back to the abbey. He thought of the looks of relief when he wandered in looking lost and hungry. What the boy did not real-ize was that he had slept for a long time and the sun had reached its peak and was starting to come down, so he was walking away from the abbey. He walked all afternoon without seeing anything familiar. He was now getting hungry and he realized that he was lost. Now, he really was in trouble.

*   *   *

The search party went into the forest in the hills south of the High Tatras. If the boy went north into the mountains, he would not be found for a day, if at all. Father Damian thought that the boy must be frightened and if he stayed in the forest past dark, he

might encounter wolves or a bear. Johan was in danger and he
must be found but there was nothing to be done but to keep on
looking. He had hoped that the search party would not go out of
the range of the abbey bell, but once it got dark, there would be
no sense in walking through the forest. If he was not found, then
they would resume the search in the morning. The sun was already getting low and once it got dark he would call off the search
for the night.

*   *   *

Johan was tired for he had walked the entire day and all that he
had to eat were three rolls and butter, some fruit and the meat he
had taken from the kitchen. He had plenty of water since the
brooks coming down from the hills contained cold clear water.
The sun was starting to go down and it would be dark soon so he
would have to find a place to spend the night while it was still
light out. He looked ahead and saw light coming through the
dense forest but when he ran toward it, he saw that it was a clearing and then a field. Maybe he would meet someone so he ran into
the field and waved his arms but he could see no one. The field
sloped down and he walked down the hill when he came to a road
which seemed to be used quite a bit. As he was walking, he heard
the sound of hoof beats and coming over a knoll, he saw the wagon
with a woman driving the horse. The wagon was full of hay and he
had never been so happy to see another human being. He waved
his arms to stop the wagon.

The woman looked down at him. "What are you doing way
out here, little boy?"

"I'm lost," said Johan. "I belong to the Abbey at St. Francis in
Ruzbachy. Is this the road to Ruzbachy?"

"Yes, it is," answered the woman. "But you are going the wrong
way. You are very close to Osturne about twenty miles away from
Ruzbachy. Come, my little wanderer and climb in the back. I will

take you to my house, give you supper and take you home. Your
people must be worried and it will be dark soon."

*   *   *

Father Damian called off the search at dark because most of the
townspeople would not go into the forest after dark. Each one
went to his own place to wait for the coming of the sun on the next
day. When the brothers returned to the abbey, Brother Theo had
a hot meal of crupi waiting with fresh baked bread. They ate in
silence even though the food tasted very good, after their long and
difficult day.

*   *   *

Johan fell asleep as soon as he lay in the hay. He was tired and
relieved to be found. The woman's house was a cottage a short
distance from the road and he had walked right past it, but did
not see it because of the new growth of leaves on the trees. She
served him pea soup, bread and a large glass of milk. Once supper
was finished, her husband started out for the Abbey of St. Francis.
Johan again rode in the back of the wagon and fell asleep so he had
no idea how far he had walked because he had no idea of how far
twenty miles was. They arrived at the abbey at about 10 pm; almost everyone had gone to sleep. The abbey was dark. They had
gone to bed so that they could get an early start in the morning.

Brother Theo was just inspecting the kitchen to make sure
that his assistants had left it clean. Two of his cooks would get up
early to bake bread and rolls before they went to morning prayer
and they went to bed at dusk while the other two cleaned up after
the evening meal. Brother Theo had nothing to do these days except to supervise the others and sample the food as it was prepared. He had gained a little weight in the last few months but
the priest thought that he needed a rest after the many years he
had served his brothers. As he prepared to blow out the lantern, he

heard the sound of horses' hooves in the court yard. Someone was in the abbey and Brother Theo went out to investigate. He found a young man on the wagon with a load of hay. He said nothing but pointed to the back of the wagon. The friar went around with his lantern and saw Johan sound asleep. He put his finger to his lips in a gesture to keep silent, ran into the abbey and rapped on the priest's door. Father Damian jumped from his bed expecting the worst and followed Brother Theo outside. They arrived at the wagon and the friar held the lantern high so Father Damian could see inside. Johan was still sound asleep. The priest blessed himself and said a silent prayer to heaven for the boy's safe return. He picked him up and took him to his room, put him to bed fully clothed. The boy did not wake up. The priest silently closed the door and went to see the man who brought him home.

Father Damian asked, "Where did you find him?"

The man said, "My wife found him on the road to Osturne about two miles this side of that town. She took him to our home and fed him. I brought him right here."

"Do you want to spend the night?"

"No, my wife is home alone and I want to return as soon as possible. We live in the counrty, far away from the town, and I do not like to leave her alone for too long."

Brother Theo gave him the lantern to light his way home and the priest asked for his name so the brothers in the abbey might pray for him. They thanked the young man, helped him turn his wagon around and he left the abbey to return home.

Father Damian went to the bell tower and rang the bell three times. The brothers came running out of the abbey into the courtyard, a few carried lanterns. The priest told them that the boy was safe and sound and was asleep in his own bed. They would see him tomorrow so they returned to their cots for a restful night sleep, now that the crisis was over.

The next day before morning prayer, Father Damian went to Johan's room and found the boy sitting on his bed. "I'm sorry," he said.

Father Damian resisted an embrace and said, "We will talk about this later this morning. I want to see you in my office after the morning meal and you are to be at morning prayers so that the brothers may see that you are all right. They spent all day tramping in the forest looking for you and now they have to do two days work in one day. You owe them an apology which you will give after the morning meal." With that he left.

Morning prayer lasted a little longer than usual as each brother said a little extra prayer of Thanksgiving. The morning meal was more noisy than usual and after the meal, at the prompting of the priest. Johan got up to speak. It became very quiet. "I want to tell you that I am sorry to put all of you through a hardship yesterday. I was being foolish and I offer no excuses. I want you to know that even though it was only for one day, I missed all of you." He looked at Father Damian when he said the last part. "That is all I have to say," he added.

The brothers got up and gathered around him. While some embraced him, others shook his hand and slapped him on his back. The brothers went to work with a smile. Father Damian went back to his office to wait for Johan to appear. He came through the door still with a smile on his face until he saw the frown on the priest's face.

"May I sit? " he asked.

"No!" came the reply. "What were you trying to do, Johan? Why did you want to put us through all the worry? Do you not know that we love you? God must love you because he brought you back."

Johan had thought of all the standard excuses an eleven-year-old would use, but decided against them. "I thought that I was old enough to take care of myself in the forest."

Father Damian got up and walked around the desk. "So you think that you are old enough to be on your own, especially in the forest. I agree, you are getting older and since you feel that you are maturing, there will be no sleeping late in the morning, and you will follow the routine of the brothers. You cannot eat in the kitchen any longer so Brother Theo can prepare special foods for you. You will eat what everyone else eats, you will sleep when everyone sleeps and you will be given extra work for a week to make up for the day you lost. You will be given extra chores to do from now on. Do you understand what I have told you?"

"Yes. Will you hear my confession now?"

"No, Johan, not this time. I will hear your confession Saturday as usual. What I have just told you is penance, we have not gotten to the punishment as yet. What you did was to disobey God's rules and my rules. We have taken care of God's broken rules and now we will talk about the punishment that you will receive for breaking my rules. I want you to go into the woodshed and bring me a piece of wood that Brother Theo uses in the cooking fireplace, one that has been split."

Johan ran out of the room and returned in five minutes with a piece of firewood. When a flat side was on the floor, the sharp edge was facing up.

"Do you have your rosary with you?" the priest asked.

"No," he replied.

"That is all right, you can use mine," said the priest. "Put the piece of wood on the floor next to my desk."

The boy did as he was told.

"Now kneel on it."

"It is sharp," Johan said.

"Yes, I know. He handed the boy a set of rosary beads. "Now you are to kneel straight up, do not sit on your heels, and say the rosary from beginning to end, out loud. When you have finished, you can get up. Be sure to say it slowly so that I can understand and do not skip any prayers because I will be saying mine along with you. You will do this in my office for the next five days. This is not penance, Johan, it is punishment for disobeying the law of the abbey. Now I would like to see you get started."

It must have been painful to kneel on that jagged piece of wood, but Johan did not let his voice waiver. He said the rosary and when he finished, the priest gave him a nod and he got up.

Johan had trouble getting up and had to hold on to the desk to get to his feet but he did so and then went to the chair to sit. He now knew what punishment was and he would never try to miss a day of school again. As he sat there getting his composure back, Father Josef entered the room.

"I hear that you found our happy wanderer," he said with a smile. "I have come to examine him to see if he is all right."

"I will leave the room. Please let me know when you are finished, "said Father Damian, who left the room to go into the kitchen.

He sat for a few minutes. "I hope I have not been too hard on the boy, "he said to Brother Theo. "But he does have to learn."

Brother Theo looked at the priest and said, "I saw him running into your office with the piece of firewood. If he had known what it was for he would not have been running. Do not be too hard on yourself because you have to discipline the boy. All of us at the abbey have undergone that punishment more than once. It is a good lesson for him to learn and it is more important than any lesson you can teach in a classroom. Most of the time it takes only one application but with Johan, I do not know."

"Thank you, Brother,"he said. "It is not easy. From now on, he is to be treated the same as the Brothers. Be sure there is a place for him at morning prayers and vespers and set a place for him at the meals, at the lowest end of the table. As he learns, we will allow him to advance. Make sure that the brothers know what I am doing as I do not want them to believe that I am putting Johan ahead of them." He then went back to his office. Father Josef had completed his examination of Johan. Once he was dismissed, he ran off to get ready for class.

"How is he?", asked Father Damian.

"Oh, he will live," was the reply. "He has some cuts, bruises and bug bites, but I put some salve on them and they should heal very soon. We Slovaks heal very quickly." He looked at the piece of wood on the floor and said, "I see that you used the old rosary and firewood routine on the boy. The wood drew blood, but not serious. Do you plan to do it again?"

"Yes, he has four more times to go." answered Father Damian.

Josef frowned, "You are being quite harsh on the boy, are you not?"

"No, he has to learn."

"Well, I put some cloth on the knees and told him that he should keep it on for a week. I will come back at that time and change them. He seemed pleased."

Father Damian smiled, "Please do not tell him that I know about your binding him up. It will make it easier for him to take the punishment. I really hated to do that to him."

Johan settled into a routine with the brothers and after that episode, he had no reason to be punished again. He did quite a bit of penance, but no more punishment. Father Josef mentioned to the parish how grateful Father Damian had been to the townspeople for their help in finding Johan. Father Damian made a trip to the young couple that found his charge. He took them a load of hay, fruit, vegetables and a bible for them. He stayed with them, blessed their home and left as a friend.

The abbey had been growing and maybe it was a good time to press the bishop for authorization to train his own friars. Father Damian knew that there must be young men in the village who wanted to come to the abbey and this thought lifted his spirits. He had been asking the bishop to allow him to train his own friars for the abbey for some time now and he spoke to the bishop each time he went to Bratislava, but the answer was always the same. The bishop would agree to it, but the Jesuits wanted to train their own friars. Privately, Father Damian felt that the Jesuits were not doing such a good job and each time he asked the bishop if he could talk to the Jesuits, he absolutely refused, saying that it was not the right time. It was a touchy subject for the Jesuits to have a parish priest in charge of one of their monasteries. The worst part about the arrangement was that the parish priest was doing a good job and the bishop did not want anything to change the status quo.

12

It was now five years since the episode with Johan. He had grown to be a strong young man of 16. He was bright and had taken to studies. Johan was a good student now and it was time to take the next step in his training. He was going be trained in the religious order of the Jesuits whether the bishop agreed to it or not. He knew the operations of the abbey better than anyone else and he had worked with all the brothers, at one time or another, so that he could assume the responsibilities of any phase of the operation of the abbey. The Jesuits required six years of schooling in their schools in order for a friar to take his final vows, so it was time now to start. He had to visit the bishop in a month and he would tell him of his plans. The time was growing short and he would either have to put Johan through Jesuit training or send him to the seminary now. He really was not ready for the school in Bratislava, and besides, he did not want to lose him. Once he came out of the seminary, they could send him anywhere and he wanted him there at St. Francis.

Father Damian made yet another trip to Bratislava. He had lost track of just how many trips he had made, but he missed the old days when he went by horseback, allowing him to take his time and think. Things were being rushed too quickly these days. Maybe it was just that he was getting older.

When he arrived at the cathedral, he received word that the bishop wanted to see him as soon as he arrived. He was ushered into the bishop's chambers without taking his coat off.

"I have some news for you," said the bishop. "You might be able to train your own friars after all. I spoke to Jan Cardinal Miesheski at a reception last week and he asked about you for it seems that a great many people have heard of you. He will talk to the Jesuits and persuade them to let you try since you have been educating this young charge of yours for the last eleven years. The cardinal would like to question the young man to see if you have done a good job of educating him. Then the cardinal will recommend it and the Jesuits would not dare to oppose him. The cardinal will make a trip here next month to speak with you and your charge."

The priest interrupted the bishop, "Yes."

The bishop continued, "He will want to question Johan alone. If he passes, then, the pathway is open."

Father Damian said, "I will have him here, your excellency. I will have him here."

He finished his business with the bishop, which was now routine, and headed back to Ruzbachy on the next available train. He sent a telegram from the train station in Bratislava to be picked up and when his train arrived in Podolencz, at midnight, there was Brother Jerome with the horse and wagon waiting. On the way back to the abbey, the priest told Brother Jerome what the bishop had said.

"We only have a month to prepare," said the friar. "You know that the cardinal will ask mostly religious questions. Another thing, how are we going to teach Johan how to be humble in only thirty days? We have quite a bit of work to do in the next month."

The following morning Father Damian met with Brothers Jerome and Voltek and Johan all morning. They will have to work with Johan well into the night to prepare him for the cardinal because the whole training program depended on the outcome of this one meeting. They arranged a schedule and the priest excused them from prayers and meals. They would eat their meals when they could and both Brother Voltek and Brother Jerome knew that their futures were dependent upon the outcome of the meeting. Father Damian alerted Brother Theo in the kitchen to the new arrangements and told the rest of the brothers so there would be no misunderstandings. He went to St. Stefan and borrowed all the books from Father Josef and Father Igor that they had brought from the seminary.

The priest did not see or hear from the student or his instructors for a whole month because he felt confident that his friars would prepare Johan. A new suit was ordered for Johan and finally they were driven to Podolencz. Johan had never seen a train before, nor had he seen a city the size of Podolencz. When they reached Bratislava, Johan marveled at the buildings and the size of the cathedral, since all Johan knew was the abbey. He knew everyone at the abbey and they knew him. He was the center of attention and he loved it but here in Bratislava, he knew no one and no one knew him. Johan would now have to show the new people, what the people at the abbey already knew: his personality, his character, and his abilities. He knew that he could not let Father Damian down. On the trip, he looked at his mentor as he sat across from him. The priest had been dozing and Johan had an opportunity to really look at him. His beard was turning gray, he had gained a few pounds and he did not look as athletic as he once did. He did not know if he could still get on a horse. He would have to help him and appear to be humble because Jesuits were supposed to be humble. Brother Jerome explained what it was to be humble and he would have to show the cardinal that he was humble.

Once he set foot in the cathedral, he was humble because he had never seen anything so large. The boy felt like a fly on the floor and some boot would come by and squash him. He now knew what being humble was and he now understood what Brother Jerome was trying to say because he had been here. As he was introduced to the bishop, he kissed his ring and told him that he was honored to be in his presence. Father Damian beamed. It was starting off well. Johan spoke only to answer the questions the bishop asked. He was well mannered, polite and accepted a cup of tea. Brother Jerome and Brother Voltek had done a magnificent job with the boy and he would have to consider a reward for them when he returned. He saw the pleasure in the eyes of the bishop as he spoke to the boy. Johan was making a good impression on the bishop and for that, Father Damian was grateful.

Soon it was time to meet the cardinal and the bishop stood up and announced that the cardinal was waiting for them in the visitor's office. Father Damian and the bishop chatted while they walked slowly towards the visitor's office, Johan followed then, listening. They did not mention Johan, but spoke of other matters. Once they reached the office, the bishop knocked on the door and a soft voice said to enter. The three of them entered a large room with huge windows and tapestries that hung to the floor and the entire room was decorated in a deep red color. It was expensively furnished with comfortable chairs, a huge heavy wooden desk and the walls were covered with pictures of former bishops. The cardinal stood up and walked around the desk.

"This must be the young man that I am waiting to meet,"he said as he took Johan's hand.

Johan did not know if he should kiss the Cardinal's ring, but he did anyway. He said that he was proud to meet a prince of the church at his young age and he would tell the brothers at the abbey of his good fortune. Father Damian was introduced to the cardinal and he also kissed the cardinal's ring to show the cardinal that Johan was taught to do this.

The cardinal smiled and said, "The Holy Mother Church is in good hands. Don't you agree, bishop?"

"Yes, your Eminence, and especially in Ruzbachy." With that the bishop took a half step toward the door and said, "We will leave young Johan in your care. Father Damian and I will tour the cathedral grounds and if you need us, please do not hesitate to summon either or both of us."

With that they passed through the door and left the cardinal alone with the young man. It was one o'clock in the afternoon. The bishop and the priest spent three hours together talking, walking and having tea. The last hour was spent in the bishop's office and the priest was sitting on the edge of his chair causing the bishop to tell him to calm down as the cardinal was not going to hurt the boy. The priest could not calm down, he asked himself why he had placed the boy in this position. The pressure in that room must be unbearable for the boy. Finally, after his fourth cup of tea, a knock came on the door and a young priest came in followed by Johan. The boy was smiling and went directly to Father Damian. He pulled up a chair next to the priest, sat and left no doubt with anyone in the room where his loyalties were.

The young priest addressed the bishop, "The cardinal offers his apologies, but he had to leave for a conference in Rome immediately. He had spent more time with the boy than he had planned and before he realized how long he spent, he had to leave without speaking to you."

"Thank you," said the bishop, and the young priest left the room.

The bishop asked them to spend the night. Johan had never seen such luxury and the evening meal was excellent. There as beef, vegetables, and bread and he ate as much as he wanted. He had never tasted food cooked with sauces but he did not know if he should mention this to Brother Theo when he returned to the abbey. Of course, Brother Theo did not have the larder that the bishop's cook had, but he put good food on the table at the abbey and he realized that Brother Theo did very well with what was given him. He could not believe the room that he was given and the large bed on which to sleep. Johan did not sleep all night because of the excitement and the pictures of all bishops and cardinals hanging on the walls. The eyes of the religious people seemed to follow him wherever he went in the room.

He did, however, explore and opened the door to the armoire that was attached to the wall. There, neatly hung up in a line were the clothes of the cardinal. He could not believe that he was actually going to sleep in the cardinal's room. He could not wait to tell the brothers. They will be very happy for him and will want to hear every detail. He would have to memorize everything in the room in order to give them an accurate description. He looked in the bottom of the armoire and found six bottles. One was opened so he took it out, took out the cork and smelled its contents. This is brandy, he thought. He put his tongue on the cork and fire burned on this tongue. This was brandy and the cardinal must need it to make him sleep. He put everything back as he found it and pulled back the covers. There were white sheets of cloth on the bed but he slept on the top of the sheets and pulled the blanket and bedspread over him. The blanket was a course weave and this added to his discomfort. It made him think of his bed at the abbey; he slept better in his own bed.

The following afternoon, they were back at the abbey. The boy told everyone who would listen about his adventure. Father Damian cautioned Johan about expanding on the food that he was served because it might hurt Brother Theo's feelings. Johan agreed but as the days flew by, he fell into his old routine, and the memories of his great adventure became dimmer and dimmer. He had new subjects presented to him in his studies and more chores to do since he was becoming older and stronger. He was given a week off now and then, to work with the brothers when their busy time came and he liked to work with them. Brother Albert worked with him in keeping of the books for the abbey and he worked in the barn with Brother Simon. He liked Brother Simon, but the smell in the barn took some getting used to. He went on one of Brother Simon's manure selling trips and met some farmers. Johan met one in particular that he liked, but he never saw him at the abbey or in church; it was Pan Pavel Valigursky.

Brother Simon told him that his wife died when she walked through the pass from Poland and the little girl that he saw helping him was the baby that he had watched being born. She was about nine years old and appeared rather big for her age but she worked like a strong young man. Her hair was cut short and she had a round ruddy face as if she spent a good deal of her time outdoors. He liked the girl, but she barely acknowledged his existence. Brother Simon told him that Pan Valigurskis herd was growing slowly, but he had used his cousin's stallion to sire two mares and he had two fine colts. One was a stallion colt and the other a mare. The farm was neat and clean and showed some promise and Johan made Brother Simon promise that he would take him there the next time he had to go. He had to concentrate on his studies, but he would find time to go out there when Brother Simon went to this farm.

13

Time sped by quickly for Father Damian, but it had been six months since Johan spoke with the cardinal and he had received no word from either the bishop or the cardinal. He had identified at least ten young men as potential candidates for the training of new Jesuit friars and he was waiting for word from the cathedral that he could begin. He had even accumulated material from the abbey itself and searched all the places in the abbey where materials were stored. The priest found some in the archives of the abbey, some in the storage area where the possessions of dead brothers were kept and he solicited all the materials that the brothers were keeping from their own training. He had enough and was anxious to start by the first of the year. One bright, sunny, summer day, he was walking with Brother Jan who was showing him the grounds and what he had planned for the fall. It had been a rather dry spring that year and Brother Jan was watering the plants from the well. The vegetable garden was also being watered from the well. A check of the remaining water would have to be made to see the amount of water that was left to decide whether Brother Jan could continue to water the flowers. The water would have to be used for the food and if the winter was bad next year they would need the food to survive. He told Brother Jan that they would all pray for rain.

A young man from Podolencz caught up to them and handed the priest a telegram from Bratislava. Father Damian tore the envelope open and read it. He was being summoned to see the bishop as soon as possible. There was no hint or clue as to what it concerned and he told the young man to go to the kitchen for some refreshments while he went to his room to prepare for the trip to Bratislava. He sought out Brother Voltec and asked him to prepare a report as soon as possible, as he was leaving in the morning. He sent a young friar to St. Stefan to tell Father Edvard that he was going to see the bishop and if he wanted something delivered, he would take it. The young brother was to wait for an answer. He would have to go to his study to take care of some matters that could not be neglected for a few days.

The following morning he was on his way to see the bishop. He arrived early in the afternoon and the bishop was waiting for him. As he sat down, the bishop told him that the cardinal, in Rome, had sent a message that he had been pleased with the young man, Johan. The boy had been trained very thoroughly and he could take his vows in a few years, but the problem was with the Jesuits who have been trying to regain control over the abbey for many years. The profit from the abbey had been substantial and although they had been getting a portion of the profit, they wanted it all. They felt that the abbey was capable of training five brothers under certain conditions. Father Damian thought, "why must there always be conditions? Did not everyone serve the same God?" He would never understand this even if he lived to be a hundred years old.

The conditions under which the Jesuits would allow the priest to train Jesuit friars were harsh. There would only be five friars trained every six years and the friars would be tested by the Jesuits before they said their final vows. If the Jesuits disapproved, then that individual would not be allowed to enter the Order. No Jesuit brother would be allowed to enter the seminary unless prior approval was given by the Order, and the priest in charge must be a Jesuit. Either the present priest must swear allegiance to the Order, or he must resign and one will be appointed by the Order. The Order would then control the abbey, the priest in charge would report to the Order and all monies made at the abbey would be sent to the Order.

Father Damian looked at the bishop in disbelief. "Cannot the cardinal order the Jesuits to do it?" he asked.

"Yes, he can," replied the bishop, "but by ordering the Jesuits to let you train their friars, he is afraid that it will cause friction between the Jesuits and the Diocese of Bratislava. There are many communities such as yours in the Diocese and your abbey is the only one controlled by the Diocese. They will make matters difficult for these parish priests in the Diocese. Matters are in harmony now, but that could change and there is nothing the cardinal can do to control it. If you agree to the conditions, the choice is purely personal and it has to be your choice and no other. I want you to think about it but I will need your decision in the morning. If you decide to join the Order, I will miss you, and I had hoped to see more of Johan. The cardinal was impressed with him and he told me that the boy reminded him of someone, but he could not think of who it was. Think about the welfare of the community. It will not be, altogether, a disaster to have Jesuits visiting you. They will come once a year to evaluate the abbey and it will probably be harvest time when food is more abundant. With all that said, I will leave you to your thoughts, and we will see what the good Lord will give us tomorrow."

They parted company and the priest went to his room. He was not hungry so he did not go to the evening meal. He lay on his bed and weighed the options. What if he accepted the Jesuit's conditions? He could have his school and probably keep the brothers that he had trained, but he would have to conduct the abbey in the strict Jesuit fashion; it could not be run as it is now. They would expect them to expand the operation, they could take out whom they wanted and send them those that no one else wanted. He could not send Johan to the seminary unless they approved and if he held off becoming a Jesuit then they will, in all probability, make things difficult for him. He is 53 years old and six years is a long time, at his time in life, to worry about Johan.

If he did not agree now, then he would have to send Johan somewhere else to be trained or send him to the seminary in four or five years. Either way, he would probably not see him again except for a visit now and then. Father Damian really did not care who received the money that they made at the abbey, but his loyalty was with the people in the abbey and in the town. They have accepted him at the abbey and have lived in harmony with him. It brought to mind the mayor, the townspeople who helped out when Johan was lost; the food that was placed on the kitchen door step when we needed it; the babies that he had baptized, the weddings he had performed and the celebrations afterward; the food and the dancing. He had to think about all the friends that he had buried. He could not let these people down.

Father Damian thought about what would happen if he said "no" to the conditions. The bishop would be happy not to lose the revenue and he was sure of that. The bishop was getting on in years and the next one may not be as easy to convince as this one, and he may transfer him to a semi-retirement parish where he would slowly go mad. Without people to serve, his life would come to an end and he could not control Johan's future. God, how he loved that boy! He could not bear to be separated from him and that, above all, is what his decision is all about. He raised his eyes to Heaven and asked God to help him to make the right decision. If he turned it down, then he would get no further help from the Jesuits. It looks like the Jesuits have won and they will finally reap the harvest of what he had sown. He remembered the abbey when he first arrived: it was run down, the morale low, some of the brothers could not read or write and everyone was hungry. The Jesuits had no one to send so they asked bishop to send a priest and Bishop Stefan sent him. How did the Jesuits become so powerful? They must have a powerful ally in Rome to be able to make this arrangement.

He felt very tired and decided to go to bed, but he tossed and turned and lay on his back with his eyes wide open. He got up and walked around the room, he wished now that he had gone to the evening meal. He went off to the kitchen but found nothing except a few pieces of bread and some milk which was on the verge of turning sour. He ate the bread, had some water and went back to his room. Maybe now he could sleep, but he dozed and then woke up again. As he tossed and turned, he felt as if it was getting lighter. His window faced the east so the sun must be coming up. He got

up, washed, dressed and went down to the dining room. The bishop
was up; apparently he had trouble sleeping because he did not
look very well. At least the bishop could take a nap in the afternoon, thought the priest, but he may not sleep for days. They ate
in silence, neither one mentioned the talk that they had had the
day before. Father Damian realized that he must look as bad as the
bishop. They finished their meal and walked to the bishop's office
without a word.

As they sat, the bishop said, "Have you decided what you are
going to do?"

"Yes, I have, your excellency," he answered. "But I have a few
conditions of my own. These have to be understood and followed,
no matter who I deal with, in the Order. I want control over the
abbey. I have built the abbey from a group of individuals with
poor morale, no food, no direction. The abbey was run down and
shunned by the townspeople and I do not want the Jesuits inter-
fering in my tried and true methods. I will swear allegiance to the
Order and become a Jesuit, but I want control of what happens to
Johan. He is not to be moved after he becomes a friar unless I give
my expressed approval. There is no negotiation on this point. I
want the five friars who will take their vows to serve in the abbey
and I want to approve the brothers who are transferred to the
abbey. When I arrived at the Abbey of St. Francis most of the
brothers could not read, write or count. One last point, I want
Father Andrej to become Pastor of St. Stefan once he has taken his
final vows. Technically, he, Father Igor and Father Josef are Jesuits,
but they are too valuable to be transferred to an abbey. The townspeople of Ruzbachy need them desperately. That is all I have to
say except that I want a decision within two weeks. I want to
prepare for a class by the first of the year when things are not that
busy. I cannot wait another nine months."

When he sat back, the bishop said, "I think that you have
made the correct decision, especially with the conditions that you
have brought forth. I must say one other thing. I think that you
have more nerve than any priest that I have seen. If the abbey is

not turned over to the Jesuits, then I would like to have you transferred here to the cathedral as my assistant. You will be bishop someday and a fine one at that."

"I do not want to be bishop, your excellency, I just want to serve my people for God, the best way that I know. If I can do this with a clear conscience, then I will die a happy man and get my reward by sitting in the presence of our Savior."

The bishop embraced the priest. "God blesses you. Leave the rest to me. I will do the best that I can."

He left for Ruzbachy later that morning and arrived at the abbey at early evening, just in time for vespers. He prayed with his brothers and again he prayed to God for a sign that he was doing the best thing for Johan and his brothers. After prayers, Brother Theo told him that he had saved supper for him in the kitchen. While he was eating, Johan came in and asked how things went with the bishop. Since he had been to the cathedral, he now had an interest in matters pertaining to the bishop. Father Damian said that everything went fine and he would know in two weeks if he was going to train new brothers. Johan then ran out because he had to prepare for the next day's lesson before he could go to sleep.

The next week was spent waiting for a message from the bishop. On Sunday afternoon when he was walking around the gardens, he met Johan. Johan knew that the priest was not himself ever since he returned from Bratislava and he tried to cheer him up.

"Do you know that little girl that was born to the woman who died?", he asked. Since he was deep in thought, he had not heard Johan and asked him to repeat the question.

"Yes, I do, Johan," said the priest. "I understand that her father bought a farm and they cannot hire anyone to help. He works very hard and far into the night."

"Well, I saw the little girl working right next to her father. I was six when she was born and since I am sixteen, she must be ten years old now."

"That's correct, Johan," said the priest.

"She works like a man. She is large for her age and she really works like a man. I like her and she will make some farmer a good wife."

"I know, Johan, and thank you for trying to cheer me up. I have much on my mind right now, but it always a pleasure to talk to you."

The boy was bubbling over with excitement, "Brother Theo and I are going fishing and if I catch one we will prepare if for your supper."

"I would like that, Johan." With that the boy ran off toward the kitchen. Johan tried to take the priest's mind from his troubles and the priest smiled. As he walked along, a germ of an idea started to formulate.

Aloud the priest said, "Now why did I not think of that before? Thank you, Lord."

Brother Jan was in the garden. He looked up and asked, "Who are you talking to father?

"God, my son, I am talking to God!" he answered with a smile. He went along the path working out the details of his new plan. A transformation came over him and he was now happy.

That Wednesday a telegram was delivered to the priest. He opened the cable, read it and smiled. All the telegram said was "They accepted, God Bless You," It was signed Mikel.

Father Damian was happy with that and he waited for the Jesuits to contact him. After the evening prayers he asked the brothers to stay for an announcement.

Once he had their attention, he started: "Dear Brothers, the abbey will soon be under the control of the Jesuits. I will be joining the order. I am not sure just when but I suspect it will be soon. There should be no major changes except that we will be adding a school to train new Jesuit brothers. They will be trained by Brother Jerome and Brother Voltekc. We are allowed five new trainees plus my good friend, Johan." Everyone looked at the boy, he blushed as he smiled. "To continue, we have identified 10 candidates of which we can pick five. If any one of you know any of the ten young men, please tell me all that you know about them. We will interview all of them in about a month from now and make a decision. This will have no effect on your everyday lives and I will do my best to see that we do not change too drastically. I do know that the new administrators will want to have the abbey grow and it will probably mean new buildings and new people. If anyone has any questions, please feel free to come to me. My door has always been open and it will remain that way. God blesses you all."

There was a buzz when the brothers left the room because many of them had been in other abbeys and life had been rigid. Some were not allowed to speak to each other so they were all thankful that they came to St. Francis. They all prayed for their priest as he was going to have a difficult time.

*   *   *

A month later, two Jesuit friars arrived on horseback and they were taken in to see Father Damian at once. They introduced themselves as Brother Domino and Brother Fredek.

Brother Domino, the spokesperson, said, "The changeover will take place after Christmas and before the New Year. You are to take your vows as a Jesuit and the transition will be complete. There will be no ceremony and the brothers will be present, if you desire. We will visit after Christmas each year to collect any profits due to the order and look over the abbey. We will make recommendations, but if you have a good reason they would not be pursued. The order will ask you to build a separate building in the abbey to house the trainees. They should take their meals with the rest of the abbey and you are to follow procedures that you have followed all along. The Jesuits do not intend to interfere with your running of the abbey. As a matter of fact, the Jesuits will ask that you train some people so we can place them in other abbeys and make them as successful as this one. We will transfer no one without authorization from the abbey and you can refuse anyone that is sent to you. We have come to audit the books to see how much is made and how much is paid out. We would also like to see the maps of the abbey confirming the amount of land the church owns, walk the perimeter of the holdings and check the livestock. Also, we would like to meet young Johan, as we have heard quite a bit about him."

"Will all of this be in writing for the future?". Father Damian asked.

"Yes, it will. Are there any other questions?". asked Brother Domino.

"Yes, I have two more questions. How long do you intend to stay and will you talk to me before you leave?"

The answer came quickly. "We will stay three nights and we should talk to each other for the entire three days. You will have the results of my findings from Abbott Dubchek, as he likes to be called, within three weeks but I will deliver it at least before Christmas. I will be your contact with the Abbott. We will start tomorrow morning. Please show us where we can stay."

They were taken to a cell with two cots and were left there after Father Damian explained the hours of prayer and meals. It seems that Brothers Voltek and Fredek went to the University at Bratislava. Brother Fredek left the University before Brother Voltek entered, but they shared a sort of fraternity since they were alumni of the same school. They talked, at some length about the school and the professors that they studied with.

After conferring with Brother Voltek, Brother Fredek said, "I find the records to be in excellent condition except for a few minor revisions that Brother Voltek found acceptable and they would make his work easier."

Brother Domino, on the other hand, spent all of his time with Father Damian. He looked into each corner, he went into the barn and noted the supply of feed, he went into the kitchen, dining room, cupboard, root cellar and sleeping quarters of all the friars. This took him two days and he made notes wherever he went. He was extremely thorough and although, he did not speak much, he observed everything. The final day was devoted to the map and charts of the abbey and they rode on horseback around the perimeter of the land holdings. He checked the grist mill and again spent time looking to see how much waste there was. The friar asked questions, but seemed to know the answers before he asked them and, finally, they rode into the abbey just in time for the evening meal. He told Father Damian that he would forego vespers because he wanted to go over his notes and make additional ones while the material was fresh in his mind. He also wanted to pack because they would be leaving right after the morning prayers and the meal.

After the morning meal, the two Jesuit brothers mounted their horses and rode south toward the Monastery of St. John the Baptist, just outside of Bratislava. Father Damian spoke to Brother Voltek about his encounter with Brother Fredek and was pleased with the outcome.

The ten candidates were interviewed by Father Damian and they were all told that there were only five openings, but they would be, in all probability, candidates again in six years since age was not a determining factor. Father Damian went to the school in town where he spoke to all the candidates' teachers. He then spoke to all the families and the mayor, who seemed to know everyone in town on both sides of the river. The priest sat starting the elimination process. He eliminated three candidates because of their scholastic abilities. If they had problems in the town school, they would never survive the rigors of training for the brotherhood. This left seven young boys to consider. Then, he eliminated one young man from vysni Ruzbachy because he detected an attitude problem. This young man was not trying to join the order to escape from problems with his parents and siblings. He was an extremely bright young man, but his motive for joining the order did not make him a candidate. This young man was lazy. He felt that the life of a friar was an easy one and he had never been exposed to life inside of an abbey. His devotion was not to God, but to himself. While going over the candidates, he placed four names aside as being acceptable candidates. He set the papers down and took a walk through the gardens but the more he walked, the more confused he became. One boy was from Nizne Ruzbachy and the others from Vysni Ruzbachy and no matter how he tried, he could not make a decision. He decided to put the papers away for a few days and look at them in a fresh light.

The very next day, the priest received a visitor who was the father of the boy from vysni Ruzbachy. He asked to speak to Father Damian and was shown into his study. Father Damian had seen the man around town, but had never seen him in church, although he might be going to St. Stefan's. The priest made a note to see Father Edvard to see if he knew him.

The man came right to the point, "I would like to have you accept my son into your school. I am prepared to make a sizeable donation to the abbey if you would select my son to attend the school to become a friar."

When the priest asked why, the man became hesitant, but finally said, "I caught my son in the company of a gypsy girl a number of times and I am afraid that it is becoming serious. If I could place my son into a confined environment, then I would be able to solve the problem. Gypsies are all alike and once one of them got his or her hooks into me, then my farm would be over run by them. It was bad enough that I let them camp on a remote portion of my property, but to have one as a daughter-in-law and have in-law gypsies running all over my farm, stealing my animals and food, is unthinkable. I have to put the boy away and that would take care of the threat.

Father Damian asked, "Why not send the boy to the university?"

The man replied, "The band of gypsies travels near Bratislava and besides that, the boy was not intelligent enough to go to the university."

Father Damian finally got the man out of his office with the promise to think about it. As a matter of fact, the priest had already thought about it and had picked the boy from nizne Ruzbachy. The school started right after the new year and Father Damian had visited all the families of the candidates and informed them of his decision. The construction of the school house was begun in April of that year. It would adapt to ten students and the Monastery of St. John the Baptist was paying to have it built.

When the foundation was complete, Abbott Franz Dubchek came to visit. This man was huge, about 300 pounds and most of his head was bald so he had the rest shaved. He wore a large brown robe tied around the middle by a cord that was six feet long. Due to his size and demeanor, Father Damian knew that he was used to the good life. He brought with him the reports of Brothers Domino and Fredek. The report was good and the Abbott had suggested some minor changes, but other than that the visit was uneventful. Father Damian could not understand why this man, who was giving him all the trouble over the years, would suddenly come to visit him on such minor points. Now that he was a Jesuit, he felt that this man would slowly erode his authority until he could replace him with one of his own trusted people. It was a shame to say, in a house of God, but he would have to watch his step to prolong the day in which his replacement would take place.

*　　*　　*

The next five years went by quickly, but each time a Jesuit came to visit him, there were small changes made. He had argued about the new changes that the Jesuits had suggested and they backed off on some of them. The changes were becoming less and less minor and he could see that the end was coming. The Jesuits needed some reason to approach the cardinal, but that was a few years away.

In the fifth year of the school, Father Damian called Brothers Jerome and Brother Voltek into his office and asked how Johan was doing in relation to his five classmates. They both stated that he was far ahead and the entire final year would be a review. All six of their charges could pass the review of the Jesuits and will be able to take their final vows at Easter of the following year. This would make it a year from the Easter that was now coming up.

The priest had gotten into the habit of visiting St. Stefan when

he was in town and in his talks with Father Edvard, he asked if Pan
Pavel Valugorski came to church. The parish priest had not seen
him in church, but his daughter, Olga, came every Sunday. She
left the church and went directly home as far as he knew. He heard
that she worked very hard.

His next stop was the cobbler's shop of the mayor to speak to
him about Pan Valugorski. Father Damian sat on a barrel and asked,
"What can you tell me about Pavel Valugorski?"

The mayor said, "Without his daughter, he would have lost
the farm to his uncle years ago. They were working seven days a
week. They were breeding horses and had having trouble selling
them. They were good horses with a good blood line, but they
were not in demand here in Ruzbachy. He had sold a few to the
landowners here, but his market was in the larger cities because
that is where the price was received for that quality of horse. They
were not plow horses as were needed in the farm community. Another problem was with Pavel, himself. He would come to town
two or three times a week and spend some time in the tavern,
while his daughter worked. She was too good a girl to talk to him
about it."

Father Damian thanked him for his frankness and decided to
go to the tavern for a beer because he had not been there for months
and he suddenly had a craving for a beer. He walked in and saw
Pavel, sat at a table closest to the man and ordered a beer. The
tavern had no longer employed barmaids since the last one disappeared without a trace some years ago.

As he sipped his beer, Pavel noticed him. "I did not see you
come in," he said, "This is the last place that I would expect to
find a priest."

The priest replied, "I have been here before. Unfortunately,
our good Lord gave even priests good taste buds. I like to have a
beer once in a while, and I prefer to have one where everyone can
see me instead of drinking one alone in my room."

He started a conversation with Pavel and learned about all the
troubles that he had since his wife died.

He said, "I had hoped that my daughter, Olga, would find a capable man to marry so we could keep up the farm but as it was, the girl could outride, out shoot, and outwork any man she met, so none came around any longer. She did not like anyone who had come around anyway."

Father Damian asked, "Have you thought of hiring a man to work on the farm to help your daughter?"

But he said, "All the men in this area wanted too much money and were interested in Olga for other reasons."

Father Damian mentioned, "I know of a young man who grew up in the abbey, has some free time on his hands and is going to take his final vows next year. If you would make a nominal donation to the church, I would send Johan over a few times a week to work on the farm. The only condition is that I want you to be at the farm all the time that Johan is there to stand in between them. I do not want anything to interfere with Johan taking his final vows on Easter of the following year."

He waited for Pavel to think about it, but he did not have to wait The farmer said, "Yes, I will have Olga put the money into the collection basket when she went to church."

That night after vespers, Father Damian met Johan and asked the boy to walk with him so they might talk. It was a chilly evening and Johan was looking forward to talking to his classmates in their nice warm dormitory room, but when the priest requests that he do something, he has to comply.

As they walked, the priest said, "Johan, there is a farmer whom I know that has some troubles and I feel, that with your training in farming, you are best suited to help the man salvage his farm."

"What about my studies?" asked Johan.

Father Damian answered, "I spoke with Brother Voltek and Brother Jerome the other day and they said that you completed your studies and all that you are doing now is reviewing the material. You could pass a review by the Jesuits now so it seems like you could make better use of your time by helping someone overcome his problems."

"Is he the one with no sons and only his daughter to work on the farm?"

"Yes, Johan, she is sixteen years old and has to work like a man and it will only be until he can pay his uncle back the money he borrowed. It should only be until you say your final vows."

"Well, if you think that I can help, I'll try."

"I know you will, my son,"said the priest.

They found themselves by the door of the dormitory and Johan said his good night and went in to tell his friends.

Johan reported to Pavel as promised and while he helped with the fertilizing and planting, Ogla found time to go into the house to clean and cook. She washed clothes, including some of Johan's work clothes becaused he did not wear his robe when he worked. He cleaned the barn, planted the vegetables, watered the horses and fed them in their stalls. He had supper with them on the days that he worked. He loved to work with horses rather than any other animal. The horse was a statuesque creature, intelligent and loyal and Pavel had some handsome horses on his farm. He and Olga worked hand in hand in the birthing of the three colts that spring.

Sitting at the meal times Johan would want to say a prayer of thanksgiving. At first, Pavel resisted, but then he realized that this was the way Johan was brought up and he actually liked the boy, so he relented. He would stare off into space, and slowly, he lowered his eyes, then his head and it might look like he was praying but no one knew except Pavel. Things went on very well all summer when Johan went over three times a week and spent three days in the classroom.

When the middle of summer came and some of the vegetables were harvested and preserved, Johan went over four times a week and he took care of the garden while Olga preserved the harvest. It looked like a good harvest and they worked side by side. Pavel was paying more attention to the farm and less and less to the tavern in the town. The second week of August, the hay had to be cut and stored in the barn while the field of oats had to be cut and processed. The dawn each day for four weeks found three shadows swinging from side to side cutting hay or oats with their scythes. The movement was so smooth and the piles were laid neatly in a row. They worked up one side and down the other until the field was cut down. The sweat just poured from their bodies but Olga brought plenty of water to drink so that they could keep working without interruption.

When the field was cut, they brought out the forks and turned the hay over so that the sun could dry out the under side. Once the hay was dry, they loaded it on the wagon to take to the barn. The barn was built on the side of a hill so the wagon could be driven into the barn. The hay was unloaded and fell down to the lower level where the animals were. The wagon was driven through the barn and into the fields for another load. The oats were processed in the field and they were cut as if it were hay, but the sheaves of oats were placed on a large cloth. The sheaves were beaten with poles until the oats had fallen from the sheaves onto the cloth. The sheaves were taken off the cloth and tied into bundles to be used on the floor of the barn to keep the dust and moisture down. Each person took two ends of the cloth and bounced the oats into the air. It was best to bounce the cloth on a breezy day because the wind would blow the chafe away and the heavier oats would fall back into the cloth. It was time-consuming and not very efficient, but it had been done this way for centuries and no one had devised a better method.

When the oats were finished, they started on the wheat and barley fields. The wheat was taken to the grist mill, while the barley was stored in a bin in a shed by the kitchen door. When food was getting low at the end of winter, barley became a staple for "crupi" which was made with barley and other vegetables even without a ham bone or any other type of meat stock. One did not eat well in Slovakia at the end of winter and the Catholic church proclaimed these days between Ash Wednesday and noon Holy Saturday as a time of fasting. Meat was only eaten once a day on Sunday, if at all and one did not gain weight in Ruzbachy over the winter. The dried sheaves of the oats were stored in the barn and used mostly to put under the animals to help keep them dry. If the hay should give out during the winter, the sheaves were fed to the animals.

Before the day's work was done, the cows had to be milked. Some of the milk was consumed by the family, but most of it was sold to the townspeople who came every day with their milk pails. The chickens, hogs and geese had to be fed. The geese were an important animal on the farm because not only did they provide meat for the winter, they provided down which was sewn into comforters and pillows by the women over the winter months. The fat from the geese that were force fed provided nourishment over the winter months. To force-feed a goose, a woman would take hold of the neck of a goose until the mouth came open. Then she would drop pellets of corn or any other grain and massage the neck until the food went down. Soon the goose would get fat and waddle around the barn yard. The theory was that the larger the bird, the more down and fat it produced when it was finally slaughtered.

When the work slowed for the winter, the root vegetables stored in the cellar, the sauerkraut fermenting in the root cellar and the glass jars full of meat and vegetables were stored in the cupboards, Johan started coming to the farm only twice a week to feed the animals and to enjoy Olga's cooking. Pavel's cousin's wife, Eva, taught her well because she used every bit of food at her disposal and made it taste very well.

When Johan came over to help feed the animals, Pavel decided to go to the tavern more often since it was the middle of December and it was cold. The barn was warm from the heat generated by the animals and the lanterns on both ends of the stall gave the barn a cozy feeling. As they were using their pitch forks, sending hay to the horses, Olga's breast accidentally brushed against Johan's elbow. Olga had been thinking about Johan all day and her nipples were very hard. Johan had no idea what to do, but a feeling came over him and he began to swell. They looked at each other and each could see the other's breath. She reached up, kissed him on the mouth and noticed the swelling in his groin.

He looked at her and said, "I do not know what to do."

"I do," she answered and started taking off her clothes. He looked at her as she undressed. As her breasts popped out of her bodice, he felt the swelling getting bigger. He started stripping the clothing off himself and when they were both undressed, he tried to get behind her.

She whispered, "That is how animals do it. We do it differently."

She lay on her back and opened her legs. "Are you sure I will fit in there?"

"I'm sure you will. You take your rod and push it into me. Keep pushing until it goes all the way in. You will feel it."

He looked at her and she was red all over. Her breasts were heaving, the nipples tight against his chest. He tried to do as she said but he hit an obstruction.

"Push, "she said. "You are my first."

He pushed and on the third time, he got through. Johan never felt like this before and he wanted the feeling to last forever when he suddenly felt an intense feeling and he deposited his sperm inside of Olga.

He wanted to get off, but she held him with her legs. "Let us enjoy this feeling for a little while longer."

Between his panting, he said, "Yes, let us stay this way forever." He finally got up, and they both got dressed.

"You had better go back to the abbey, father will be home soon," she said as she kissed him.

She patted his groin and whispered, "Take care of our friend, he does a good job."

She left the barn and he put out the lights, closed the doors, got on his horse and left. The next morning while Olga was preparing the morning meal, Pavel took a walk through the barn when he saw an indentation in the hay. As he looked closer, he saw the telltale sign of what had happened.

He smiled and said out loud, "The plan worked and it is about time. I will have to tell the priest."

When Johan got back to the dormitory, he did not know whether to feel guilty or joy as. He tried to feel quilty but he could not. If this was what life was all about on the outside of the abbey, then life was not too bad. There were problems to solve as there were problems to solve everywhere and he must explore this further. He did know that he loved the young lady and he loved the way that she had taken charge. He lay awake for half the night thinking about it, trying to relive the events leading up to the lovemaking. Johan decided that he would not tell Father Damian, even in confession, but would see where the events would take him.

Father Damian said Mass as usual the following Sunday. He looked up after reading the opening prayer and saw Pavel sitting in the back row. He smiled at him and Pavel smiled back. When the priest finished Mass he went looking for Pavel, but he had left. He must have left before Mass was finished but the message, however, had been sent and received.

Johan had no reason to go to the farm as things quieted down for the next three months for it was time to prepare for the Christmas season. He went down to St. Stefan to see if he could help the priests decorate the church. They had more help than they needed so he went back to the abbey to talk with his friends and read. Some of his classmates did not like to read and they went to their homes between Christmas and New Years to spend some time with their families. When Johan should have been happy in the season because of the Birth of the Christ Child, he was sad that he had no excuse to see Olga.

The third week of January, a familiar face stood in the doorway of Father Damian office. It was Brother Andrej, now Father Andrej with his contagious smile.

"Good morning to you," he said.

Father Damian smiled and said, "Good morning to you,"

"I have been assigned to St. Stefan and Father Edvard has been transferred to the cathedral to spend the remaining days of his priesthood. I take over on the First of March and Father Edvard will stay until then. Isn't life wonderful? I am so happy to be here."

Father Damian walked over and embraced him. "Now my family is together again," he said.

Andrej saw a tear forming in his eye and asked, "Where is my favorite pupil?"

"You will be surprised when you see him. We have had a few changes since you left. I am now a Jesuit priest and we have a school of six students who will be taking their final vows at Easter Mass and Johan is one of them."

"I cannot wait to see him. Where is he?"

"I'll take you there and later we will talk." He led the new priest to the school building and they walked inside. As soon as Johan saw Father Andrej he leaped up and ran to the door. He embraced his former teacher and Brother Jerome excused him from class.

"Thank you, "Brother," came the response, and the trio left the building.

In Father Damian's study, they talked for hours until finally Father Andrej excused himself and left to go to St. Stefans. When Johan left, Father Damian thought that the bishop was true to his word and he would have to send him a telegram and thank him. This has been a good day and he felt very happy

When the middle of March came, Johan went to the Valigursky farm. He had been there six or seven times since Father Andrej had arrived. Father Damian had asked Johan if he had seen the Valigurskis and when told that he had not been over there in two months, the priest told him to go over and help plan the planting season. He now had an excuse to go see Olga and on his first day at the farm, he and Olga took a walk and talked.

"Are you sorry about what happened?" she asked.

"No," he said, "I am happy that it happened. It was the most joyous day of my life. I feel that I want to spend the rest of my life with you and we can have a good life together."

She lifted up her eyes and said, "It is a serious decision for you to make."

He said, "I have thought about it and nothing else since that day." He stopped her and turned her to look at him. "I want you to marry me."

She said that he would have to ask her father, but before that she had something to tell him. With her head held high, she looked him right in the eye and said, "I am pregnant."

"You are what?", he asked.

"I'm with child."

He turned his head to heaven, raised his eyes and said, "Wonderful! Where is your father?"

"He is at the tavern. I will not be here when you ask him."

Johan waited until he saw Pavel walking up the path to the front door. He went into the kitchen and told Olga, who left to go into the barn. Supper was on the hearth when he walked in.

"Where is Olga?", he asked.

"Out feeding the stock," he replied. "Please sit down, there is something I want to discuss with you." As Pavel sat, Johan started. "I will not be taking my final vows into the brotherhood and I will leave the Abbey with all my belongings. The books that I am studying will be floating down the Poprad River toward Polodencz. I wish to marry your daughter."

"What does Olga say?"

Johan smiled, "She will marry me."

"Have you told Father Damian?"

"No, but I will tell him in my own way."

Pavel thought a respectable length of time, put both of his palms together and placed his fingers under his chin. He stood up and reached across the table with his hand outstretched. "I would be honored to have you marry my daughter. Treat her well, my boy, and we will get along just fine. She is a fine strong woman and will give me many grandsons to play with in my old age." They embraced and Johan went out to tell Olga.

14

Pavel Valigursky was born in the town of Nowy Targ in the southern most area of Poland where the Dunajec river and the Bilay Dunajec separated on their journeys south to the Danube. The Bilay Dunajec went due south and the Dunajec went southeast toward the pass that went through the High Tatras. He was the youngest of nine children and when he was born, his mother did not know that she was pregnant until Pavel was delivered in her home. When she saw her son, she said, "Now that he is here, I imagine, we will have to keep him."

His oldest brother, Anton, was 20 years his senior and was already working the small farm. As he was growing up, he did not remember being included in any family discussions, nor was he ever included in the decision-making processes. He usually sat away from the others as they sat around the table discussing what was to be planted, which mare to be mated and other matters pertaining to the running of the farm. He sat there, he listened and he learned. Many times, he felt that they could be making better use of their land and resources, but he kept his thoughts to himself. Since he was assigned to the menial tasks, he completed them quickly so he could watch his five brothers work at their tasks. He asked many questions and received the answers.

When he was sixteen, his father passed away and Anton became head of the household. He married right after Pavel was born and that union produced Pavel's nephew a year later. There were now twelve mouths to feed and the good earth did not provide enough to feed them all. The three girls married and went to live with their in-laws while the boys, one by one, left the home and went south to try to find their fortunes in other lands. At this time, Pavel became more important because help was needed on the farm. Slowly he began to see more responsibility, more respect and he was able to join in on the family discussions. Anton had two more sons and his wife could not bear any more children. Pavel's mother took care of the children, while Anton, his oldest son, his wife and Pavel worked the farm.

While lying in bed one warm night, Pavel thought of his future. He was nineteen years old, he had three years of schooling, and he had no future on this farm. He could not share his feelings with Anton who did not have too much to do with him. Anton would go into town once or twice a week to have a beer at the small tavern. He did this to see his fellow farmers, to talk over any innovations or ideas that would make their work easier. One day, Pavel asked to go with him and Anton consented. The talk sometimes turned to women and Pavel had never heard his big brother talk this way before. At first he was embarrassed, and the older men teased him, but gradually he became one of them and listened. Pavel knew nothing about women even at this stage of his life. He saw animals mating and helped deliver a colt and several calves, but he did not understand how one obtained a wife and lived with her. As he had gotten older, his life became more complicated and he still had this terrible feeling about his future.

One evening as he was sipping his beer, one of the men came over to him and said that he knew of a sweet young lady who was looking for a husband. She lived in town and was trying to get married so she could leave her mother and father. Her father had trouble finding work because he drank some and word had gotten around that he was unreliable. The man, who was a friend of Anton's, offered to take Pavel over to her house to meet her mother and father. Anton was watching and listening to this conversation a few feet away for he had put his friend up to getting Pavel to make some commitment. He might even get the boy to leave home and it was about time since he did not want his brother living with him for the rest of his life. The next time Pavel went into town, he wore his best shirt and trousers, the ones his next older brother had outgrown and he went to meet Anna Grobitch.

Anna was seventeen years old and she worked as a maid or

kitchen hand whenever she could find work. When she returned home from work, she would find her father waiting at the door to take whatever she had earned. He would keep enough to buy some beer and give the rest to her mother. Anna had worked for Anton's friend and confided in him that she wanted to be married because there was never enough food in the house and unless she cleaned up at home, it was never cleaned. She was happy when she worked in someone's kitchen for she could find something to eat when she cleaned up the kitchen. Anna went to church alone each Sunday; she had thought of going to a convent, but quickly discarded that idea. She did not see herself spending the rest of her life as a nun. What she wanted was a home, with a husband and babies. Her mother could not understand why no one came to see her. She was pretty, blonde, had a slim figure, a beautiful smile and she knew how to dance very well. She never realized that the man who married her also married her family.

As Pavel came through the door of Anna's small cottage, he was impressed at how clean it was. The furniture was old and hastily repaired, but the home was clean. He saw her mother who must have been attractive at one time, she had dark circles under her eyes and two teeth were missing in front. When he looked at her closely, he noticed a faint growth of hair on her upper lip. Her father's clothes were old and torn, his shirt was missing buttons and it was soiled in front. He had a grey beard which looked dirty from food stains. Pavel thought to himself that he could still turn around and go out the door, but he would wait to see Anna. He came all the way to her home, so he would stay and see what happened. If he did not like what he saw, he would never come back. He was thinking these thoughts when Anna came out and he knew at once that he had made the right decision. He would stay for a while longer and he felt at once that he could love this girl once he began to know her. After the introductions, they spoke for about ten minutes when Anton's friend asked Pavel to step outside while he spoke to her father, Pavel left the house. He wondered what they could be talking about and at last, the man came out and started to walk toward the tavern.

"What did you talk about?" asked Pavel.

"Her father agreed to let you court her and even to marry her under certain conditions," he answered. "He does not want you to give him any money, but he does need furniture. Also, if it comes to getting married, he wants you to live with them so you can help with the expenses. You and Anna can work on your brother's farm but you would have to live here. I'll tell Anton and you had better talk it over with him."

As Pavel walked home from the tavern, he thought about Anna. She was a lovely woman, but being married to her did nothing for his future. He would, in all probability, end up supporting her father and mother for the rest of their lives. The future looked bleak at this moment and when they reached home, Anton told his mother what had happened, and she felt that they should talk about it after the evening meal. She had always wanted Pavel to stay home, but she knew that Anton would not consent to that much longer.

After the kitchen was cleaned up, they each lingered over a cup of tea and Pavel told the family about the arrangement that Pan Grovitch had proposed.

Anton said, "I am sure that the conditions could be negotiated but you would have to go live in the cottage with your in-laws. I have a bed, a table, an armoire that I could give to you and I will give you both an honest wage. When I pass on, the farm will be turned over to my oldest son. That was the nature of things and it has been done this way for a thousand years. You were just unlucky to be born last."

Pavel said that he wanted to think about it and went outside. He sat on the railing of the porch and soon his mother was sitting beside him. He was her youngest child and she had to help him.

"I have some money saved," she said. "I was saving it for a decent burial, but you are welcome to it if it will help. Do not give it to Pan Grobitch. You should save it and use it if you need it. Do not tell anyone that I gave it to you. It is only thirty crowns."

"Thank you, mother," he said, "I can use the help."

She went on, "You know that you do not have to marry this girl, I will still give you the money. We will let Anton worry about putting his mother into the ground. I have a brother who left Nowy Targ before you were born, he settled in Ruzbachy which is over the High Tatra mountains. If you follow the river, you will come to a pass that will take you through the mountains. You could leave now and find a nice Slovak girl to marry. Don't waste your life feeding that old man and woman." She put her hand on his. "Think about it, my son." She kissed him on the cheek and left.

Pavel could not get to sleep as he kept thinking about that lovely woman in town and how it would be to sleep next to her for the rest of his life. Then he thought of her parents and tried to foresee when they would die, but he would own only a cottage and he wanted land, a farm that he could work and raise children on. He could just pack up and leave and visit uncle Pavel but he wanted to wait and see how Anna felt about moving away. Sometime during the night, he formulated a plan that would give him both options. He could marry Anna, move in with her family for a short time and then move to Ruzbachy. With that he fell asleep, he would work out the details tomorrow.

When he got up and came into the kitchen, his mother was taking a pan of hot bread out of the little oven that sat on the coals of the fireplace. He told her that he would court Anna for the next three months and if at that time she still wanted to go through with it, he would get married. If her family was too much of a problem, then he would vanish and go to live with Uncle Pavel. He swore her to secrecy and put the money she gave him into his pocket. He would find a suitable hiding place for it later. He went out to find Anton to tell him so he could strike a bargain with Pan Grobitch. Anton was overjoyed. He could now get rid of his brother for he had planned to let Pavel work for a year and pay him well and after that, he was going to tell him that he could not pay him any more and release him.

That night, Anton went to the Grobitch cottage and spoke to Anna's father. He told him what he had proposed, they agreed and shook hands. Anna burst through the door to the kitchen where she was listening to every word.

"What about me?" she asked. "I suppose that I have nothing to say about this arrangement? What happens after three months of courtship and I find that I cannot live with him? What happens then?" Her father spoke, "You can either marry him, or leave the household because you will embarrass me. You will not go against my word and nothing will change hands until you are married so nothing is lost except my honor."

His daughter calmed down somewhat and said, "I have one condition and it is important to me. Pavel and I must be married by a priest in a church. If we have children, then they will be brought up in the church because I want all of us to go to church as a family."

Both her father and Anton looked at each other and said in unison, "Agreed." They shook hands and Anton left.

He rushed back home to tell Pavel. The next arrangement to be made was the amount of money that Anton would pay for the services of Pavel and Anna once they were married. He was generous since he would not be paying them any longer than a year. Pavel agreed and the courtship of Anna Grobitch began.

Pavel went to see Anna once a week at first and then twice a week. Soon he was seeing her every day. They found that they were well suited for each other and she told him that she wanted him to start going to church now and he agreed. They went to church every Sunday and talked to the priest right after Mass. The more time that went by, the closer they had become and Pavel thought that this was the woman with whom he would gladly spend the rest of his days. He told her of the generous amount that Anton was going to pay them but he told her to tell her father that it was one half of the amount. That way, they could save one half and buy their own home sooner. She agreed because she wanted to leave as soon as they were able. The three months went by quickly and before they knew it, the wedding day came and they were married. It seemed like a perfect arrangement until the furniture was moved into the cottage.

Once the furniture was moved in and the couple moved into the cottage, Pan Grobitch became unbearable.

The first night at the evening meal Pan Grobitch spoke, "I demand all the money that you make so we can use it to support the household."

Pavel answered, "I will match the amount that you bring into the household."

A loud argument followed as Pavel walked out, but Anna asked him to return and discuss it with her father. This did not suit Anna's father since he planned never to go back to work. Pavel returned and they finally reached still another agreement with Pavel paying one half of their earnings into the household, this still left Pavel with three-quarters of his wages.

After four months of married life, Anna announced that she was with child. Pavel outwardly appeared happy, but he was thinking of leaving with Anna as soon as he was sure that he could make it through the pass. They had a long hard winter to contend with before they could leave and he counted the days. Each day they would trudge through the snow to be sure that they would work and be able to collect their earnings. Pavel's mother gave Anna lessons on how to cook Pavel's favorite foods and they grew to love each other. His mother would tell Anton that Anna did more than she actually did so she would be sure to be paid. Anton smiled because he planned to release both of them next spring. The couple, however, had planned to leave right after Easter and that would put Anna in her eighth month. Pavel would carry the bulk of their belongings and, if they traveled slowly and made frequent stops, they should be able to get to Uncle Pavel's farm in a week. On Easter Sunday, as they were walking from church, Pavel told her of his plan. She agreed and said that they would travel very slowly as she was heavy with the baby and it was going to be a large baby.

The Sunday after Easter, they left the house very quietly at three o'clock in the morning. Pavel had seventy-four crowns in a bag tied around his waist. He carried all of their belongings strapped to his back while Anna carried the food. If it was any day but Sunday, they might have met a wagon and gotten a ride for part of the way, but since it was Sunday, no one was out this early. They would stop every hour for five minutes and rest. The first three hours they would walk without resting as they were fresh from sleep and excited.

*   *   *

Pan Grobitch and his wife awoke on this Sunday later than usual for Pavel and Anna were not down yet. They decided to let them sleep as they needed time together without their boarders. At about nine o'clock, the couple still had not been seen. Anna's mother became worried and knocked on the door of their room. She opened the door a crack and peeked into the room, she found the room all clean, the bed made, her daughter and son-in-law were gone. She ran into the room and opened the armoire, and it was empty. She went downstairs to tell her husband that they were gone but he went to see for himself and came back, looking puzzled. All he did was shake his head back and forth and wonder how they were going to get along. They were never to see their daughter or son-in-law again.

*   *   *

The Saturday before the young couple left the farm, Pavel kissed his mother goodby. He saw a tear on her cheek and, brushing it off, he told her how sorry he was that she would never see her grandchildren. She told him that was what had bothered her the most about their leaving. She pressed him close to her and told him that he would always be her baby. He tore himself away and went to Anton to collect the last of his earnings.

Sunday afternoon, Pan Gorbitch went to the Valigursky farm, looking for his daughter and her husband. They seemed to have disappeared and no one had seen them since the previous Saturday evening. Anton seemed relieved as this solved a problem for him. When he thought about sending the couple away, it seemed easy, but when he actually had to talk to Pavel, he did not know how he would get the nerve to tell him. They all agreed that they must have gone on a picnic or an outing of some kind and that they should wait for them to return.

*   *   *

On Monday morning, the couple saw a wagon and were given a ride for about ten miles. They had spent the night in a barn. It was cool but they cuddled and kept each other warm. It would get colder as they went up higher in the pass. The farmer who gave them a ride also gave them food and an old horse blanket. They were grateful for the way that rural people helped each other. The couple came to the mountains and the higher peaks had snow, but it looked like the pass was clear. It was now Wednesday morning when they started up the pass and the weather looked clear with no storms in sight. The road was muddy which made the walking more difficult and the higher they went, the colder it became. The walking became less difficult as part of the road was frozen but that night they huddled under the blanket in a small hut someone had built for travelers. They put all of their clothes on to keep warm and at daybreak they started down. They would stop to eat something as soon as they found a brook coming down from the mountain. They had run out of water, but it was plentiful on the trail.

On Friday, they came to a clearing with twelve crosses standing in a row and Anna wanted to stop and say a rosary, but Pavel said there was no time. He wanted to be in Ruzbachy on Saturday

but Anna complained that she was tired, her legs ached and she
was starting to feel warm in the cold air. They were almost out of
food and they had to get down from the pass to an area where it
was warmer. They slept in a strand of pine where Pavel made a bed
of needles and they slept soundly. When they woke, the sun was
up in the sky and Anna had difficulty standing up. She felt dizzy
and he put his arm under hers to help her to walk. They looked for
a cart to go by, but none showed up so they had to keep walking.
They stopped often to rest; they saw a farm house, Anna wanted
to go for help, but Pavel kept walking because they were not making good time. Saturday came and went and they did not know
where they were. Suddenly Anna fell by the side of the road, she
looked up,told Pavel that she could go no further; he ran down the
road where he found a small cottage. He must be close to town, he
thought as he went to the door and started banging.

A large woman came to the door and he told about Anna. She
hitched up her wagon, got a lantern and they rode out to where
Anna was lying. The woman said that there was an abbey close by,
and they struggled to get Anna into the wagon. It took the two of
them, along with an old friar to take her into the kitchen and put
her on a table. The woman sent Pavel into a large hall and she
seemed to know what she was doing as she barked orders to the
friars running around. After about an hour, a priest came to the
hall with the newborn baby. He said that he was a doctor and as
much as he tried, he could not save the woman. Pavel could not
remember what he said to the young priest, but he took the baby
and walked out of the door. He said that he would come back for
the body of his wife as soon as he could. Pavel asked directions
from a friar who was pacing back and forth and he gave him directions to his Uncle Pavel's farm.

Although it was dark, he found his uncle's farm. It was further
then the friar told him it was going to be. When he banged on the
door, a short stout woman came to the door.

Pavel asked, "Is Pan Pavel Dombrowski at home?"

The woman looked at the baby before she answered, "Yes, he

is, please come in. Where did the little baby come from? It looks like it was just born? Where is the mother?"

Pavel replied, "I'll answer all of your questions, but I must see Pan Pavel Dombrowski as soon as possible."

Pan Pavel came in just at that moment and looked at his nephew but did not recognize him. He had familiar features, but he could not place him.

Pavel introduced himself. "I am your nephew, Pavel from Nowy Targ. I am your sister's son."

Pan Pavel embraced his nephew and pulled him toward him. "I am happy to see you. Marta said you were coming. She told me to open my house to you. I expected to see you and your wife, Anna. Where is she?"

"It is a long story, Uncle, I will tell it to you later. All I know right now is that the baby is hungry and I do not know what to feed it."

Eva took the baby and looked, "You have a little girl, Pavel and she looks healthy. Let me get her some food."

She took the infant and ran out of the door. Pan Pavel smiled, "She is taking your daughter to our daughter, Lita's house. Lita had a baby three weeks ago and she has enough milk to supply half of Ruzbachy. Your daughter will be well fed."

The men sat down and Pavel went on to tell his uncle the entire story. He did neglect, however, to tell how he pushed his wife the last three days until she could travel no further. He asked his uncle about the priest in the abbey who appeared to know medicine. Pan Pavel told him that both priests were good men. The older priest, Father Damian has been here for many years and he could be trusted. The younger one, Father Josef, was educated in Bratislava and went to Vienna for his medical training and he also could be trusted.

Eva Dombrowski came back with the baby who was now asleep. She placed the little girl down and looked at Pavel. "You must be hungry, let me fix you some soup. We have a bed for you so you can go to sleep. We will worry about the details tomorrow."

After two bowls of soup, Pavel went to his room with his daughter but he could not sleep. Every time he thought of Anna, his eyes filled with tears and he thought, "How things could have been if I had not been so stubborn and, now, I will never see her again." He had such fine hopes and all that he had was a baby girl, not even a boy, but a girl to take care of and who will not be of any use to him on a farm. How did he get into this predicament? He trusted God to get them safely through the mountains and He failed him. "I will never put his trust in religion again," he thought.

The more he thought, the more he tried to put the blame on someone else and the more he felt sorry for himself. Being the youngest in the family did not prepare him for this tragedy. He would drop off to sleep for a few hours and then stay awake for five or six more. This pattern continued for four days and Pavel did not leave his room. The pot that was under the bed was full and the room smelled.

As he was lying on his bed, he could hear voices coming from outside. Apparently Eva and Pavel had left the house so that he would not hear them arguing.

He heard his uncle say, "Give him a little longer. He has had a difficult time."

Eva's reply came out in an angry voice, "He has to leave that room and get on with his life. I will cook for him, clean after him, wash his clothes that he has worn for four days, take care of his daughter, but I absolutely refuse to bring his food to him. That will only encourage him to stay up there until his daughter gets married. He probably will not even see his grandchildren."

"All right," Pavel said. "I will talk to him. I should empty the pot anyway."

As he listened to the couple, something that Eva said suddenly came back to him. "All is not lost." He said aloud, "The girl will grow up and marry, then I will have a son and I will have grandchildren."

As he laid back on his big downy pillow, a knock came on the door. It was Uncle Pavel, who came into the room, took the pot from under the bed and left. He said that he would return shortly and he did with the pot all cleaned.

Pavel got up and the nephew and uncle faced each other. The uncle spoke first. "Pavel, we have to talk about a few things. First of all, you look terrible. You have lost even more weight. Your face is gaunt and you have hollow black eyes. You need food, fresh clothes and sunshine. Come down for the evening meal and we will eat sooner than we usually do because I want you to meet your family."

"You are right, Uncle. Give me a few minutes to clean up and I will join you. How is the little girl? We do have to find a name for her and I just cannot think of a name."

"Eva had a suggestion," Pan Pavel said. "She always liked the name Olga and we have no one in the family named Olga. We have to consider the baptism and Father Damian took care of the burial of Anna. He is having a headstone cut for her but we have to get you out and about. Your daughter is waiting to see you."

With that he left the room. Pavel got up and washed and shaved in the bowl of water that had sat there for four days. He had not noticed, but the room that he had spent four days in was pretty and, no doubt, it was a woman's room, probably Lita's room. She must have left it when she got married. He looked into the faded mirror, combed his hair with his fingers and left the room. Pavel went downstairs and saw the table laid out for five places.

He found his uncle and aunt in the kitchen as he entered and the aroma of food hit him full in the face, telling him that he was famished. Eva told him that it would be a few more minutes and Pavel took him into the dining/sitting room area. The kitchen comprised one-third of the second floor and the first floor was devoted to the prize animals while the third floor had three bedrooms. The house was built on the side of a knoll so that the bottom floor was covered on three sides by dirt. The front door was on ground level and opened into the kitchen. There were curtains on the windows, pictures and little shelves with knickknacks on the walls. This was a fine-looking home and Pavel hoped to have one like it someday. As they sat in the sitting room, a young, short, stout woman entered carrying a baby and following her, was a young man taller than the woman. He was slender and muscular and he looked like he worked outdoors all day.

The woman introduced herself as Lita and handed Pavel the baby. "This is your daughter," she said. "I just fed her so she will sleep for a while. She is a beautiful baby and your wife must have been beautiful."

Pavel's eyes started to water and she put her hand on his arm. "I'm sorry," she said. "I did not mean to bring up a painful memory."

Pavel was looking at his daughter. He looked up and said, "I have decided to name her Olga."

He looked at Eva who had just entered the room. She heard the last of his conversation and smiled.

Lita looked at the young man and said, "This is my husband, Midtj and my daughter, Eva. It looks like my daughter will have a playmate."

"Let's eat before it gets cold," said Eva as she set a large pot of steaming food on the table.

There were two identical baskets on the floor and Lita put Eva in one while Pavel put Olga into the other. They all sat down and Eva said a prayer to thank the Lord for the food. She noticed that, the younger Pavel did not participate.

The meal was a stew with bits of beef along with carrots, beans, and potatoes. The family did not eat this way on every week night, but this was a special occasion, Pavel had come back from the dead and he was entering life again. Pavel ate more than he should but the fresh baked bread was just like his mother baked. Midtj appeared friendly and he offered to take Pavel down to the tavern when he wanted to go.

Pavel said, "I am not ready to do that sort of thing, just yet, when I am ready, I will let you know."

He was sitting across from Lita and could not help but notice her ample breasts. Yes, she could feed half of Ruzbachy with those breasts; for the first time he felt his lips part in a half smile. This did not go unnoticed by Eva, who was watching him and she also smiled.

After the meal, they sat around the table while the women cleared it and then Eva brought some tea. They had to get a plan into action to take care of Olga and Eva suggested that she stay with her, then Lita could visit them at various times of the day to feed her. She should be weaned from breast feeding as soon as possible because this will be difficult for Lita but she said that she did not mind and would help as long as she could. Pavel said that he would probably never get over mourning for his wife. He told his story, once more, for the benefit of Lita and Midtj and again left out the part where he pushed her to finish the journey. He thought to himself that he would have to come to grips with that someday. Before they realized it, the sun had set and it was well into the evening. Lita and her mother went to clean up the kitchen and Pavel went up to his room. Olga would sleep in Eva's room for a while as she might need attention during the night. As Pavel laid his head on the pillow he fell asleep and slept soundly for the first time in ten days.

When he awoke, he heard activity downstairs and got up, dressed and went down. He felt that he should work for their keep for on a farm of this size, there was much to do. His uncle had a good farm, he raised mostly horses with a few cows and other animals that were used for food. Pan Pavel's horses were known all over the area and he boarded a few for people in town because he was well-known as a trainer of horses. People from Podolencz brought their horses to him to train for racing because he had a track and stables on the farm. His prize stallions were kept on the bottom floor of his home and were not allowed to mingle with the rest of the horses. This is where he made the bulk of his money, from the stud fees he obtained for his Arabian stallions.

He had a roll and tea and then went on a tour with his uncle. He liked what he saw and he had much to learn but he still could not get the memory of Anna out of his head. Eva and Pan Pavel were helpful. They talked to their nephew and tried not to leave

him alone for any length of time. He slowly spent less of his time
in his room and more on the farm. Pavel loved his daughter who
would grow up looking just like her mother; she would keep re-
minding him of her.

Slowly, the patience of his aunt and uncle was being rewarded
for he was working more and was settling down to a routine. One
day his uncle told him that the older priest, Father Damian, had
stopped over and baptized Olga and he took the news with not a
hint of pleasure or displeasure. He simply shrugged his shoulders
as if he did not care. He still had not visited the grave of his wife
even though Eva told him that the headstone was set up and someone had been tending the grave. They had even put some flowers
on it. Pavel vowed that one day, when he could develop enough
nerve, he would go to the cemetery. This might help him resolve
his guilt problem but he still kept on putting off the visit. Olga
was getting bigger and before long, she would walk and talk. She
had been given milk from the cows that were on the farm and Eva
had started her on solid foods. Lita had stopped coming over as
often for she had her own household to run and her own baby
required more attention.

One day, Pavel and his uncle had fashioned a small bed with
sides on it so that Olga could use that instead of the basket. She
outgrew the basket and needed her own bed, one where she would
not fall out. The bed was placed in Pavel's room so he could get
closer to his daughter. She recognized him and smiled when she
saw him and he started feeding her at night. She knew who her
father was and who to go to when she wanted to play. One day
when he came in from the stables, Eva had a surprise for him. She
stood Olga up next to a chair, went a few feet away and called her.
Olga took three uneasy steps toward her and Eva said that they
might be sorry that they taught this young lady how to walk. She
was a bright child, she learned very quickly and she had energy to
spare so there was nothing that she would not try. The little girl.
She was also very persistent, she would keep trying until she was
successful and as Eva had predicted, she was into everything. Eva

had placed all the breakable objects out of reach. Once in a while Lita brought little Eva, as she was now known, down to play with Olga and Olga tormented her unmercifully. She was impatient with Eva's inability to master some of the activities that Olga had mastered. Eva predicted that this child would be riding a horse at the age of five years.

Pavel had not gone into town until two years after the death of his wife. He was not interested in getting married again and he had resigned himself to the fact that he would be a widower for the rest of his days. Midtj and he had spent a rather exhausting day in the fields on an unseasonabily hot day and they left work early to go back to the main house. Pan Pavel was feeling the effects of the hot day and suggested that he treat them to a beer at the tavern. Midtj accepted readily but it took a little persuasion to get Pavel to go. They hitched up a wagon and left for town.

There were about ten men in the tavern and Pavel introduced his nephew to everyone and the more beer that was consumed, the higher the noise level became. The door opened and in walked Father Damian and when he saw Pan Pavel, he went directly to their table. Hands were clasped by everyone and it was evident that this was not the first time that the priest had been in the tavern. He was in the circle of comradeship with the men that frequented the place. Father Damian spoke nothing of religion but talked about the same subjects that the rest of the farmers found interesting and there was no mention of the incident that happened over two years ago. Midtj and his father-in-law left Pavel alone with the priest and went outside, to the big tree, to relieve themselves.

Pavel looked up and said, "Thank you for taking care of the burial of my wife. He had been very careful not to use the term "father."

The priest answered, "I am happy that I was in a position to help. How is the young lady doing? What is her name, Olga? That is a pretty name."

This brought forth a long talk about the exploits of Olga. She was driving poor Eva to insanity, she was big for her age, had now been walking and talking for a year and was getting into everything. He had taken her into the barn to see the horses, and she left covered with manure. Eva was beside herself. She took the child, washed her and then washed her clothes. Eva had pretended to be angry, but she loved every minute of it. The priest smiled through the discourse and did nothing to interrupt the young man. The best thing he could do now would be to talk about his daughter but when the other two returned, it was time to go home. Eva would be furious if they were late so they said goodbyes to the priest and left.

Riding back to the farm, Pavel looked at his uncle and said, "You were right when you told me that the priest was a good man. While I was talking to him, I forgot that he was a priest." Nothing more was said on the way home.

When Olga was five years old, her father put her on a horse. It was an old mare that Pavel loaned to the fairs and the schools so young children could ride her. She was very gentle with children. Pavel once had tried to sell her to a band of gypsies, but they would have taken her for nothing and eaten her, so Pavel kept her around for the children. Olga was delighted to sit upon the horse, her father had put a small saddle on the mare and sat her up on it. He gave her the reins, let go and the horse started and walked very slowly as she had done countless times with young children sitting on her. Her father told her that if she wanted the horse to go left then she should pull that rein a little. Olga gave the rein a little tug and the mare turned left and when she tugged a little on the right rein, the mare turned right. He told her to pull both reins for the horse to stop and to lean forward and loosen the reins to go forward. He told her to practice and watched her for about an hour without interference. She did not want to get off the horse, but he pulled her off anyway. He unsaddled the animal and took her into the barn. Next he brought a step stool to the mare and gave Olga a brush. He told her that anytime she rode a horse, she must brush it down and there were no exceptions to this rule. The horse would get to know her and they would become friends. If she treated the horse as a friend, then the horse would treat her as one.

He asked her, "Do you like riding the horse?"

She told him, "Yes, I like riding the horse. When can we do it again?"

"In another month you will be starting school and she will be riding down with little Eva. As long as you went to school and did well, then I will allow you to ride the horse. We might even take a ride in the fields when you learned to ride better."

From that time on, Olga loved horses.

Pavel, occasionally, would accompany his uncle and his son-in-law to the tavern. On one of these occasions, he was talking to the bar keeper about the possibility of buying a farm. The barkeeper had said that he knew of a farm owner who was thinking about going to America. He and his wife had no children to whom they could leave the farm so they thought that they might sell it and spend the rest of their days in America. They had relatives there who could help them find work. All this landowner needed was a push, the promise of ready cash and he might just go to America.

Pavel went to his uncle's table and asked to speak to him privately and once alone, he told him the story as he had heard it from the barkeeper. "It sounds interesting," said Pavel. "Let's go talk to him."

They both went to the barkeeper and found the owner was Hiedl Braski. They thanked the man, bought three more beers and went to the table where Pavel told his nephew that he knew the farm. It was small, with only a small amount of livestock on the farm. There was a small house in good condition but the barns could stand a little work. There was some land but it had not been worked for some years; it could be a fine farm with a great deal of heavy work. Pavel promised to help his nephew, as did Midtj. Midtj was not worried about competing with Pavel for he had been told that his wife would inherit that farm and all he had to do was to wait it out. Besides, Midtj liked young Pavel and, over the length of time that he knew the young man, they had become friends. There was really no one in the area for companionship and he was grateful that Pavel was there.

Uncle Pavel looked at his nephew and asked, "How much money do you have?"

Pavel answered, "A little over one hundred crowns."

His uncle was amazed; he had been giving Pavel a few crowns now and then, and he must have been saving all of it. "Fine," he said, "I can loan you some, but it all depends on how badly Pan Braski wants to go to America. We will ride out to see him tomorrow."

Right after the morning chores were done, Pavel told his nephew, "Saddle up, let us go see if we can buy you a farm."

They rode out to see Pan Braski and found him in the barn milking a cow. Pavel pulled up a stool and pointed to another one which his nephew pulled over, sat down while Pan Braski did not miss a stroke in his milking. Pavel introduced his nephew and waited for the farmer to finish.

When he was done, the farmer asked, "To what do I owe the pleasure of this visit?"

Both uncle and nephew did not see very much milk in the pail and they knew that cow must be going dry. Pan Pavel spoke first: "We understand you are thinking about going to America?"

Pan Braski knew exactly where he had gotten his information. He said, "So you have been to the tavern with the talkative bar-keeper."

Pavel asked, "How serious are you in going and would your farm be up for sale?"

The reply came, "We have talked about it, but I would have to get enough for my farm to make it worthwhile."

Uncle and nephew looked at each other and young Pavel asked, "Do you mind if we look around at the house, stables, barns and fields?"

"No, I do not mind," he answered. "I have some charts and

maps in the house and I will get them for you if you want to make an offer."

They all went into the house where Pan Braski's wife made them a cup of tea. Pavel told his nephew, "anytime you enter a Slovak's home, you will be offered something to eat or drink. You accept, because if you do not, you have made an enemy for life. This is good advice, do not forget it."

He had noticed that Pavel was hesitant about taking the cup of tea and finally accepted it. Armed with the charts, they rode around the perimeter of the land, inspected all the out buildings, the house and the animals.

Young Pavel asked, "Well, what do you think?"

His uncle answered, "Everything is in worse condition than I remembered it and it is not worth much."

They found Pan Braski in the barn again and they asked him what he wanted for the farm. He told them to make an offer so he would know if they were serious or not. On the ride out, Pavel told his uncle to do the talking and he would abide by any bargain that was struck.

Pavel looked the man right in the eye and said, "We are prepared to offer you fifteen hundred crowns for the farm, land, out buildings, house, furniture and livestock. The buildings are run down and since you do not have anyone to which you can leave your farm, it will go to the state when you die. What would happen to your wife if you should die? You would have some money to take you to America to be with your relatives until you pass on from this life to the next."

"I will have to talk it over with my wife, but I can tell you that fifteen hundred crowns is not enough money for this farm."

Pavel said, "Well, we'll keep looking because there must be a farm we can buy in Ruzbachy."

They left the farm and went home to wait for Pan Braski to make the next move. They waited a week when he came riding into the Dombrowski farm. He came into the house, Eva made him a cup of tea and she went to find her husband.

When they were all seated around the table, Pan Braski said, "I have discussed our meeting with my wife and we agreed that if the offer was raised to two thousand crowns, we would accept. All we want to take from the farm are our clothes."

Pavel looked at his nephew, "We also discussed it and we will be prepared to pay you cash money in the amount of 1750 crowns and no more. If you agree, we will go to the notary tomorrow and transfer the title, but if you do not accept our final offer, then we will stop our quest to buy your farm."

Pan Braski stood up, put out his hand and said, "We will accept your offer. Give us two weeks to pack, make transportation arrangements and we will go to America."

Pan Braski left, pleased that he was able to obtain another two hundred and fifty crowns for his farm. He would have accepted the fifteen hundred crowns if they had not wavered and he thought that the negotiations were like two gypsies selling a horse over a campfire. He was pleased with himself. Pavel told his uncle that he would only need 1650 crowns, but Pavel offered him the entire 1750 crowns since it would take some time to fix up the farm and he would have no money coming in for a while. Two weeks later, the three of them met in the notary's office. Papers were signed, money changed hands, and Pavel took the Broskis to Podolencz to catch a train. He wanted to move into the house a week later without Olga. Eva suggested that they wait until the house was repaired and furniture from the Dombrowskis was in place in his new home. Besides, Olga had to go to school every day.

Pavel worked on his new farm for a year. Eva had them over for meals often for she was teaching Olga how to cook and the girl was learning quickly. The following year when Olga was seven, she moved in with her father. She had to be taken, each morning, to the Dombrowski farm which was on the way to school and picked up every night. She cooked the meals, cleaned the house and sometimes helped in the barn. Eva would send them some food for the evening meal with Olga when her father picked her up. Pavel wanted Olga to stop going to school and keep house for him but

Eva would not stand for it. School was important, Olga was a bright young lady and it would help her in later years. Pavel had learned much from his uncle and the one thing he learned was not to argue with Eva. The farm had begun to look good, the crops were in and in the fall, Pavel would mate two mares with his uncle's stallion. He would also need calves, sheep and chickens but that could wait while he worked on his herd of horses. During the winter, Pavel went into the woods to hunt with an old cap and ball rifle. He shot a deer and a boar which he hung in the barn frozen all winter. He would cut off a piece of meat as it was needed. He had taken Olga with him on his hunting expeditions and taught her how to shoot. At the fairs in town, she could outride most of the young men, and outshoot all of them. She was strong willed and intimidated the young men she met, so no one visited her after the first time. Pavel sold his first horse in his third year, bringing in some cash to pay part of his loan to his uncle. His uncle sent some horses for boarding to his nephew when he had more than he wanted to handle and Pavel also took in some horses to train. He was beginning to gain a reputation as one who knew how to train horses.

One fine sunny, Sunday afternoon in April, Pavel and Olga took a ride on their horses. They had no route planned to ride, electing to go where the horses took them, to the edge of their land and beyond. Pavel wanted to talk to his daughter about men women relationships but he did not know how to begin. He thought that Eva had talked to her, but he could not be sure and he wanted her to know certain things that a young girl should know. He knew that she felt relaxed while riding and this would be a good time to talk.

Pavel started out by saying, "How are you doing in school?"

She replied, "I am doing well. I am ahead of all the boys in my class. They are such stupid creatures. All they ever think about are girls and I really have no interest in them."

She made it easy for him to approach the subject. "Why do you feel that you have to be better than all the boys in your class?

You will be interested in boys when you are a little older and you will never have any suitors if you keep doing what you are doing. You have to let them win once in a while because boys have to feel superior even if they are not."

If Olga had been on the ground, she would have stomped her foot but she still let her anger come forth. "Why should I let them win? If they beat me fair and square, that is one thing, but to let them win to appease them, no, I cannot do that. They will have to work to beat me and I am not going to let them." She prodded her horse to go a little faster. It still might be too early to talk to her but he would talk to Eva the next time he saw her. He looked up to see where they were heading, saw the abbey in the distance. They were heading right for it. Since Olga was a good distance in front of him, he followed her until he caught up. By this time, they were fairly close to the abbey.

"Let's stop at the abbey," she said.

He answered, "All right, but only for a little while. We have to start for home."

They rode through the gate of the abbey and she though that it was a beautiful place with its well-kept gardens and pathways.

They stopped the horses and heard a voice behind them.

"Welcome to the Abbey of St. Francis." They turned to see Father Damian coming toward them.

"I am very happy to see both of you. I have been looking for company. I walk these paths on Sunday to organize my thoughts, and they're organized now." He smiled at them and said, "Please, come into the kitchen for a cup of tea. You can leave your horses here. They will be fine." Pavel thought back to what his uncle had said once. "If you visit a Slovak, he will offer you food or drink. If you refuse, you will have made an enemy for life." He did not feel that the priest would be an enemy for life, but he accepted anyway. They tied the horses to a pole and walked with the priest. As they rounded a corner of the building, they saw the cemetery in a corner of the wall. One of the graves seemed to have better care than the rest, but no comment was made. They were having a cup of tea and enjoying the conversation when a young boy came through the door. Father Damian introduced him as Johan Janek when he stopped for a few minutes and went to the pump to wash his hands. He looked like he was planting some flowers, his hands were covered with dirt.

"What have you been doing, Johan?" asked the priest.

Johan answered, "Brother Jan gave me some flowers and I was planting them in the cemetery. I hope that they will grow." He dried his hands and left the room.

Olga looked at the priest and asked, "Is that the cemetery where my mother is buried?"

"Yes" he answered, "Would you like to see where?"

"I have never seen it," she said. "I would very much like to see it." She turned to her father, "You can come, too." Pavel turned pale and looked at the priest. Father Damian knew that it was a difficult moment for Pavel, but if anyone could make him visit the grave it was strong-willed Olga. He did not press the issue with Pavel but remained silent. Finally Olga stood up, took her father's hand and led him out the door. He resisted some but allowed himself to be led to the cemetery. When they approached the cemetery they discovered that the well-kept grave was Anna's, the tears rolled down Pavel's cheeks.

"Who takes care of it?" he asked.

"The boy you just met," answered the priest. "He was in the doorway on the day Olga was born and Anna died. Johan was left on our doorstep when he was born and we do not know who his parents are. We raised him in the abbey. He is a fine boy and sensitive; he wanted to take care of the grave because he never knew his mother either and someone had to step in to care for her."

Olga said, "It is beautiful. I want to thank Johan."

"There is no need to thank him," said the priest. "I think he is doing it for his mother as well as Olga's mother. Let him continue to plant the flowers. I have asked Brother Jan who takes care of the grounds to give Johan the flowers to plant there and it is a good thing for Johan."

Pavel felt a sense of well-being float over his body and his color returned to normal. Olga took the priest's hand and squeezed it, the message was given and received.

There was no conversation on the way home,for they rode in silence, each with his and her own thoughts. It was dusk when they returned and they changed their clothes to take care of the animals. Olga left the barn early and warmed up some leftover "crupi, And there would be no leftovers after dinner. They were hungry when they sat to eat and once fed, they were tired. Olga went to bed, Pavel sat in his rocking chair and smoked his pipe. Life appeared to be all right, he thought. He had a farm which belonged more to his uncle than to him; he had a beautiful daughter and relatives that he could count on, and yes, he even took a liking to the priest. He still had problems with his religion but the priest, as a human being, was a fine man and he would have to see more of him. It was this night, with the help of his daughter, the priest, a young man, with sympathy for his plight, and his God, who he still would not acknowledge, that Pavel made peace with his guilt. He would go to bed and sleep without interruption.

When Olga was fifteen, Pavel had a decision to make. She was still in school but he needed her on the farm desperately. The farm had grown and there was more work to be done. She did her share but going to school and doing the work was taking a toll on her. She appeared tired after the evening meal and went right to bed. He thought that this was no life for the girl and he would ask Uncle Pavel and Aunt Eva for their opinions. While Olga went to school, he rode over to the Dombrowski farm. It was midday and they were sitting on chairs under the large tree in the rear of the house. Pavel had planted the maple tree to provide shade for the house.

Pavel took a cup of tea from Eva and said, "I am worried about Olga."

Eva said, "I think that I know what you are worried about but

I have been talking to Olga about boys in general and the repro-
duction process and there is very little danger of her going too far
with a boy as she had not been able to entice any suitors. In a year
or so, she will be of marriageable age but there is no one to marry.
I, too, am worried about this but Olga likes school and this is the
place where young girls who lived out in the country met suitors.
The other place is church and although we take her into town for
church every Sunday, no suitor has come forward."

Pavel told them of the conversation he had with Olga, the day
that they were riding.

Eva said, "I expected as much. Olga is a headstrong young
lady and she gives no quarter to anyone, especially the boys. She
can outride them, outshoot them, outwork them and outsmart
them. I think she will eventually find the one and only, but I hope
that it will not be too late. Once a girl gets to be eighteen or
nineteen and was not pursued, then word seems to circulate that
she has a problem. We will have to look for a suitor for her because
nature is not taking a true course."

It was decided that after 10 years of schooling, Olga should
not return to the school the following year. She would finish this
year, but she was needed on the farm. Pavel had hoped that she
would meet someone at church or a festival at one of the holidays
but all Pavel knew was that he did need help on the farm. One
rainy day, Pavel decided to ride down to the tavern for a beer or
two. He was limited in what he could do when it rained and he
arrived in late afternoon. He planned to leave in time to pick up
Olga at his uncle's house. The tavern was deserted so he sat by
himself at a corner table. The door opened and two more farmers
stopped in. Right behind them Father Damian entered. He saw
Pavel sitting alone and sat at his table. They talked for a few minutes and Pavel told him about his problem with Olga and about
needing help on the farm. The priest knew of no one that he could
recommend as a suitor for Olga, but he might have someone who
could help with the work on the farm and he would not have to
pay him. The young man had year and a half to go before he

would take his final vows as a Jesuit brother and he had completed all of his studies. He could send him over to help, if he wanted him.

Father Damian said, "the boy's name is Johan Janek and you had met him the day that you and Olga visited the abbey."

Pavel could not turn down an offer like that because the young man was young and strong, he knew every phase of farming, having been trained by the Brothers, and he was well educated. This was the ideal suitor for Olga, but it was too bad that he would be taking the vow of celibacy, he would make a perfect husband for his daughter. A few days later, Johan rode up to the farm in his working clothes and Pavel put him to work.

He came only a few days a week but Pavel could see the impact that he was making. He would come when Olga went to school and went back before she returned. She was riding her horse to his uncle's home and she went to school with little Eva. Little Eva was not a pretty girl, she was short and inclined to be on the plump side. She was helpless to a fault so all the boys at school tried to help her. Once they arrived at school Olga did not see her until it was time to go home and she had trouble riding a horse so Olga drove a wagon. Pavel had discussed the matter of leaving school and working on the farm and Olga was delighted. She felt that school was now boring. She loved her animals, she loved caring for them and she did not mind getting dirty. In a few months she would not be going to school any longer and she was counting the days. On the last day of school, Olga said goodbye to the students and the instructor and left, never to return.

Olga spent the first few months cleaning the house, washing all the clothes and scrubbing floors. Gradually, she was spending more and more time with the animals. Johan liked Olga and he began coming three times a week. When harvest time came the following year, the three of them worked side by side in the fields, cutting hay, rye, barley and wheat. Johan had gotten some seeds from Father Damian and had planted maize. Pavel was happy to see his daughter so happy and was impressed with Johan for he was a hard worker and he worked well with him and his daughter. Once the harvest was in, Johan helped Olga preserve the vegetables for the following year.

At this time, Pavel spent some of his free time at the tavern because he wanted to talk to the priest, but he did not want to visit him at the abbey. Instead, he decided to try and meet him by chance at the tavern and on his fifth try, Father Damian came in. He came right over to Pavel and asked, "How is Johan doing?"

Pavel said, "Johan was doing a good job but there was a problem. The two young people were seeing too much of each other and I do not want to be held responsible for any attraction that they had toward each other."

Father Damian smiled and said, "I suspected as much when I sent Johan over to your farm because I felt that Johan may not be suited for the brotherhood. I really trained him too well and at some late date, many years from now, he would most likely turn to the priesthood and find himself in a small parish in a remote village. The Hungarians or Magyars had taken over the church and they were not putting Slovaks in any position of authority. If God saw fit to bring this young couple together, then I would not stand in their way."

Pavel sat there with his mouth open in amazement for he had never heard a priest speak in this manner before. This is, indeed, an extraordinary man, he thought.

He finally spoke, "I would not be against a union between the two and I hope it comes about."

Thus, the futures of this man and this woman were sealed by a priest and a widower in a tavern at a remote little town of Ruzbachy in the shadow of the High Tatra mountains.

When Pavel left the tavern he was bursting with joy. He had to tell someone, but he dared not reveal the plans to anyone, less word would come out and the plan would fail. He would have to watch these two very closely and he had hoped that Eva had educated Olga enough for the union to take place. The next few months, Pavel left the couple alone as much as he could. He noticed that Johan kept looking at Olga when he thought that she was not noticing. It worked the other way around as Olga watched Johan when she felt that he was not watching. He noticed that Olga was dressing better, she spent much more time in combing her hair and he caught her daydreaming and humming to herself. Yes, there definitely was something going on but the young people were doing a great job of controlling their emotions. It was only a matter of time that they would break down and passion would take the place of their self-control. He had hoped that they knew what to do when the moment finally arrived. He had been asking them to feed the horses in the stable and this meant throwing a mound of hay down from the upper loft into the stable next to the horses. Then they would take a fork load to each horse until the mound was gone. Each day, Pavel walked through the stable and the mound of hay would be gone. One day in December, he noticed that the mound was only half gone and there was an impression in the hay. He put his lantern closer and noticed a tiny red mark in the hay. He really had to look hard to see it, but there it was. The chain of events had begun.

He left the hay alone, and said to the horses,

"Some of you will go hungry tonight, but I will take care of you tomorrow night." He went into the house and looked at his daughter and she showed a definite glow; yes, he thought, no doubt about it. He would have to go to church to tell the priest. This will be the first time that he had been inside of a church in over seventeen years, but it was a special occasion. That Sunday morning, when Olga had gone to church with Eva and Pavel, he rode to the abbey and sat through Mass.

Pavel did not see much of Johan after this episode and he thought that he sensed a bit of nervousness on the part of Olga. Things were fairly quiet on the farm and Pavel and his daughter could take care of the animals. He met Johan at the Christmas feast at the abbey, but he did not have a chance to speak with him for very long; it appeared that Johan had tried to avoid him. Toward the middle of January, Johan started to come over once in a

while. He helped out some, but most of the time was spent talking to Olga. Pavel was waiting for an announcement from either of
them, but it was not forth coming. By the first of April, Olga's
Sunday dress was starting to rise in the front and she was beginning to show. There were only two more weeks until Easter when
he would take his final vows. Pavel did not want to bring up the
subject, but the suspense was making him very nervous and if he
did not hear by Palm Sunday, he would bring it up.

On the Wednesday before Palm Sunday, Johan came to the
house and asked to talk to Pavel. They sat at the table. Olga made
a pot of tea, put it on the table and she left the room.

Johan looked haggard, but he cleared his throat and spoke to
Pavel. "I will not be taking my final vows into the brotherhood
and I will leave the abbey with all my belongings. I wish to marry
your daughter." He breathed a sigh of relief.

"Have you told Father Damian?" asked Pavel.

"No, but I will tell him in my own way."

Both he and Olga had discussed what would happen if he
refused but Pavel put both of his palms together and placed his
fingers under his chin as if he were in deep thought and finally, he
reached across the table with his hand. Johan took it and looked
into Pavel's eyes which were moist.

Pavel spoke to him and said, "I would be honored to have you
marry my daughter. Treat her well, my boy and we will get along
fine. She is a fine strong woman and will give me many grandsons
to play with in my old age."

He ran from the house toward the barn, where Olga was waiting. When she saw him running toward her, she knew what the
answer had been, let out a scream and rushed to her intended.
They walked arm in arm to the house where she embraced her
father.

She looked at her father and said, "There is one last thing that
I must tell you. I am with a child. You are going to become a stary
otec (grandfather)."

Now it was Pavel's time to scream. "Tell me the details," he said.

The following evening was quiet except for the sound of the river and the rush of the wind as a gust went by. It was a cool night in April when the door opened in the abbey wall. It creaked slightly when it opened and a lone figure came out pushing a cart. The cart was heavy and he had trouble holding it back on the declining pathway. The path wound its way to the bottom of the knoll and this made his job even more difficult. The figure was small in stature, muscular and was dressed in a heavy brown robe with the hood pulled tightly around his neck. Johan Janek was to take his final vows as a friar at the Mass of Easter. He had been studying for his vocation for eight years and as he made his way down the pathway, he could feel the tears rolling down his cheeks. He had told no one what he planned to do, because he was not sure that he could go through with it himself.

The wind was cold, but he did not feel it except where the tears made his face wet. He had been asking God for guidance for the last five months and since he had gotten no sign, he believed that he was about to do His will. As he got to the middle of the bridge, he paused, asked God's blessing, took off the side panel and listened. He could hear the bell of the abbey calling the brothers to prime prayers as he shut his eyes tightly and dumped the contents of the cart into the rushing river. The river swallowed all of his books, clothes and papers that he had accumulated over his eight years of study at the monastery. He sighed, raised his arms to Heaven as he watched all of his worldly possessions float under the bridge. He felt that God had taken the weight of the world from his shoulders and he raised his eyes to the Heavens to thank Him for showing him the way. He put the side back on the cart and slowly pushed it toward the monastery. As he went up the path, he went over in his mind how he was going to tell Father Damian what he had done.

Once inside the door, he took the cart to the stable and went to Father Damian's study. The door was open and he went in, sat and waited for the priest to come in. He noticed that the sky was getting brighter and after a short wait, the priest appeared at the door. Father Damian was a creature of habit and he always came in after the morning meal. He noticed Johan sitting there with his hands folded and resting in his lap.

He stepped behind his desk, moved some papers from one spot to another and said, "We missed you at morning prayers and the morning meal, Brother Johan. Would you like to tell me where you have been?"

All the way back to the abbey, Johan had thought about how he was going to break the news to Father Damian. He felt that his best approach would be to ask the priest to hear his confession and to tell the truth. He would beg for absolution and a penance. This way, the priest would be told and he would be bound by Cannon Law not to repeat what had transpired in the confessional.

"Father, will you hear my confession?", he asked

"Of course, my son," replied the priest

Father Damian put on his vestments and closed the door.

Johan started the confession by making the sign of the cross.

"Bless me, father, for I have sinned."

The priest sat down, frowned and said, "What is your sin?"

"Father, I have taken all of my worldly possessions, including my books, papers and clothes, and dropped them into the river. I am leaving the brotherhood and I am going out into the world."

The priest said in a calm voice, "Those books and papers were valuable. Some have been copied, by hand, by brothers that have come before us."

"I know, father."

"Then why?" asked the priest".

"I want to leave my past behind me and look only to the future," he replied.

"But your future is with us and you are going to take your final vows at the Easter Mass. Your future has been planned since we found you at the kitchen door when you were only a few weeks old!

You were left there with no mother or father to care for you. We took you in and raised you to be what you are today. We did that with the hope of sending you to the seminary at Bratislava in a year or two and now, you tell me that you are going to give all this up?"

The priest looked up for the first time, "I have failed you, Johan. I have not instilled the zeal of religion in you." A tear formed in the eye of the priest and his eyes became red and watery.

Johan looked at his mentor. "Father, you have not failed me. You have taught me well, for which I am grateful. The Lord has directed me to follow another path."

"And what path is more important than the one that I have chosen for you?" asked the priest.

"For the past year, you have directed me to spend time and labor at the farm of Pavel Valigursky which I have done to the best of my ability. Pan Valigursky has a daughter, Olga, and she and I have worked together for the last twelve months. We have become lovers and Olga is with child."

The priest looked shocked.

"I offer no explanation, father, except that I am twenty-two years old and she is seventeen. We have urges and I did not know how strong these urges were until that day. I did not know that they would be as strong for Olga as they were for me."

"Does Pavel know?", asked the priest.

"Yes, he knows. He has asked me to live with them. I have asked Olga to marry me and Pan Valigursky has given his consent. I am leaving today."

The priest got up from his chair, walked around his desk and stood in front of Johan. He put his hand on the young man's head and said, "I absolve you of your sin before God and man. For your penance, you are to raise this child and all the children that you will have in the Catholic faith. You are to instill in your children all the values that I have instilled in you. You will attend Mass with your family at least once a week and you are to bring Pavel Valigursky back into God's church."

Johan looked at the priest and said, "Thank you, father. Will you marry us as soon as possible?"

"Yes," the priest answered.

The young man stood up and embraced the priest. "Father, I will make you and God proud of me."

Father Damian searched for words, but the only words that came out were, "I know."

*   *   *

Johan moved into the house. He went with his new family to Mass at St. Stefan's on Easter Sunday; Pavel went at Olga's insistence. She told him that he would have to set an example for his grandchild and what better time to start than now. Pavel went to church, but did not receive communion, that could come later because he was going to have to take his reunion with the church one step at a time. The following week, they were married in the abbey by Father Damian. The Mass and the wedding ceremony were simple, Father Damian heard Olga's confession the day before and gave her the same penance that he had given Johan. The brothers were all there for the wedding, Midtj was best man and Lita was matron of honor. Eva cried all during the ceremony, but they were tears of joy. The wedding feast was at the abbey and Brother Theo supervised the preparation of the food. The Mayor, Alexander Kopec, came to the wedding and brought a suit of clothes for Johan that he had made by his friend Volek Benerik. Olga and Johan started their life together and if they could have seen into the future, they would have been amazed.

15

Pavel was proud of his son-in-law and they worked hand in hand with some help from Olga. This was a happy time for this family because with Johan's help, he could now finish pay off the loan from Uncle Pavel. Nothing was ever said, but the debt had been outstanding for too long. He had two colts born last spring, which were filling out quite well and he was waiting for a stallion of his own one day, then he could breed his own horses. Uncle Pavel had his barn full of horses most of the time, and sent people to his nephew who followed the example of his uncle. He taught Johan everything that his uncle taught him and with his mild nature, Johan was a natural at training horses. The animals seemed to sense the love that Johan had for them, making the training easier. With Johan's help, they cleared and planted more acreage and Olga's garden became larger since she planted maize that could be eaten by them instead of the animals. Johan's hard work was contagious; Pavel attempted to keep up with Johan, but it was difficult. It had been a wet spring so the crops had taken hold nicely and one day, Pavel startled Olga when he told her that maybe this was a test by God to see if they could survive and move into the good life.

*   *   *

There were hard times coming over the horizon. They did not affect the small towns on the outposts, but they did affect the Slovaks in the larger cities especially Bratislava. The menace was the Hungarian (Magyars). When the Austrian/Hungary Empire was declared in 1867, Slovakia came under its domain. The Magyars controlled Slovakia and the Austrians had their influence spread over the Czechs. The empire controlled the church, the bishops were being influenced by the powers in the empire and especially hard hit were the Slovaks in Hungary. They were compelled to speak the Magyar language which was being taught in the schools. The Slovak language, customs and traditions were phased out and an attempt was made to uproot the Slovak culture. The Magyar government followed a carefully calculated plan to surpress all Slovak activity in Hungary, which slowly crept into Slovakia and even into the smaller cities. Slovak teachers were replaced by Magyars. Slovak figures of authority, such as notaries, a most important position in the Slovak scheme of things, were replaced by Magyars. Prison terms were given to Slovaks for using their own language. The names of Slovak cities, towns, landmarks, rivers and castles were changed to Magyar names. The Magyar government was determined to absorb all the people in the empire, under its control, into a single nation with one culture.

When the stubborn Slovaks fought the cultural revolution, the Magyars started to ship the children to their schools. They soon found out that this program was doomed to failure because when the pupils returned home, the Slovak culture was returned to them. The people in the towns and villages along the High Tatras ignored the laws and regulations and the Slovak spirit lived and even gained strength. Only the government agencies and public offices were controlled by the Magyars; the Slovaks clung to their culture as they had over the thousands of years before the Magyars came into power. From the Agars who overran the country in the 790's A.D. to the Germans, Mongols, the Romans, Tartars and Turks, they had survived. They had fought the Magyars for over a thousand years and they were still practicing their traditions and cultures. It was just a matter of time before this course would run itself out.

*   *   *

Father Damian was being pressursed from the Magyars through the Jesuits, but he absorbed it himself without passing it on. He

discussed the matter with the priests from St. Stefan's and they
agreed to continue as they had been and even if they were placed
in prison, they would not conform. They felt that even the Magyars
were not stupid enough to put the clergy in prison. They did not
know it, but they were wrong for there were parish priests, abbots
and bishops in prison. The Magyars had bigger problems than to
put their resources into changing little Ruzbachy in the foot hills
of the High Tatras. Johan and his family knew nothing of the problems that were surfacing around them for they were concerned
with their own problems of planting the crops, getting them to
grow, harvesting them and storing them for the winter. The days
were long and the night's sleep was short. Johan became muscular
and tanned; he had callouses on his hands and a smile on his face.
Everyday that he came into the kitchen he patted Olga's stomach,
which was getting larger and larger, and asked how little Johan
was that day. Olga hoped and prayed that the baby would be a
boy. Eva and Lita said it would be a boy because she was carrying
the baby high and that usually meant that she was going to have a
boy. She dismissed this as an old wives' tale, but she hoped anyway. She was not ill at all and did all of her work without com-
plaining. Little Eva came over once in a while to help, but all she
did was sit and talk. Olga suspected that Lita had sent her over
and she obeyed her mother. Besides, Eva liked Olga because she
was the only one that listened to her talk for hours. Little Eva
thought that Olga was interested in what she was saying and understood what she was telling her but Olga thought that little Eva
had never really grown up. Her problems were petty because she
was not confronted with life's real problems and Olga thought
many times that she would not trade places with little Eva. She
could not understand why everyone called her little Eva, for little
Eva was much bigger than big Eva and she could not help but
smile every time she had to say her name.

One August evening Johan announced that a hay field was
ready to be harvested so he and Pavel would go at first light to start
the mowing while Olga was to come to the field to provide water.

This was the first harvest of the year and it started a very long season. They would work seven days a week until the middle of October to get all the crops in. Olga suddenly announced that she was going to help because it would take only five days if Olga helped.

Johan was against it and said, "Your time is too close."

Pavel smiled and said, "I know my daughter; there is no sense arguing. If Olga has made up her mind, there is no changing it. This daughter of mine is a true Slovak. You know how stubborn they can be."

The next morning they set out for the hay field and Johan was still trying to get Olga to stay in the house, but she told him that she had a month to go according to her calculations and she would be fine. They worked side by side all morning. The sun was high in the sky and Johan kept watching Olga, as he marveled as to how smooth her stroke was and how neat the piles of hay were in her row. They stopped for a rest and drank some water in the shade of a large tree. Johan wanted to rest longer, but Olga jumped up, picked up her scythe and motioned to them to follow. The work went smoothly for a few hours when he saw Olga grimace. He ran over to her and, from the look on her face, knew that it was her time.

Johan called to his father-in-law as he laid Olga down on the ground. "Pavel, unhitch the horse and ride into town and get Father Josef, quickly, now! It is time!"

Pavel did as he was told, thinking that he did not want history to repeat itself. Before long, he was pushing the horse as he rode bare back holding onto the mane. Johan lifted up her dress and, with his knife, cut away her underclothes. He raised her knees and opened her legs all the while telling her that everything was going to be fine as he knew what to do.

He asked, "Can you feel the baby coming?"

She said, "I felt the baby drop and it was time."

She grimaced every few minutes and he knew that she was having contractions. From delivering fouls and calves, he knew he had to wait and he prayed that the baby was born head first so he would not have to turn the baby around. He was calm as he talked to Olga and he gave her a stick he found in the field to bite on as he feared that she would bite her lip or tongue.

He must have been there an hour when he noticed the top of the baby's head. "Here it comes," he exclaimed.

"Yes," she said, "I know."

Slowly she opened wider and wider and the baby's head appeared followed by its shoulders. When it got to its hips, it stopped.

"You will have to help, Johan," she said. He looked up at her and she was drenched in sweat.

He gently took hold of each side of the head and tugged. "It's a boy!" he exclaimed. "We have a son and a rather big son at that."

She sighed, smiled and said, as he lifted up his son and showed him to her. "He's beautiful,"

"How do you feel, Olga?" he asked.

She answered, "I feel fine but tired."

He set their son down on the inside of her skirt and went to get water to bathe and clean out the baby's mouth so he could breathe. As he did so the baby started to scream and got blood all over the front of him, the baby was breathing. He looked at his hands and they were all covered with blood. She pointed off into the distance and saw a wagon coming toward them very fast. In no time at all, Father Josef was kneeling beside her in the middle of a hay field. He worked quickly, bound the cord in two places and cut it. He cleaned up the baby and, Olga, as best as he could. Pavel came riding up, all out of breath and saw the doctor finishing his work on Olga. They lifted her into the wagon, hitched the horse back up and started for the house. Once there, Father Josef took charge, and Olga was in her bed, feeding her son while the three men sat in the kitchen talking. Johan was exhausted from the mental strain and Pavel was breathing easier since Olga did not suffer the same fate as his wife.

Father Josef looked at Johan and said, "How did you know what to do?"

1

Johan smiled, "I was looking through the door when Olga was born. I saw what they did and even though I was only six years old, I remembered her being born. I have loved her ever since."

Father Josef looked at Pavel, shook his head and said to him, "God does work in mysterious ways."

He left the Janek house and went back to his patients in town. Pavel left to tell his aunt and uncle the good news. Within a few days, Father Damian arrived to see the new baby. He brought a gift, a bible with a page in front to list the names and dates of births of the Janek family. Already in it were the notations of when Johan and Olga were born and where they were born. The next slot was for the son born three days before. The name had already been chosen and it would be Johan Janek, the same as his father. He was to carry on the family name for future generations. While the priest was visiting, Eva, Pavel and Little Eva came in. Eva had a huge bowl of soup to be heated and brought three loaves of bread. She also had clothes and a basket, the same one her mother had used. Eva took charge. She told Little Eva what to do, shooed the men out of the kitchen and started to clean the mess that the two men had produced. Uncle Pavel had brought over a few bottles of beer and the men celebrated the birth of the first born.

Johan was baptized the following week and Olga rode in the wagon to the abbey holding her son. Her husband followed while her father watched his daughter all the way for any signs of fatigue. Uncle Pavel and Aunt Eva were godparents and the brothers were all present and were given the day off. After the ceremony, each brother lined up and shook Johan's hand. A few of the older ones embraced him and there was happiness in the abbey this day. Brother Theo, although too old for everyday work, even, supervised the food for the baptismal meal. Father Damian did not say much, but his face showed his happiness. He ate with the celebrants and then excused himself to pray.

As he went out the door to the church, Pavel went after him. He stopped him and asked, "Father, will you hear my confession?"

Johan and Pavel worked on the harvest. Little Eva came to

help but she did not help very much. Lita had not shown her how to do many things and had not prepared her very well for family life. She had to be told what to do and when she was finished, she would stand there, waiting to be told what to do next. Olga got stronger and was able to do much more. She harvested food from the garden and between the two women, they preserved quite a bit. After a few weeks, little Eva went home and the household went back to normal.

Johan went down to the town to record the birth of his son. He went to the notary, found a new one there and spoke to him in Slovak. Hoverever, the man told him that he would not respond to any language except the Magyar tongue. Johan did not know the language and the recording became difficult because even though the notary spoke and understood Slovak, he would speak only Magyar. The forms were in Magyar and the familiar ones he had seen before were gone. Johan was trying to reason with the man, but he became very cold and would not discuss any argument except those presented in the other language. Father Igor happened to come in and observed the heated discussion and he volunteered to act as an interpreter even though the notary could speak both languages. Once the form was executed, the priest walked out with Johan and explained what was happening. Johan remembered the lectures that Father Damian had given him all of his life about the Slovaks. Here again was an attempt to dominate the Slovak people and Father Damian had told him not to fight the oppressor, but to agree with him and to do the things that he had always done. He could not understand why the priest was telling him this all the time, but now he understood. He felt like a second class citizen, he had really wanted to confront the official and it was a good thing that Father Igor came in.

The next Sunday, the Janek family went to St. Stefan's for Mass and Pavel went with them. At communion time, he got into line behind Johan and received communion with his family. It was the first time he had taken communion in seventeen years and he felt relieved for he had made his peace with God and he had made peace with himself about his wife's death. He had taken over the care of the grave and went to the abbey as often as he could. He ever talked at the grave site, telling Anna what had transpired. He told her that he would be there to join her and that she should wait for the day that he would be with her. His life had changed with the birth of his grandson. When he came in from the farm, the first thing he did was to check on him and once he assured himself that his grandson had no problems, then he would continue with his life. He made the boy toys and talked to him as if the baby was an adult and he promised to take him hunting and fishing when he was older. Pavel was going to be a good grandfather.

On the first of December, Johan announced that he would have to kill one of the hogs to have meat for the winter. This was done every year at this time and meant a great deal of work for the whole family. Eva and Pavel would be over to help and when their turn came to slaughter a pig, then they would expect help from the Janek family, including Pavel.

Pavel and Johan had been cutting trees down for wood to be used for the winter. The trees cut this year would be allowed to sit and dry out for use next year and the wood that they used this year was cut last fall. They cut the wood with the large cross cut saw, they saved the sawdust. Each day, they would deposit the sawdust on a pile and put a cloth over it so it would not blow away. They did not want the snow to fall on it as the heat from the sawdust would make it wet and later it would freeze. If they did not have enough sawdust, they would drive the wagon over to the saw mill and bring home as much as they needed. Sawdust was used to preserve the ice that was gathered in the winter.

Johan built a little hut about six feet by six feet and eight feet high. It was a four-sided structure where they would cure the pork. The roof was loosely attached and the floor was dirt with a hole scooped out. A wooden tub was placed in an inverted position over the hole. The tub had holes drilled into the bottom and was used only for this function.

Johan waited for a cool day and then cut the hog's throat. The blood was saved and used to make blood sausage. The head was then removed and given to the women to clean and boil. It was boiled for two days until the bones and teeth could be extracted and the meat in the head would be boiled down to little fragments. This would become head cheese. The men brought out a large trough which they placed in the yard under a tree. They had a rope with a pulley on the end of the rope and the pig was pulled up until it was off the ground. The trough was placed under the animal and the pig was lowered into it. They hand rubbed resin, which they obtained from the pine trees, all over the pig. The men and women poured hot water over the hog. The water was heated over an outdoor fire in a large cast iron tub. Sharp sticks were used by the men to scrape the skin until all the hair was removed and the skin was clean.

They pulled the pig up with the rope and washed it down and when it was clean, Johan took a knife and slit the animal from the throat to the very end. The women caught the insides of the pig and took them aside to clean them and the organs were preserved to be cooked later. The men started to cut up the pig. The feet would be pickled in large pots, the ham and bacon sides were put aside along with the ribs to be smoked. All the roasts were cut and placed aside, while the tenderloin was deboned and brought inside to be roasted for the evening meal. After all, as the helpers had to be fed.

The women cleaned the intestines and ground up all the excess meat and fat. That was stuffed into the small intestines and made into rings that were tied at both ends. This would become kielbasa. The large intestine was cleaned and put into an earthen pot, to be stuffed with potatoes, cheese and spices to bake into kishka. A sauce was poured over the kishka just before it was served. It took two days to process a pig of this size and once the work was completed, the utensils were cleaned and stored for another day. Now it was time to get the smoke house going.

Johan built a fire in the pit inside the smoke house. He had hung all the hams, bacon, shoulders and kielbasa and once the fire was going, he poured sawdust over the fire so it would burn very slowly. He put the tub with the holes over the pit and, once he was assured that the fire would keep smoking, he secured the door to keep out the animals. He would go into the smokehouse each day to add some sawdust to the fire and he would continue to do this until all the meat was eaten. It was a hectic two days but everyone sat down to a good meal of fresh pork. If one Slovak offered another money, the helper would be insulted and would never offer to help his friend or relative again. One did not ask for help, as the person who helped was expected to know that help was needed and he offered his services. His reward was a good meal and the satisfaction of knowing he had helped someone.

Christmas came and went and the problems between the Slovaks and the Magyars deepened. Father Damian, who now had a small school for ten students, was told not to teach his lessons in Slovak any longer. He flatly refused. The teacher in town with twenty-five pupils followed his example and also refused. Relations between the notary and the teacher became strained and when someone threw a stone through the window of the notary's home, he backed down. After all, he was only one Magyar in a sea of Slovaks. Everyone seemed to know that unless something drastic happened, they might not be able to hold out in the future and they might be speaking Magyar, but they would never abandon their language, traditions or culture. The priests were telling the people of Ruzbachy to speak their old language, not to abandon the old traditions and to hold out as long as possible. They offered to teach the children Slovak in their homes if necessary and when the notary saw what he was up against, he backed down awaiting new instructions.

Matters calmed down and life went back to normal. No one wanted to go out into the cold winter wind; it was bitter cold and much more snow than usual had fallen. Pavel and Johan made a few trips to the tavern, but the Janek family stayed warm and well fed on their farm. Little Johan was growing and would be a big man. It seemed to Pavel that with each generation, the men and women got bigger and bigger. Pavel was now happy with his life and family and he doted on his grandson who knew his grandfather very well. Pavel told Johan one day that he had hoped that he would not spoil the boy too much but Johan told him that was what grandfathers were for.

Two years after Johan was born, Olga announced that she was again with child. Both Johan and Pavel were overjoyed and Pavel could hardly believe it. He would have another grandchild to play with on cold winter days. Little Eva, meanwhile had married and had a miscarriage. Father Josef had tried to save the baby, but it was too early in the term. Olga said that she should try again as soon as possible, but Eva said that she would wait. She and her husband Lech were having a strained marriage and Johan said that if she did a little work to help her grandmother out, then she would feel better. In June, Olga began to show her pregnancy, but she was not going to have this baby at harvest time.

In the spring of the year after young Johan was born, his father went into the field and on the spot where his son was born, he planted an oak tree. He wanted his son to know where he was born on the land and the tree was growing just as Johan was growing. At two years of age, young Johan was into everything and Eva said that he was just like his mother. Johan Jr. was given the freedom to wander around the farm just like his father was when he was that age and being so active, he ate everything in sight. At meals when Olga did not make enough, she would give little Johan more food and leave less for herself. When everyone would be out of the kitchen, she would take a piece of bread, spread lard over it and eat it. This made her full, but it also made her gain weight. Once, when she saw Father Josef, he told her not to eat so much as the baby would be heavy and difficult to deliver; she made more food for the evening meal. She remembered when she delivered Johan in the hay field in the bright afternoon sun and she did not want to go through that again.

The baby was born in January, another little boy and he was

named after his grandfather. Pavel was a perfect baby, he slept through the night and smiled all day as long as he was well fed and dry. When he did scream, Johan could hear him in the barn and Pavel said that his newest grandson would be a singer with the set of lungs that he had.

In March of that year, Uncle Pavel died. They found him in the barn and when he did not come in for the evening meal, Eva went out to look for him. She found him sitting up against a stall and he had been dead for a few hours. She sent Lech to fetch Father Josef who said that he had died of a heart attack. His face was all blue and he had died without suffering. Father Damian held the funeral in the abbey. He was buried next to Anna, and Pavel said that he would now take care of both graves. After the funeral, Eva took Pavel aside and told him that now that his uncle had died, she would need the rest of the two hundred crowns that he still owed them. Pavel told her that he would sell two of his best horses and give the money to her. Two months later he handed her the money. He did not tell her that he borrowed it from Johan who had gotten it from Father Damian. Lita and Midtj moved into the main house and Midtj became its master, while Eva and Lech lived in the other house. Without Pavel, Eva became frail as if she had given up on life, Olga brought her sons over to visit more often to cheer her up somewhat; if only Eva would have a child, it would give her something to do. She would just sit in her rocking chair and rock back and forth looking into space as if she was waiting to join her husband.

*   *   *

Johan had not heard anything further from the Magyar in town, but the rest of the town had heard that the notary still wanted to drop the Slovak language in the schools and substitute the Magyar language. The sermons in church spoke against it and told the people to hold their ground. The people of Slovak decendants living in Hungary were being persecuted and even some of their children were scheduled to be taken away to the Magyar boarding schools. Again the notaries backed off. A few months later, the notary wanted to rename some of the streets because he said that the names of the streets had no meaning to the Magyars and therefore they had to be changed. He even went so far as to change the name of a few of the larger streets. The next morning, the signs were gone and someone had seen them floating down the Poprad River. The streets remained unnamed, but everyone knew what they were.

At harvest time when both Lita and Midtj were out in the fields working, they came home to find Eva dead in her rocking chair. Midtj cried more than Lita did because it was the passing of an era. Olga was stunned. It was like losing her mother and she mourned her until Christmas. They buried Eva beside her husband and Pavel now had three graves to care for.

The Janek family could be seen in church every Sunday and there were fewer and fewer middle-aged people at Mass. Johan started to notice that people, whom he had known for years, were suddenly gone. He asked Father Damian where they were going.

The priest replied, "To America, England, Canada and South America or any land where they can practice their old traditions."

"Why do they leave their homeland, the place where their people have lived for thousands of years?" asked Johan.

"They go for freedom," answered the priest. "They have been oppressed for thousands of years and they want freedom."

The priest could not explain it any further because he was also being pushed by the Jesuits to comply. The outposts of the empire did not see the extent to which the Magyars went. They had pushed back every attempt and would continue to do so, but the day would come when the Magyar could no longer be pushed back. He had been pushing the Serbs and Croats, who are Slavic brothers. Once they had been put in line, then the Magyar would devote his full attention to Slovakia. The Slovaks had no military training to fight the Magyar, they could only hope to delay the takeover of the culture of Slovakia and hope that something would happen to help their cause. That was the reason that the country-men of Johan were fleeing the country. Johan had said openly that it would be unwise to bring any more children into the chaos, but three years after Pavel was born, Olga announced that she was pregnant again. She went to see Eva (she was now called Eva instead of Little Eva) with her two sons. Johan could drive the horse at the age of five, but Pavel could not understand why he could not, at the age of two. Eva told Olga that she was also pregnant and she was four months into her term. Father Josef had warned her about doing any labor. She had lost some weight and looked radiant, but Lita told her to be careful and, if necessary, she would come and stay with her for the final two months of her term. Eva said that Lita had volunteered and was coming to see her every day and the next five months went by very slowly. Eva delivered a little girl who weighed twelve pounds. The baby girl was given the name of Anna, Pavel was delighted, especially since he would be the godfather and Olga would be the godmother. Johan congratulated his in-laws and said that they made a very good choice. Two months later, Olga delivered another boy who was given the name of Karol. Johan wanted to name him after the most intelligent man he knew and he chose the first teacher that he had ever had. Johan pulled at his suspenders and told everyone who would listen that the Janeks were becoming quite a family. He was proud of his sons and he wanted young Johan to go to school in the abbey because there was a better chance of that school not being changed from the Slovak language to the Magyar language. Even if they were forced to do it at the abbey, Father Damian would see to it that his sons would always be taught in Slovak. Little Johan went to the school at the abbey, when he was five and one-half.

Olga still had two young boys at home during the day and Pavel was a handful. Her father, who was getting older, was not able to work as hard as he once had so he would watch the boys while Olga worked alongside her husband. When harvest time came, Johan had to hire one of the men from town to help; this was the only way that they got through the season. Johan had hoped that Olga would not get pregnant for a while, but they knew nothing of birth control and three years after Karol was born she announced that she was with child again. Johan wanted a little girl to help Olga, but, again, she carried the baby high and another little boy was born while Pavel jumped with glee, with four little men. Olga looked as if she could have a dozen. She was healthy and the birth of this boy was much easier than the other three. This one was named Josef after the priest who delivered him and they were running out of godparents, but they managed to find some for Josef. Johan and Olga were to have one more son, Stefan, who was named after the church and a girl, Marta.

When Marta was born Olga said, "Now that I have a girl to help me, that is enough children."

Johan Jr. was seventeen years old when Marta was born. He was out of school and was helping his father. Pavel was fourteen and would be in school one more year while Karol was eleven. He stayed home from school to help only at harvest time. Josef was eight years old and he helped with the animals. Stefan was four years old and was going to start school the following year. When they went to church, they would take up a whole row and Father Andrej would smile every time he saw them come in a single file, with the oldest being first and the youngest being last.

Father Andrej looked at the pride in Johan's face and he often said, "The Magyars are trying to change this and it would be a sin."

As Johan was working in the garden on a bright clear day, he looked up to see a friar riding toward him. His robes were flying behind him and he left the garden to meet the man. It was a young friar that he had never seen.

"Please come quickly. Father Damian needs you!", he gasped.

"I will get my horse and will be only a minute," he replied.

He ran into the barn and threw himself on his fastest animal. He stopped at the kitchen and told Olga where he was going and he told her to gather the children and meet him at the abbey. As he got there, he was met by Brother Karol.

"Go to Father Damian's room as quickly as you can," Brother Karol shouted. He leaped from his horse and ran to the priest's room. He found him in bed with Father Josef at his side.

The priest looked up and said, "May we be alone for a moment? I have something to tell Johan." Father Josef nodded, left the room and shut the door.

Father Damian coughed and said, "Please sit, Johan, there is something that I must tell you. Something that I should have told you years ago. I would appreciate it if you did not interrupt me as there is so little time. I arranged to have you dropped off at the abbey right after you were born. You see, Johan, I am your father. It was I all along who was your real father and I have taken care of you all these years. I would let no harm come to you and I made sure that you would grow up to be strong in body and spirit. I knew that you were never destined to become a friar or a priest. I was happy that you left the abbey, but I was not happy when you destroyed all those good books. I am ready to meet my God. The bishop heard my confession and I was given absolution so I can leave this earth with a clear conscience. The only thing that I had left undone was to make my peace with you. Whether you choose to tell anyone, will be your decision, but it will not affect me after I am gone. I am seventy-seven years old and I have had a good life. I look at you and I am fulfilled." He coughed again and laid back on his pillow and sighed.

Johan spoke, "Am I allowed to know who my mother is?"

"Yes, your mother was the woman behind the bar at the tavern. She used me as a trophy and when she realized that she was pregnant, she came to me for help. I arranged to have her go to a convent in Poland and I had her drop you off at the abbey so that I could take care of you. She died about twelve years ago. My mother's maiden name was Janek."

Johan looked at his father, so frail, waiting to die. He thought back; the time they went to Bratislava and he he looked frail then. He knew that Father Damian was his father.

Johan said, "I knew who you were for some time, but I never

realized it until I saw a painting of you, right after you were ordained. We have the same nose, the same eyes and the same chin.
Look, even my hair line is receding like yours. I knew that you
grew the beard to disguise yourself. I have waited for you to acknowledge me and you will never know how many times I wanted
to tell you in the confessional, but I held back. My children are
here and I will bring them in shortly. When they come in, pay
attention to the youngest boy, Stefan, and you will be able to see
yourself at his age."

Johan went to the door and opened it and Father Josef was
there with Olga and the children. As they filed in, the eldest first,
each went to the priest and said, "Bless you." Young Johan said it
first and the younger ones did not know what to say so they did
what Johan did. The last was Olga who did the same thing.

Father Damian looked around him and said, "It is good for a
dying man to have his family with him when he passes on."

He closed his eyes and laid there quietly while the Janek family stood around him. Father Josef went to him and put his fingers
under his chin and a tear rolled down his cheek.

"He is gone," whispered the priest.

After the funeral, Johan rode home with his family. He was
depressed over the death of his most powerful ally and although
he never looked at the priest as a father, he thought back to the
many times that he had been there when he had needed help. He
remembered the brothers' uproar when he was punished for running away and he thought about kneeling on a piece of wood
while saying the rosary. It must have hurt him to make his son
endure the punishment. He knew that it had hurt him when he
used that punishment on his sons, but it only took a few times in
saying the rosary, in this manner, to cure bad habits. Olga had
become angry when she first saw it, but later relented when she
saw how effective it was in instilling discipline in the boys. He had
not used it with Stefan, as yet, but he could see the day coming for
this young man was a Slovak. He could see quite a bit of his father

in the child and he was the youngest male, but he would be an asset to the family.

Olga had asked Johan, "Where did you get the idea for this type of discipline?"

He told her, "It was the manner in which I was punished in the abbey as I was growing up."

She never mentioned it again. When they returned home, clothes were changed and they went back to work for there was much to be done to feed nine mouths. Olga was doing well in preparing the meals, but she had to have the food to make the meals. The smoke house was almost empty, along with the cupboard and the root cellar. Food at this time of the year was very expensive, but he had paid Father Damian back for the loan of two hundred crowns and they had saved some for a rainy day, although he did not want to use it. He had a stallion and he would have to raise some money by putting the horse out for stud.

One problem that arose with the death of Father Damian was that of educating his children. No one from the church had come to the funeral except the local clergy and the brothers, of course. No one wanted to align himself with the controversial priest from the Abbey of St. Francis. The Magyars must have been watching closely, the notary was at the funeral and he would, no doubt, report his findings to his superiors. He did not know who the Magyar-dominated church would send to take his place. It still was too early to tell, but Johan felt that whomever the church sent would be a problem because he did not want his children taught in the Magyar tongue, but rather in the Slovak one. There was no compromise on this issue. They had been successful in delaying the transition, but the town of Ruzbachy was at a crossroads. He took some time on the following Sunday to talk to the three priests at St. Stefan and they all were concerned by the same thing, but they could not venture an opinion. He spoke to the school teacher who now had two assistants. One taught arithmetic and the other science and agriculture. The teacher reserved the subjects of history and languages for himself and he showed that he would hold out as long as possible. Next, Johan spoke to Brother Voltek who taught at the abbey. He was less optimistic. If the replacement was a strong-willed Magyar, then he would have to follow the vow of obedience and conform to his superior's wishes. The teacher at the abbey was worried and he promised to send word to Johan as soon as he heard anything.

It was not until harvest time in September that a new Abbott was appointed and everyone breathed a sigh of relief when they heard that he was a Slovak. He had addressed the brothers and told them that he had come with instructions to replace the language of Ruzbachy from Slovak to Magyar. His name was Feliks Bross and he was in his late forties so he had been ordained prior to the establishment of the empire. The new Abbott told his brothers that the change would be long and drawn out and he would not make any changes for the time being. Privately, he told Brother Voltec that the Magyars had trouble with the Croats and Serbs in the south and as long as they did not give the Magyars any cause to notice them, they would not bother them. When Johan spoke to Brother Voltec, he thought to himself that this was the typical Slovak attitude; you wear down your opponent with kindness and agreement, but you do what you want to do anyway. This is how the Slovaks survived for thousands of years. Something always happened to change the status quo and then they would capitalize on it to their own advantage. Johan wished that Slovakia could be an autonomous state, and they could govern themselves, but he doubted that this would happen in his lifetime or even in his children's lifetime. It was good for the Slovaks that their brothers, the Croats and the Serbs living in Hungary, were occupying the resources of the Magyars so the outlying outposts of Slovakia could live in virtual peace. He felt better after talking to Brother Voltek and he related his conversation to Olga who suggested that he visit the Abbott as soon as he could.

* * *

It had started to snow early that year, but the harvest was in and the family had an opportunity to rest. Johan took his father-in-law and his eldest son to the tavern for a beer and young Johan found some friends very quickly. Pavel wanted to keep a tight rein on the boy, but Johan said that the boy needed people his own age and let him sit with his new friends. When they returned home, young Johan had many stories to tell his family that his new friends related to him. He disagreed with some of their opinions and had apparently told them so. The discussions became a bit heated, but young Johan enjoyed the give and take. He said that a good Slovak had an opinion about everything and he allowed Johan to go to the tavern alone to meet his friends to discuss current events. Johan learned a great deal from his son as to what was happening in other areas of the empire. The young men in the tavern were becoming fired up with Slovak nationalism. They wanted to be an autonomous state so that they could govern themselves, but since their up bringing did not include any direct action against the oppressor, it was only talk. Young Johan suspected that this group was responsible for throwing the street signs into the river and a rock through the notary's window. When Johan told his father of his suspicions, Johan told him not to become aligned with this group in the event that they did do something foolish and to his surprise, young Johan agreed. Maybe he did not want to say the rosary while kneeling on a split piece of wood.

Young Johan spoke about the Slavs in the southern provinces of the empire wanting to join neighboring Serbia, but this was causing friction in that area with the empire's Germans and Magyars. Germany had aligned itself with the empire against Russia which brought Italy into the triple alliance. Russia created an alliance with France and everyone knew where Great Britain stood with its most powerful navy. Russia pledged itself to help Serbia in case of war and the people of Slovakia felt more of a kinship with the Slavs of Poland and Russia rather than to the Germans and Austrians. The whole region was becoming unsettled and the people of Slovakia were torn between their kinship with the Slavic people of the region and the German people in the Empire.

No one knew where America stood in all of this because they maintained a shaky neutrality. If dragged in, they would probably be with France, Great Britain and Russia. Russia, with its great number of people, was still backward and no one knew how much it could influence the empire without France and Great Britain. Deep in the outpost town of Ruzbachy, no one really paid attention to the events outside of the immediate sphere of everyday life, for the object was to survive; let the politicians handle the world problems. There were many discussions around the table at the Janek household. The problems were not solving themselves and they were getting worse. Young Johan had thought about leaving Ruzbachy and going to America but he had put off discussing this with his father for some time.

One Sunday afternoon while they were sitting alone in the backyard enjoying a glass of beer, young Johan brought up the subject. After the second beer, he said, "Father, there is something that I want to tell you. I have been thinking about leaving for the last few years. I am twenty-two years old, I have no prospects of getting married, this part of the world is in turmoil and I might be dragged into a war for which I have no sympathy. One of my friends has an uncle in the state of New York and my friend has been over there for the last year. He had written to my circle of friends that there were jobs in the woolen mills and I could stay with my friend until I got settled. I do not want to work the farm for the rest of my life and I do not see any future in Ruzbachy."

His father let the revelation sink in and asked, "Have you discussed this with your mother?"

Johan said, "I did and she approved. Mother wants me to be happy but the big problem I have is that I do not have enough money for passage or money to live on until I find work. I have about fifty crowns saved and I would need another two hundred crowns more but I would make every effort to pay it back."

Johan said, "If this is what you want, I will loan you the money and I agree with your mother. I would do anything for you so long as you were happy."

Young Johan added, "I have thought about this decision thoroughly and I will stay until after the harvest. Grandfather could not help any longer and by next year, you will have Pavel and Karol to help."

It was agreed upon therefore that Johan was going to America. The harvest was a good one that year and they were planting more land since they had more animals to feed. They were selling more, training more and boarding more horses since his father-in-law's uncle had died. There also was more work to do so Pavel took care of Marta and Stefan while Olga went out to work with the men.

Finally, the time came for Johan to leave. He had purchased a steam boat ticket from Bremerhaven, Germany. He took the train to Bratislava, a boat up the Danube and onto Bremen. The whole trip would take fourteen days. His ocean liner would dock in a place called Boston and he would take a train to Albany, where his friend would meet him. Johan was excited to begin a new adventure, but sad about leaving the only world he ever knew. He had countless second thoughts, but he knew that he had to go.

Two days before he was due to leave from Polodencz, he disappeared in the afternoon. He was not in the house, the barn or the stable and Johan finally realized where his son had gone. He saddled his horse and rode out to the hay field where Johan was born and there seated against the oak tree in the middle of the field was Johan with tears running down his cheeks.

He looked up at his father and said, "I am like this oak tree. It is very difficult to pull up my roots and leave."

Johan got off his horse, sat next to his son and said, "If there is one thing I want you to remember, son, is that you are a part of this family. We are a Slovak family and we do not take our obligations lightly. You will always be a member of our family no matter where you are, we will help you if you get into trouble. You are indeed like this oak tree. Your roots go deep into the Slovak traditions, so do not ever forget them. Use the language and teach it to your children; the core of the Slovak tradition is the family. When family values die, then tradition disappears. You are a Slovak and you have the blood of your grandfather running through your body! Keep that close to your heart. Do the things that you were taught and you will be fine. I raised you, my son, and I have confidence in you. God Bless you."

They rose and embraced each other, but they spoke no more as they rode back to the house. Two days later, he said goodbye to his mother, brothers and sister. That was the last time Johan would see his first born son.

It was two months later that they received a letter from Johan.

"Dear mother and father. I am living with my friend in a place called Cohoes, New York. There were many factories. I have found work in the woolen mills and I hope to rent a room of my own very soon. There is talk of war in Europe. Please take care of yourselves."

Olga could see his face when he left and started to cry.

Johan put his arm around her and said, "In a year, he would run the factory."

She wiped away the tears, managed a smile and continued to read the letter, "There is more food in America than you could eat. You could buy meat, bread and potatoes on every corner and the factory paid enough for you to buy them. I even managed to save a little, but I am eating so much that I will get fat and need a special bed to sleep in."

Olga knew that Johan had tried to sound happy in the letter, but she detected some homesickness. Once Johan had read the letter, she took it and read it to herself a few times. She put it next to her heart and went up stairs to put it in a special place. She would read it over and over again until it became frayed and the folds began to rip apart.

That summer, grandfather Pavel died. He had been riding his

horse when his heart stopped. He fell from the horse and struck his head on a rock. The horse came in riderless and Johan, Pavel and Karol went to look for him. Pavel found him about fifty feet from the oak tree, in the middle of the hay field. He went to get his father and brother and they took him home for the last time.

Johan had gone to meet Abbott Feliks some time ago and had a long talk with him as most of the brothers had mentioned Johan to the new Abbott. He was waiting to meet him. Nothing had really changed in the abbey. Brother Jan was taking care of the cemetery now and the graves of his loved ones looked very well kept. The funeral was held in the abbey and Pavel was buried next to his Anna. Father Damian had two names on his head stone. One was his, one was Johan's and all that was needed was the date. Johan thought that even from the grave, Father Damian touched them. Johan sent a letter to his son telling him that his grandfather died and was at peace.

At first Johan wrote quite often, but the letters grew further and further apart. Olga looked for a letter every day, but Johan told her that he probably found a girl friend and she was using up all of his time. Olga said that she hoped so, it was about time that they had a grandchild. Two weeks later a letter came from Johan and as was the custom, the whole family gathered around Johan as he read the letter out loud. "I am sorry that I had not written sooner, but I am quite busy. I have found a two-bedroom apartment that I can afford and my friend and I rented it. It was a half of a large house and there are people living on the other side. We do not have much furniture but we will make do. I have met a wonderful girl."

"See, I told you so," Johan said to Olga.

She blushed and he then went on reading to his family. "The girl's name is Hanna Baranowski and her people had come from the city of Presov. There was a large Slovak community living close to each other in Cohoes. She came up to me and asked if I knew Father Andrej Baranowski, pastor of the church of St. Stefan in Ruzbachy. He was her great-uncle, her grandfather and Father

Baranowski were brothers. She helped me find our apartment and
her father had given me a bed and table. I use a crate to sit on and
I will have to get another crate so I can have Hanna come over and
cook some "galumki" for me."

Olga looked at Johan and said, "So now she is coming over to
cook galumki for him? Is that proper?"

Johan looked at her and rolled his eyes. "Olga, they are in
America now. They do things like that."

He finished the letter and handed it to his wife. She took it
and read it carefully and he was looking at her waiting for a reaction. As she got down to the bottom, she saw how he signed it.

"Johan, have you seen how he signed it? He says your loving
son, John Janek. His name is Johan."

Johan shrugged his shoulders and said, "Olga he is an American now. This is how they spell Johan in America."

She wrinkled up her nose and muttered, "I do not like it. His
name is Johan. Look on his birth papers."

The family found that there was more food to go around with
two fewer mouths to feed. Pavel was now taking his brothers to
school at the abbey. Next year he would be finished and it would
be Karol's turn to take his brothers to school. Marta still had a year
to wait before she started to school, but by custom, girls did not
go to school as late as the boys; girls were finished two years before
the boys. The girls furthered their education at home by learning
to cook, sew and keep the home together. Olga had been an exception. Since there were no boys in the family when she was growing
up, she might be expected to run the farm. Marta was already
picking up after her brothers and being the youngest, they teased
her when their parents were not around. The boys all worked on
the farm and it was making some money to put aside. Johan was a
good money manager as he was still getting a discount at the grist
mill owned by the church and sometimes the brothers "forgot" to
take the one fifth of the flour for milling it.

Life was getting better except that they kept hearing that conditions were getting worse in the cities. Russia went to war with

Japan and was beaten and there were revolutionaries in Russia that wanted to take control of the government from the czar to create a new system of government. The Magyars were watching this very closely and were waiting to pounce on any small protectorate that Russia left unguarded. This took some of the pressure off the people on the outer edges of the Austria-Hungary Empire. The notary in town, feeling that he would not be able to obtain support from the empire if he tried to enforce the decrees, had little physical contact with the people. He sat and waited thinking that his day would come; it never did. He was one lone Magyar in a mass of Slovaks and he did not want to come to physical harm.

Since Johan was getting established in America, Pavel felt that it was his turn to go. He had written a letter to Johan expressing his desire to go to America. He received a letter back from Johan that he was able to keep away from his mother, saying that Johan would be happy to have his brother join him in America. He had better get permission from their mother and father as they might not want the entire family to move to America one by one. Pavel approached his mother first and she started crying at once, however, she agreed and Pavel went to his father. Johan had paid back the fare and he agreed to loan that money to Pavel so he waited until the harvest was in and made his arrangements to travel to America. He had sent him instructions and things to look out for in the journey since there were many people in America who could take your money, giving nothing in return. Johan was going to meet Pavel when he got off the boat in Boston because he would have a difficult time finding the right route from Boston to Albany and he did not want Pavel to get lost. This departure was less painful for the Janek family because they knew that there was someone on the other side of the ocean to meet him. Pavel left on November first of that year and he would be traveling on All Saints Day so Olga felt better. But the goodbyes was still tearful. They were losing another son.

The family received a letter from Johan a month later, "Pavel had arrived and was living with me. Hana and I met Pavel when he got off the boat but it had taken two days to process him and another day to drive the wagon to Albany. I have good news for the whole family. Hana and I are getting married. Pavel will be best man and her father is going to provide the wedding reception with much food. Life in America is good, and I am happy that Pavel came. I am promised by my father-in-law to be that he would have a photograph taken of the wedding and I will send it to you. Hana's father is a foreman in the woolen mill. He has gotten Pavel his job and it seems as if there are only Slovaks working in this mill."

At the bottom of the letter were some words not in Johan's hand writing. The words said, "I love you all," Pavel.

Olga looked at Johan's signature and said, "Again, he signed it John."

At the evening meal, Johan told Olga that her wish to become a grandmother might be coming true and she just smiled.

Pavel paid off the loan quicker than Johan had and he added a little extra. It seemed that each time they received a letter from Pavel, there was some money in it with instructions to buy something for the children. Olga looked at Johan and told him that her sons missed their brothers and sister and he had to agree with her.

One Sunday while they were leaving church, Father Andrej stopped them and asked, "How are the boys getting along in America?"

Johan asked Father Andrej, "Do you have any relatives in America?"

Father Andre smiled and asked Johan, "Do you have time for a little story? Johan nodded.

Father Andrej started his story, "Father Damian built St. Stefan's church almost single handed, but he was short of money and I wrote to my brother in Cohoes, New York. He organized the parishes and with the help of the Bishop of Albany, they raised the money. My brother, Michel, came over here to deliver the money personally and then went to Bratislava with Father Damian to attend the installation of the new bishop and to obtain authorization to build the church. I went to Polodencz to pick them up and on the way back we were accosted by two robbers who were after my brother's money. Quick as a wink, Michel took a revolver that he had hidden under his coat and shot one robber in the shoulder and the other in the leg. We had to take them to the police for medical attention and although Father Damian looked calm on the outside, he was angry on the inside because of the use of force."

Johan said, "So that is how this church came to be built. Your brother Michel supplied the money from America."

Father Andrej spoke, "Why do you think that I am pastor of this church? Father Damian arranged it or otherwise, I would be just another brother in the Abbey of St. Francis."

Johan asked, "Do you have a nephew in America who has a daughter named Hanna?"

The priest answered, "Yes, he has three daughters and the oldest is named Hanna."

Johan smiled and said, "Then you and I will be related. My son Johan is going to marry Hanna."

The priest was overjoyed, "I knew that she was getting married to a man who came from Slovakia, but I did not know that it was Johan. I will write to my brother and tell him that Hana has made an excellent choice."

The Janeks now had one son working on the farm. Stefan was helping with the minor chores and it looked as if this arrangement was to continue for a while. When he left school, Karol went south to Roznava. He went to work in the coal mines, about sixty miles away so he came home only on weekends. Karol was becoming muscular and hard from working in the mines. The pay was good, but the work was hard. He rented a small room from a couple with no children because the room was going to waste and the rent was cheap. The older couple would feed Karol twice a day and they were happy with the arrangement. Karol ate well and he had a place to sleep, so he was content. At the end of each month, he had a few crowns to give to his mother so she might save it for him. He had written a letter to Johan to ask if there were any coal mines in America. His brother wrote back to tell him that coal mining had a Slovak community in Barnesboro, a short distance from Altoona, Pennsylvania where there were many mines. Hana's grandfather knew of a man from Presov, now living in Barnesboro. Perhaps he could help Karol. He had given Karol the man's name and address so he could write to him. When Karol had amassed his fortune of three hundred crowns, he wrote to the man to explore the possibility of moving to Barnesboro. The man wrote back and said that there were jobs in the mines, but it was hard and dangerous work. The pay was good, as no one but Slovaks would work in the mines. Karol decided to follow his brothers and settle in Cohoes until he could decide what he wanted to do. That Saturday Karol drew his last pay, took his belongings to his parents home and announced that he was going to America. As soon as he had made his travel arrangements, Karol left and his parents were now resigned to the fact that all their children would leave. They had hoped that Stefan and Marta would stay to run the farm because Josef had gotten the wander lust some time ago and he was waiting for his schooling to finish. He was counting the weeks until he would leave.

One day a man from the post came with a package containing some canned goods, some shirts for the men, some sweet smelling soap and an envelope. Olga hurried to open this while the rest of the family looked at the goods and Olga started sobbing when she looked at the photographs of Johan's wedding. There were her two boys dressed in black suits and black ties, their shirts were white and each had a white flower in his lapel. The woman was dressed in a white gown with lace over her head while another woman stood next to Hana. She had a dark dress in the same style as Hana's and they all were smiling at the man taking the photograph.

Olga, still sobbing, said, "How handsome they look. Those suits must have cost a fortune. Hana is so beautiful and the woman standing next to her is beautiful. Johan, we have a new daughter-in-law."

Johan took the picture and studied it carefully noting every detail. When he finally spoke, his voice showed as if he was on the verge of tears. "I have to make a frame for this so we can display it on the wall."

Johan read the letter out loud; "There were one hundred people at the wedding and it was held in the Slovak community hall. We had a band that played polkas and obereks for two days and on Sunday night, everyone went home tired. No one went home hungry for there was much food. There was beef, chicken, lamb, glaumbi, keilbasa, pierogi, pies made with potatoes, cheese and kapusta and all kinds of pastries. There were breads made with nuts, prunes, cheese and potatoes. Hana's father paid for all of the food, the wine and the beer. I will remember this day for the rest of my life and I only wish that you were all here to share it with us. Pavel met a young lady and they danced together for the entire wedding. She seemed to like Pavel and he definitely liked her, maybe something will come of it."

Olga looked at Josef as he was studying the picture and she knew that it would not be long before he too would go off to America.

It was now 1910 and the melting pot of eastern Europe was boiling. Germany was building up its armed forces and it wanted to challenge Great Britain on the high seas. The British were building bigger ships with bigger guns while the Germans were trying to keep up. As the larger nations were making alliances with each other, the smaller nations were drawn into these pacts. Europe became divided into two armed camps. Austria was annexing land to the extent that Russia, to help stem the expansion of Austria into the Balkans, pledged to help her "Little Sister" Serbia in the event of war with Austria-Hungary. A crisis developed when Austria-Hungary annexed the provinces of Bosnia and Hercegovina. Russia backed Serbia while Germany supported Austria-Hungary, but armed conflict was avoided and the Serbs, who had many of their people living in these provinces, became outraged with the empire.

*   *   *

It was in the shadow of these events that Josef left for America and
Johan and Olga agreed to allow Marta to accompany her brother.
The plan was to have Marta stay with Johan and Hana. She would
not have to go to school any longer for she was fourteen years old
and would have been out of school if she had stayed in Ruzbachy,
anyway. They did not know that things were different in America.
Her parents wanted her out of Slovakia should war begin. This left
only Stefan to help his mother and father so they would have to
hire some help during the planting and harvest seasons. For the
rest of the year, they would be able to handle the farm. Of all her
children, Olga missed Marta, the most because of her personality.
Marta bubbled all the time, when she was talking, doing her chores
or helping Olga cook. She was small for her age, but what she
lacked in size, she made up in personality. Marta was excellent
company for her mother, joking with her, teasing her brothers or
sitting on her father's lap.

Once she asked her father, "Do you think that I am too old to
sit on your lap?"

He answered, "You will never be too old to sit on my lap."

He smiled and patted his knee and when she sat down, she
gave him a great big hug. Olga remarked on more than one occasion that the home had gotten too quiet and someone had to make
some noise. With all the work to do on the farm, Johan and his son
were out of the house a great deal of the time. When they did
come in from the barn, they were too tired to be much company.
They ate their meal, sat down to relax while Olga cleaned the
kitchen and, when Olga came out of the kitchen, the men were
discussing the work to be done the following day. They went to
bed early, beginning the next day before dawn. The farm had grown
from the early days, the herd of horses had grown and the barns
were full of horses being boarded. There were now fifteen cows to

be milked every day, and the other stock had to be fed. The buildings on the farm were in need of repair and one morning a week had to be devoted to maintenance of the farm. Even if Stefan wanted to leave, he could not since he was the youngest and he had an obligation to stay and help his parents until they too went to America or died.

The cows were now giving so much milk that they had to sell it quickly or it would spoil. They had dug a cave in the north side of the hill at the rear of the barn some years ago and now, they were going to make use of it. When there were many consumers of milk in the household, they really did not have a problem with the surplus. They would feed some to the calves and colts and sell the rest. But now with everyone gone and the amount of work that had to be done, there was little time left to sell the milk. The winters were fine, because they could store the milk in the cave. It would not freeze and Stefan would take the surplus in large cans to town on Sunday and sell it by the liter door to door. The problem was in the summer time, when the milk would spoil before they could sell it. The time that they had to cool it was from April until October and this was their busiest time. They had to milk the cows, which had to be milked every day. The cave was large enough to store ice for about four weeks. In the dead of winter, Stefan and his father would take the wagon and go to the lake ten miles north in the High Tatras. They would saw the ice with a large cross cut saw into blocks weighing about 100 pounds each. This was backbreaking work; they would slide the ice onto the wagon until it was full. Then they would store the ice in the grass-covered cave. The ice was packed with a space between each block. Sawdust, obtained from the saw mill, was put into the spaces between the blocks. The blocks would stay frozen until April before beginning to melt. The sawdust, which was used from year to year, retarded the melting process and the milk or other perishables would stay cool. For four years, they managed to keep the farm in the black and they put away money, but at a cost to Johan. He started to lose weight and he was tired all the time. He was now fifty-nine

years old and was working as if he were twenty. A decision was
made to have someone come in to help and Johan went to see
Father Andrej after Mass on the following Sunday. He asked him if
he knew of a man and woman who would come to work for them
six days a week. The wages were not too much, but they would
have extra benefits such as food to feed their entire family. They
would have to go to church and be trustworthy and Olga would
like to meet them before they decided. Father Andrej said that he
had the ideal couple for them, they were brother and sister and
they would work hard. The girl, Kada, had a hard life until now
and she was fifteen years old while her brother, Andrej, was seventeen and would work hard. The next day, the priest brought them
to the farm and Kada reminded Olga of her own daughter, Marta;
she smiled all the time. She had developed a fine sense of humor
and, even though, she was only five feet tall and weighed about a
hundred pounds, Olga could tell that the girl knew what hard
work was. She could milk cows, cook, clean and preserve food.
Andrej was taller and heavier. He had worked at the saw mill, off
and on, for the last five years. He too knew what hard work was.
Olga approved and they were hired on the spot. They would report for work at six am. on the next day and leave for home at six
p.m. The following day they came to the Janek's farm ready to
work but Kada did not realize how this job would have an influence her for the rest of her life.

16

Pavel Podorski was born in nizne Ruzbachy and he was a true Slovak since his mother and father were both born in nizne Ruzbachy. It seemed like the family was always short of food where they lived in a little cottage near the edge of town. Pavel's father never learned a trade, nor did his son learn a trade because there was no time to learn when he had to live from hand to mouth all his life. He made some money guiding people through the pass into Poland and he worked for the abbey at harvest and planting time. If someone needed a minor repair, such as a door or window, he would fix it. They got by, but barely.

He had five children: of which were two sons. He would have to wait until they grew up so that they could bring some money and food into the house. When he worked, he worked very hard. The people who hired him liked him, but there was only so much work to go around. He worked in the saw mill when he was younger, but he could not keep up with the work once he got into his forties. He had sent Andrej into the saw mill when he was fifteen, but he knew that the youngster would not be able to do that type of work for long and he would turn out exactly like his father.

His wife Anna was also a hard worker and when they were at a rock bottom low, he would send her to the Marianske Spa in the High Tatras. She would find work as a maid, cook attendant, or any other job that was available. Anna would work for a few months and then come down from the mountain with her money and they would live well for six months. The employees would pay nothing for food at the spa and all the money she made was hers. She did not like to work at the spa, she did not like the people that came to the spa and she did not like being away from her children for such a long time. When her oldest daughter was old enough, she took her to the spa to work. Marta would hide from her mother because she did not want to go but she always did.

When Marta was sixteen years old, Pavel met a man in his forties whose name was Josef Krupchik. He had inherited a large piece of land from his father with a house and some farm buildings on it. He did not work, but had hired hands that lived on the farm. Josef's wife had just passed away and left him with three young children and he was looking for a wife. Actually, he was looking for someone to take care of his children, to cook, clean and be available to warm his bed on cold winter nights. His oldest child was a boy who would inherit the farm, but Marta would have a place to live for the rest of her life.

Pavel reached a bargain with Josef where Marta would marry Josef and in return, Josef would give Pavel some furniture, a wagon, horse and two hundred crowns. He would also give Pavel's fourth born a job when he was old enough to work. They shook hands and when Anna and Marta came back from the spa, he told them what he had done. Anna did not say a word, but Marta cried for three days. She contemplated running away, but where would she go? She would have to go live with that ugly old man until she thought of something else. The marriage took place in the church and Father Andrej suspected that she had been sold by her father, but neither of them would admit it so he performed the ceremony and Marta went to live with her new husband.

With Marta gone, Anna started taking Kada to the spa when she was eleven. On one of her trips, the management said that the system that they were using, with the temporary help, was not working. She and her daughter would have to stay there for a two-year period or they would have to stop coming. When Anna went home, she left Kada behind for her two-year tour of duty. She told Pavel when she returned that it would be good training for Kada and she would bring home good money. Pavel assured himself that he could get along without the girl for two years but he was already looking for someone to take her as a wife if he could work the same arrangement as he had with Marta.

Things were looking up. His two hundred crowns would feed his family for two years and when Kada returned, he would have more money to use. With what his son was bringing home, they could even put some money away and buy a horse and he could go into business of hauling goods for people. Yes, it was good to have children. Pavel started to slow down and he would work enough just to keep up appearances. He was hoping that Jacob would get bigger so he could go to work and he still had one other daughter, Hana, but she was only nine years old. When Kada returned he would be able to have her take Kada's place his future seemed to be set.

Kada came back from the spa two years later and was replaced by Hana. She gave all her money to her father and now he would have enough money to buy a horse. Kada was thirteen years old but she had aged more in experience than she had in years. She was still small and thin and he would have trouble finding a husband for her. He looked for about six months and found an older man in his fifties who would be willing to marry her. The man was wealthy and he was looking for someone young to share his bed. He was willing to marry her and to watch her grow up but she did not bring as much as Marta did. He would wait and, once the man became dependent on Kada, then he would talk to him some more. He called Kada and her mother to talk to them about the agreement and Anna was outraged at her husband, Kada said nothing but left and went to her room. She gathered a few personal things together and put them in a shawl. Her brother, Jacob, watched her and asked her what she was doing; she did not answer as she put the bundle under her bed.

She finally turned to him and said, "I am leaving tonight and I will join a gypsy caravan that I saw parked in a clearing up by the river from town. You must swear not to tell anyone where I have gone."

He looked at her and said, "I swear!"

After the evening meal, she took her bundle and left the house and went on her adventure. She found the encampment by the light of the fire, around which there were eight or nine people sat around talking. She saw six wagons parked around the fire and one of the children, sitting on his mother's lap, pointed to Kada as she stepped into the light of the fire. A man stood up and approached her and she kept telling herself not to be frightened. The stories that she had heard about gypsies stealing children and eating them were old wives' tales, she mused. They were people just like everyone else. A man, with a thick accent, asked what she wanted.

She told him, "I ran away from home because my father had promised an old man that I would marry him. I haved no place to go so I would like to join your band."

He looked over this frail, frightened youngster who was to be sold to an old man and he told her, "Go to the wagon right behind me. The wagon belongs to a man named Kafka who has a daughter about your age."

She went in and found a neat little travel wagon with a woman and a girl in it. A lantern hung from the ceiling and the woman asked her to come in and sit on the side of the bed. There was a bigger bed on one side and a smaller bed on the other; multicolor cloths covered the beds and pots and pans, hung everywhere. Every bit of space was used in the wagon. The woman motioned for her to look out the back of the wagon where six men sat around the fire. The man she had spoken to, was standing up and was speaking in a language that she did not understand. She knew a little of many languages that she had learned from working at the spa but she did not recognize this one. Another man got up to talk and the first man sat down and, in this way, each man, in turn, got up to speak. After all the men had spoken, the first man got up, waved his arms in the air, struck his chest with his fist. All of the men got up and went to their wagons.

The woman turned to Kada and said in Slovak, "I am Belina and this is Naja. My man's name is Kafka. It appears that you will be staying with us. You will share the bed with Naja."

A man came into the wagon; he did not appear to be pleased as he blew out the lantern and went to bed. There was barely room for one on Naja's bed, but the little girl pulled her down next to her and told her to be quiet. Kada slept very little that night. The next morning she woke to the smell of breakfast cooking on the fire. Naja was already out of the wagon. She looked at the other bed and it was empty and made up. Kada got up, made her bed and went outside. Naja was eating and put her bowl down to fetch Kada some breakfast. A dog came too close and she kicked it, sending it away.

As she was putting some white substance into the bowl for Kada, she said, "You cannot let a dog eat from a bowl that a person uses. If you do, then we have to throw it away. A person cannot eat from a bowl that a dog has used and we cannot wash it, so it has to be thrown away."

She handed Kada the bowl with a wooden spoon and some type of barley porridge, sweetened with honey. It was very good and she ate it all. She looked for more, but Kada told her that there was only enough for one bowl per person. Kada looked around her and saw that everyone was busy but Belina stopped just long enough to tell her that because they were taking her with them, they would have to leave or people will think that she was stolen by them. She saw Kafka arrange four stones, with one on top a little off center.

Naja said, "We are expecting another tribe, but since we are leaving, we have to show the tribe where we are going so they could follow us."

Kada asked if a little pile of rocks said all that and Naja just nodded her head. Within fifteen minutes the caravan was on the move and they were heading south, across fields and keeping away from the roads.

Naja said, "The leader of the tribe is King Farrah and his wife is Queen Fatima. We have to make a circle around the town because of you. If we crossed the bridge at Ruzbachy, then someone might see you and we would be accused of taking you by force. This was a serious offense and would bring much trouble for the tribe. King Farrah was taking a big chance by taking you with us.

The caravan will go to a shallow spot in the river where the wagons will cross because we will have to be far away by nightfall."

The girls settled down to the noise of creaking wood, the clanging of pots and pans and the noise of the wheels as one of them struck an occasional stone in the field. The wagons rumbled all day stopping only once outside of a field. It was a field of maize and the women went to gather armfuls. They took only one from every fourth stalk so the farmer would be less likely to see that any were missing. There was a brook nearby and the men filled all the water skins with fresh water. They stopped for only fifteen minutes and the women relieved themselves in the field among the stalks while the men went into the woods next to the brook. Kada was glad that the wagons stopped for she had to go very badly, but she did not know how to ask and she had never felt so relieved in all her life.

They later stopped in a field by the edge of a forest. When Kada asked Naja where they were, she said, "It makes little difference where we are but, to answer your question, we are north of a little town of Rudnany. A coal mine is nearby and the women will go into town to tell fortunes and try to buy some food. The gypsies carry no food except what we find during the day because we have no means for preserving it."

Kada and Naja would have to stay in the encampment with the men and they would have to wait for the women to come back before they could eat. Some of the men, used the time to go into the forest to set snares for rabbits or birds. The gypsies baked no bread, they either stole it or bought it. As they sat in the "vardo," the wagon where the gypsies lived, Naja gave Kada a piece of bread and told her to put it into the pocket of her dress for good luck. When that piece got moldy she was to throw it away and put a fresh piece into her pocket; that way, luck would never desert her. The men had caught one rabbit, which they skinned, put a stick through it and placed it over the fire. It was Naja's job to turn the rabbit so it would cook evenly.

The women came back from town with a few loaves of bread

and some tea. There were twenty-three people in the tribe, ten adults and thirteen children, including Kada. Everyone received a small piece of meat, an ear of corn which had been placed in water and put into the fire, husk and all. The bread was passed out and Kada saw a few people stick a piece into their pockets before they ate. It would appear that if a choice needed to be made as to whether to eat the bread or put it into one's pocket, the person would go hungry that night. Everyone ate and the leftovers were given to the three dogs that ran behind the wagons. The dogs were useful as an early warning to approaching strangers and Naja told Kada that strangers were allowed in the encampment.

An old gypsy proverb said, "You should beware of your neighbors but strangers will not harm you."

After the meal the women cleaned the utensils, and more wood was placed on the fire. Everyone sat cross-legged around it as King Farrah sat on a box that he brought out of his vardo (wagon). It was story telling time and they listened to him with respect. He looked at Kada and said that she would have to learn the gypsy's language or "Rom." He said that she could learn much from the language a person was using as there were many dialects and she would be able to tell where a person was from by listening to the language. Everyone around the fire was anxious to hear what story King Farrah would be telling tonight. They had all heard the stories many times, but they never tired of listening to them. He spoke in Slovak for Kada's benefit. The "paramitscha" is the traditional folklore of the gypsies' tales that were told around the fires at night.

He started off with the basic tale that related to the origin of the gypsies. "We gypsies believe that we come from Egypt and are direct descendents of the Pharaohs. We left Egypt and went to all four corners of the earth. Some of us went to western Europe and then across the little ocean to England where we roam the countryside much as we did in the olden times. Some of us went to eastern Europe where we are now and this tribe was descended from those people. Some of us went to Italy, Greece and Turkey.

Those who went to India are starting to come into Russia and eastern Europe and they are known as "Colo Gypsies" or Black Gypsies. There are three types of gypsies who roam eastern Europe. The dark gypsies or "Colo" who are considered barbarous, the light brown, or true gypsy who is considered more intelligent, and the gypsies of the yellow pine complection. The latter may have come from China. They do not mingle with the light brown gypsies."

The hour was getting late and the two girls were told to go to bed. Belina told Kada that gypsies do not sleep as late as she did this morning and she would have duties assigned to her tomorrow to help the tribe. The rule in her vardo was that the last person out of the bed has to make it and that went for her and Kafka also. Everyone around the fire laughed except Kafka. He would hear about that later.

The next morning, Kada woke early, but Naja was already gone so she made the bed. She wondered if Naja slept at all and when she asked her when she got up, Naja said that it was before dawn. Gypsies did not require much sleep because they had to train themselves to be alert. After a bowl of barley porridge, Naja showed her how to braid her hair with pieces of silk interwoven in. The hair was heavily oiled prior to the braiding and at night, the braids were taken out and redone the next morning. King Farrah said that this was a good place and that they would stay there for a while.

King Farrah stopped by to see Kada and asked, "How are you getting along?"

Kada answered, "Fine, except for not understanding the language, I am doing fine."

His face broke into a smile, "You know that as a "Parno," (a white person who was non-gypsy), the language is going to be difficult to learn, but I have instructed Naja to give you lessons in our dialect."

Kada wondered why Naja was spending so much time with her. She learned quickly that a suggestion made by the "viovode" or tribal chief, was actually an order said in a polite manner, and one which dared not be disobeyed. After the meal, she saw some of the men take pieces of leather and leather crafting tools. They worked on a stump or three legged tables. The women took out reeds and soaked them in water, so that they would be pliable enough to weave into baskets. The gypsies who traveled less would fashion charms out of silver or copper and those who lived permanently in a town would practice the blacksmith's trade, repairing metal tools and equipment or working as coopers making kegs or barrels. A gypsy passed the art of making the objects down to his sons, but a gypsy would never pass it on to a non gypsy as they did not want competition from a parno. In the afternoon they would try to sell their wares in town.

In one of her lessons with Naja, Kada asked, "Why was I taken in so quickly by the tribe? I had understood that the gypsies were very secretive and would have nothing to do with a parno unless the gypsy could foresee a way of making some money."

Naja answered, "Although you have yellow hair, it has a red highlight to it and the gypsy believe that a member of the tribe with red hair assured the tribe of good fortune. Red hair is called "bala kameskro," or sun hair. King Farrah felt and convinced everyone in the tribe that you would bring us all good fortune."

Things were falling into place for Kada. She was learning the gypsies' language, their customs and beliefs and she was traveling around the countryside. She had never been through Hungary where they were heading for a warmer climate. Before they finished their annual loop, they would have traveled south into Bosnia and around Belgrade. There was a natural valley to the south of Belgrade where various tribes met to exchange information and to warn each other of pending problems in an area. The gypsies were like shadows because they were in and out of an area before the residents knew of their presence. After the annual meeting, the tribe would go east through Romania, then north through the Balkan countries to Poland. They would spend the summers on either side of the High Tatras and when summer was almost over, they would head south. They had mostly a warm climate, little snow and food for the entire year. When people in Ruzbachy were worried about having enough to eat, the gypsies were well fed in the south.

The meeting place gave the gypsies an opportunity to make any repairs to wagons and other equipment, to repaint the wagons, if necessary, and to gather material for the next year's trek. The stop also gave the young men or "shavs" a chance to look over the crop of marriageable women and horses, which the gypsy considered equal. This is also the time for King Farrah to learn new stories that he could tell around the fire. Kada attracted quite a bit of attention but even though she was below the marrying age by about a year, the young Shavs were trying to get her to notice them. It seemed that the reddish tint to her hair attracted them to her. She did not compete with Naja because she had her eye upon a slender young man from another tribe but he would wait until next year when he would talk to her. Naja could wait until the following year and she was amused by the antics of the Shavs going after Kada. Naja told Kada that she had picked up a piece of red string one morning and that was a powerful symbol of good luck. She had given the red string to her intended, so she is, therefore, bound to this man when she becomes of marrying age. She told Kada, "Do not encourage any shav because if you do and do not marry him, he will be insulted, you will have made an enemy for life. He would tell his chief who would bring it up to King Farrah and it could end by having both tribes become enemies because this is how blood feuds began."

Kada did not acknowledge any advances and spent most of her time in the wagon with Naja; they were becoming as close as sisters. They shared each other's secrets, did each other's hair, and went to the river to wash. One stood guard while the other bathed.

Once a man and a woman decided to get married, the parents would sit down to discuss the terms. The woman's mother would be expected to provide the necessary items that the woman needed to provide a happy home. This would include bowls, eating utensils, pots, pans and bedding and the man's parents were to provide a wagon, or tent if they could not provide a wagon, and a horse. When the terms were agreed upon, a date was set for the wedding. The mother of the bride would make her a wedding dress and a nightgown that was sure to entice the groom. After all, grandchildren were at stake here. Members of both tribes would start stockpiling food for the wedding feast. The groom's mother would start making her son's wedding suit but it would probably be her husband's wedding suit used by four or five brothers before him and she would cut and sew until she made it fit.

The groom's father would work with his family to make the wagon, paint it and bargain for the horse. Once the day arrived, the chief of the bride's tribe would officiate at the wedding. The "voivode," would call all the members of both tribes and they would make two lines; the bride's relatives on one side, the groom's on the other. The couple would walk in between them, arm in arm, and once they got halfway down the lines, they would jump over a broom that was laid by the voivode. The chief would yell, "You are married! Let us feast!" Everyone would clap and go to the table for food. A fiddle, guitar, or an accordion would start the lively music and the dancing would last for three days. That evening the bride and groom would retreat to the wagon or tent, made up by the bride's mother. They would make love to the music and if a child could be conceived this night, then the child would be blessed with good fortune for the rest of its life. The couple went to live with the bride's tribe. The gypsy says, "If you have not been a part of a gypsy wedding, then you have not experienced life."

Kada could hardly wait for the following year so she might be at Naja's wedding. They talked about it when they were alone and Belina spent time with the girls explaining what was expected of them before, during and after the marriage. She said that Naja was conceived on their wedding night and the tribe has had good fortune since for it had brought a sister to Naja. Belina explained that she could not have any more children after Naja. Kafka and she had tried for many years and just as they gave up, Kada walked into camp, a girl with yellow hair tinted with red, and King Farrah had known right where to put her. Some of the members of the tribe were against letting a parno join their group. It would draw attention to the tribe, bring the wrath of the towns down upon them. They would never be able to come this way again and this way was paved with food just for the taking. The vote was tied when King Farrah raised his arms and struck his chest with his fist. He shouted, "I am King and I say that she will stay and become one of us. I have spoken."

All the members of the tribe got up and went to their wagons, the decision had been made. They accepted her as one of their own because if one of the tribe had challenged King Farrah, he would have been banished. He would have told everyone at the winter meeting that he had been challenged and no tribe would have taken in the challenger unless he had some extraordinary talent to be shared. Once he was abandoned, he was no longer a gypsy and he would have to travel in the world of the parno. Since all he knew was to be a gypsy, he would either have to work for a living or starve because discipline was harsh in the life of a gypsy. Kada asked Belina if she would ever get married and her adoptive mother told her that she had no doubt that Kada would. Since she was not in love with anyone yet, she should learn to love someone who would bring the most, both in material things and other things to the wedding. She winked and both girls giggled, the message had been received by both.

After spending two months at the Valley of the gypsies, as it was called by the parno, King Farrah decided to leave. They would travel east into Romania but life would be hard because there would be no crops from which they could steal their food. There were forests where they could trap food and if they could snare a deer, they would eat until they finished it or the meat turned rotten. Even then, they would cut the rotten part off and cook the rest.

The tribe had put the two months in the valley to good use. They made leather belts, leather hats and vests to sell and they bought some silver ore, extracted the silver and made some charms.

The women gathered reeds so that they could make baskets and because the baskets were so tight that they almost held water, they were in demand. They would keep these and sell them as a last resort when there was no food to gather. The women would go into town to tell fortunes, to predict the sex of a pregnant woman's child, or to give the outcome of some future transaction. This tribe did not have a trained bear that would dance for money and they did not play music at weddings or other feasts. No one in the tribe was an acrobat, so they could not put on shows to make money that way.

Once in a while, they would catch a stray goat, sheep, pig or even a cow in the forest and they would have a "pativ" or feast. They would gorge themselves trying to eat as much as they could before the meat went bad. The farther north they went, the longer the meat kept. The people in the area knew that if an animal strayed into the forest, it was gone because if the gypsies did not get it, then the wolves did; they kept their distance from both of them. The townpeople had many sayings about gypsies. They felt that every gypsy woman was a witch and they did not want to confront one in the forest. The gypsies felt that they were as free as a bird or a deer in the forest because they were very rarely followed there. They did not carry guns and felt that if someone knew you were going to shoot at them, then they were going to shoot at you. They relied on methods that have worked for them for centuries, on their wits and their knowledge of what people believed that the gypsy could do.

*　*　*

Kada had mastered a basic knowledge of the language and was blending into the life of the gypsy. The best time of the day was at night, when the fire was dancing and King Farrah told one of his stories. He told a rather frightening one one evening when there was a full moon with long black clouds running across it. The fire flickered from the faces of the people as they sat on rocks or stumps and waited eagerly for the story to unfold. As he looked at the people, he waited for the right moment to tell his story.

Then he finally started, "I am told of a tribe of gypsies called the yonesti whose chief was Yono and this tribe lived in the caves in the High Tatras. They lived there year round and did not wander. The tribe rarely left the High Tatras except when food was scarce. Since food was always scarce in the winter, they would come down, usually in a snow storm, because it was easier to get into the barns and steal a sheep or pigs and the falling snow would cover their tracks. They would take the animal into a cave, kill it and eat it and there were only ten people at any given time in the tribe. The hide of the sheep would be cured and sewn into a blanket. The meat lasted a long time because they froze it and used only a little at a time.

They knew all the edible herbs and plants on their mountain and supplemented their diet with what they could find. Summers were times of plenty and they made large snares from young trees that lifted a boar or a deer into the air, where they would club it to death. Life was good on the mountain; they saw few people and few people saw them. Legends sprang up about this man or that man seeing a deer or a boar hanging by his hind legs high in the Tatras and people avoided the area while the gypsies wanted only to live in peace.

Yona and his wife Koho lived in one cave and their two sons, Maki and Yuki each lived in a cave. Both were married. Maki had two children and Yuki had one. Yono and Koho had a daughter about eighteen years of age who spent most of her time with her mother, but slept in her own cave. She wished she could find a husband but it was highly unlikely."

King Farrah took a long drink from a mug that was on the ground next to him and went on, "The daughter, Hona, had long black hair, large dark eyes and a slender body. Her olive skin was as smooth as a pitcher of warm cream. She was very beautiful and when she moved, she walked with grace, like a panther, but with the slyness of a wolf. A few people had seen a glimpse of her gliding noiselessly through the forest and labeled her a witch. A young man whose family was very wealthy decided that he wanted to find this woman and talk to her so he set out with provisions for a week. At dusk on the third day into his trip, he walked under a cliff. He was only about one-half way up the mountain when a noise stopped him. He thought that he heard a slight rustle of the leaves, but everything seemed quiet and he sat down to rest. There was a huge she wolf on the edge of the overhang that had been tracking him all day and she was ready to pounce on him, but she dislodged a rock in her attempt to get to the edge. Hearing the noise, he looked up just in time to see the rock before it struck him in the head rendering him unconscious.

The she-wolf had to run around the side of the overhang. As she reached the fallen man and had just sunk her teeth into his neck, the wolf felt a sharp pain in her eye. She looked up to confront Hona who had a sharp pointed stick in her hands. The wolf jumped up to lunge at her when Hona stuck the point of the stick through the wolf's heart. She looked at the young man who was bleeding from the neck and wrapped her kerchief around his neck to stop the bleeding. She went into the woods to find a certain leaf and when she found what she was looking for, she wet the leaves and placed them on the wound. She tied the kerchief around his neck and the bleeding stopped. The woman tried to carry him, but she could not. If she tried to treat him where he lay, then the blood of the wolf would attract other wolves so she had to get him away from this area. She knew of a cave not too distant, yet far enough away from their homes.

Hona cut two saplings and stripped off the branches. She took off her clothes and with a little rope she carried, made a carrier to haul him to the cave. She put the poles on her shoulders and pulled the man through the forest. It was a sight to see a naked woman with poles on her shoulders, hauling an unconscious man through the forest. Once she got him to the cave, she propped him up against the ledge and left him resting on her dress while she went out to look for more herbs.

He was still unconscious when she returned and she continued to treat him. She built a fire to keep the animals away. The man would awaken once in a while to see this beautiful naked woman giving him herbal tea to drink. She spent a week with him and when he appeared better, she took her clothes and put them on. He awakened once so that she could talk to him and she gave him directions to the village. He fell asleep and when he woke, she was gone. He called out to her, but there was no answer. He left the cave and followed her directions to the village. He was treated by a doctor and within a few weeks, he returned to the forest to find his love. After wandering around for a few days, he found the ledge but there was no sign of the she-wolf or any other tracks. Someone had taken care to eliminate all signs of his ordeal. The young man did not return home and he has not been seen since. He disappeared without a trace. While some say he found her others say he did not. There are reports that he was sighted running through the forest on all fours; the bite of the she-wolf, which bit him on the full moon, turned him into a werewolf. When there was a full moon his body grew hair, his eyes turned red, his ears grew and he developed hideous teeth. He still runs on all four feet looking for his love. When there is a full moon in the High Tatras, the wolves howl. There is one howl, however, that comes from higher up the mountain and is much louder than the rest."

As King Farrah was telling his story, he looked at all the wide-eyed people watching him. When he got to the part at the end of his story, a wolf howled nearby and Kada screamed and jumped up. Everyone but Belina laughed and she pressed Kada's head against her bosom and kissed her on her head.

*   *   *

Two days later the tribe packed up after a quick meal and headed north. A road went through the forest and they followed it. The forest was thick and dark and Kada rode up front with Kafka. Belina and Kafka did not speak to each other often for each knew

what had to be done and did it. Betina got news from the women
and Kafka got his from the men. Both received the same news so
there was no need to tell each other. Kafka welcomed the company
and he spoke to Kada as they moved along the road. The horse
seemed to know where he was going so Kafka exerted little effort in
managing him. When the wagon got close to the wagon in front,
the horse slowed but when it lagged, then would go faster.

Kafka loved the forest and he told Kada, "When I am in the in
the forest, I feel free. The darkness in the forest is the light for a
gypsy and the forest is the church. A gypsy would go to a parno's
church only twice, once to be baptized and once when he dies;
maybe not even that. Most gypsies never enter a parno's church for
they are baptized by the chief and buried by the tribe. When a
gypsy dies, no one may touch the body and the entire tribe will
fast until the body is buried. The women will keep a vigil around
the body to ward off any evil spirits, ghosts or witches. They burn
all of the deceased's possessions, sometimes even the wagon and he
is buried at the edge of the forest, marked by a pole. There are no
markings on the pole and it is buried deep enough to where it is
almost touching the head of the corpse."

All that was said to Kada was designed to accomplish one
purpose;to educate her in the ways of the gypsy. The tribe grew to
love this young lady who was always smiling, always willing to
help and to learn. No one loved her as much as Betina who accepted her as she was; she asked nothing of her past and looked
only to the future.

She once told Kada, "Good luck always follows bad luck and
no matter what has happened in the past, we do not know what
tomorrow will bring, so we have to make our own luck."

She gave Kada a little black bag with a piece of a bat in it. She
wore this around her neck to ward off evil spells and to bring
good luck.

Kada asked Betina one day, "Do you and Kafka argue at all?
You speak so seldom that you appear you are not getting along."

Betina answered, "A wagon will hold more people if there is

peace among them. All we have to do is to look into each other's eyes when we want to communicate and we know what we want to do."

Kada thought that if she could, somehow, bring this peace to her parent's home in Ruzbachy, then she would even consider going back there. This life was so much more simple; she loved to stay with these people. The only problem she had was with the marriage. She did not know if she could wed a shav because this meant a commitment and she could never leave.

When the tribe was sure that she would become a gypsy, Fatima took over her education. Kada rode in front of King Farrah's wagon while Fatima drove it. This wagon was always first in a line and Fatima usually drove it while King Farrah rested in the back. He had so many decisions to make, in the course of the day, that he grew tired and while travelling often. Fatima instructed Kada in all the secret signs that gypsies had.

"One such sign," Fatima said, Is that we display a sign when a gypsy is amoung non gypsies and did not want them to know that he was a gypsy. He would put his hand in his pocket and leave his little finger sticking out. If someone saw it, they would display the same sign and they would speak later. Many times, a gypsy would enter the parno world to buy or sell an animal or to conduct other business. Many people on the outside would not deal with a known gypsy because, when a gypsy dealt with a non gypsy, the gypsy always got the better of the bargains, for he was better prepared. It made no sense for one gypsy to deal with another on the outside for they could handle their affairs within the encampment of the gypsies."

The art of predicting the future was always a mystery to Kada. She had been with them for nine months now and she had watched many gypsies tell fortunes, by either palm reading or by the cards, but she could not find a pattern.

She mentioned this to Fatima, who only laughed. "There is no pattern and you have to know what questions to ask and what to notice about the subject. You have to talk to him for a time to

learn as much as you can about the person. If you see a man arguing with another man and he came in later to have his fortune
told, you could tell him that he was going to reach a bargain with
another man. You have to notice what is going on and use this to
your advantage. There was no such thing as predicting the future
because no one knows what will happen tomorrow. The non gypsy
thinks that every gypsy woman is a witch and can foretell the
future, but the gypsy woman makes the best estimate about what
is going to happen with the information that she has managed to
learn. Sometimes she is right and sometimes she is wrong. If she is
right then the person will think that she knows the future and will
come back. If she is wrong, then she has to ask the person what
happened and she has to tell the person that he did not do what
the gypsy told him to do."

Kada asked, "What would happen if the gypsy did not tell
him the correct thing to do?"

Fatima smiled, "Human nature being what it is, the person
would not remember what was said to him and automatically would
believe that he was wrong. The most important thing is to get the
money first. The amount is determined by what you think the
person will pay."

The next subject covered was the curses and evil eyes against
someone whom they attempted to harm. Fatima said, "Certain
signs are used by the women and each tribe has its own set of
signs. The ones used by our tribe are simple. I would extend my
little finger and index finger, holding the other two fingers in my
palm with my thumb. I extend my arm, palm down, and utter my
oath in a voice that I reserve for just such an occasion."

"How do you know that the oath would come about?"

Again Fatima smiled, "You do not know if the oath will come
true and if it did, then you are a witch. Even if it did not, then the
person would feel that all the bad luck he was having was due to
the curse. The curse would be on his mind when bad luck happens and he will seek you out to have the curse taken off. This is
when you demand money to take the curse off. The person is vul-

nerable now so you get as much money as you can. To take the curse off, you use the other hand and utter an oath taking the curse off, but be sure to take the money first."

Fatima was a good teacher and Kada traveled with her for three days through the forest. They saw many animals, such as a bobcat, deer, racoons, rabbits, squirrels and even a bear. They had plenty to eat because, while they were going through the forest, one of the men rode ahead on a horse and set traps and snares where the tribe would stop for the night. There were clearings in the forest that showed signs that the gypsies used them regularly and when they stopped for the night, there was food waiting for them. Kada was learning all of the gypsies' secrets and Fatima promised to let her sit in the next time she read a palm or took the cards out to tell a fortune. She told Kada to stay close to her and to learn how to put the evil eye on someone because the trick was to make it look and sound convincing.

As soon as they stopped for the night, the women would leave the encampment and go out into the forest. They would come back with various plants and roots. The leafy plants were boiled and spread with a sauce made from any animal fat and flour while the roots were baked in the fire. These vegetables supplemented the roasted meat that was caught in the traps and snares. There seemed to be plenty to eat and they took what nature provided. It was no wonder that the gypsy loved the forest. It provided safety because people were afraid to venture into it; it provided food since they were the only ones to go deep enough to go through it. Non gypsies went into the fringes of the forest for the hunting that it provided, but they did not go very far because of the imagined witches, goblins and ghosts.

Once they left the forest, food became scarce so they had to go into the villages to tell fortunes and to remove hexes in order to buy bread and other supplies. Kada watched the masters of their craft at work and the women would darken her face and hands so she would not be noticed as a non gypsy. The first thing that everyone did when a loaf of bread was brought into the camp was to break off a little piece and put it in his pocket and then eat the rest.

The small caravan went through Poland and came to the High Tatras. King Farrah decided to camp in a spot that they used before, just on the edge of the forest. They had a river in which to fish, they had food from the forest and, if need be, they could steal an animal from one of the farms nearby. It was a good place to spend a few weeks and they needed some repairs on a wagon. At the usual camp fire that night, one of the women in the tribe announced that she was pregnant. At the time of an announced pregnancy, everyone suspected that she might have gotten pregnant at the meeting in the valley and usually that meant that the woman's husband was not the father. King Farrah called the couple aside and spoke to them to confirm who the father really was. There was much hand waving and shouting at the meeting, but the group was just out of earshot so no one could make out what they were saying.

Soon they all got up and returned to the camp where King Farrah had an announcement to make. He stood up before his tribe and said, "As Chief of the tribe, I have determined that the baby was indeed that of the husband and this becomes the law of the tribe."

Betina whispered to Kada, "We will have to wait until the baby is born to see what it looks like."

Kada thought that these women of the tribe knew everything that was happening. Everyone got up and went back to their wagons, but there would be more discussions about this later, among the women.

If the chief determined that the father of the child was not the husband, they would wait until the baby was born. The woman would be an outcast in the tribe; she would not be spoken to by the members of the tribe. she would eat alone, wash her clothes by herself, use the same utensils every day. Once the baby was born the marriage would be destroyed and the woman banished. King Farrah would declare the marriage void and she would be free to remarry in another tribe if one would have her. No man wanted a "soiled" woman so her only alternative would be to go to a brothel in one of the large cities of Budapest, Bratislava or Vienna. This was harsh treatment, but infidelity was not tolerated by the gypsies. The baby would be given to another couple until it grew either enough to be cared for by the father, or the father remarried. Many women, unknown by the husband, would sell themselves in one of the towns that existed around the meeting valley. She would give the money to her husband telling him that she earned it by fortune telling or some other way.

After they had been in this camp for a week, Kada became ill. Her nose was stuffed up, her throat hurt, she felt lame and her eyes watered constantly. Belina knew it was a cold and they set up a small tent for her to sleep. King Farrah did not want the sickness to spread to her family and then to the rest of the tribe. If everyone became ill, then there would be no one to gather food. He sent Belina and one other woman to find the remedy. They went high into the Tatras to look for a plant and they searched all morning until they found it, a tiny plant called thyme. They searched the bush until they found a small sack full, made a fire and boiled some water. The leaves of the thyme plant were crumbled into the boiling water. The water had to be boiled in cold air which meant that they climbed even higher. Once the herb tea was brewed enough, they strained the brew through an undyed cloth they had brought for this purpose. They put the tea in a container and started down the mountain.

When they arrived at camp, the woman made a fire outside of camp and Belina went to fetch Kada. She brought her to the fire and sat her down with a blanket around her, reboiled the tea, put some honey into it to make it taste better and made Kada drink most of the boiling brew. They each had a small amount and threw the rest away for it was bad luck to bring thyme into camp. Kada was helped back to her tent, blankets were put under and over her and she was told to sleep. Kada had no trouble in falling asleep and she slept from three o'clock one afternoon until noon the following day. Her foster mother checked her once in a while and she put her hand between the blankets to feel the dampness from the sweat. At noon the following day, Kada came out of her tent and declared that she was hungry and the thyme had done its work. It had sweated the fever and virus from her body. The women took the blankets to the stream and washed them with cold water and lye, they were dried and put away. Kada had asked Belina what was in the brew and she made a mental note so she would not forget it.

Belina told her, "If you had been a child, we would have made a salve or poultice. We would have mixed the tea with flour, kapusta, animal fat from either a dog, bear, chicken, wolf or a frog. We would have spread this poultice over the body and left it there for three days and the poultice would suck all the sickness out of the body. Once the poultice was removed, the baby would be washed in warm water and the contaminated poultice would be buried."

The gypsies had a cure for every known ailment and Queen Fatima had a book that told of the various cures. Since the gypsies could not read or write, the formulas were in picture form. There were pictures of the plants that were used, pictures of the mixing of the ingredients and how they were applied. The book was passed from generation to generation. While they were at the meeting valley, the Queens of the various tribes would get together and exchange new remedies that had worked and Queen Fatima would draw the pictures in the book and explain the procedure to the other women of the tribe. A tribe that had a Queen who would keep up with the remedies was fortunate for there was sickness in many of the tribes and those who had no cures were wiped out.

King Farrah stayed at this location longer than he wanted because he was worried that Kada's illness would come back to her and he also wanted to make sure that no one else in the tribe was infected. Sometimes the symptoms did not show up for several weeks. They had enough food and water and wood was plentiful for the fires. They would have to stay at the other spots for shorter periods of time to get to the meeting valley on time. Also, he was worried that Kada would become homesick and leave them when she saw familiar grounds. He set a course that would make a wide berth around Ruzbachy so she would not be tempted to return home. Another reason why he did not want to go near the town and that bothered him ;if someone stumbled on their camp and saw Kada, he could recognize her and tell the authorities and they could all be placed in prison for stealing a girl. The gypsies, although, they had never heard of such a thing happening, had the reputation for stealing children and selling them as virtual slaves. He had to protect the tribe so he told no one, not even Fatima, about his fears. He just took steps to avoid any problems.

When they reached the fork of the Poprad and Dunajec rivers, he went right and followed the Dunajec river south. He was not as familiar with this route, but he was a gypsy and the whole world was his route. Once he started to the right at the fork, a number of eyebrows went up, but everyone learned, a long time ago, not to question the word of King Farrah. They suspected that it was because of Kada but no one said a word and besides, they wanted her to stay with them so they followed their leader. Kada, knew nothing of what was happening because she was happy to be well and to see that no one else caught her illness. The new route meant that they would be going a longer distance and would be on the road longer than usual. This also meant more work to pack and unpack, less food and less time in the villages making money. King Farrah picked up the pace a little bit to be sure that they arrived at the meeting valley on time.

When they reached the valley, everyone was tired. They had been on the road longer than usual. On the morning after they arrived, they noticed that there were many shavs, or young unmarried men, waiting for Kada.

King Farrah came to her one day and asked, "Have you made up your mind about marriage. I have had a few very good offers and it would benefit the tribe if you married a wealthy shav. He would bring much wealth and prestige to the tribe and the people who married each other from different tribes formed alliances."

She remembered what Naja had told her last year that if she did not intend to marry, then she should not encourage anyone. When she turned him down, she will have made an enemy for life.

"Before I answer," she said, " I want to talk to Naja and Belina."

King Farrah found that understandable and told her they would speak some more. At their first opportunity, the three women sat on the beds in the wagon and Kada told them what King Farrah had said to her.

Belina said, "You should be careful about picking a husband because the ones that brought much wealth into the tribe tend to dominate the wives. The wives of these husbands were generally not happy, but those that had nothing made their wives sleep in a tent, on the cold hard, ground. Once she wedded this type of man, they would be sleeping on the ground for the rest of their lives. You, Kada have plenty of time to decide upon a husband. You should choose a husband with a wagon and, more important, one with whom you could fall in love. I knew, as soon as I saw Kafka, that he and I would be happy."

Naja agreed with her mother, "I first saw my intended, Mika, and we have been eyeing each other for the last five years. It was not a decision to be made lightly for Mika will bring a horse and wagon to the marriage and his tribe is large so they would not miss one wagon. All these things are taken into consideration when we agree to the marriage. Kafka talked to Mika's father last year and, although, the bargain has not been made, all they have to do is to shake hands."

Kada waited two days and then talked to King Farrah, telling him that she was not ready to be married. She was fourteen years old and she wanted to wait for a year to decide. He took her at her word and spread the news that Kada was out of the running. One father was rather disturbed and said, "As chief of your tribe, you are bound to order her to be married."

King Farrah replied, "No one is going to tell me how to run my tribe and since this girl has no gypsy mother or father, Kafka would act as her father, and I would not order her to be married."

There was a confrontation for a few minutes when their eyes met and neither man blinked. He said, "My son will marry someone else and Kada will lose my son."

King Farrah had calmed down and said, "So be it."

He went back to Kada to tell her, "Do not marry that man's son, ever. He was used to getting his way and he would treat you badly and he will not be an asset to our tribe, either."

Kada was relieved that the crisis was over.

A bargain had been struck between the fathers of Naja and Mika and the marriage was to take place in two months time.

Belina said, "there was not enough time to do everything. The comforter has been made and everyone from the tribe donated what they could to furnish the wagon, but there is not enough time to do everything."

She was running around trying to do everything at once. In all the excitement, the woman in the tribe finally gave birth to an eleven-pound baby boy; the delivery was three weeks late.

Belina said, "Nature is never late, the brain is late because it miscalculates."

This meant that the baby was conceived after the couple left the meeting valley and the boy had traces of his father's looks so everyone was relieved. King Farrah baptised the boy and was happy that he had made the right decision. Queen Fatima took charge of helping the mother with the baby while Belina made wedding arrangements. A dress had to be made, food gathered and prepared, and the wagon to be outfitted. She could not let this young couple start life together unless she furnished their wagon. Kada helped all that she could, but she did not have skills in sewing or making the leather boots for Naja that was the traditional footwear for a gypsy wedding. She was a very good cook so she foraged for food. Kafka bargained for a pig which would be cooked on a spit, but the problem was that everyone wanted this wedding to be better than the last.

The day finally arrived, the pig was being turned on the spit and the fat from the pig was dripping into the fire, sending up puffs of flames and an aroma that could be smelled all over the camp. The wedding was to take place on a Saturday. The pig was put on the fire the night before and someone tended it all night. At noon the following day, the people lined up, the groom's friends and family on one side and those of the bride on the other. A broom was placed across the lines somewhere in the center where the parents of each stood across from each other. The accordion and the fiddle began to play as the bride came out of one side of the line and the groom the other. Naja looked beautiful and Kada worked with her all morning. Mika wore a suit of dark gray tweed, a stiff white shirt and a tie. They walked between the lines with everyone shaking hands and clapping them on their backs. When they reached the broom, they looked at each other and jumped across. King Farrah jumped between the lines, raised his right hand and pronounced them married. The music got louder, the beer started to flow, and the food came out.

The celebration would last until late Monday evening when all the food and drink was gone and the musicians could not play any more. The night of the wedding, the couple stepped into their wagon and they waved as they went in to try to conceive a child. The crowd cheered as they went in, then went back to the dancing.

Tuesday morning found little activity in the large encampment except for the women who went looking for wood to build a fire for their men. It was going to be a long day for most of the men and, slowly, they limped out of their wagons looking pale and tired. This was the one time that the women could vent their feelings on the men without retaliation of any kind. Kada watched the activity around her and even Belina was talking to Kafka as she never heard her speak before. Kafka seemed to ignore her tirade and asked if the newly-weds had come out of their wagon; no one had seen them. Kafka told Kada that Mika would not recover for months. This brought a smile to Belina's lips, and she turned around so no one could see it. Women were down at the river, pounding clothes with a board to get them clean. They used a soap that they made by boiling fat and lard together with lye until it became thick. They would spread it on a small trough until it hardened and would then cut off pieces as it was needed. Belina had washed her clothes and those belonging to Kada but she went to another part of the river to wash Kafka's clothes. The gypsies never washed men's clothes at the same time as those of women and no one seemed to know why it was done this way, but it had been passed on from generation to generation. The reason was forgotten. At the wedding, King Farrah danced a little, but he had to keep his senses so he would be needed if one of his tribe had gotten into trouble.

The tribe of King Farrah still had a month to go before they went north and Kada looked forward to the time that they spent in the forest. Those were happy days when no one was looking over their shoulders to see if they were being followed. No one ventured into the forest because this was the one area where the gypsies exerted control. Someone spending the night in the forest would wake up to find the juice of the fruit of the elder tree smeared on his saddle. This was the sign of the curse put on by the gypsies and this was feared by everyone. The person would reason that the gypsy was close enough to do him in, but put the evil eye upon him so he would perish slowly and he would now have to find a gypsy woman and pay to take the curse off.

The time in the forest was a time for story telling, laughter and plenty to eat. Six weeks after the wedding, the tribe departed to go north and goodbyes were said to the old friends and the new ones made this year. Some gypsies met every year as some came after an absence of a few years because there were many winter meeting places. King Farrah had come to this valley because Naja asked him to come. He did not ask why, he just knew that he had to come. When they left, there were now seven wagons in the caravan. King Farrah told Kafka that possibly next year they might have eight wagons and they went, single file on the road that this tribe, and the ancestors of this tribe, had traveled for fifteen hundred years.

Everyone breathed a sigh of relief when they entered the forest. Kada was riding on the seat next to King Farrah while his wife was taking a nap. Now that Naja had her own wagon, Kada felt lonely, sitting in the back of the wagon that Kafka was driving.

Kada asked, "Why do the gypsies feel safe in the forest?"

King Farrah looked into the canopy of trees and said, "It is about time that I tell you about the legend of Vila, the gypsy witch who lives in all forests. In the forest the gypsy does not accept the parno or new gypsy ways. They accept no religion, no laws, no customs and no traditions of the outside world. The forest supplies the gypsy with wood free of charge, fruit from the trees, grapes from the vines, fish from the streams. We have good water from the fountains that the streams make going over the rocks, shade from the sun, fresh air from the mountains and caves for shelter. At the campfire tonight, I will tell the story of Vila, the witch."

They rode on in silence for some distance. Kada was anticipating the story of Vila, the witch because she loved the stories even though the stories frightened her. She got off the wagon while it was moving and jumped on Kafka's wagon. She told Kafka and Belina that King Farrah was going to tell the story of Vila, the witch, tonight and she asked them to tell her if they had ever heard it. They answered yes, that they had heard it, but she had better let King Farrah tell the story.

*   *   *

After the meal, Kada helped clean up and was among the first to sit down in front of the fire. The women and children came out next and the men finally came out. The women usually found their place and were seated first for a gypsy woman never walked in front of a man while he was seated. Finally, King Farrah came out puffing on his short stemmed pipe. The gypsies sat in a semi circle and the leader placed his box in the open space across the fire. The fire danced over the red coals and someone put fresh wood on the fire so the flames would leap even higher. The fire was at the edge of the trees and the chief had his back to the woods while his audience was looking into the forest behind him. He looked right at Kada and said that he had been requested to tell the story of Vila, the witch of the forest. He looked around to see that he had everyone's attention and he saw all the eager faces as he began.

"About four hundred years ago, give or take a hundred years, as we gypsies have no idea of time, the Catholic Church was holding trials for everyone who was suspected of not following the Catholic faith. On the edge of town, in a field, a band of gypsies had camped for a few days and they camped there because it was on the edge of a huge forest. The tribe's leader was King Dohlec, his mate's name was Vila. The bishop heard of the gypsies and he asked the policeman to bring the leader into town so he could question him.

The bishop asked, "King Dohlec do you believe in Christ?"

The leader said, "I believe that there is a prophet by that name, and since my tribe is Moslem we believe in a Supreme Being, which is the same God that the bishop worships."

The bishop told him that he wanted to consider this further and sent him back with instructions not to leave or he would be tracked down and burned at the stake. The bishop was trying to have King Dohlec commit some blasphemy against the church so he could condemn him for heresy and execute him. This would enable him to condemn all gypsies and they would stay out of this area. The bishop needed time to trap him.

After he left, the bishop summoned the policeman and asked, "Have you any reports of the theft of any swine?"

The policeman answered, "I have one report at the other end of the city."

The bishop, familiar with the ways of the gypsies, knew that they would never steal anything close to their encampment. He commanded, "Visit the gypsies at meal time and check the pots. If you find pork, you are to bring the king of the tribe back to me."

The policeman did as he was told, found the remains of pork in each pot and brought King Dohlec to the bishop. The bishop passed the death sentence and that evening, Dohlec was burned at the stake while his tribe watched from a distance. Vila was outraged and conjured a curse on the town, the bishop and the Catholic church. The bishop told the law to gather the entire tribe and bring them in the next morning because no one would go out to a gypsy camp at night.

The next morning, the policeman went out to the camp with his men and found the wagons empty. The people, horses and all the posessions were gone. They followed the tracks to the edge of the forest and went back to report to the clergy.

The bishop was furious and commanded, "Go into the forest with supplies to stay for an extended campaign and bring back as many gypsies as you can find. There will be more burned at the stake."

About thirty men went into the forest for the hunt. They came to a steep rocky slope and were ready to go around when they saw Vila, in her multicolored dress, taunting them from the top of the ledge. The leader sent three men up the slope, but when they were half way up, an avalanche of boulders came tumbling down, killing all three men. The police surrounded the area, but Vila was gone. Meanwhile, the gypsies took the three dead policemen and buried them, leaving no trace. The men camped for the night, with guards posted, and when they went to saddle their horses, they found their saddles smeared with the berries of the elder tree. They all knew that it was the evil eye put on them by the gypsies and they wanted to turn back. The leader, fearing the wrath of the bishop, urged them on. They all went in different directions to have a better chance of spotting the gypsies and within two weeks, all were dead and buried without a trace of them. The gypsies had killed every one of them, one by one, and disposed of their bodies. On the next Easter Sunday, when the people were coming out of church, they looked up and, on the hill, stood Vila with her dress blowing in the wind. She shouted another curse at the town telling them that misfortune would follow them until the town turned to dust. The people went to their homes, afraid to come out.

In the years that followed, people venturing close to the forest would see a glimpse of her colored dress running through the forest. The people in the town found animals missing, gardens picked clean and clothes taken that were set out to dry. No one would go after her and soon people began leaving the town; no one wanted to live in a town that was hexed. The church started to lose revenues and closed its doors and after a few years, no one was left in the town. People who passed the edge of the large forest could still see glimpses of the witch, Vila, running through the forest mourning the loss of her man. Word had spread that she was seen in other forests so no one ventured into the forests any longer except gypsies."

As he finished talking, he looked to his right and all eyes followed his to see what he was seeing. In the light of the large fire they saw a glimpse of red flashing through the trees. Kafka looked up and saw that Belina's place was empty. King Farrah had a reason for reinforcing the legend of Vila, the witch because he wanted his people to be comfortable with the forest. Vila would not harm another gypsy. They were protected in the forest. In the forest, they were as free as a deer and their God is in the forest, not in the church because, to a gypsy, heaven looks like a forest because it is safe.

*   *   *

They spent two more weeks in the forest before they followed the trail through the fields of the Ukraine to a small town. The names did not mean anything to Kada any longer, they just seemed to blend one into another. They made camp on the edge of town and had just lit the fire when another caravan rode into view. King Farrah knew who it was by the paint on the lead wagon.

He called Kada to join him in the lead wagon and said, "The chief of this caravan is the one who was difficult with us about his son wanting to court you. This is a powerful man and he has followed us to this site. I have been putting out pativ, or signs that we had passed this way and the other chief has followed us to this spot. The son's name is Kota and the chief's name is King Abdul. There has been bad blood between us since I sold him a horse that later became sick and died. King Abdul accused me of selling him a horse that I knew was sick. Now, go to your wagon and do not come out unless I ask you to come out personally. You will be safe in there because it is against gypsy law for one gypsy to enter another's wagon without permission."

The wagons came closer and King Farrah had rearranged the men of the tribe so that they all sat up against Kafka's wagon. The other tribe pulled in across the fire and made camp. There were ten wagons and King Farrah's tribe was badly outnumbered. After supper, King Abdul came over with his son, Kota, and asked permission to share the fire. As a good gypsy, King Farrah could not turn him down. Kota asked where the red headed young woman was, as he looked at every female face in the tribe.

Queen Fatima stood up and looked the young man in the eye. She said, "The red-haired woman is in the midst of her female problems this time of the month and when she is in that state, she will not eat, cook or do any of her duties. She just lays in her wagon for five days and will not speak to anyone. I will be happy to see this woman in another tribe because she did not contribute anything to this one. She brought nothing but bad luck to our tribe and we are thinking of leaving her in some parno church and going on without her."

She could see the man's father pulling his son by the arm to go back to his own tribe. King Farrah stepped in and said, "As I am a good gypsy, I would not cheat one of my brothers and that is why I am determined not to let Kota court this woman."

Once they had left, the chief thanked his wife for stepping in to solve the problem. They had embarrassed the other leader and made him feel that they had done him a favor. King Farrah did not mind making an enemy of a non-gypsy, but he had to live with

King Abdul. They would meet many times in this lifetime and he did not want a confrontation each time. Kada was told to stay in the wagon until they set up another camp. Word would spread among the tribes and she would not be bothered again.

Early the next morning, they broke camp and followed the foothills of the Carpathian mountains. The next night they camped in Poland and since they did not see King Abdul's tribe again, they assumed that he went north into the heart of Poland. The matter was soon forgotten by everyone except Kada who was now having second thoughts about staying with the tribe. Her difference in color showed that she was not a born gypsy and this was starting to create problems. While the gypsies had a reputation for kidnaping children and taking them into their families, if the parno could see the number of children in the gypsy camp, he would have realized that they could produce enough of their own and did not have to kidnap other people's children. Kada was tired of hiding whenever any non gypsies entered camp and she would have to make a decision when they crossed over into Slovakia. The tribe had just camped outside of the city of Sanok, in Poland, when three local policemen entered camp.

The leader demanded, "I want to see the white child that you are holding."

Kada was brought out and the policemen asked, "What is your name and where are you from?"

She answered, "I am from Slovakia and my name is Kada Podorski."

He said, "You are not a gypsy. Why are you staying with these people? Did they take you away?"

Kada replied, "I ran away from home. I was hungry and they took me in and I am like one of the family. I am here of my own free will and I can leave any time I want to, but I choose to stay."

The policeman talked to King Farrah, "A chief from another tribe had come to the station and reported that you were holding a white girl against her will so we had to come and look into it. I do not see a problem here."

King Farrah asked the policeman, "What did the chief look like and what was the color of his wagon?"

King Farrah knew who it was and determined that there was bad blood between him and King Abdul and he would find a way to even the score. The tribe continued moving until they reached the area where Kada was ill the year before. It was a good place to camp for a while and there could be work done on the leather crafts, the women could make beads and other trinkets to sell in Nowy Sacz. They could even spend the rest of the summer there. Clothes were washed and mended and the children were allowed to run free and play all day. This was the time to bond friendships which would last a lifetime. Kada went from family to family learning new skills and perfecting the ones that she had, and time flew by.

King Farrah announced, "it is time to leave this place. I want to be in the meeting valley by autumn and I need to be there before King Abdul. I want to see if the council will even his score." Nothing was said to Kada because it did not concern her, but King Farrah's honor had been breeched and he would have to get even to restore his honor. Kada knew that it was because of her that the tribes were in conflict and she was leaning toward leaving the gypsy's life and returning to her family. She would see how things progressed in Slovakia.

The tribe had gone through the pass into Slovakia and the twelve crosses were still there, but they could stand some work. King Farrah felt it was safe to follow the trail that they had followed for years instead of going around Ruzbachy as he had done the year before. They camped near the edge of the forest north of the Abbey of St. Francis because the friars tolerated them and usually left them alone. They were camped for a few days when King Farrah and Kafka left late one evening and came back before dawn. At noon the next day they went to the abbey where they met the priest who took care of the animals. He told them that a large pig had died suddenly during the night and he could find no reason for its death. He was in the process of checking the herd for any tell tale-signs when the gypsies told the priest that they would take the carcass off his hands since they had animals that would eat the swine. They rode double and draped the pig over the other horse and once they were back at camp, Kafka slit the animal's throat to allow it to bleed. They dressed the pig, put it over a spit and roasted it. There would be a feast that evening and, while Kada observed all of this, she asked Belina what was happening.

Belina smiled and showed her white, even teeth, "King Farrah and Kafka had stolen into the abbey the night before, picked out a pig and fed it "Drao" which is a poison. The poison does not affect the blood, but paralyzes the animal until it dies. They asked the priest for the animal and the blood with the poison in it was drained making the pig good enough to eat."

Kada looked at the pig on the spit being turned by two boys and almost became sick. Her mind was made up at that moment. She would leave the tribe, but she waited until the feasting had begun and approached Belina and Kafka to say goodbye. She told them that when they returned to the wagon she would be gone. She said goodbye to Naja, took her belongings and walked down to Ruzbachy.

She crossed the bridge, went to the kitchen door of her parents' home and looked through the window. She could see her mother at the kitchen table with a cup of tea. She could see no further signs of life in the house so she rapped on the door and waited for her mother to answer it. Her mother took a look and almost slammed the door in her face because she saw a gypsy in a multicolored dress.

Kada spoke to her mother, "It is I, Kada. Do you not know your own daughter?"

Her mother turned pale as if she had seen a ghost as she recognized her and tears flowed on both sides as they embraced. Kada entered the house for the first time in two years and she sat with her mother at the kitchen table until dawn, each relating to the other what had happened in two years.

Her mother said, "Your Father died when his wagon got stuck in the snow and he tried to push it out. The exertion was too much, his heart stopped and they found him frozen the next day. Andrej is helping to support the rest of the family and Anna married the son of a land owner from vishe Ruzbachy and has gone to America. I have not heard from her in three months, but they settled in a little town on a river. His name is Petro Dulac. He treats her very well and she loves America. Marta's husband died and she is staying at the house with her stepson and his family. She is now doing fine and she is like a mother to them. Jacob is old enough to work and he helps Andrej. We are getting by better than when your father was alive.

Kada told her mother of her travels with the gypsies and what had finally caused her to leave.

Her mother asked, "Are you home to stay?"

"Yes, mama, I am."

Her mother said, "I did not hear from you in two years, and I blamed your father for your disappearance. He realized his mistake as soon as you had gone, but no one could find you to bring you back home and he died with guilt on his soul."

Once the talking had stopped, Anna got her daughter some food, some less conspicuous clothes and made her sleep. It was an exhausting night for both of them and Kada slept for ten straight hours. That evening, she met with her brothers when they returned from work. She would see Marta later. The following Sunday, the family went to church and her brother introduced her to Father Andrej at the end of Mass. She told the priest that she and Andrej were looking for work and the priest said that he might be able to help. A few days later, he visited them and told them that a family in vishe Ruzbachy was looking for help on their horse farm. The only people working on the farm were Stefan Janek and his mother, Olga. The terms were arranged and Kada and Andrej began work at the Janek horse farm about six months before the outbreak of World War I.

17

The situation became very tense between the Serbs and the Magyars and with all the pacts and alliances being made, the people in the outlying districts did not know to whom to pledge their allegiance. Stefan was the only one left to manage the Janek farm and it did not appear that he would be there very long. In order to make their armies mobile, horses were in demand and the Janek farm had a surplus. Prices started to rise when the horses were bought to go into the armies. One day, a representative of Archduke Ferdinand visited the Janek farm and said that he was looking for war horses, large and well-trained. He liked what he saw and offered Stefan a price beyond his wildest dreams. Stefan sold all of his horses except five of his best mares and his two stallions. Olga was able to put the money away to be used to build up the herd and it looked like the farm would show an excellent profit, even with the wages of Andrej and Kada.

It was too late to start the herd this year so they waited until the following year. In July of 1914, word reached Ruzbachy that a Serb named Govrilo Princip murdered Archduke Ferdinand and his wife in Sarajevo, Bosnia on June 18, 1914. The Archduke was in line to take over the throne of the Emperor Franz Joseph when he passed on. Austria had accused the Serbian Government of having planned the assassination and on July 28, 1914, declared war on Serbia. The next day Austrian artillery bombarded the capital of Serbia, Belgrade.

Russia ordered mobilization against Austria, and Germany declared war on Russia. Russia's ally, France, mobilized. This caused Germany to declare war on France, and Britain joined France while Bulgaria sided with Austria. This was to be the first great conflict to involve most of the world. Sixty-five million men were to become involved, and eight million five hundred thousand lost their lives. The war was to be fought on two fronts: the Germans, Austrian and Bulgarians fought against the Russians on the Eastern Front and the Germans fought the French and English on the Western Front. Italy temporarily remained neutral along with the United States.

In July of 1914, the notary went to the Janek farm and handed Stefan a piece of paper saying that he was now in the Austrian Army and would have to report to Vienna in five days. Failure to comply would mean that he would be caught and shot as a deserter. His term of duty was six years. The notary did not stay long as he had a great many more papers to serve. Stefan decided that he would have to go by train and Andrej would have to drive him in the wagon. Four days later, he kissed his mother and father good-bye and left in the wagon for Polodencz with Andrej.

The train took him into Vienna at five in the afternoon. Wagons were waiting to take him and others to the staging area. Once he got there, he found that he was one of the thousands who had reported. Signs were set up for Austrians, Magyars, Slovaks and Czechs, so he got into a line that said Slovaks. Once it became his turn, it was ten o'clock. He gave his name to the soldier seated at a table and was told to join a group of men under a sign that read "Slovak Volunteers." When there were about thirty in the group, they were lined up and marched to a row of tents set up on what used to be a parade ground.

Two men behind a table passed out uniforms and equipment. They were given a jar for water, a helmet, a tin dish and a gas mask. There were only enough gas masks for one out of every three men and Stefan did not get one. There was no food this night and he was assigned to a tent with six men. They would be called out of the tent at five am. the next morning and they would be expected to be fully dressed in their uniforms when they reported. The first day, they would be shown how to use their equipment and pack it into their backpacks so they could carry all their gear with them. When he went into the tent the first night, there were no cots, and only three blankets on each side. When he got to the tent the second night, even the blankets were gone. They were expected to sleep on the ground with no blankets and only their clothes to keep them warm.

He woke up the next morning to a shout from a bearded face in the flap of the tent. He got up, brushed himself off, smoothed his hair and left the tent. His uniform was too big. When he looked at the man next to him, he could not button his because it was too small. Stefan asked permission to go back into the tent and exchange uniforms with the man so they would fit better. They came outside to line up with the rest of the men and when they were lined up, a corporal came out to stand in front of them. His superior told them that he was Corporal Hadarek and first names were not important. Their first military lesson began at once, they were taught how to line up and how to pack their equipment so that they could carry all of it. They would have to make do with only the equipment that they could carry and were marched to a field where an officer stood on a platform. He told them that there would be two weeks of training and then they would go to the front. They would be given weapons after one week and they would have one week to learn how to use them. Each corporal would be responsible for his six men and he would teach them the make up of the Slovak volunteers and how they were attached to the Austrian army. As he was speaking, a thunder storm drenched all of them, but the officer did not stop talking and Stefan could not hear him. He hoped that the corporal would explain it.

They were given a meal of bread, sausage and water right after the speech. Corporal Hadarek took charge and explained the fundamentals of living in a tent and the tent would be a luxury compared to where they were going. There were exercises to be done and classes on gas masks, bedrolls, helmets, marching and the chain of command. As they were resting under a tree, the man next to him said that he never volunteered to come into the army. He was from a little town of Nizne Slavkov. Stefan thought that the worst part of standing in the rain listening to an officer talk was that the officer was a Magyar and everyone knew that they had no regard for Slovak lives. The first day ended with a meal of bread, sausage and beer, and a welcome sleep.

The first week of training went by quickly for there was no time to think; you did as you were told without hesitation. Hesitation meant a stick in the ribs with the riding crop that the corporal carried. The second week, they were given rifles and bayonets and they spent that week learning how to load the weapons, clean them and attach the bayonets. They were settling into a routine of sleeping on the hard ground, getting up and training all day. There was not a shot fired in their training because ammunition was in short supply and only used in combat. At the end of the second week, they were issued ammunition and told that the next day they would take a train to the front. The train trip was short, only four hours and they were herded into cars like cattle. The cars were so crowded that it was difficult to sit so Stefan stood up for the entire time. They were unloaded and combined with the other troops. Stefan estimated that there were four Armies of 100,000 men each. He felt better when he saw all of these men and they would surely be able to push the enemy back. He lost his enthusiasm when he learned that they would be fighting the Serbs and not the Russians. He knew that the Russians were ill-equiped and not trained as well as they were, but the Serbs who had fought in the previous war were properly trained. They had seen combat so they were veterans and the rumor was that the attack would be the next day.

At dawn the next day, they marched across the Sava River and the Drina River and it was obvious that the target would be Belgrade. Their commanding officer was General Oskar Potiorek and the attack would begin on August 12. They spent three days in the trenches getting their equipment in order and waiting for the signal to attack and invade another country. Stefan thought to himself that the Serbs were Slavs just as he was. This was a funny war, brother fighting against brother, and he could really see no sense in it. While they were in the trenches Corporal Hadarek told them that if they see a comrade die and he had a gas mask, they should take the gas mask in the event of a gas attack. On the 11th of August, the Austrian artillery opened fire, with round after round aimed at the Serbian trenches.

At dawn on the twelfth, a flare went up and Corporal Hadarek leaped out of the trench and his men followed him. There was no gun fire for the first one hundred yards and until they came upon the barbed wire fence. The Serbs opened fire. Since Stefan was first, he fell on the wire so his comrades could go over him and advance. He looked up to see soldier after soldier fall and when no one else came, he got up and got through the wire. The ground was strewn with dead bodies; he found one with a gas mask and took it. About fifty yards ahead, he fell into a trench used by the Serbs. It was time to regroup for another attack. There would be less barbed wire from now on. They had advanced through three trenches and it was getting dark, so fighting stopped. Patrols were sent out. They would attack in the morning.

The attacks continued for another day with the Slovaks advancing and the Serbs retreating. The following day, the Slovaks were anticipating entry into Belgrade when suddenly they saw the Serbs counter-attacking. Hordes of brown uniforms were coming at them. Stefan ran out of ammunition so he had to retreat into the next trench. He searched every dead body to get as much ammunition as he could and put it into his shirt. They were pushed back at Cer Mountain and Sabac River where the Serbs were preparing for a final assault. After ten days of bitter fighting, the Serbs suddenly pulled back and drew a defense line. By this time, Stefan was a seasoned soldier. He learned how to defend himself and reduce his chances of being hit.

The troops sat in the trenches for two months while reinforcements were brought up and the army was re-supplied. The trenches were so close to each other that the foot soldiers could talk to each other; some even tossed food and cigarettes to each other. Once in a while a hand grenade would follow, but that was a rarity. The patrols were sent out and the periscopes went up, but there was no

Legacy of the Priest

activity until November 5, when another offensive was started by
the Slovaks and Austrians.

The offensive began when the reinforced troops climbed out
of their trenches and by December 2, they occupied Belgrade.
The Serbs, who were also reinforced with supplies from France,
counter attacked and drove the Austrians and Slovaks out of Serbia
and recaptured Belgrade on December 16th. Austrian and Slovak
casualties totaled 227,000 men killed or wounded out of 450,000
troops who took part. The Serbian casualties amounted to 170,000
out of 400,000 troops who took part. Corporal Hadarek was killed
and Stefan was promoted to corporal. He had no one in his origi-
nal squad who was still alive, so he was given six new men to command. Three hundred and ninety seven thousand men were killed
or wounded from August 12, 1914 to December 15, 1914 and
the two armies were still back where they started. The first year of
the war resulted in a stalemate.

Stefan and his unit were sent to Vienna for a rest. He could
write to his mother and receive mail that was waiting for him. The
first thing he did was go to the Slovak post where he found a letter
from his mother. She missed him, but Andrej and Kada were doing a good job and his father had suffered a fall and broken his leg.
Father Josef fixed it and the would be as good as new. Kada and
Andrej were now living with them. They were not leaving until
late in the evening, they had the room, so now they were almost
like part of the family. They mated the two stallions with the five
mares, and they hoped to see some colts in the spring.

Stefan wrote a letter telling his mother that he was in the
Belgrade campaign, but he was not hurt. He told her that Slovaks
are survivors and he will come home as soon as he could but he did
not know where he would be sent. They promoted him to corporal but he did not tell her about the details of battle as he did not
want to alarm her. He held the letter until he could obtain a Mass
card from St. Stephan Cathedral in Vienna so he could send them
both to her. The rest of his leave was spent sightseeing and sleeping in a bed. The highlight was when he went to midnight Mass

at St. Stephan. He was given a little money so he was able to buy some food and drink. Midnight Mass at St. Stephan on Christmas Eve was unbelievable and he would remember it for the rest of his life no matter how short it was. He took advantage of his free time as rumors were flying that they would be going to the front after the first of the year.

Turkey declared war on October 19, 1914 against the Allies and they bombarded the Russian Black Sea coast, closing the supply routes from France and Britain to Russia. Stefan was sent to the Russian front at Bolimov and on January 31, 1915, the German ninth army made up of Germans, Austrians and the Slovak volunteers faked an attack on Warsaw. It then pushed against Bolimov where for the first time poisons gas was used. Stefan had his own squad of eight men and the Germans used the Slovak volunteers on the front lines. The German high command felt that the German troops were better trained and held them in reserve so the Slovaks were sent in at the beginning when the fighting was the most fierce. The Germans would advance over the bodies of the Slovaks to press the attack. The weather was bitter cold and that is what saved the Slovaks from the poison gas. The gas shells were not effective in freezing temperatures. Since they were not effective, no one reported the gas attack.

Stefan realized that this was not the type of fighting they were used to on the Serbian front with the trenches, but they would pursue the retreating Russians through fields and forests. Once in a while they would come to a small town and clear it of Russians. They chased the Russians for seventy miles when suddenly the Russians counter-attacked. Stefan and his men were in the front lines as usual, when the Russians came. They managed to get back to the main army to warn them of the coming Russians so the Germans were able to dig in and stop the Russian advance. By now, Stefan was a seasoned soldier and, although he took orders from them, he considered the Germans arrogant. He came to realize what his role as a Slovak was in the German Ninth Army and that was to do as he was told, report what he saw, but he did not volunteer his men for any missions. His men found food, and casualties were light, for he took care of his people and they took care of him. The ninth army was ordered to keep the Russians occupied just north of Warsaw while the German Eleventh Army made the thrust at the Russians.

This allowed Stefan and his men to rest. They went out on an occasional patrol at night, but their main duty was to find food and to keep warm. Stefan found that he had frostbite and went back to the infirmary where he was kept for a few days and then sent back to his men. Although it appeared insignificant at the time, his feet would bother him in cold weather for the rest of his life. Once in awhile, they received food on the front lines and Stefan rationed it to his men. They were resentful at first, but when other squads went hungry, they at least had food.

Toward the end of March, the days were becoming longer and there were days, now and then, when the sun was warm. The men knew that with the coming of warmer weather, the fighting would renew. On May 2, 1915, they were ordered to attack the Russian Third Army on a twenty-eight-mile front and they broke through. The southern end of the front began to crumble by the end of June. Stefan and his men crossed the Dnestr River where they suspected a gas attack, although none came. Stefan expected the worst at all times and held a drill at unexpected times. Warsaw fell in early August, and by the first of September, they reached Grodno.

When Stefan reached Vilna, he had traveled three hundred miles since the drive began. Stefan wondered when it would stop or when reinforcements would arrive so he and his men could rest. He asked his superiors, but was told only to keep moving forward. To add to his problems, the rains came and the roads turned to of mud. Supplies could not reach them at the front but it was harvest time and Stefan knew how to gather food from the fields. There were soldiers who were reared in the cities and they had to be taught how to survive. Stefan would always look for the fires because the Russians would burn the fields so the enemy could not use them. The German Army stalled and without supplies and freedom of movement, they could not advance. Ammunition was getting dangerously low, but Stefan reasoned that the Russians must have the same problem. He was hoping to be in the rear before the winter threw its full fury at them. He felt that he could not survive another winter on the front and he had to get away from the arrogant German officers who were putting the Slovak troops into the front lines while their soldiers rested. He knew that many more Russians died in this campaign than German, Austrian and Slovak troops put together but what he did not know was that Russian casualties on this front in 1915 were two million men. The combined German, Austrian and Slovak casualties were in excess of one million men. He and his men made it through the campaign with only minor injuries.

The weather turned cold so neither side attacked until the middle of March when the Russians tried to retake Vilna, but it bogged down when the roads turned to a sea of mud in another thaw. The Germans lost about twenty thousand men, while the Russians lost between 70,000 and 90,000 men. The morale on the Russian side was low and they were surrendering in droves. It was better to be a prisoner than to die in the mud of Vilna.

Fearing another Russian attack, the Germans sent reinforcements with fresh supplies. Most Slovak troops were taken off the front lines to rest. Stefan had spent nearly sixteen months on the front lines. They went into a rest area in the rear of the lines where they were given warm food, blankets and new uniforms. They were also given gas masks which were supposed to be a new and improved versions of the old ones. Stefan still had the one that he had taken from a dead soldier when he crawled into a trench in Serbia. They rested for about two weeks when they were notified that the Russians, under General Brusilov, had attacked and had broken through their lines; they were needed at the front.

The men gathered their new equipment, left the rest area and were transported once again to the front where, this time, they were attached to an Austrian unit. The Russians had come through in two different places but the front where the attacks took place was three hundred miles long and both armies were spread thin. The Austrian army was especially battered. Stefan was trying to hold a small hill, when an artillery shell exploded ten feet away. Three of his squad were killed, three others were wounded, and two died enroute to the medical station in the rear lines. The last thing he remembered was asking the two remaining members of his squad to get help. One ran for help while the other one wrapped Stefan's sleep roll around his waist. As he was talking to his comrade, he drifted into unconsciousness.

He woke in an aide station well to the rear of the front lines. A man shouted that Stefan was awake and a young doctor came to talk to him. The man was about twenty-five years old and he had a surgical mask tied around his neck. His hands were covered with blood but he managed a smile and told Stefan that he would recover. Stefan's comrade had carried him on his back to the rear of the lines and left him on a litter that was attached to a truck. He had decided that the truck was going to the rear medical station. Stefan had taken a piece of shrapnel in his mid-section and in order to get it out, the doctor had to cut off a section of his stomach. The doctor told Stefan that he would take a long time to heal. He would rest here for a few weeks but, because of the severe injury, he would be sent to a large hospital for war wounded in Vienna. Stefan thanked God that he was alive, for a few inches higher and the shrapnel would have entered his heart. He would be off the front lines for a long time and the war might be over by the time he healed.

The doctor was correct and within a month he was in a hospital in Vienna. He heard news from the front; it was all bad. The Brusilov offensive almost knocked Austria out of the war and casualties were huge on both sides. His Slovak volunteers were almost wiped out so if he had stayed at the front, he would be dead. The Romanians had entered the war on the side of Russia. He was wounded, but he was fortunate to be alive and, most important, off the firing line. As he was lying in a bed with sheets, being fed and washed clean, a woman walked in with four letters from his mother. He had two letters written, but he had lost them and he suddenly realized that he had not seen a woman for twenty months.

It was now the end of August in 1916 and he had been in this war for two years and two months. He read his mother's letters and they were basically the same except the last one. The Magyars came one day and took all of their animals, including the stallions. They had managed to save a few cows, chickens and sheep that were out in the fields, but they had kept the valuable horses in the barn and they were taken. Andrej and Kada were still with them and his father was showing his age. He got tired very fast and it was a good thing that they had help. They had not been able to pay Andrej or Kada for some time, but they stayed on anyway. They were like her own children and Stefan read the letter with tears in his eyes. If only he could go home to help them.

He wrote his mother a letter and told her of his wounds and he reassured her that he would recover. He was in a hospital and getting excellent care and he had even gained some weight. He did not go into details about the battles he fought because he knew that it would upset her. Since he had plenty of time, he would be able to write to her often and he gave her his address so she might write him. He finished his letter and laid back in his bed with his arms folded behind his head. He was able to bathe and shave, now the meals were good. A man usually came by and he would paint a picture of the soldiers for a small fee. All he wanted was enough money to buy frames and materials. The next time he came, Stefan decided to have his picture painted. He would have to dress in his uniform, but it will be a good present for his mother.

While in the hospital, other men came and went. He was in a large dormitory style room with twenty beds on one side and twenty beds on the other, and the room was almost full. More men were coming than were leaving and the ward would be filled soon. He had his picture painted and it was stored beneath his bed; he had now been in the hospital for six weeks and he was feeling much better. It had been ten weeks since he was wounded, and he did not know how long he could enjoy this life of leisure. Each day a team of doctors and nurses would talk to each patient, they would ask the nurses questions and make notes of the answers. One day a man came to his bed and asked Stefan where he lived. Stefan told him that he lived in Ruzbachy, Slovakia and it was a half day's ride by train from Vienna. The man told him that he could just as well recover at home, because they needed his bed for someone else; he should prepare to leave in two days. When he arrived in Ruzbachy, he should report to the notary and spend thirty days at home. After thirty days he was to report to the camp where he went into the army and he would be reassigned to new duties. Stefan was given train fare to go home and the return trip to Vienna. He immediately telegraphed his mother to have someone meet him in Polodencz.

*   *   **

When he arrived in Polodencz, he found Kada and his mother waiting for him. His mother cried when she saw him and she embraced him so hard that he had to pry her arms from him. When she embraced him, he felt a shooting pain in his abdomen, but he did not let on that he hurt. He looked over and saw Kada a step away, she was small, about five foot two inches and she hardly weighed a hundred pounds. She looked solid as if she could do anything that she wanted, she smiled at him. He walked over, embraced her and whispered a thank you for helping his parents. They rode to Ruzbachy with Olga doing all of the talking. She brought him up to date on everything that had transpired since he had left and she told him that he looked thin but she and Kada would have to fatten him up. When they arrived home, his father embraced him and there were tears in his eyes. He then saw Andrej and thanked him also.

The five of them had a meal, sat around the table and talked for hours. Stefan looked forward to sleeping in his own bed. Stefan had looked at Kada for some time and he knew of her past with the gypsies, but she had turned into an attractive woman. She was now seventeen and would be married soon and he had hoped that she would wait for him to come home from the wars. The next morning he reported to the notary and showed him the papers that the army had given him. The notary made a note of the date that he was due to report to Vienna and made sure that Stefan knew when. Stefan went home and tried to help around the farm, but the stitches had not fully healed in his stomach and he was afraid that he would pull them out. He did help with harvesting the garden and they had brought the few animals that remained into the barn to try to start a new herd. It would take time.

Stefan rode over to see Midti Kostrek who was running the farm belonging to Midti's late father-in-law, Pavel. They had managed to hide a stallion and two mares and he told Midti that if he could buy a mare, would he consider letting him use his stallion. Midtj would allow him to use the stallion at no charge. He did not charge vzajomny (relatives) a fee for the use of his stallion and he also knew of a bull that he could get for a nominal fee. Stefan was pleased with his visit. Olga was happy to see her son return because he knew what to do. Stefan tried to buy a young mare and take her to the Dombrowski farm to be put in with his stallion. He went down to the tavern to see if there was a mare for sale. He did not find a one mare, but the word was out that the Janeks wanted a mare.

Stefan spent a great deal of time with Kada because he liked her. She was small, but determined; she made up her mind very quickly and did not allow anyone to take advantage of her. She had her own opinions, she did not force them on anyone and she never expressed them unless someone asked. He could tell that Olga liked her, but Johan did not. He treated her like the servant girl, which she was and he went out of his way to keep them apart. The closer they became, the more time Johan found to do something with his son.

Once, while he and Kada were in the barn alone, Stefan asked, "Do you have any male friends?"

She said, "No, I have none since I had lived with the gypsies.

They all considered me to be a witch and were afraid of me."

She could see that he was trying to suppress a smile, "If you will wait for me to come home from the war, I would like to court you."

She nodded yes.

The month went by quickly and Stefan was to report to Vienna on November 1. He thought about deserting, hiding in the mountains and living in the caves, but that would make him a hunted man so it was best to get his obligation finished. The day before he was due to report he left, it was a painful and tearful goodbye. When Stefan thought of his life on the farm with Kada, he knew that he would have to be careful for the rest of the war. He had already been wounded and now he had a greater desire to stay at home. He did not know how long the war would continue, but he thought that if he would be captured, he could wait out the rest of the war. He did know that he would not be captured by the Russians because they had no food for their own troops so no one could survive the war in a Russian prison camp. They sent their prisoners to labor camps in Siberia where they either froze to death or starved, but they never came back. Finally, his train pulled into the station in Vienna and he got off to look for a military vehicle.

*   *   *

Unknown to Stefan, such events were happening all over the world that would change his life forever. The United States, though President Wilson, wanted his country to adopt a policy of neutrality but most of the people in Washington sympathized with France and England. Great Britain had begun a blockade of Germany. Germany established a war zone around the British Isle and told the world that their submarines would sink all vessels in the area. The Germans sank the British liner "Arabic" in August of 1915 and President Wilson protested the needless slaughter of civilian lives. The Germans, fearing entry into the war by the United States, on the side of Britain, guaranteed that submarines would not sink passenger liners without warning. Despite this, another liner, the "Sussex" was torpedoed by German submarines and several Americans were killed. Germany then announced that they abandoned the entire submarine campaign.

Great Britain, still seeking to maintain the blockade of German ports, started seizing American vessels and President Wilson threatened to provide armed escorts for all American merchant ships. In 1916, Wilson was reelected. His slogan was "He kept us out of the War." The Germans, in a complete reversal of policy, announced that they were resuming unrestricted submarine warfare and in February of 1917, President Wilson broke off all diplomatic relations with Germany. Germany tried to enlist the aid of Mexico. The pact said that if Mexico went to war against the United States and aligned itself with Germany, then Mexico would receive Texas, New Mexico and Arizona for their efforts against their neighbor. The message was intercepted by British intelligence, decoded and sent to the United States. In April of 1917, the United States Congress approved a war resolution against Germany.

The United States was not prepared for war, but the regular army units of 200,000 men were sent to France in June. The draft law, the Selective Service Act, was passed in May of 1917 to build up the American army and General John J. Pershing was selected to command the American Expeditionary Forces. He planned to send a one-million-man army overseas by May of 1918, with a total of three million men in Europe by a later date.

*   *   *

Stefan was assigned to the Austrian Army on the Italian front and since he was a corporal, he was assigned a squad of eight men. He was part of the new Austrian Fourteenth Army and he spent the next few weeks being retrained, for the fighting was different from that which he did on the Russian Front. He was going to war in mountainous terrain and this meant different gear, warmer clothes, Austrian leadership instead of German leadership and he could speak to his superiors in his own language. The Austrian Fourteenth Army was dug in to defend the city of Isonzo and they were sure that the assault would come from the Italians. It finally came on the 12th of May and after seventeen days, the lines moved back and forth, with the Italians making small gains. The Austrian army lost about 75,000 men in the 17 days of fighting as each army pulled back to lick its wounds. Stefan had come close to death a number of times. In the mountainous terrain, the Italians had heavy guns on the higher ground so they rained shells down on the Austrians before each assault. Stefan had learned from his experience, because of the shelling that had wounded him. He sought shelter until the assault arrived. He fought bravely but he came face to face with an Italian soldier and both stared at the other in disbelief, before either of them could make a move, one of Stefan's men shot the Italian dead. Stefan fell to the ground as a heavy rifle fire came from a tuft of trees. He crawled back to his lines, thankful that he was alive.

In the middle of August, the Italians decided to make an all-out assault which was to be called the eleventh battle of the Isontio. They came with a vastly superior force and forced the Austrians back to the Bainsizza Plateau. The Austrian army was about to collapse and they asked the Germans for help. With their aid, the Austrians moved the Italians moved back to the Livenza River. This time, the Italians asked the French and British for reinforcements and the Austrian's advance ground to a halt.

Stefan was happy for the rest and because none of his men had been killed or seriously wounded. He liked all the men of his squad and they, in turn, trusted their corporal. He treated everyone alike, got them food, and took care of them, so they did not want to lose Stefan. Nor did he want want to lose the trust they had in him. He would eat what they ate, go on patrols with them and even assumed some of the dangerous assignments himself. The Sargeant sent his squad on patrol across the lines to determine if there was any activity on the other side. He left with three of his men and, under cover of darkness, they went from tree to tree to get to high ground; they would have to look on the enemy encampment to complete their mission. The Italians would set traps and sometimes mines, so they had to be careful. They avoided all the sentries and were going up a small knoll when they spotted a small building. It was made from logs and it looked to be a hunting lodge used in better times. They could use the building for shelter and they had a view of the enemy camp. They slowly made their way to the building and there was no moon so the only light came from the stars. Stefan posted two men as guards and he and the remaining soldier approached the building and went in. Suddenly a light came on and they were confronted with four rifles aimed at their heads. A minute later, the two members of his squad, posted as sentries, entered the building at gun point. The four were now prisoners of war.

They were taken down the other side of the mountain and taken to a tent. All of the equipment that they carried was taken away but they were allowed to keep their warm coats since it was very cold in the mountains. Stefan was separated from his men. Since he was in command of the squad, he was interrogated. Once he got into a lighted tent, he tried to see who captured him, but his captors did not wear British, French or Italian uniforms and he did not recognize them. They spoke English, but it was somehow different. He had learned a few words of English, but he could not understand this language. One of the officers spoke to him and he gave his name, rank and number as he was instructed to do. They spoke to him in French but he shook his head indicating that he did not understand. They tried German, but Stefan was not German and he was not going to admit that he spoke the language.

The man pointed to himself and said, "I am American."

Stefan pointed to himself and said, "Ja Slovensky."

One man looked at the other and asked what a "Slovensky" was and the other said that he was Slovak. It was part of the Austrian Hungary Empire, but he did not know that the Austrians had Slovaks in their army. They decided to find an interpreter when an Italian officer came into the tent and demanded the prisoner. Stefan did not want to be turned over to the Italians for it meant physical harm and he had heard that the Italians were just as hard on their prisoners as the Russians. After a brief argument, the Italian left and Stefan did not know what to expect next. It appeared that his captors were going to wait for someone who could understand Stefan to come in. As they waited, a young man came in with a tray, a pot, two cups and some milk and sugar. The man was sent out only to return with another cup. Three cups were poured and one of the men handed a cup to Stefan. They poured some milk and sugar in theirs and Stefan did the same. It was hot, strong coffee and it was good, but he might have put a little too much sugar. Stefan looked at the two men, even though he was a prisoner of war, they treated him with courtesy. They did not beat him or force him to lie on the ground. This was Stefan's first impression of Americans and it was favorable. He now knew why his four brothers and a sister had gone to America.

He was kept separated from his men. They had already gone to the rear and for them the war was over. Stefan was taken to a building and they locked him in. A guard was posted out front but Stefan sensed that it was more to keep the Italians out rather than to keep him in. He slept on a cot, was awakened at sunrise and a tray of food was brought in with boiled eggs, ham, burnt bread with butter, and more coffee. Stefan thought that these Americans ate very well but the surprising thing was that he ate the same food that they did. The Italians would have starved him until he told them everything he knew. They hated the Germans and to them, Stefan was a German. He sat in his locked room for half the morning and because it had no windows, he could not see what was happening outside. He heard loud voices in Italian and the same English that he had heard on the first day. A young American soldier came in, followed by another who stood guard by the door with a gun. They told Stefan to step to the corner of the room while the young soldier retrieved the tray. Once they left, he sat to wait for their next move.

About midday, the door opened again and the officer that he

had met the night before came in with another American. The other soldier spoke excellent Slovak. His name was Jan Oberek, who came from Roznava down near the Hungarian border. He told Stefan that he went to America with his mother when he was ten years old. He and his parents had become American citizens and he had been drafted into the army only six months before. Stefan was most happy to see another Slovak so he might be able to tell his story. He had been drafted by the other side to fight in a war that he knew nothing about, he was just doing what he was told. They both settled down for a long talk. More food came and they talked while they ate.

Jan told him, "There are only a few Americans in Italy and you have been fortunate to be captured by us instead of the Italians. The Americans were special troops experienced in mountainous terrain and most of us came from a place in America, called Colorado. There were many mountains there and we volunteered to come to the Alps. We have not been in any battles, but we are used mainly for intelligence gathering. That is what we were doing in the mountain cabin, we were spying on the Austrian troops. We are attached to the Italian Army but we take our orders from General Pershing who was in France and this was the reason you were not turned over to the Italians. Your men are going to be transported south in a few days and they will be treated as any other prisoners of war."

After his talk, Jan settled back and told Stefan to tell him about himself. Stefan felt at ease with this young man and he had a kinship toward him since he was a little younger than his brother Josef. He tried to make sense out of this war and it could have been Josef sitting across from him. He could not figure out what could be so important, that they made a brother fight a brother. He reported, "My home is in a small hamlet of Ruzbachy. My brothers and sister are in America and my mother and my father are trying to survive when all their livestock was taken away from them. I fought in the campaigns in Poland and the Baltic. I was wounded and went home briefly to get better. I was assigned to the Italian front recently and had fought in the great battle to gain control of the Bainsizza plain. Then we were reinforced with German troops and artillery and we beat the Italians back. The Germans use the Slovak troops in the front lines and when there was a lull in the fighting, they would send in the German troops. I do not know how many soldiers were fighting or what the makeup of the armies are, for the Germans never took the Austrian or Slovak troops into their confidence. I had been on an intelligence gathering mission when I was captured. If my men arrived at the hunting cabin first then we would have been there to capture the Americans."

They talked about Slovakia and America for hours and Stefan was getting more information than he was giving. He let Jan talk all that he wanted, it was apparent that Jan was not an experienced interrogator. Stefan had to convince the American that he did not know anything and he was just a foot soldier. Finally, Jan got up and walked around the room. He told Stefan that he would leave, but would return in the morning. He opened the door and Stefan saw that it was dark outside. He thought that they must be in a valley with mountains around them because it got dark very early in the valleys of the Alps. He did not tell Jan that the reason he was chosen to go on this patrol was because he grew up in the High Tatras and he knew how to survive in the mountains. Once Jan left, another American came in with a tray of food and Stefan thought that he must be crazy to consider escaping from this to go back to the fighting. He would convince Jan that he was no threat and reasoned they would send him south where it was warmer. The food was good and he did not have to place himself in danger. Unless his situation changed drastically, the war was over for him, he just might come out of this alive.

He slept well that night even though it had turned very cold. He had to call the guard twice so he could relieve himself outside but he had no trouble with that. He wished that he had some water to wash himself because he was beginning to smell. He would talk to Jan in the morning. He settled back in his cot and dozed off thinking of Kada and the farm.

The next morning, Jan and the officer he had met the first night, entered the room. Stefan talked to Jan, who spoke with the officer, who then spoke to Jan in American. By listening to the officer speak and the translation made by Jan, Stefan was beginning to pick up a few words of English. The officer's name was Captain Louis Mitchell and he was from Denver, Colorado. He told Stefan through Jan that the Italians wanted to interrogate him, but he was not bound to allow them to do so. He had passed on the information that he had received from Jan and he was going to send Stefan to a prisoner of war camp far to the south. There were some Slovaks there so it would not be too bad and he would be fed three times a day by the Americans and not the Italians. Part of the camp was partitioned off for the American prisoners and part for those captured by the Italians and he would leave either the next day or the day after. He left the room and allowed Jan to stay and talk.

The trip through the mountain passes was difficult since there was a shortage of wagons. Each wagon was overloaded. The prisoners were mostly Austrians with a very few Slovaks. He looked at every face, but did not see any of his men. They were in the foot hills of the Alps after two days and traveled two more before they came to a row of buildings surrounded by barbed wire. There was a smaller compound also with barbed wire and across a field he saw another row of buildings. This must be the command post for the camp, he thought. He could see barns and stables behind the row of buildings across the field and he saw a circular fence with horses running loose. The prisoners of the Italians were taken to the large complex while the American prisoners were taken to the smaller one. He looked to see if his men were taken there but they must have been taken to another camp, for he saw no one he recognized. The American camp held about fifty men while the Italian camp held over two hundred. The Italian camp had two rows of barbed wire fence with a space of about eight feet in between and through this space, large black dogs roamed. The American camp had only one fence of wire but there were towers on each corner of the camp where guards sat with powerful lights.

Stefan could not understand why anyone would want to escape from the American camp but he had not lived there yet. The routine was a simple one. They woke at dawn each day and lined up outside of their building. They were counted and then dismissed back into the buildings. The man who ran the camp was Captain Alton Bush and he was regular army; he chose to make the army his career. He had charged up St. Juan Hill with Theodore Roosevelt's Rough Riders so he had seen combat. He wanted to command a company of first line troops, but they assigned him to run the prison camp. He had hoped to see action before the war ended because that is what a soldier does. The camp ran smoothly. Each prisoner picked up a tray and food was put on it three times a day. On Sundays, they got either beef, chicken or pork. After the meal, they would all line up in front of their buildings and do exercises and they were free to either volunteer for a work program or spend the time in the barracks.

Once lunch was over, they exercised some more and the same routine followed in the afternoon until the evening meal. They were free to do what they wished until nine pm when the lights were shut off and everyone went to bed. The food was good compared to the way they ate on the front lines. The morning meal consisted of a boiled cereal with milk, bread and coffee; at noon, they received cheese, bread, fruit and coffee; at dinner they had a bowl of soup made out of vegetables and pasta, bread, fruit and coffee. The big problem for Stefan was boredom for he did not have anything to do. The Red Cross came once a month and they brought books, mail and magazines, but none was in Slovak. Stefan, who could read a little German, would not take any German books on principle. If they could not provide Slovak books, then he would read nothing at all. The American camp did not associate with the Italian camp at all because the captain did not get along with the Italian commander so each ran his own camp in his own way.

One day, the captain asked for volunteers to rake the debris in the center of the track that ran along the fence. This was used to exercise the horses and since he was a cavalry officer, he had brought four horses over with him. He would ride one around the track every day, rain or shine but he did not leave the camp to ride in the countryside as he did not want an Italian to mistake him for a German or Austrian and shoot him. Stefan volunteered for the cleanup duty just for something to do and he was raking the clumps of grass when a private came out pulling a horse. Apparently the horse was not used to the soldier and was being difficult. Stefan raked closer to the horse so that he could see him. He had not been this close to a horse since he left Ruzbachy. The soldier was pulling the horse and the horse was rearing backwards and since it was a large Arabian stallion, the man could not hold him. He had a riding crop in his hand and once in a while he would strike the horse just above the front legs. Stefan watched this for a while and as he drew closer, he saw that the bridle was too tight. He caught the soldier's attention and pointed to the bridle and made a fist to show that it was too tight. The soldier took this to mean that Stefan was going to harm him and hit him with the riding crop across the head. Stefan took the handle of the rake, shoved it between his legs and moved it so that the soldier lost his balance and fell to the ground. He took the crop away and looked up to see the captain running toward him. He handed the commander the riding crop, went to the horse, loosened the bridle, spoke to him softly and stroked his neck and the horse calmed down immediately. He asked Stefan's name and told the soldier to get up. By that time, there were four other soldiers there. The captain told one of the men to escort Stefan to his building and lead the horse to the stables.

Once in the barracks, Stefan thought that he was in deep trouble and he kept waiting for the axe to fall. Nothing was said to him, so he followed his routine but the next afternoon, after exercises, a soldier came to take him to see the captain. As he walked to the headquarters building, he felt as he had before he went into battle; he was sharp and noticed everything around him. He wondered what his punishment would be for knocking the soldier down and he was told to wait outside of a railing while the soldier knocked on the door and went in. He came out a few minutes later and escorted Stefan into his office where another man was sitting. He was not an officer, but he acted as if he was in charge. The man introduced himself as Sargeant Malik and said that his parents came from Slovakia. He spoke Slovak, but not very well and his speech was interjected with words that Stefan did not recognize. They did talk and after a while it became easier.

Captain Bush spoke through a Sargeant Malik, "Why did you knock the private to the ground?"

Stefan replied, "The man hit me with his riding crop when I told him that the bridle was too tight. I only wanted him to stop hitting me and the horse."

The Sargeant relayed the message in English and Stefan went on, "Such a beautiful animal should be treated with kindness because he would respond to that quicker. The horse is not stupid."

He waited until this was relayed to the captain and waited for the answer.

After the captain and the Sargeant talked a while, the Sargeant asked, "Do you know anything about horses?"

Stefan smiled and said, "I grew up with horses."

The captain said through Sargeant Malik, "This horse has been giving me trouble ever since I brought him over. Can you train him?"

Stefan said, "All this horse needs is a friend and I could train him to be gentle."

The captain said, "You have the job. Sargeant Malik will work with you. You will start tomorrow after exercises."

As he was taken back to his barracks, Stefan could not believe his good fortune. He was captured by the Americans, fed very well and now he was going to do work that he loved. He could not sleep that night as he planned his training program for the horse. He would feed him, reward him and befriend him. He got up early, ate his food, exercised as fast as he could and showed some impatience in getting to work. The first thing he had to do was to gain the horse's friendship and confidence. Sargeant Malik had told him that the horse's name was "Blaze." Stefan did not understand what the name meant, but he told him that it meant "fire", Stefan understood.

Stefan took the horse to the circular track, walked him for half an hour as he talked to the horse in low tones. When he brought him back to the stable, he gave him some water and bits of carrots that he had gotten from the cook and broken into little pieces. He kept these in his pocket so the horse could smell them and know a reward was waiting for him. After the drink and carrots, Stefan washed him down and brushed him for an hour while talking to him. Blaze appeared to be skittish at first but the brushing made him feel good and he quieted down. It would take some time to bring this horse under control, but Stefan was in no hurry. He was here for the duration of the war, and he might as well make the best of it. He would bring the horse around very slowly.

Stefan noticed that no matter what he did, Sergeant Malik was not too far way and watched him carefully. This reminded Stefan that he was still a prisoner of war and he would have to be very careful not to overstep his bounds. He stayed with the horse every chance that he could and once in a while, his guard would bring him some food so he would not have to go back to the area where the prisoners ate. He always included some food that Stefan could give to Blaze as a reward. Stefan went to bed late and rose early to be with his companion and soon Blaze became his life. He did not want to put a saddle on him too early, because this would destroy all the work that he had put in with the horse. He decided to give it more time since Sargeant Malik had told him that this was an unusual horse. He had destroyed his stall on the boat coming over and he told Stefan to be careful. Stefan felt that he understood the horse. He suspected that someone, at another time, had tried to break the horse's spirit and failed.

About a month after Stefan had started training Blaze, Captain Bush came into the stable to see Stefan and the horse. He saw progress with the horse and asked when Stefan had planned to put a saddle on him. Stefan, who was learning a few words in English, told him that he was almost ready but it would be just a little longer. Captain Bush assumed that he had the patience to work with the animal. Stefan felt that the longer he took to train Blaze, the longer he could stay away from the prison population and the longer he could stay with the animal. The captain told him that there were many more German and Austrian troops surrendering and there was a shortage of beds in the dormitory so he asked Stefan if he minded staying in the stable with his horse. Stefan thought that his captor could have ordered him to stay in the stable, but rather asked if he "minded" staying in the stable. He wondered what kind of people that these Americans were, they treated everyone the same. That country might be a good place to live.

The weeks turned into months and Stefan had been riding Blaze for some time. The horse was intelligent and responded very quickly to commands and he was exceptionally strong and fast. Captain Bush was pleased and had told some of his officers who owned horses about Stefan. He was now training three horses in the stables but his favorite was Blaze. They had developed a kinship for each other and seemed to anticipate each other's wants. Stefan no longer went to the exercise programs with the rest of the population and he found that life in the stable had its own rewards. Sargeant Malik no longer shadowed his every move. There was no reason for him to try to escape and go back to the front.

Sargeant Malik was keeping him up to date on the progress of the war. There had been a revolution in Russia in March and Tsar Nicholas had been abdicated and was replaced by the government of the new Russian Republic. The government was unstable, even though they vowed to continue the war against Germany. Many felt that it was just a matter of time before Russia gave up the war since the Russian troops were demoralized and surrendering in droves. In December, Russia signed a truce and all fighting stopped on the Eastern Front. There was heavy fighting on the Western

front where American troops joined British and French forces, they
were fighting the Germans who were virtually on their own. The
Americans in the war had proved to make the diffence and fresh
troops from America had battled tired German troops. The American President had established fourteen conditions for the surren-
der of the German forces and the collapse of the once mighty German war machine was slowly becoming a reality.

Stefan listened to the accounts of the progress of the war. He
had to hold out for just a little while longer before he could go
home. Each day that went by, the Americans appeared to be more
lax. Sargeant Malik was spending more time in the stables talking
about America, where he had a woman that he intended to marry
once he got back home. He wanted to leave the army and settle
down to a life on a farm, raise children and animals. He had learned
quite a bit by watching Stefan working with Blaze and he thanked
him for the training. He told Stefan that if he ever came to America
and needed work, he should go to Colorado where he could easily
find work training horses. There were not many Slovaks in Colorado, but who could tell what the future would bring? Stefan was
wary about getting too close to the Sargeant for he still did not
understand the Americans. What he did not understand, he stayed
away from. Rumors were flying about the end of the war. Some
said the end of the war was only a few days away; others said that
it had already ended. Stefan awaited official word that he could go
home since the prisoners were still prisoners until they were re-
leased by the Americans. There were celebrations in the little Italian towns in the area, but nothing official came through Captain
Bush. He still kept strict control over his prison camp while the
Italian prison camp became lax. There were rumors that an uprising would take place there and some of the more hated guards
would be punished by the prisoners, but as far as Stefan could see,
no such uprising occurred. Stefan was patient and waited for the
official word.

In the middle of November in 1918, the entire prison population was called into the compound and Captain Bush mounted

a platform to speak to the prisoners. He told them that Germany had agreed to President Wilson's fourteen points and an armistice was signed on November 11, 1918. Hostilities had ended on the Italian Front on November 4, 1918. World War I was over. The captain was given no provisions for helping the prisoners reach their homes, but the following morning at six am, the doors of the prison would open and they were free to go home. He had given orders to his men that if they were attacked, they could defend themselves by force. There was a loud cheer from the Italian camp and it was assumed that they had received word also. There was none of the wild cheering in the American camp for the prisoners felt that they were treated fairly, there was food and the guards were just doing their jobs. The guards were looking forward to going home just like the prisoners. Stefan thought that this was a strange war, brother fighting against brother and his best friend now was Sergeant Malik who invited him to his home.

He went back to the stable and started to collect what belongings he had but he had no idea how he was going to get home. It meant a long walk through mountain passes, through hostile territory and he had no money for trains or other transportation. He was going over his options when he smelled smoke. He jumped up and ran to the other side of the stable. The horses were jumping and neighing because of a fire in the straw in an empty stall. It had started to burn the wood. Realising that he could not put it out by himself, he ran to each stall, opened the doors and started to release the horses. By the time he reached Blaze at the end stall, the smoke was black and he could not breathe, but he got the horse out. They all gathered in the center of the training track. Stefan was coughing, his eyes burned and he could not catch his breath. He was aware of someone dousing him with water. His uniform was burnt and smoking. Someone had thrown a blanket around him, knocked him to the ground and was rolling him, in the blanket, on the ground. He looked up to see Sargeant Malik puting out the fire on his clothing. He noticed people running around and passing buckets to each other trying to put out the fire in the stables. They managed to contain the fire and Stefan had gotten up to help but Captain Bush told him to sit; all the horses were safe thanks to him. Stefan was relieved to hear that none of the animals were harmed.

He was then taken to the Captain's home where the doctor treated his burns. He was told that the dressing would have to be changed daily so infection would not set in; Stefan did not realize that he was burned so badly. Once the doctor left, Captain Bush and his wife entered the room.

Captain Bush said, "The fire was caused by two American soldiers who had gone into the empty stall to celebrate. They had hidden a bottle of whiskey there, and while they were drinking one of the soldiers dropped a cigarette in the straw. Before they knew it, the straw was on fire, they panicked and ran away. It was a good thing that you were there to get the horses out or we would have lost fourteen animals. I am grateful to you for getting the horses out. Mrs. Bush and I want you to stay in our home until you are fit enough to travel. Mrs. Bush wants to take care of you herself because she is a trained nurse and worked in a large hospital in Denver. You have Sargeant Malik to thank for containing the fire on your body. Without his quick thinking, you would have been burned badly and would have had to go to an Italian hospital. This would have delayed your going home by some months."

Once more, Stefan was laid up with injuries because he did not think of the danger; his only thought was to release the horses. He loved the animals too much to see them perish in a fire and as it was, Blaze suffered some superficial burns but he would heal.

Stefan asked the captain, "May I see Blaze to be sure that he is fine?" There were tears in his eyes when he asked.

Captain Bush and his wife helped Stefan to the window and Sergeant Malik led Blaze past the window so that Stefan could see for himself. The horse seemed to sense that Stefan was looking at him and he put his head down and snorted as if to thank him for saving his life. This did not go unnoticed by the captain and his wife, who saw the mutual love between Stefan and the horse. After he was laid back in his bed, Stefan felt relieved that the horse was indeed all right and now he could sleep.

The camp emptied out quickly with some of the prisoners fleeing the following day before someone changed his mind. Others stayed a little longer to gather their possessions. The camp looked deserted except for the Americans waiting to be reassigned. Captain Bush would be the last to leave since he would formally turn the camp over to the Italian Commandant of the other camp. It would be sometime before that happened because both commandants had to await orders from their headquarters. First, however, the material would have to be packed, shipped to America and arrangements made for the animals to be shipped. By that time, Stefan would be able to travel.

Sargeant Malik came to his room every day to visit. He helped Mrs. Bush take care of Stefan when the captain was away but the days passed slowly. There was nothing to do accept to wait for their visits. They spoke for hours on life in America and Slovakia and the Sargeant could not get enough of the information about his homeland. One day when Sargeant Malik came to visit, he brought Stefan some clothes.

Stefan said, "the doctor has given me permission to go outside so I can finally get a chance to touch my friend, Blaze."

Sargeant Malik helped him get dressed, put him in a wheelchair that was borrowed from an Italian clinic in town, and wheeled Stefan out doors. He took him to the fence around the track where Blaze was held and as he approached the horse, the horse reared on his hind legs, trotted over to Stefan and lowered his head into Stefan's lap. Stefan talked to the horse in low tones and the horse responded by snorting. Looking from the second story window, Captain Bush with his arm around his wife's waist, watched the event taking place at the fence. They looked at each other and smiled. This man had made a bond with the horse that was not meant to be broken.

Stefan met with the horse every day. He brought treats and the horse responded. When he could stand, Stefan asked for a brush. He groomed the horse, using Blaze as a brace so he would not fall down. He was using the muscles in his legs now more often and he was getting stronger. Soon, he would have to leave and would never see the horse again; he tried not to think about the time when he would have to say goodbye. That day would come soon enough without his having to think about it. He brushed the horse and talked, the horse seemed to understand every word that was said. He told Blaze that he would be leaving soon and they probably would never see each other again. Blaze would have to remember his training and treat his master well. He would have to go back to America by boat, but he would be well fed and would have the best of care. Each time Stefan left the horse, he wondered if this would be the last time they saw each other.

Finally, the day came to leave when the Americans received their orders and prepared to leave within days. Wagons were packed with furniture, hay for the horses, personal belongings and all of the other military equipment. There were no heavy weapons, only side arms and rifles and a few machine guns. Everyone was excited to be going home. Stefan had few things to pack because most of his meager personal belongings were destroyed in the fire. He was ready to leave anytime and he picked a Saturday so he could go to church in town. He had not been in church for 18 months and he had to thank God for all of his guidance and good fortune. He planned to leave at noon but when the time came, all of the Americans lined up to bid him goodbye. Mrs. Bush had given him a new set of clothes and some food for the trip. Sargeant Malik had given him his address in America, one of his blankets, a cooking pot and eating utensils. He said that the American government would never miss them. Suddenly from behind the line, a soldier led Blaze up front and the horse had a large American saddle and polished bridle. He stopped right in front of Stefan. He looked around at the captain and his wife; both were smiling.

Captain Bush looked at the young Slovak and said, "Stefan, Mrs. Bush and I would like you to have Blaze as a gift from all of us."

Tears burst from Stefan's eyes, "I do not know what to say except thank you."

Mrs. Bush stepped forward and embraced him. She pulled him close to her as she said, "It is we who should thank you. You risked your life for this animal and he should be with you. No one will ever take your place with him because he was yours from the minute you saw each other. God bless you, Stefan."

Sargeant Malik helped him up into the saddle as everyone clapped. This was the most wonderful day in his life. Each one shook his hand and said a few words. While he could not understand all that was said to him, he was grateful. Captain Bush reached into his pocket and took out an oil skin pouch. He told Stefan that the pouch contained papers that showed the horse now belonged to him and it also gave the blood line of the horse for breeding purposes. Stefan took the pouch, shook the captain's hand and rode toward the town. He did not turn around because he was crying and did not want the Americans to see a Slovak weep. He raised his eyes to heaven and gave his thanks. He was finally going home.

He came upon a little town by nightfall. He had planned to stop at the little village near the camp but because he was on horseback, he could travel faster. In Italy, it was reasonably warm but he knew that he would have to travel through the passes in the Alps, near Christmas when the weather would be cold. He remembered the story of his grandmother who gave birth to his mother in the Abbey of St. Francis. If she could travel over the mountains, so could he since they came from the same stock. Stefan went to church that morning, not understanding Latin or Italian, but he was sure that he had spoken with God. He spent the daylight hours traveling and the night hours sleeping. When he finished the food that Mrs. Bush had put in his sack, there was something in the bottom. She had put in an envelope with some lira in it. He had no idea how to count lira or how much they were worth so he hid it in the bottom of his saddle bag and pushed on.

The road was getting steeper and he was getting into the foothills of the Alps. The sun was setting so he stopped at farm houses to ask if he could sleep in the barn. He was never denied, and occasionally, people gave him some food. He still had all of the liras because he knew that his parents would need money. He could convert them into crowns, when he was home. The road climbed, going higher and higher; it was getting colder and there was snow on the ground. Everywhere he went, people looked at his horse and he had a few offers to sell him, but there was no chance of that happening. Once he met a gypsy caravan and was allowed to sleep under a wagon after he pushed the snow away. He could tell which roads were the best through the Alps by the usage that they received and he always took the well-traveled routes. The travelers in this country would know what the best routes were, so he would follow their example.

Finally, on a cold, windy, snowy day, he started down the mountain. Blaze was tolerating the trip very well for it was much easier going down than it was going up and they made better time. As he went through a small village, he remembered it when he was traveling south and he felt that he must be on the right road. The people on this side of the mountain spoke German and he told everyone that he was captured by the Italians, spent time in a prison camp and he was trying to get home by Christmas. He had some scars from his burns so he used them to get sympathy. The people did not have much in the way of food, but they still shared with a soldier who was wounded. He was given bread and milk but the last time that he tasted meat was in the prison camp. He had lost weight and his eyes had sunk back in the sockets, but he kept moving. He finally got to Vienna, went through it in one day and crossed the bridge into Bratislava. He was on Slovak soil and this gave him added strength as he went through the city. He could finally speak to someone in his own language.

He stayed in a barn that night without asking since he did not want to wake anyone up. The next morning, he awoke to the slight prick of a pitch fork against his neck. He looked up to see a huge man with a black beard and a stocking hat pulled over his ears. He looked even bigger with the heavy clothes he had on. The man said nothing, he was waiting for an explanation.

Stefan told him in Slovak, "I am a soldier returning from the war in Italy and I did not want to wake up anyone to ask permission. It was late and I had to find a place to spend the night. I mean you no harm and all I want is to be on my way to see my family before the birth of the Christ child."

The man relaxed his grip. He could see that Stefan did not present any danger so he took the fork away, saying, "Get up so I can see you."

Stefan came up to the man's shoulders and the man looked him up and down, he smiled. "Where are you heading and how long have you been on the road?"

Stefan said, "I am from a little town in the foothills of the High Tatras called Ruzbachy and I have been traveling for ten days so that I could be home for Christmas. My mother does not know if I am dead or alive and I want her to have a joyous holiday."

The man put the pitchfork away; "My name is Petra Kobeck. You are welcome in our home. Please come meet my Pani."

Petra's wife was almost as large as her husband and she had huge breasts that rose and fell as she said, "we have lost a son in the war and we are happy that you will be able to be with your mother and father for Christmas. Sit, my son and I will feed you for you are nothing but flesh and bones. We do not have much but we will share what we have."

A huge bowl of oatmeal was placed before him. He was given bread, butter and milk, and he told them his story while he ate. After he ate all that he could, he stopped, for his stomach had shrunk from the lack of food and it was easy to fill. Pani Kobeck gave him a sack with bread and butter for Stefan to take with him.

Stefan asked, "Before I leave, may I feed my horse?"

Petra said, "That has already had been done. I have sent my son to the barn to feed the animal. I know that a true Slovak would be worried about his horse and such a beautiful animal he is."

As Stefan rode away, he sighed, he was finally in Slovakia and had spoken to a Slovak. He rode a little faster as Christmas was only two days away. It looked like it was going to snow, he slept in a barn that night and ate the bread and butter the woman had given him. The next morning, at first light, he continued north, it had started to snow during the night and was still snowing, but he put his blanket over his head and trudged forward. He could hardly see, relying on Blaze to follow the road. At about five in the afternoon, he passed through Polodencz, and it was still snowing. It was dark now, but he knew the road. At about nine o'clock he crossed over the Poprad River and headed for the Janek farm and home. He saw the house with the candles burning on Christmas Eve, went to the kitchen and looked in. His mother and father were sitting at the table saying the rosary. He took a deep breath before he rapped on the door.

His mother got up, opened the door and cried, "Stefan." She turned to her husband and sobbed, "Johan, our youngest has returned home from the war! He is here!"

18

The first thing that Stefan did, after he embraced his mother and father, was to take care of his horse. Blaze had saved his life by his constant movement toward home in the blizzard. Stefan could have waited out the storm and continued after it blew itself out but he wanted to be home on Christmas Eve. He took Blaze to the stable, fed him oats and water, then brushed him until he had a high shine, talking to his horse constantly in his low voice. The horse seemed to know what his friend was saying because they had built a bond a long time ago. Johan sat on an overturned bucket and listened to his son and his horse and he saw all the years of training put to use. He was proud of his son, he had gone through four years of war and came home with his body intact. He had all of his senses, both arms and legs because Johan had seen other men coming home from the war with various disabilities who could not support themselves. The tavern was full of these men every afternoon.

Johan and his son went into the house, each carring an arm full of wood. There was much to discuss and it would be a long night. Stefan was chilled to the bone, but his mother had hot food waiting for him. She had a pot of pea soup with pieces of ham in it along with a loaf of bread she had baked that morning. This was left over from the Christmas Eve dinner that they ate at noon. They were alone because Kada and Andrej had gone to spend Christmas with their mother who was now alone. Johan had wanted to go to the abbey for the traditional Christmas Eve celebration, but the snow had stopped them. They decided to stay home and pray for Stefan's safe return. Stefan ate one bowl of soup and some bread.

His mother looked disappointed. "Eat some more, you look starved."

"I cannot eat more. My stomach is smaller now because of my wound and I have not had much to eat in the last ten days. I will have more a bit later, but for right now, I just want to be warm and look at you."

Johan asked, "Where did you get that magnificent horse?"

Stefan started his story from the time that he left home eighteen months before and reported for active duty in Vienna. He had been sent to the Italian Front with the Austrian Army and was captured by the American Alpine troops. He described his life in the prison camp, the fire in the stable and especially how he had worked with Blaze for the last year.

Johan asked, "What does Blaze mean?"

Stefan replied, "It is an American word that means fire. I was fortunate to be captured by the Americans. The Italians would have shot me so they would not have to transport me back. I had heard of such stories in the prison camp. We ate what the Americans ate and I was treated as a human being should. I had a good place to sleep, and they allowed me to work with the horses so I had so much time with the stallion. I realized that the horse would not respond to anyone else, but I never thought that Captain Bush would give me the animal."

He showed Johan and Olga the papers that Captain Bush had given him. They were in English so he did not understand them, but he would take them to the school in the abbey to be translated. He showed them the lira that he had not spent and they could convert them into crowns to be used when needed. Stefan got up and put some wood on the fire while Olga got him another bowl of soup.

"We will fatten you up now that you are home."

As he ate his soup, Stefan heard the news from the town. Johan had tears in his eyes, saying, "The Magyars came and took all the men to fight in the war. They took all the livestock and much of the food last fall. Olga had managed to hide some for our use, but there might not be enough to last the winter. The abbey had some food and was giving it out to those who needed it. The celebration this year was subdued because of the lack of food. This has been a somber Christmas."

Olga went on, "Most of your friends never came back and there are not enough men left to do the planting in the spring. I saved enough seeds to start the planting and there were seed potatoes that I had put into the root cellar. We will not eat these potatoes unless we are in danger of starving during the cold, hard winter."

"I am happy that I have come home when I did because the stallion may be our salvation," Stefan said. "We can charge a good fee for stud service and we will receive it because only a few stallions are left in the area with good blood lines. Blaze will demand good money. When word gets out that he is available, the farmers will beat a path to our door." They finally decided to go to bed because Stefan had been through a hard ordeal and Olga wanted to go to church as a family.

The next morning, Olga got up early, baked a low, flat bread with sauerkraut on it, and she made a cream sauce from animal fat and flour to put on it. She made another bread with raisins as she had a small amount of butter which she had saved for Christmas. Her yeast was running low, but when the lira was changed into crowns, she could buy more in town. They ate their morning meal and for the first time in eighteen months there was laughter in the Janek kitchen, Stefan looked forward to going to church with his mother and father.

The church was full when they arrived, but they found three seats together near the front. Stefan rode his horse to church while Olga and Johan drove the small wagon. All heads turned as Stefan walked down the aisle, but he was looking for Kada who was not there. He thought that she must have gone to the midnight mass. Before the mass had begun, Stefan looked around to see if there was anyone his age there. There were many women, but very few men. He saw a few that had only one arm and saw some with a leg missing, they were supported by wooden crutches. There was no joy in the church this day, for all of the people were thinking of their own problems and how they were going to survive the winter. Stefan was at peace during the Mass and his mother and father looked pleased. Everyone had their finest clothes on and the few children who were there. They looked scrubbed and neat. There were three priests saying Mass and they all seemed older than their years. Father Andrej, the youngest, was the pastor of St. Stefan, with Fathers Igor and Josef assisting.

He went up to communion with his parents and while he was kneeling at the altar to receive the Host, he raised his eyes to Heaven and said, "Thank you God for allowing me to return to my parents and to my beloved town of Ruzbachy."

The priests were all lined up to greet the people as they left the church. They had noticed Stefan and they wanted to greet him. The more people he saw, the more chances there would be that Kada would find out that he was back. Father Igor left the reception line when he saw the large horse tied to the Janek wagon and examined the horse very carefully.

Stefan came over,

"How do you like my horse? I have papers to prove the blood line. We have been through a difficult time together and I would like to have the horse examined some time."

Father Igor said, "I will make it a point to stop in since there are so few animals left in the area."

It was a short ride to the Janek farm. When they left the church, Stefan thought that it would be good to take some time and rest, but it was not to be. There was a steady flow of people moving in and out of the Janek home and a Slovak never visits without bringing something. They brought food, clothing for Stefan, and crafts that were homemade. Everyone greeted Stefan with an embrace and a kiss on both cheeks and he was getting tired of all the fuss made over him. He wished that he could just sit in front of the fire, with a cup of tea. Toward late afternooon, he looked up to see that Kada and Andrej had arrived and she came to him and embraced him. He got a kiss on both cheeks, as was the custom, by both Kada and Andrej. As soon as the people thinned out, Kada and Stefan took a walk outside.

She said, "You look thin and pale, but knowing your mother, she will put some meat on your bones."

"You do not know how wonderful it is seeing you again."

She sighed and said, "I almost gave up on seeing you again as no one had heard from you for eighteen months. No one had gotten any word about you, but if you had been killed, your parents would have been notified, and no word was received so I never gave up hope."

He told her, "I was a prisoner of war of the Americans in Italy and, apparently, the Americans never notified the Red Cross so no one knew where I was. I like the Americans and I would like to go to America one day. How do you feel about going to America?"

She said, "I will go, but the only problem would be to leave your parents and my mother."

He stopped walking, took her face in his hands and asked, "Will you marry me?"

She told him, "Let us wait for a few months. If you still want to get married then I will, but we should not commit to marriage until we are sure."

They agreed to keep things just as they were for six months and they would not tell anyone, but after that time if they still wanted to get married and go to America, then they would. The courtship of Kada and Stefan had begun.

Stefan made a tour of the farm with his father on the day after Christmas, St. Stefan's day. St. Stefan was the first Saint and he was stoned to death by the Jews for his beliefs in Jesus Christ. He was Stefan's patron Saint and he looked forward to this day each year. His brothers often told him that unless he did not work harder on the farm, he would follow the same fate as his patron Saint. The farm appeared to be in fairly good condition; Andrej had done a good job in maintaining it. The hay was in the barn, along with two mares, a few chickens and a cow. Stefan would have to start all over again, but there was only a short time before the planting season came and he would have to make plans. His father was not able to do much because of his age and a problem with his lungs. Father Josef told him that he must not do any heavy labor. He would only feed the animals and would run out of breath. He had to sit and rest so he could breath again. Because of this, Andrej usually sent him back to the house.

Stefan and Andrej worked together very well and Stefan asked, "How did you avoid getting in the army?"

He answered, "When the Magyars came, your mother hid me in the barn and since I was never home, they did not know where to find me. Out of respect for your mother and father, the townspeople never told the Magyars where I was. I managed to elude them until they stopped looking."

They made repairs on the barns, worked on the equipment and gathered wood for the fireplace. Olga did wonders with the food and they did not miss a meal. Stefan went to Polodencz to exchange the lira for crowns and found the exchange rate unfavorable due to the inflation in Italy. He took what they offered and gave the money to his mother. She bought her yeast so that she could bake bread and other essentials. She hid the rest without telling anyone where.

Around the end of March, Johan's breathing became labored and Olga sent Andrej to fetch Father Josef.

The priest sat with Olga and said, "Johan's lungs are full of fluid. He must stay in bed until they cleared."

Trying to keep him in bed was difficult, but they did manage to keep him from going outside; his breathing became worse. Kada suggested that they boil some thyme and have him drink it with some honey. He drank it one night and the next morning he felt better. Dr. Josef said that the lungs had cleared considerably, but he must remain in bed. His breathing became better as the days went by, and Kada continued giving him the tea. Johan did not credit Kada with getting better. He said, "Father Josef's drink of sugar, fruit juice and vinegar has made me well. The tea that Kada made me drink was just an old gypsy concoction that worked on gypsies, but not on real people."

Kada was sad to hear Johan speak this way. She always had the feeling that he did not like her much. He avoided eye contact and went out of his way so he would not have to speak to her. If he wanted to convey a message to Kada, he told Olga what to say. On more than one occasion, Olga told him, "If you have anything to tell Kada, tell her yourself because I will not play this game any longer." He would not say anything so the message never got to Kada. Finally, to avoid a confrontation with her husband, she decided to convey the orders for work to be done. Kada, of course, knew what was happening, but she kept it to herself. She thought about talking to Stefan, but decided against it. This was the reason that she gave the provisional "yes" to Stefan's proposal of marriage. She wanted this problem resolved before she made a commitment. If she had told him that she would marry him, she might force Stefan to choose between the two of them and she did not want to put him through that. She wanted Johan to accept her as an equal and he would not, because to him she was a gypsy girl, tainted by living with them for two years. She was a servant girl and would always remain so.

Johan knew that there was a shortage of young men in Ruzbachy and Stefan could have his pick of all the young ladies in town. He had hoped to make a marriage with a woman whose parents owned a farm so that they could combine the farms into one large one. However he knew that if he confronted Stefan and forbid him to marry Kada, his son would challenge him and marry her anyway. He planned to make life so miserable for Kada in the Janek household that she would leave voluntarily.

Olga loved Kada as a daughter because she reminded her of her own daughter, Marta, now married and living in America. For all that Johan did to discourage Kada, Olga reversed the process by treating her as a daughter. She gave her all of Marta's clothes, and taught her how to sew, so Kada could alter them to fit her slim figure. Olga would be very happy to have Kada as a daughter-in-law. She had no grandchildren in Slovakia and this was her only chance. She did everything she could to encourage the union and in a confrontation between Johan and Olga, the smart money would bet on Olga.

*   *   *

There were events happening in Europe that would hastened the decision of Kada and Stefan to marry. At the end of World War I, Stefan and the others assumed that Slovakia would be a free and autonomous state. There were actually three groups confronting each other; one group favored autonomy within the Hungarian kingdom; the second wanted to create an autonomous state consisting of the Czechs and Slovaks, and the third, with which Stefan allied himself, wanted Slovakia to be a free and autonomous state governed by Slovaks. Funds were being raised in America on behalf of the Slovaks in Europe to gain their own free state. On May 4, 1919, Stefan's hero, General Milan Rastislav Stefanik was returning home to Slovakia after World War I. When his plane flew over the small town of Vajnory, it burst into flames and the general was killed. The exact cause of the crash had never been determined but Stefan suspected that it was caused by the Czechs, who opposed the freedom of Slovakia. Without the leadership of General Stefanik, the hopes of a free state of Slovakia waned.

The union of the Czech Republic and Slovakia gained momentum and Stefan felt that the Slovaks were powerless to prevent it. He could only hope that his people would have a vote in the government if the two nations merged. In all of history, this was as close they had ever come to seeing that the Slovaks would be independent and free to govern themselves.

*   *   *

Stefan felt that unless there were free elections where his people were represented in the newly formed nation of Czechoslovakia, he would be better off in America with his brothers and sister. He had to consider many things before he could decide on going to America. His father's health was failing quickly; he had his mother to consider and he could not leave either one behind. He felt as if he were being stretched in two different directions. He wanted to make the farm profitable, but he did not know if he would be there to reap the harvest of his labors. Kada had become distant and he could not get a feel as to whether she would marry him or not. He had noticed that Kada kept out of his father's way. His father had never really spoken to her directly. Stefan suspected that something must have happened while he was away and at the first opportunity, he would talk to his father. He wanted to know what the problem was because the six months were almost up and he wanted to marry Kada. He had asked his mother, who was very easy to talk to, and she told him to speak to his father. This was the first bit of evidence that there was a problem. Why had he not done something about it before? He told his mother that he would take the matter up with his father at the first opportunity. That time arrived sooner than expected but Stefan had no way of knowing that Olga had arranged it.

One afternoon, Stefan came in from the fields and found his father sitting alone at the kitchen table. Andrej and Kada had gone to visit their mother since it was Saturday and they usually spent Sunday with her. They took her to church and then went on a wagon ride to the edge of the forest and back. Olga had gone off to visit her cousin Lita and she promised to be back in time to make the evening meal. She had not returned as yet. Johan was drinking a glass of beer and Stefan joined him. The shadows had begun to creep into the kitchen and in the candlelight, Stefan looked at his father and saw that he must have been sitting there for a while.

Stefan looked at his father and asked, "Are you and Kada having some sort of a problem?"

Johan took a drink of beer then wiped his mouth with the back of his sleeve. "Do you plan on marrying this woman?"

"Yes, I do," he answered.

"I wish that you would find someone else."

"Why?" asked Stefan.

The old man settled in his chair which creaked as he moved, "This girl has lived with the gypsies for two years. Who knows what they have done to her? She is no longer one of us. She was exposed to their wild ways, ate all manners of disgusting foods and she is tainted. Once a gypsy, always a gypsy. Look at the brew she gave me to drink when I was sick. It almost killed me. She is a servant girl and will always be a servant girl. She is not of our status and you can do better than her. I want you to promise me that you will not marry her, ever!" He banged his fist on the table.

Stefan was shocked. His eyes shown like glass, he was angry and yet, he could not openly defy his father. Yet, he knew that he must marry this girl.

He asked his father, "What status are we? Why is she so different than the other women? Is it because she has worked for other people and she has no money for a dowry? I cannot make such a promise. It is my life to lead and I must make my own way."

He got up and went to his room to consider the conversation he had with his father. He wanted to discuss this with his mother because he realized that he had accomplished nothing with his father. He would go to see Father Andrej for his advice, he was overwhelmed with guilt for defying his father. This would be a long night and he hoped that he would be able to sleep. Stefan did not come out of his room until it was time to go to Mass. He asked Father Andrej to stop by the farm when he had an opportunity to stay and, in the meantime, he must speak with his mother.

Since he and his mother were alone on the ride home, Stefan took a longer route.

He told his mother about the conversation with his father and she said, "I suspected as much, but I want you to work it out with him. I know him better than you and if he did not relent during your talk, then he will never relent. Your father does not change his mind very often and I doubt very much if he will change his mind this time. You are on your own and if you do get married, you could not live in your father's house. You would have to live elsewhere. Your father knows that you will not do that since you would not be there to help on the farm. This has turned into a problem and a solution would have to be found. I have no objections to your marrying Kada because I would like her for a daughter-in-law. She is intelligent, young and strong. She would bear you many children and I only hope that I would live long enough to see them."

The matter never came up again. Stefan talked to Father Andrej who told him the same that Olga had said; he really was no help. Stefan avoided the subject and threw himself into his work. He left before dawn and came back after dark. His father went to bed early and he ended up eating a meal by himself. Many times, Kada waited for him to come back before she ate so he did not have to eat alone. It was in late June and he was weeding the garden when he looked up and saw Kada running toward him. She was shouting for him to come to the house; his father was ill.

He ran into the house, up to his father's bedroom and found him lying in bed coughing uncontrollably. Andrej had already left to fetch Father Josef and Kada had brought him some thyme tea, but he refused to drink it. It took about an hour for Father Josef to arrive with his little black bag. He checked Johan's lungs and said that they were full and he was getting very little air. He gave him some medicine and told Olga to make some hot tea. Since there was already had hot tea in the room, they tried to make him drink, but he refused. He finally fell asleep, with Olga holding his hand.

Father Josef took Olga aside and said, "Your husband has an infectious disease of the lungs called tuberculosis. No one should go into the room except to feed him and attend to his needs. No one should get too close to him and you will have to wear a mask when you enter the room. There is nothing else to be done for him except to keep him comfortable. I will come by each day to give him his medicine."

He left the house and Olga to administer to her husband. She sent Andrej to town to send a telegram to Marta in America. Since the town now had a telegraph station, he did not have to go all the way to Polodencz. Marta would pass the message to her brothers.

When everyone went to bed, she sat at the kitchen table and cried. She did not want anyone to see her weep for he was going to die, this man who had almost been a priest. He had watched her being born. They had sent four sons and one daughter to America and he would never see them or his grandchildren. This was the saddest day of her life and she had to appear strong for Stefan's sake, but she did not know how she would cope.

Johan lasted fifteen days in his bed with Olga taking care of him before he died in her arms. Olga spoke to the mortician about arrangements and was told that Father Damian had reserved six grave sites in the abbey cemetery for Johan and his family. Father Damian had also paid for Johan's funeral so that he would be sure that Johan would be buried next to his father. Olga had no prior knowledge of these arrangements and when she questioned the mortician, he told her that he was bound by an oath of secrecy until Johan had passed away. Father Andrej, who had known Johan in the early years, said the eulogy and Fathers Igor and Josef helped at the Mass. None of the children now living in America could come to the funeral and the only family that Johan had at his funeral was Olga and Stefan. Stefan was especially sad since he did not resolve the problem with Kada before his father died, but he was thankful that he did not promise to exclude Kada from his marriage plans. He would wait a respectable time for mourning before he brought up the matter again.

*   *   *

In the months that followed, the people working the Janek farm settled into a routine. Johan was missed because even when he was doing nothing, his presence was felt. Now his favorite chair was empty, no one sat at the head of the table and Stefan had to make the decisions pertaining to the farm. The harvest that year was good and Kada and Olga put away a good amount of food for the coming winter. Stefan loved hunting and as soon as the first dusting of snow came, he and Andrej went into the forest looking for a wild boar. They brought back two large ones, the smoke house was rebuilt, sawdust was gathered and the curing of the meat had begun. Christmas was coming and it looked like the celebration was going to be better than the previous year for there was more food and much more to be thankful for. Olga was getting pressure from some of the ladies at church who had daughters of marrying age since Stefan was a good catch. Olga did not tell Stefan about the ladies because she felt that she knew what the future would bring for Stefan.

It was Christmas of 1919 and Stefan had to make some moves to protect his future because, although Kada had been patient, he did not know how much longer he could keep her waiting. The European countries recognized Czechoslovakia as a state, but it would not become a republic until February of 1920. The writing was on the wall and he would have to do something soon.

Stefan's four brothers and sister had sent Mass cards to Olga, promising Masses to be said in America for their father. He received no further correspondence from his siblings in America until a letter was received for Christmas from Marta. It was addressed to Stefan:

> "Dear Brother,
> "Life in America is good. We work hard, but there is enough money to buy food and some left over to save for our son's education. My husband, Michael, is good to me and even though we now have only two children, we are hoping for more in the future. We work in the woolen mills, Michael in the card room and I in the factory store selling sweaters and carpets. We work six days a week for ten hours a day, but we spend Sunday with our children. We have been following the events that have been happening at home and we cannot understand why Slovakia is not an independent nation.

We are wondering what your plans are now that father has
gone to heaven. Do you plan to come to America? If you
should decide, we will have work for you and you can own
your own home someday. You have to work in America, but
you keep what you earn. We know that money is scarce for
you since you are still recovering from the war. Michael and
I have some money saved and we would be willing to loan it
to you so that you could come and we would want you to
bring Mama with you. We have been reading about the
'Land Reform Act of 1919', and if this is true, then the
government will take the farm anyway and you could not
leave her there. Please write back and tell us what you want
to do. Let us know how much money you will need and if
we do not have enough, we will get more from one of our
brothers. Mama could take care of all our children while we
all work and you could live with us until you found a place
of your own. We all want you and Mama to come and live in
America. All of your brothers asked me to write this letter.
We will all wait to hear from you. Your loving sister, Mary
(Marta)."

Stefan decided to speak to Kada first and if she agreed, then he
would speak to his mother. He read and reread the letter many
times because he wanted to be sure that he understood what Marta
was saying. He did not want any misunderstandings when he arrived in America. He met with Kada on Christmas day. She had
gone to midnight Mass with her mother and brother so she could
visit the Janek farm the next day and help Olga. Olga bought little
gifts for Kada and Andrej, to be exchanged after the Christmas
meal. This year, Kada bought a small gift for Stefan also. When
Kada and Andrej arrived for the meal, Stefan invited her to go for
a walk. It was a clear cold day, the sun was out and there was little
snow on the ground. They put on their coats and left through the
kitchen door. Olga was happy to see them leave because she loved
this day and it gave her an opportunity to fuss with no one else in

the kitchen. Kada and Stefan walked slowly toward the stable because he still brushed Blaze as often as he could. They could talk while he worked on his horse.

He showed Kada the letter and once she read it, he said, "I do not want to go without you. I want you to marry me next spring and the following year the three of us will go to America."

Kada did not hesitate because she was waiting for Stefan to ask her and she had an answer all prepared. She said, "Yes, yes, yes!" She wrapped her arms around his neck, kissed him on his cheek, his nose and his mustache. He finished with Blaze so they could get back to the house and tell the others. Kada was beaming, her face was red and she had a smile showing her straight white teeth.

The meal was being put on the table and, upon strict orders from Olga, Andrej was all set to go after the two of them. They went to sit at the table as they had done countless times before, but there was no place setting for Stefan. Olga told him that it was time that he sat at the head of the table. Stefan gave the blessing and before they started to eat, Stefan rose and said that he and Kada had an announcement, "Kada and I are getting married in the spring and I have a letter from Marta. I will let you read it, but Marta wants her mother with her in America."

Olga asked, "What about the farm and what would happen to it?"

Stefan told her, "Under the law, all land over 618 acres that was owned by one person, would come under the control of the state. This meant that our farm, because of all our work will, be under government control and I would be nothing more than a manager on our own farm. I do not want that to happen."

Olga wiped away a tear and said, "I will think about it and I will give you my decision on St. Stefan's day, the day after Christmas."

They ate the meal and spoke of other matters, but Olga expressed her happiness at having Kada as a daughter-in-law. She noted that Kada and Stefan were looking at each other during the entire meal and when they finished, Kada and Olga cleared the table while Andrej and Stefan rolled some cigarettes and had a cup of coffee. The women went into the next room and brought out their gifts. Andrej and Stefan had their gifts under the tree so they all sat around the tree and exchanged them. Olga give Andrej a new pair of suspenders, as she noticed his had broken and he was always repairing them. Olga received a carving of The Infant of Prague from Andrej who had found it in a shop in town and had saved for it. Kada gave Olga a babuska that she found in town while Olga gave her a mug of her own so she could sip her tea at night. Kada gave Stefan a scarf and he gave her a music box that played a Straus waltz when it opened. This was a happy time because they did not let the thought of their leaving the only home they knew dampen their spirits. Stefan brought out two bottles of beer, for him and Andrej, and they talked into the evening.

The next day, Olga said, "I am ready to go and see the rest of my family so we can all go to America. I recommend that Andrej manage the farm. He could get married and live in the house." Stefan said, "As a going away present, I will give Andre my horse, Blaze."

Olga detected a tear in Stefan's eye when he said it. The pact had been sealed and they were going to America. Stefan would obtain fare rates and he would write to Marta to tell her how much money they would need to make the ocean crossing. The government would take between twelve and eighteen months before they took control and this meant that they could be able to sell some things to raise more money. They agreed that no one should know of their plans until the tickets were bought because they did not want to call attention to themselves.

Life went on as usual and Stefan and Kada set a wedding date of May 30, 1920. They went to the church and asked Father Andrej to perform the ceremony. Kada's brother was going to be best man and Kada's cousin, Anna Kupchak, would be the matron of honor. They would have a few friends and relatives over to the Janek home for a celebration of the marriage.

Stefan went to Polodencz and found that each of them could

book passage from Hamburg, Germany for $190 in American money.

He wrote Marta, "We are coming to America and we will need $750 for the three of us to come to America. This would give us more than the fares, but we might need more for unforseen expenses. We do not plan to leave for at least fifteen months because Kada and I will be getting married on May 30 and we will start making plans for leaving the farm sometime after that. It would probably be in the spring of 1921 because I do not want our mother to make the ocean crossing in the winter. You should not send the money until after Christmas. We are leaving the farm with Kada's brother, Andrej, and we want to leave the farm in good condition. I want to be sure that the planting is under way for the following year's harvest. We will wait for your answer."

The spring came early that year. They started spreading the fertilizer in April and the first of May, they were ready for planting. Olga had to buy food for the marriage reception and she started about the middle of May in the preparations. Stefan and Kada had invited about forty people, relatives on both sides. Kada and Olga had worked on the bride's dress, started right after the new year and finally it was finished. It was beautiful with the traditional embroidery over much of the dress. Stefan would wear his father's embroidered suit.

Olga had given Stefan her wedding ring to use in the ceremony. She told him, "I am too old to remarry, I will not need it any longer and its rightful place would be on Kada's finger. The ring had been my mother's and my father had saved it for me to use when I married and no one knows how many women have used the ring to wed."

The day of the marriage finally came and the "March of the Matriarchs" had begun. The women took the bride's belongings along with donated items of clothing and bedding, from the bride's home to the groom's home. This was a happy time, with much laughing and joking and many predictions as to how many children the couple would have. The night before, the couple had said an emotional farewell to their parents in front of the wedding guests. The bride was escorted to church, in a decorated cart by the women in their carts while the men rode horseback. They would leave the church with their horses tied to the back of the wagons. Stefan rode his horse, Blaze, who in fact, was paying for the wedding. Stefan had sent Blaze out for stud the previous fall and had collected the money for the service. He had gotten two colts which would help Andrej when they were gone because he wanted to leave Andrej with something to bargain with.

The ceremony was long, as Father Andrej insisted upon a High Mass. All of the women cried, while the men wished that the ceremony would end so that they could get down to some serious dancing and drinking. When it ended, Stefan lifted Kada into the wagon while the guests cheered and all followed the newlyweds to the Janek home while they sang songs and joked among themselves as they recalled their own weddings. It was a sunny day and that was a good sign for, legend has it, rain would have translated into tears and it would be a stormy marriage. Sunlight was definitely a good sign and someone saw a hawk gliding in the sky when all fingers pointed to it; for this was another good sign. This marriage was starting out very well. While everyone thought that Kada was a lucky woman, it would turn out that Stefan was the lucky one.

The music and dancing started as soon as they entered the house as Pan Grabowski had brought his violin and the celebration had begun. Women deposited food on a long table and there were tubs of beer. Someone also brought the ingredients for a non alcoholic punch for the children. There were men in embroidered suits and the modern three button suits while, the women, without exception, wore their embroidered dresses. Stefan and Kada sat in the chairs of honor and all of the guests stopped in front of them, wished them a happy marriage and many gave them gifts to start their married life. The celebration lasted until the next morning when the married couple, as expected, excused themselves and retired to their bedroom. There were giggles among the women and shouts of good luck by the men.

Kada woke up the next morning and still did not believe that she was married. She thought of the old sayings among the women, that a woman who did not marry turned into vinegar. She got up to make her husband's first meal, but Olga was already up and Andrej was feeding the animals. She allowed Kada to make her husband his meal because she gave up dominance of the kitchen to the new woman of the house and sat at the table with a cup of tea. They spoke softly so as not to waken Stefan because he had a long day with the toasting by every man at the celebration. Stefan could not eat or drink as he had at one time, and it would take him a day or two to recover from all the celebrating. He danced quite a bit and danced the tsardice, a very difficult dance even for a younger man. He would be stiff and sore from all the new activity.

He finally came into the kitchen. His head hurt, every muscle in his body ached; it had been a good wedding. He went over and kissed his bride and then his mother, but no one said a word. He sat at the head of the table and Kada put a bowl of oatmeal in front of him. She had beaten in two eggs as it was cooking and there was a pitcher of fresh milk on the table. Stefan did not feel like eating, but he ate everything and said that it was very good. Olga watched what was happening and thought that this marriage would be fine for they had taken each other's feelings into account. When Stefan finished his coffee, he kissed Kada and went out to help Andrej. It was a long day and Andrej knew how Stefan felt, so he took on the heavier tasks without being asked. When they went in to wash for "Vecera" or supper, they found that Kada had prepared a large meal. She had some sliced "shunka", "Kielbasa", "slutka kapusta", and some fresh baked bread. She had made some "platsky" (potato pancakes) for a side dish and some beans with mushrooms cooked in them. The meal was excellent and it lifted Stefan's spirits. It took his mind off the illness he felt. They sat around the table and talked for a full two hours after the meal was finished. Stefan and Andrej had a cigarette and a beer before they went to bed.

Stefan lay in bed waiting for Kada to finish in the kitchen and he thought that this would be a good life if they could stay. He knew that he could make the farm pay, but it was out of the question for the farm would not even be theirs in another year. Kada finally came to bed and they discussed the family that they were going to have. Stefan wanted as many children as they could and Kada agreed, but she suggested that they wait until they arrived in America. They reached an agreement, but since they were now married, they did what married people do. They were young and loved each other, not a marriage of convenience as most of those in Ruzbachy were. The men were limited due to the war and only those women who could offer a large dowry were being married. This was only one of the prices that people in small villages paid for the ambitions of the leaders of the empire.

The summer passed with Stefan and Andrej working in the fields and the women working in the house. Stefan planned to put Blaze up for stud service again in the fall and he had heard that there were some wild cows roaming the upper pastures. When the Magyars had come to take the animals, some of the farmers had turned them loose rather than give them up. They had planned to round them up after the Magyars had left, but did not capture all of them. They now belonged to those that dared to go into the hills to capture them, and the newlyweds decided to take a few days off and ride to the high country to be alone for a while. Stefan went to the abbey and asked where he could find Brother Augustus who was herding the flock of sheep in the high pastures. This would save some time in looking for the cattle because no one knew the area better than he did. Stefan knew the high country and Kada had traveled with the gypsies so she had been in this territory before.

Kada packed some food and they left before dawn on a clear cool day. Andrej could handle things until they returned. They headed north and followed the trail of the gypsies and Kada could tell when the trail veered off when Stefan could not see the signs left by them. The first night, they camped by a small stream. They had followed the stream for a while and went by the spot where Stefan's father had slept when he wandered away from the abbey many years before. They found a likely spot and Stefan made a small fire while Kada got supper ready. The night was cool and darkness came early in the shadows of the High Tatras. She boiled some water for coffee and heated some sausage on the open fire. It was pleasant being there alone and after the meal, they bundled up in the blankets and slept soundly.

They woke up in full sunlight, finished the coffee from the night before, ate some bread, saddled their horses and rode north. Stefan had an idea where Brother Augustus was tending his flock, but it would take them another two days to get there. That night, Kada said that she wanted to try something and after they took care of their horses, Kada went off into the forest. She made a snare as the gypsies had done for years, she caught a rabbit and while she went off into another area to skin it, she reset the snare. When she had finished with the first rabbit, she went back to the snare and she now had two rabbits. She dismantled the snare, went back to camp, made a spit, rubbed the rabbit with oil and spices that she had brought and went to skin the second animal, while the first one cooked.

When the first rabbit was cooked, they took it off the spit and put the second one on as they ate the first. The rabbit had cooked slowly and when it had cooled somewhat, Kada broke it apart and she gave Stefan a piece to try. It was excellent and a new experience to Stefan. They sat across the fire, eating roasted rabbit, gypsy style. When Stefan looked at Kada with oil dripping from her chin, he started to laugh. Kada pointed to his chin with the oil dripping down and laughed with him. It was a unique sight, two people sitting next to a fire, eating rabbit, oil dripping down their chins, laughing out loud. Once they were finished and tired of laughing, they decided to go to bed. Kada told him to rub the oil on his hands so they would not get rough. With the gypsies, nothing was wasted.

Their trip turned out to be more of a holiday than a working trip and they learned a good deal about each other. Stefan learned that Kada had been taught well by the gypsies. She had learned patience such as waiting for a rabbit to get caught in the snare, she was resourceful and frugal. She brought a great deal of knowledge into the marriage that other women in town were lacking and he knew that he had made the correct choice in picking his wife. She learned that Stefan had a sense of humor that he had never shown before and he also had patience and trust when he allowed Kada to go into the forest by herself. He realized that he had married more that just a housemaid; he married an intelligent, caring woman. As the days on their trip melted one into the other, the love that they felt for each other deepened.

On the fourth day, they came out of the forest and into some lush pasture land. They heard the bleating of sheep and the ringing of the bells before they saw the friar sitting on a rock, watching his sheep. He had built a crude "buda," or hut, out of dead trees and branches. It was made with three sides and a roof while the fourth side was open, overlooking his sheep. There were about a hundred and fifty sheep milling around his camp, some had bells on and all had a heavy growth of wool. In another month, he would have to start herding his flock to the pasture in the lower ground. As they approached the camp, the sheep parted and made a path allowing the horses to go through. Brother Augustus saw them and waved to them to come in.

Stefan introduced himself and his wife to the friar, but he knew who they were and he knew that Stefan was Johan's youngest son, for the story of Johan was well known at the abbey. The friars always considered Stefan's father as one of them and it was as if he had never left the abbey.

He told Stefan, "I see cattle once in a while, but I was not able to catch any and even if I did, I do not know how to handle them."

The meadow they were in was a massive pasture and he knew

that there were cows in it somewhere. Stefan and Kada decided to
ride through the center of the meadow, but they would keep each
other in sight and when one saw a cow, he or she would motion to
the other and they would try to get a rope around it. They would
have to put a rope around each one, or they would never get them
south. Toward late afternoon, Kada came across a low hill and
looked to her left and she saw a small herd of seven animals grazing
on lush grass. She motioned to Stefan and he rode over slowly so as
not to startle them. He counted six cows and one bull and if he
could capture the bull, then the cows would be easier to bring in.
They rode slowly down the hill, one on each side very slowly.
Stefan was about ten yards from the bull, when the bull saw them,
and challenged them while moving backwards. Stefan had a looped
rope ready and when the bull started to run, he kicked blaze in the
side and took off. The bull was no match for this horse and Stefan
realized why the cattle ranchers in America used this saddle in
their work. It was comfortable and well suited for this type of work
and he ran the bull back to his herd when Kada joined in the
chase. Soon they had the animal between them and Stefan dropped
the rope around its neck. He had Blaze rein and the animal was
captured. They took him to a lone tree in the pasture and tied
him. It would be dark soon so they did not chase the cows because
they would not stray very far from the bull. They could be rounded
up in the morning.

They did not make a fire that night, but slept on the cold
ground looking up at the stars. Stefan did not sleep much for there
was enough light from the moon and he could watch the bull. He
did fall asleep a few hours before dawn and awoke to see the six
cows milling around a few feet away from the bull. Stefan got up,
saddled Blaze and rode over to the cows. He got down and slipped
a rope over each head and when they had seven animals, they
started south. They did not expect to stay away this long and they
had to get back to the farm. Kada had three of the cows while
Stefan had the bull and the rest. They made better time going

home, since they did not go slow to enjoy the scenery as they had on the way up.

They got to the farm after sunset on the third evening, Stefan put the animals in the outside pen and brushed the two horses down while Kada went into the house to tell her mother-in-law the good news. She ran out to the pen with a lantern followed by Andrej. The animals looked well fed, but the bull was extremely wild. If it could, he would have broken through the pen and escaped into the wild, but Andrej took some hay and threw in into the pen. There was water in the trough so they were set for the evening and they would examine them further in the morning. For the last three days, Olga had food ready for them, waiting for their return and she set it out on the table. Stefan and Kada were tired because it was a difficult two days and they did not rest much so they ate their meal and went to bed.

The next morning, Stefan woke and Kada was already gone. He looked out the window, saw the two women looking at the cattle and he got dressed to go out to join them. Olga, after her inspection, said that the bull was older, about eight years old, two of the cows were heifers and the other four ranged in age from two to six years. The bull could be used for at least four years more since he was in such good shape. It was good work and she kissed them both. There were no marks on the animals, so no one could try to lay claim to them. The farm now had two bulls and ten cows. They were slowly building the herd taken by the Magyars. Although they would never see the farm after they went to America, they worked it as if they were going to stay.

A month later, they had to turn their attention to the fields for the hay had to be cut, dried and stored before anything was harvested. Olga now stayed in the house most of the time while Kada went out to the fields with the men. She worked just as her mother-in-law had done when she was young and she handled the scythe as well as Stefan. Once the hay was stored, they started on the grain fields and these were finished by the middle of September. Kada went inside to help Olga process the cabbage and other vegetables, while Stefan and Andrej killed two hogs that went into the smokehouse after they were cut up. From the outside, appearances were such that no one expected them to leave for America because they appeared to be preparing for the future.

Andrej had met a young lady by the name of Anna Klobeca. He had met her in church and he would visit her on Sundays. They would go for rides and picnics on the edge of the river and when there was a celebration of any kind, they would always be seen dancing and sitting together. Andrej did not talk about her very much, but he had brought her to the Janek house a few times. She seemed to be in love with Andrej, but nothing was ever said of their plans.

Stefan told Kada when they were alone, "I think that Andre was waiting until we left before he would commit to anything. He did not technically own anything, while her family owned a small farm with few animals. I think that once we leave, Andrej would be able to marry her and bring her into the house. If they married before we left, he would have to live at his mother's home and come to work each day from there."

Kada wondered, "Why do events become so complicated because all he had to do was to plan the marriage for April or May and they would know what to do."

Stefan countered, "What would happen if, for unforeseen reasons, we do not go to America? The situation would become more complicated. It is better to handle it this way because they are still young and they have plenty of time."

Kada had known for some time that she was pregnant and she and Olga had calculated that she became pregnant about the first of July. That would bring the delivery date around April first and Kada swore Olga to secrecy. She did not want Stefan to know because she was afraid that he would not allow her to work in the fields. That was fine with Olga because she felt men did not understand such things and she told Kada that she had delivered Johan in a field where that large tree grows. Johan had planted that tree after his son was born to mark the exact spot and he said that he wanted Johan's roots to go deep into the ground. Kada felt that it was no time to tell Stefan so she decided to wait until she was starting to show before she told him.

A few weeks went by. There was nothing further to be done in the fields, so she decided to tell him. They were lying in bed one night when Kada brought up the subject. She looked at him and said that there was something that she wanted to tell him. He sat up in bed with all kinds of thoughts running through his head, from her being ill to her changing her mind about going to America.

There was a silence and Kada finally blurted it out . . . "I am pregnant!" She waited for a reaction, but there was none. Stefan was actually relieved that it was something that he did not have to argue about.

He asked calmly, "When is the baby due?"

"Your mother and I figure that it is due on April 1," she answered.

"You told my mother, but you did not tell me."

She was almost in tears when she replied, "We were not sure until now and I did not want to get your hopes up."

He calmed down again and started to count on his fingers. "It takes you three months to be sure?" he exclaimed.

"Yes," she replied. "It takes sometimes three or four months to be sure. You men know how to make babies, but you do not know what goes on afterward."

She turned her back to him and pretended to go to sleep.

"I am happy that you are going to have a child," he said, "and it will not interfere with our trip across the ocean but I want you to see Father Josef as soon as possible."

Kada breathed a sigh of relief and tried to go to sleep while Stefan lay on his back with his eyes wide open, thinking of the implications regarding the news she just gave him. He wanted the child to be born in America so it would be an American citizen but this meant that they would have to depart by the first week of March. That would allow ten days for the trip over and another two days to get to Marta's house so she could have some help.

That, of course, was assuming that she would be on time and he tried to think back to what he was doing on July 1. It must have been while they were up in the mountains, snuggled in their blankets. A smile came across his face and he fell into a deep sleep.

When he woke the next morning, Kada was already gone so he dressed and went into the kitchen. She was outside getting water when he walked up to his mother, kissed her, "I know of your little secret."

"And what is the little secret?"

"You are finally going to see one of your grandchildren."

After they ate, he put Kada into the wagon and took her to see Father Josef. There were a few people waiting to see him. When it became to their chance, Stefan got up to go into the other room with the doctor and Kada.

Father Josef said, "Fathers are not allowed in the examining room."

Stefan allowed himself to be pushed out and he found a vacant chair. He sat and imagined that all eyes were on him. He wanted to tell everyone who came in that it was his "zena" or wife, who was seeing the doctor, and he was going to be a father. He tried to look as calm as possible, but an hour went by, and he started to worry. He wondered why it was taking so long because, how long would it take for him to examine her? What he did not know was that Father Josef and Kada were just talking, because it was a pleasant visit so they both enjoyed it. She did not have any problems, but they let Stefan sit in the waiting room while they enjoyed themselves, after all, he was only the father. When she came through the door, Stefan jumped up and led her out the door and they went to the church and talked. He wanted to know what the doctor had done to her and what the results were, but all she would tell him was that she was fine. He took her home and spent the rest of the day cleaning out the stable. He brought out his brush and started to groom Blaze. He needed to talk to someone and speaking to Blaze seemed to soothe his feelings. The horse did not argue with him, but he grunted once in a while to let his master know that he was listening. Sometimes, Stefan would take the horse out for a ride because the saddle, given to him by Captain Bush, was comfortable. He had many comments on it and many of his friends at the tavern asked to sit on the horse. He had many opportunities to sell it, but he and the horse were fond of each other and he could not part with him.

Since the amount of work was slowing at the farm, Stefan and Andrej went down to the tavern for the latest news. The most popular subject was the land reform act of the last year. Some of the people at the tavern were going to deed one-half of their land to their children. Their farms would fall under the 618 acres and this would allow them to get around the transfer of the land to the State. They felt that they could control their own future but some of the men did not feel that it would work. If the state had the power to take the land, it had the power to void the technicality and take the land anyway. This caused much discussion in the tavern; Stefan and Andrej just listened. Rumors were flying and it was difficult to tell what was fact and what was fiction and at one point, Stefan asked Andrej if he understood what they were discussing. Andrej shrugged his shoulders, shook his head side to side.

Another point of discussion was the new Constitution that was going to be voted on in the early part of the following year. Since 1918 all of the universities as well as other schools, had become state institutions and the state would now control what was taught in the schools. Attendance was compulsory from age six to fourteen. What disturbed Stefan the most, was when the new constitution was approved, there was going to be no, or very little, representation by the Slovaks. The Slovaks wanted self rule, but from the way matters were progressing, they would, again, be ruled by someone else. This time it would be the Czechs. One of the men said that he heard that the communists were getting stronger and maybe they would be able to help the Slovaks get some representation in the nation that they were forced into. The more Stefan heard, the more he felt that he had made the correct decision to leave this new nation. Matters never seemed to get better, but worse. He would miss the farm, but he knew that he had to go and give his child an opportunity for a better life.

Stefan made more trips to the tavern although he never drank much because of the war wound to his stomach, but he wanted to hear and understand the latest news. He heard that the notary, who now reported to the Central Government in Prague instead of the Empire in Budapest, was making the rounds of the farms and taking inventory. From the reports of farms that he had visited, Stefan learned that the notary was recording all of the assets, including the livestock and the food storage. The farms were allowed to keep enough to feed the people, but the surplus was going into government storage to be either sold or passed out to people in Bohemia and Moravia. In exchange, the Central Government was supposed to mechanize the farms with tractors. The gasoline used to power these devices could only be bought from the government. Stefan calculated that if the government was going to take the surplus food and other commodities, what would be left to sell to obtain money to buy the gasoline?

Slovaks were being used again to feed other people and things had not changed from before the war; they were still becoming worse. Instead of being trod upon by the Magyars, they were being trod upon by the Government of Czechoslovakian Republic with very little representation by the Slovaks.

He went home, after each night at the tavern, to report the developments to Kada and his mother. They usually talked around the kitchen table with a cup of tea and Olga was disappointed with the changing events. She could not understand why Stefan spent four years of his life in foreign countries fighting for a better life, when the world chose some other government to dictate to them. She spent all of her life building up the farm only to see it taken away and the only thing about which she expressed some happiness was that her husband, Johan, was not there to see what was happening. He had such hopes of seeing a free Slovakia, free from foreign domination after the war and now they were to leave everything to some bureaucrats in Prague. Their discussions disturbed her so that Stefan held back some information about the notary since she would know about it soon enough. He stopped going to the tavern and concentrated on holding their last celebration of Christmas.

This Christmas was not a happy time on the farm because they knew that it would be their last one. Kada went to get her mother and the two families became one because of the holiday. They all got into the wagon and went to midnight Mass and Father Andrej gave an excellent sermon on families and how they should come together at the Birth of Christ. After Mass they went back to the farm and Stefan lit the candles on the spruce tree that was decorated with brightly colored ribbons and glass crystals held on by strings. As the crystals moved, they reflected lights over the entire room. They drank hot tea with a little honey and rum and as the fire was blazing, everyone exchanged small gifts. Andrej announced that he and Anna set a date of June 20, 1921 to be married and Kada's mother, Anna, was overjoyed because there was now going to be another woman in the family. She saw Kada quite often, but she had not received a letter from Marta or Anna for quite some time and she was worried about them. She did not know that Kada would be leaving her within three months.

The celebration continued until the small hours of the morning until Olga told everyone to be up by nine am for the traditional Christmas breakfast. She usually made enough to feed an army since tradition dictated that any visitor to their home on Christmas morning must sit at the table and share their meal. People visited each other on that day and some wanted an early start. They wanted to cover as much ground as possible for once a visit was made, it was difficult to tear oneself away to go to the next place. Food was saved for this feast and Kada and Olga had been cooking for three days. It was Andrej's job to see that the fire was kept hot for the cooking because Slovaks associated a celebration with food and the sharing of it with their friends and relatives. Everyone in town was invited and many came, for the Janek household was known around town as having the best food and drink.

Kada was up when Stefan woke so he got dressed and went into the kitchen and he took a deep breath, for the smell of fresh baked bread was all over the kitchen. Olga was busy kneading bread on the table and there was flour up to her elbows, in her hair and on her nose. Stefan laughed at seeing his mother, but she had no time for him. Kada was brushing butter over the top of a freshly baked loaf. She cut off the heel, put butter on it and handed it to her husband. His eyes said "thank you." The butter was melting over the hot bread and as he took a bite, he burned his mouth. Taking a pitcher of water, he took a long drink. He looked at his mother and from the look he got back, he knew that it would be best to leave the room. He went out to feed the animals since it was about eight o'clock and he would have to find to something to do for an hour.

When he reached the barn, he found that Andrej had already fed the animals so he went to the cows, milked two of them and then took the milk to the kitchen. It was a good excuse to go back in and get another piece of bread, but he opened the door to see all four of the women busy at work. Andrej's mother was putting the ingredients into a new batch of bread, the other Anna was taking the bread from Olga and putting it into pans. Kada was putting the pans of bread into the oven. When Stefan returned from the war, he had seen an oven in Vienna and he had gone down to the blacksmith and had him build an iron box with a door on it. The box was placed into the fireplace about a foot and a half from the floor. A fire was built under the box and the hot ashes would bring heat to the oven.

The women would not use the oven at first because they did not know how to regulate the heat. To use it properly, one had to monitor it constantly while turning the bread to be sure that it baked evenly. They soon adapted to it and now they used nothing else. The blacksmith made a few of them when work was slow, sold them quickly and he now had enough orders to keep him busy until spring.

Stefan left the pail of milk on a chair and caught Kada's eye and she knew what he was looking for. He told her that Andrej was in the barn so Kada put two pieces on a cloth and pushed him out the door. He gave Andrej the larger piece since he had already eaten one and Stefan ate his while he sat next to Blaze. Of all the things that Stefan would miss, he would miss the horse, the most. He wished that he could take Blaze with him, but that was impossible; he never brought it up.

When they thought that it was safe, Stefan and Andrej went back into the kitchen. The women were cooking ham, kielbasa, bacon, a gravy made from the bacon drippings, and eggs. They cooked the eggs in water, in and out of the shells and there were fried eggs, scrambled eggs and a large plate of plaske (pancakes). These were made by shredding potatoes and adding an egg to hold them together. When they were mixed throughly, they were dropped on a hot skillet, flattened and then turned. The different kinds of breads were put on the table prune bread, raisin bread, sauerkraut bread and potato bread. The sauerkraut bread and potato bread were flat. The bacon gravy was thickened and served on top of the breads and there was coffee with fresh milk and tea to drink.

As they were into their meal, a knock came at the kitchen door and Olga opened it to Pavel Dombromski's granddaughter, Eva with her husband, Lech and four children. The two girls were dressed in native dresses made for the occasion and the younger boys were dressed in suits, white shirts and ties. They were invited to sit at the table and Lech gave the usual greeting for the occasion, "Happy Birth of Jesus Christ and may He bless this house." Room was made at the table and they sat to eat. About an hour later other people came to the door and were invited into the Janek home and more food was laid out on the table while the four women did some more cooking and washed dishes. At about noon, people started to come in more frequently and by mid-afternoon, the house was full with people spilling out of doors into the yard. Some of the visitors brought food and drink knowing what a strain it was on the Janek family and Stefan saw old friends that he had not seen for years. He had planned to visit the abbey in the afternoon, but with the amount of people that had come, that visit would have to wait until the next day.

By the time most of the people left, the Janek household was a mess. There were dishes over the entire house and the women must have washed each dish five or six times. Most of the people ate well but the Janek family did not have any food since the morning meal. There was some food left so each person washed a dish, dried it and ate what was left. Olga would not go to bed without cleaning the house so as soon as she started to clean the mess, everyone helped and before long the Janek home was spotless and everything was washed, dried and put in its place. The floors were scrubbed clean, the furniture wiped and more wood was put on the fire. By ten o'clock, they were all ready to go to bed. It had been a long exhaustive day but it was worth it for everyone had a good time and this Christmas would not soon be forgotten. Stefan banked the fire so they would have hot ashes from which to start the fire in the morning. At last, all the lights were put out and the Janek household was quiet.

Stefan awoke to a cold morning. He was the first up, so he put wood on the fire and went to the wood pile to bring more in. He got water boiling, and threw in a handful of coffee. Once the coffee boiled for a few minutes, he took it from the fire, the boiling stopped and he dropped an egg into it. The egg cooked at once while surrounding the grounds. He reached in with a large spoon and took the cooked egg out and threw it out the rear door. This left a pot of hot clear and almost ground free coffee. He took a cup with him and went out to the barn to feed the animals. He wanted to do that before he rode to the abbey because, on the Janek farm, the animals came first. It was now only eleven weeks before they would leave their home forever.

When Kada woke, she found Olga sitting at the kitchen table

drinking a cup of coffee. She asked Kada, "Has anyone commented on your condition?"

Kada laughed and said, "Everyone noticed that my dress was riding up in front and that was a sure sign that I am pregnant. I told everyone, even if they did not notice, that I was with child. The gypsies have a test that we performed after five months to see if it would be a boy or a girl. The woman would lie on her back from north to south. A needle is tied to a string so it is suspended over the woman's stomach and spun around. If the needle went from east and west, it will be a girl, if it went from north to south, it will be a boy."

Olga smiled and said, "We will try the test when the men are out of the house."

Kada's stomach was getting bigger so she wore her dress higher in the front and Slovak women tended to notice these things about other women.

Stefan ate his morning meal of leftovers, saddled Blaze and rode off toward the abbey. On the way, he made a slight detour and found the solitary oak tree in the middle of the hay field. The tree had become a symbol of the Janek family's roots in Slovakia, but in another eleven weeks, the last of the clan would be leaving Slovakia forever. He had instructed Andrej to cut the tree once they left and to use it for firewood. There would no longer be Janek roots in Slovakia, but he again wanted to see the tree where his brother, Johan, was born. He would report what he had done to his brothers and sister when he met them in America.

The abbey appeared to need work once again since there had been no repairs made on the building since before the war and that was almost six years ago. He had no doubts that the repairs would be made at some later date because there were many brothers now and once the priorities were completed, work would start on the abbey. The brothers were trying to get the farm back in shape, build up the herds and bring in enough food for the winter. They had a surplus this year and, in the event someone in town needed it, they would pass it out because the brothers wanted no one in Ruzbachy to go hungry. As he got nearer, it looked like it was worse than what he saw at a distance.

The mortar on the masonry needed pointing, the roof on the barn and stable needed replacement, all of which was going to cost a great deal of money. He noticed the windows as he went by and he could see space where the windows met the building. His grandfather must be up in heaven watching this; he would not have let things go so far if he were still alive, he would have found a way. The Abbott, now running the Abbey of St. Francis was not a priest. The abbey had become a political plum and it did not matter if the Abbott had the skills to run the abbey. Everyone was pushing their allies toward positions of authority and he thought that the Czechs would soon be running the church.

He stopped in the cemetery, went to father's grave and talked as if his father was still alive.

He told his father, "I ordered the tree in the field cut down because I am taking my wife and your wife to America to be with the rest of the family. The most important matter that I want to tell you is that you were wrong about Kada because she is a good wife and she will be a good mother. There will be no one left to visit your grave, once we leave, so I want to say goodbye and to thank you for all the sacrifices that you made for your children. You went without so we would have a better life and, for that, I am grateful."

He went to the next grave where his grandfather, Father Damian, was buried. He said, "Thank for starting the Janek family because from your one night of passion has sprung the entire Janek clan. You will be pleased to see how your future generations will fare and you will be proud of them. Goodbye, grandfather, I am sorry that we could not stay in Czechoslovakia and we will not be back. I do not want my sons to fight in a war on behalf of the new Republic. I fought for the empire and now they are going to take away my mother's farm. I would not be angry if my own government did it, but to have the people in Prague, where we are not even represented, do it is unpardonable. I could not stay in a country that did not give the people a voice in the government and I am tired of living that way. I want to give my children the opportunities to be masters of their own fate. The most important resources that people have are their children and I am going to give mine a chance."

He said good-byes to everyone who he knew in the cemetery and left, never to go back. The next morning, Andrej took his mother and his fiancee to their homes, Kada and Olga ran their test to see whether Kada would have a boy or a girl. The needle was tied to a string and lowered to about three inches from Kada's stomach as she lay on her back. The needle pointed from north to south and that meant that she would be expecting a boy. They decided not to tell Stefan about it since he would only laugh. If it turned out to be a girl, they would never hear the end of it. They decided to engage Stefan in a conversation so that they might be able to determine what his preference was. They had plenty of time to do this so they would wait until Stefan brought it up. It would be their secret. Olga and Kada were becoming friends and Olga would be close to her daughter-in-law for the rest of her life.

In the middle of January, they received a letter from Marta. It contained instructions for getting seven hundred and fifty dollars from the bank in Polodencz and Stefan was to book passage on the first steamship that was available. He went to Polodencz a few days later and got the money. He went to the steamship company and booked passage on the "S.S. Mongolia.", a ship carrying four hundred passengers. Stefan booked a room since, Kada was pregnant and he did not want his baby born with passengers looking at the delivery. He confirmed with the steamship line, that there would be a doctor on board. The ship would leave on March 14, 1921 from Hamburg, Germany and he was told to be there a day early so he could be processed on board.

The fare did not include meals and he could either buy food on board, bring his own or not eat for the voyage. The agency did not seem to care one way or the other what he did. He could take all the luggage that he could carry, but no more. With women traveling, he was told not to take too much as there were people who made a very good living taking away property that could not be taken on board. The room on the ship would be small, but it would have three beds. He bought rail tickets from Polodencz to Hamburg. The train left on March 11 and even allowing for the poor record in keeping to a schedule the European rail system had, they should arrive in plenty of time.

Stefan rode his horse back to the farm but he still had misgivings. This was the only life he knew. His fears disappeared when he arrived home. His mother told him that the notary had stopped in to make an appointment to come back and inventory the farm and Stefan did not have any doubts from that day on they were going to lose the farm anyway. Olga told the notary to come back when Stefan was home but he did not make an appointment.

The next day, the notary came again; he was not a Slovak. The new government had changed the requirements for notaries and they now reported to the land committee in Prague. He was a well-trained auditor, specializing in farms.

He told Stefan, "You or someone that you recommend will manage the farm, but accountings and profits will have to be sent to the government. The government will control the use of the land."

Stefan thought that there was no difference between this government and the communists since both took the land and profits and there was no incentive to improve the farm. The notary confirmed what he had heard in the tavern that the country was moving down the path toward communism. The Czechs would take the food and sell them the goods in order to produce the food. He did not see any future in Czechoslovakia because, through its actions, the government encouraged people to leave the country. It helped with the problems of overpopulation and it permitted those who stayed to make better use of the land with fewer mouths to feed. The way to America was made less difficult from Europe but what Stefan did not know was, that between 1890 and 1924, twenty million Europeans emmigrated to America. Stefan and his family were just three of many that left their homeland.

The notary returned within a week with three other people who went over every aspect of the farm. Stefan kept Andrej close so he would be familiar with what was happening when he left. The notary wanted projections on how much was going to be planted in various fields.

He wanted to leave nothing to chance and said, "You may plant a garden for your own use. Any surplus could be sold and you may keep the profit. I will give you written instructions, which have to be followed to the letter. We have a map of land owned by the farm with the wooded acreage and that acreage suitable for planting. We will tell you what will be planted because the government understands the whole situation with the country and if there is a good market for export or internal consumption for barley, then you will plant barley."

They were making it easier for Andrej to manage, but Stefan would never be able to bear it. Stefan and Andrej worked on the projections for two weeks and finally thought that they could satisfy the notary.

The weather had turned bitter cold and everything was freezing. There was no water for the animals and they had to crack the ice in the well to get water every day. It was a time to work in the kitchen where it was warm and they got all their papers together and went to see the official. As they approached the river, they saw that there were thin streams of smoke rising from every chimney, as if strings were coming down from the sky to be attached to each home. The river was frozen over and the ice was so thick that the wagons did not need the bridge. Young children were skating on the river, playing a game with sticks pushing flat rocks around. The cold did not seem to bother the young boys for they had taken off their heavy jackets and were skating around in their sweaters. They went into the town office and found the notary sitting at a desk. They gave him the papers and while he was reading them, Stefan looked around his office. There were papers piled everywhere and Stefan did not know how he could find anything, but that was not his problem.

The notary looked up and told them, "These projections do not go into enough detail."

The notary gave them a map of the property belonging to the farm. He told them to draw the areas where certain crops were to be planted and they were to show where the untillable lands were on the map. This would give him an idea as to the amount that will be planted for each crop. Stefan gave the map to Andrej and told him to complete it because he would be the one to answer to the notary after he was gone.

The cold weather continued, there was very little wind, but the temperature was well below zero. Stefan had a few of the pots that were designed by his grandfather and they seemed to help them get through this difficult period. Kada went to bed early while Stefan stayed up a little later to help Andrej on the completion of the map. As he was getting undressed and into bed, he happened to look out the window and saw a glow over the town. There appeared to be a fire across the river in nizne Ruzbachy. With the severe cold weather, the people in town would need all the help that they could get so he dressed and knocked on Andrej's door.

He shouted, "Hitch the wagon and drive into town. There is a huge fire and I am going to saddle Blaze and go on ahead."

He rode as fast as he dared because the road was covered with ice and he did not want the horse to slip and fall. As he approached the bridge, he saw that the fire was behind the cobbler's shop. That was where Andrej's mother lived so he pushed the horse to go faster. The men in town were trying to put out the fire, but water in the well was frozen and people broke the ice from time to time, but it started to freeze again as soon as it was broken.

The house was almost burned to the ground and Stefan stopped one of the women, "Is Anna was all right? Where is she?"

The woman said, "She was pulled out of the house by Alexander Kopec who was working late in his cobbler shop. He had smelled smoke on such a still night and saw that it was coming from Anna's house so he rushed in and got her out, they could not save the house. Anna was taken to Alexander's home a few doors down and Father Josef was seeing to her now."

Just then Andrej pulled up and Stefan told him all that he knew. They both went to see Anna and found her sitting in the kitchen of the Kopec home drinking a cup of hot tea. She had been burned, but it was not serious. Father Josef had put some salve on the burns and that was all that was required. Andrej kissed his mother, but she had a glassy look in her eyes as she had gone through a traumatic experience; she was in shock.

Andrej asked, "How did this happen?"

His mother spoke very slowly, "I could not sleep in the bedroom because it was too cold so I took my bed clothes and put them on the floor, in front of the fireplace in the kitchen. I laid down on them to sleep and I must have slept soundly, because a spark had jumped from the fireplace to my bedclothes. A chair caught on fire from the clothes and that spread to the table that was against the wooden wall. When I awoke, the wall was in flames and Pan Kopec had broken in to get me out. I was burned from the bed clothes, but he carried me out and before help arrived, the building was in flames. They tried to get water from the well to put out the fire, but they had trouble breaking the layer of ice to get at the water and by that time, it was too late to save the house. It was an old house, and rather small so it did not take long for the house to burn to the ground. Pan Kopec saved the life of your mother."

Stefan told Anna, "You are welcome to stay with us. Stay here with Pan Kopec and we will come in the morning to see what we might salvage from the fire and then we will take you to your new home." Anna managed a faint smile and nodded in agreement.

The next morning, Stefan and Andrej hitched up the wagon and started down to the town. Kada insisted upon going even though the weather was still bitter cold. They spent the morning going through the ashes and they did manage to salvage some furniture that could be refinished, some dishes, pots and pans and other household items that were spared in the fire. They loaded the wagon with the items that they had found and, as they were sitting in the Kopec's kitchen with Pani Kopec, people came to the door with items that they wanted to donate to Anna. There were clothes, blankets, pots, pans, boots and food. They all said how sorry they were for the tragedy and some even offered to take her in until suitable arrangements could be made for a permanent residence. Stefan told them that arrangements had already been made. Father Andrej stopped in and said that there would be a special collection taken up for Anna at the Mass the following Sunday. Stefan watched these events and thought that these people were the finest people on earth and he would always be proud to say that he was a Slovak. He would go to America, but he would remain a Slovak until he died.

Anna was welcomed into the Janek household and in a short time it appeared that she had always lived there. She did her share of the chores and even left time for Kada to help her husband and brother in the barns. Kada could not do much since she was getting rather large in the waist. She told her mother that she and Olga had performed the test which said that it was going to be a boy. They decided to tell her that the three of them were leaving for America in three more weeks. It did not mean much to Anna as she assumed that they were going to visit and they would return, but Stefan explained that she would be living with Andrej and his wife, Anna, once they were married, and that Olga, her daughter Kada and Stefan would not return. She did not take the news very well until Stefan assured her that her son was capable of running the farm and dealing with the notary.

Once Anna was settled and calmed down, the Janeks began their preparations to leave. They picked out the belongings that they wanted to take and those that they had to leave behind.

Stefan said, "It is better to leave our property with Andrej than to an unknown German on the pier in Hamburg."

Since the passage fare did not include meals, Olga set aside one piece of luggage for food so they would not have to buy as much.

Stefan said, "We have only enough money for either a room or food and I elected to buy the room aboard ship."

Olga argued, "Kada will be eight months along in her pregnancy when we leave and the last month is all important for the nourishment of the baby; Kada will require more food than the two of them."

Kada said, "It will only be for ten days and I will manage."

Olga hid some money that neither of them knew about, just in case. She did not want a puny grandson to start his life in America."

19

On March 11, 1921, Olga, Kada and Stefan left Ruzbachy forever. Andrej took them to the railway station in Polodencz. They finally told all their friends and relatives about their departure and Father Andrej said a special mass the Sunday before they left. Stefan and Andrej went to the tavern for one more night so Stefan could say goodbye to his comrades. They retold old war stories and Stefan was feeling very good when Andrej helped him into the house. The weather was warmer and the roads were turning into mud when they left and they allowed for this by leaving early. Stefan gave Andrej instructions on how to handle the notary; Andrej was not to take the word of this man as the truth, but was to see everything in writing. If he disagreed, he should consult Father Andrej who would advise him or send him to someone who would. Not much was said for most of the wagon trip to the train. Andrej helped them load the baggage and the goodbyes were painful. Olga and Kada cried and even Stefan grew misty-eyed.

They rode in silence for many miles, looking out the window of the train where they saw the landscape of Slovakia with its forest and fields slipping by. Every so often, they went through a small town; sometimes they stopped, and sometimes they did not slow down.

Olga sighed and said, "When my sons and daughter left, I did not ever consider following them and here I am with my youngest son and his pregnant wife sitting on a train going to America. I am happy to be going to see my children and grandchildren."

Olga did much to bolster her son's spirits because he felt better after listening to her. She seemed to be enjoying the ride because this was the first time that she had been further than Polodencz. He had not realized that before, but to her, this had to be the greatest experience that she had in all of her life. But if

Stefan could read Kada's mind, he would have returned to Ruzbachy. She was worried about the birth of her child. She prayed quietly every chance that she could and she would have plenty of time to pray by the time they arrived in America.

The train pulled into Bratislava and they had to change so they could take the one to Vienna. In Vienna they would have to change trains to go to Prague but the last change they would make was in Prague for that train would follow the Elbe river and finally reach Hamburg. The schedule called for them to reach Hamburg the afternoon of March 11, but with the number of stops that they made, it probably would be later. They had to wait two and a half hours for the train to Vienna so they found a stand that sold sausage and bread. They each had one sausage and a piece of bread for the evening meal and Stefan would have loved to have a beer, but he wanted to conserve the money that they had taken with them. They washed the meal down with water, went to their track and waited for their train.

The train finally came, two hours late, and they were tired. It was now ten o'clock in the evening. They knew that the trip from Bratislava to Vienna was only about an hour and if the train was late, then they would not be leaving Vienna until early morning, on the twelfth of March. It seemed that the train had just started when it stopped and someone said that it was a customs check. Austrian police came on board and walked through the train questioning people at random and a short stout officer spoke to Stefan. He looked at his papers and then at Kada but he did not want to upset her, in her condition, so he did not question them, and walked to the next seat. It took almost an hour for the police to do their work. The train started again and within a half an hour, they pulled into the station in Vienna. Stefan knew this station as he had been there twice before and when they got off the train, Stefan asked the ticket seller when the train to Prague was to leave. He told them that they missed their train but another one left at five o'clock in the morning and they could catch that one. They had three and a half hours more to wait and Stefan found two benches close together where he guarded the women while they slept. Stefan would sleep on the train to Prague.

He had to wake the women, but they caught the train to Prague and no one told them that it was a "milk" train until Stefan asked the conductor. The train stopped at every stop to pick up milk and other food to be delivered to the city. The train seemed to go back and forth over the countryside and Stefan swore that they had gone over the same track twice. He tried to sleep, but the jerking motion of the train kept waking him up so they bought some bread from a vendor who came up the aisle and had their morning meal. A man in the next seat told them that they could buy coffee or tea a few cars back. Stefan went to explore. He no sooner returned when the train stopped again. They were leaving Austria and were returning to Czechoslovakia so there was another customs check and police boarded the train. When their time came, he showed the officer his papers and spoke in Slovak; the policeman looked at him suspiciously and asked where they were going.

Stefan proudly said, "We are going to America."

He looked at Kada and wished them good luck and moved on quickly, before Kada started her delivery.

While the train was stopped, Stefan dozed off because he had something in his stomach and the train was not moving. The last thing he remembered hearing was the sound of the steam engine. He woke up three hours later while they were only an hour out of Prague and it was ten o'clock in the morning. It was time to get ready to leave this train and then find the one that went to Hamburg. When they pulled into Prague, he was surprised to see such a large city for it was bigger than Bratislava, and about the same size as Vienna. He knew that they missed their connection for the train to Hamburg, and he wondered how long they would have to wait for the next one.

In Prague they found that they would have to wait five hours for the next train to Hamburg so they found a place to store their luggage for very little money, and decided to walk around Prague. Olga wanted to see the Cathedral and they really needed to get

some exercise after being seated for the last twenty-four hours. The
cathedral was large and beautiful: they had never seen anything
quite like it before and never realized that such things existed.
Stefan said that their adventure was just beginning since they have
yet to spend ten days at sea before they got to America. They
found Prague to be clean and well-maintained but Kada said that
her neck hurt from looking up so much. They found a small family restaurant, went in and sat down. Olga said that Kada needed
food so they ordered some pierogi with soured cream and bread
and Kada had a big glass of milk. When the bill came, Olga paid
for it out of her money that she had put away for just such an
occasion. They felt good when they returned, got their luggage
and found that the train was on time.

They boarded the train ahead of time and Stefan slept for an
hour. When he woke, they were moving toward Hamburg. The
train made a stop in Karlovy Vary for about one half hour and then
headed north to the Elbe river. They would follow the river to
Hamburg but they seemed to stop every half hour until they got
to the border when the police came on to do another customs
check. This did not take too long and the first stop in Germany
was Dresden which took some time because they had to change
engines.

They arrived in Hamburg at five in the morning; it had taken
them twelve hours to travel from Prague to Hamburg. Being so
tired, they had to hire a wagon to take them from the train station
to the docks. They were in awe at the size of the ships, the equipment to load them; people were everywhere. The wagon dropped
them off on March 13. The ship was scheduled to leave at three
pm on the next day. It was an old ship. Paint was peeling from the
hull and there were two black smokestacks in the middle of the
ship. It looked big to Stefan but it was not the largest one at the
docks. He walked up to the bow and saw the words "S.S. Mongolia."
It was the right ship all right, he did not want to end up in Africa
or any place like that. He wanted to go to America.

Stefan went up the gangway and saw an officer, the first black man he had ever seen. He spoke to the officer in Slovak but the man shrugged his shoulders and called to another man. He was a Czech who could understand Stefan and Stefan asked if he could board and stow his belongings, but the officer said no one could come aboard until five o'clock that night. Stefan pointed to Kada and said that he could not have her carrying luggage for twelve hours. The officer looked at Kada and said that, due to his wife's condition, he would allow them to lock their luggage in their room until they boarded. This seemed to be working out just fine for no one wanted to be responsible for harming a mother-to-be. He was given a key, was shown to their room and was assured that it would be safe. Stefan thanked the officer and made three trips with their luggage.

The room was very small but there were two bunks in it and a cot in between. There was barely enough room to walk around it, the good thing about it was that the cot could be folded up when not in use. There was a little room with a toilet but nothing else. He noticed that it was a trough with running water and he assumed the water carried the waste out to sea. He deposited all of the luggage on the bed and went off to join the women.

They spent the day walking around the waterfront. They marveled at the huge cranes used to load the ships and looked this way and that to see the sights. As each saw something new, they pulled the others over to see it. The day flew by and Olga said that she had been fortunate to live to see such sights. The women had rarely ventured outside of the boundaries of the farm but Stefan got to see some large cities when he was in the army. But, even he had not seen anything like this. They went back to the ship at five in the afternoon, Stefan showed the officer his tickets and the key that was given to him earlier and they were allowed to board the ship. There were no windows, but there seemed to be air circulating through the room and Stefan made a note to ask someone how they did that.

The next morning they walked around the ship and noticed that it had been loaded with cargo and the cranes were moved to

other ships. They found that they were on the next to lowest deck
and Kada mentioned that she hoped the engines were not so loud
as to interfere with their sleep. There were people coming and
going, pulling young children and carrying packages up the gang
plank and helping elderly people on board. By the time the ship
was ready to sail, it would be full. They found the dining room
and had some rolls and coffee. Olga said that they would have a
good meal that night because they have not been eating much
since they left the farm. It was fun exploring the ship, but Olga
and Kada became tired and they went down to their cabin to rest.

Stefan found a crew member in uniform and asked, "Where is
the doctor's office? My wife is eight months pregnant and I want
to be prepared in the event that she needs medical attention."

The officer took him to the doctor's office on the main deck
and told Stefan that on the ship it was called the infirmary. The
doctor was a tall German with a small mustache right under his
nose. His hair was cut very short, only one-half inch was visible on
the top of his head. His monocle hung around his neck and rested
on his chest and he had on a tailored ship's uniform. His eyes were
pale blue and gentle and Stefan liked the man right away even if
he was a German. He was relieved to know that there was someone
on board that he could trust if Kada had any problems.

The doctor introduced himself as Dr. Shent and asked, "May I
have your names and cabin number? Bring your wife to the infirmary at nine o'clock tomorrow so I can meet her and examine her."
Stefan breathed a sigh of relief and went back to the cabin where
he found both Olga and Kada asleep.

At two o'clock the engines started. The noise was not so loud
that they would not be able to sleep. The women woke up and
they all went on deck as the ship was leaving the pier. They found
the deck crowded, but the people made way for Kada so she could
stand by the railing for support. Right on time, the gangway was
lowered, the ropes were taken off their poles and two little boats
started to push the ship around so that it faced north. They started
to push the ship up the Elbe River and the two powerful little

boats, were pushing the ship with ease. They were doing most of the work even though the engines on the "S.S. Mongolia" were helping. The city of Hamburg was sixty miles south of the North Sea on the Elbe river and the ship moved slowly enough so that they could see all the people waving goodbyes for a short time.

Before the gangway was lowered, Stefan saw men throwing packages and luggage into wagons. These were the belongings that could not be carried aboard. Stefan was pleased that he was allowed to make three trips because of his pregnant wife. He thought that Slovaks do not knowingly break the rules, they just bend them a little. They sat in the chairs, next to the outside wall of the deck and watched the country side move past. A woman came by and told Stefan that she was a trained midwife and she gave them her name and cabin number. She spoke Czech and told them that if Kada had trouble, they could call on her to help. Her name was Pani Dubchek and she reminded Stefan of Pani Benerik in Ruzbachy. She was a large woman and looked as if she had delivered many children herself for there were six children of various ages standing to one aide. They were all well dressed and well mannered. She wrote her name and cabin number on a piece of paper and gave it to Stefan. They had made their first friend on the way to America.

Once she had left, Stefan said to Olga, "I do not see a husband around and this woman has courage traveling on a steamship, on her own, with six children."

Olga replied, "It took no more courage than to travel on a steamship with a wife who was eight months pregnant."

She looked Stefan squarely in the eye when she said it. Stefan knew which side his mother was on. He decided to keep the name of this woman and her cabin number just in case they needed her. An announcement came over the loud speakers that if they looked north, they would see the city of Weden with its castle sitting on the hill. The castle was built to protect the German people from an invasion from the north.

Stefan sat in his deck chair and watched the people parading in front of him. He saw whole families of three, four and even five children and they were all well dressed for the start of the journey. He could tell who the farmers were by looking at their hands for they were rough and calloused from years of holding reins, cutting wheat in the fields and using the hoe in the gardens. He could tell the professional people by their haughtiness and bearing and they looked as if they had not done a day's work in their lives. He recognized soldiers or military men by their precise manner and their stiff appearance because they walked as if they were on a march to nowhere. There was nothing to do on the boat except to look at what was around them so they sat in the deck chairs until dark and then went into the dining room.

They were led to a table with a white cloth and a small vase of flowers upon it and since there was no way to keep the flowers fresh, they should enjoy them as much as possible. It was an elegant table, set with a dish, three forks, two spoons and two knives, one large and one small, and a white cloth folded in the shape of a butterfly for each place setting. There were not too many people in the dining room because many people brought their own food on board.

Olga said, "I have put aside money for this meal, so order whatever you want. I have saved a few crowns over the years and the most important matter at hand is to get Kada to America so that my grandson will be born a citizen of the United States."

Stefan looked puzzled and asked, "How are you so sure that it will be a boy?"

He never did get an answer. The women just looked at each other and smiled.

They ordered roast pork to the waiter with the black bow tie and short white coat. They had no idea what it would cost since the price was printed in German marks and they did not know what the exchange rate was. The waiter brought them each a small bowl of soup made with vegetables and tomatoes. He took the bowls away when they were finished and brought a small dish of raw green vegetables with a sauce poured on them. Next, they were served a plate of roast pork, boiled potatoes, some carrots and a small serving of a stuffing. The waiter brought bread, butter and a bowl of gravy to be poured over the meat and potatoes. They ate everything on the table because they had usually not eaten anything as tasty as this in their lives. They did not know which utensils to use so most of them remained clean. They watched other people unfold the white cloth and put it in their laps. When they were finished and felt that they could not eat anymore, the waiter brought them each a piece of pie. It looked like some cooked apples between two crusts of bread. They noticed other people eating the pie with forks, so they did the same, tasting the pie. Kada liked it so much she ate her piece, Stefan's piece and would have eaten Olga's if Olga had not eaten it quickly. They each had a cup of coffee with real cream and sugar and after the meal, they were ready to go down to their cabin and go to bed. It had been a long day and when the waiter came with the bill, Stefan asked what it would be in Czechoslovakian crowns and the waiter came back with a bill in crowns. It was three crowns for all that they had eaten and the waiter told them to take their crowns to the pursers office to exchange them for German marks. It seemed like with the amount of food they had eaten, they would not be hungry for at least a few days, but they knew that the growling would come to their stomachs by morning. They spent some time walking around the deck to help settle their meal and to discuss the day's events.

The next morning, they awoke before dawn. They had only gotten to the mouth of the Elbe and had not entered the North sea but they wanted to see the dawning of the day on their first full day of their journey. The ship had just begun to make the left turn into the North Sea, toward the English Channel when the first sign of the sun made its appearance on the horizon. They went around Guxhaven and Duhnew with their resorts and health spas and Kada remembered when she worked at the Marianske Spa in the High Tatras. When she left that spa, she vowed that she would never work in that type of service ever again. She told Stefan and Olga of the hardship she had to endure in the two years that she had spent there, for Kada had a hard life until she met the Janeks. She did not mind living with the gypsies, but she would never go back to the work at Marianske Health Spa.

The sun was now rising quite rapidly and they could almost see it move. There were a few clouds on the horizon and they turned colors as the sun came up. They heard a few "Ohs" and "Ahs," and looked around to find that they were not alone. Many people had the same idea and had gotten up to see the sunrise. It was a spectacular sight, the dawn of a new day for the world and the dawn of a new life for the Janek family.

Olga had a lump in her throat and she almost started to cry. It caused Stefan to look at her and ask, "Are you all right, mother?"

She suddenly embraced her youngest son and wet his jacket with her tears. "I am finally on my way to see my family, all in one place, at one time and if only Johan had been alive to see this. All of my grandchildren that I have never seen will now be in my arms. God has been good to me. I did not get to know my mother, I did not know my grandparents, but God has gotten me this far. He will surely carry me the rest of the way."

They did not speak, but just stood there and enjoyed the sight.

At nine o'clock, Stefan took Kada to see the doctor. Olga insisted on being present. She was not going to leave her daughter-in-law with a strange man, no matter who he was. He examined her and said that he felt that she was further along than she claimed but Olga and Kada had counted the days and they felt that Kada still had three weeks or more to complete her term. The doctor just shook his head and smiled and after the examination, he took them on a tour of the infirmary. There was a room with four hospital beds and the whole room was painted white, even the walls. He told them that he was equipped to handle an emergency and he had delivered many babies on the high seas. While Kada felt at ease, Olga was worried. When they left the doctor's office, she wanted a second opinion so they went down to see Pani Dubchek in her room. She was not in, but a girl of about fifteen said she would give her the message. Olga told her that they would be sitting in the same area where they first met.

Stefan brought back some rolls and coffee while they waited for Pani Dubchek. About an hour later they looked up to see the large woman moving down the deck and for a large woman, she moved rather quickly. She gave the impression that she did every-thing quickly and she did not like to be contradicted. She took one look at Kada and reached for her hand to take her pulse. She felt her forehead and asked her to step into the woman's lavatory. She pressed on her stomach, listened to her heart beat, took out a very primitive stethoscope and found the baby's heartbeat.

She listened to Kada's heartbeat and asked, "Have you carried the baby low for all term?"

Kada said, "The baby seems to be lower now than it was before."

Pani Dubchek asked, "When is the baby due?"

"According to our calculation, the baby is due on April 15."

Pani Dubchek shook her head and said, "Your delivery process has started."

Kada told her what the doctor had said and Pani Dubchek would make herself available in the event she was needed. When they returned to Stefan and Olga, Kada asked that nothing be said since she would tell her family in her own way. Kada did tell Olga, but did not Stefan, because she did not want him to worry.

They sat outside for most of the afternoon when they passed the resort islands of Wangerooge, Langeoog and Norderney. The sea became rougher as they were now in the North Sea heading for the English Channel. Once past the channel, the sea was calmer but the weather was becoming colder when the wind came out of the north. The north wind helped to push the ship ahead so they were making good time when Kada decided to go to the cabin to lie down and Olga went with her. She was not going to leave her daughter-in-law alone for any length of time. Stefan continued to walk around the ship asking questions. He went to the purser's office and exchanged his crowns for German marks and the officer told him that sometime before they docked in Boston, he should exchange his German marks for United States dollars. This would be the last time that Stefan used his money from his homeland.

When he returned to the cabin, had picked up some rolls to be added to the evening meal. Olga had opened the suitcase that contained the food which had kept fairly well. She had some dried beef, hard-boiled eggs, some canned peaches, beans, carrots and smoked sausage and ham. They ate the food that was the first to spoil. The only money that they spent on food was the rolls and coffee that Stefan had bought and the meal that Olga had paid for. For the remainder of the evening, they sat on the beds and talked. Stefan had found a wash room that was to be shared by six cabins. He and Kada found the door unlocked so they went in to wash. There were towels there, but it looked as if some of the towels were missing. After they washed, they took their towels plus one for Olga back to their cabin for use the next day.

Olga went to the washroom and this gave Kada and Stefan time to be alone. Kada said, "Your mother is like my shadow, she will not let me stay alone at all."

Stefan smiled and told her, "My mother is just worried about you and wants to be near you in the event something happened. Do not mention it to her, but let the woman do what she wants to do. The voyage will be over in another week and then she will have her other children to occupy her. I have other things to do and I do not want to drag you around in your condition. I would rather have you rest and if my mother wants to be with you, so be it."

Kada nodded her head and said, "I will allow your mother to do what she wants."

The next day turned out to be a perfect day. The sun was out and the wind had shifted, now coming from the west, and the day was warmer. They chose the side of the ship that faced the sun but when the sun was overhead, they went to the other side. Everytime an officer would go by, Stefan jumped up to ask him a question. Finally, the first mate offered to give him a tour of the ship. Stefan was excited and asked Kada if it was all right for him to go and she replied that Olga was with her so it would be fine. The two went off together with Stefan asking questions as they walked.

The first mate's name was Kirchoff. He was a white Russian who spoke Slovak along with four other languages. He took Stefan down to the engine room where there were two large furnaces. The doors were open and men were shoveling coal into the red-hot ovens. There were gauges on the furnaces and once the temperature went down, the men shoveled more coal into the fire. This went on for twenty-four hours a day; the fire heated the water that turned into steam. The steam expanded and pushed the pistons which were geared to the propeller. The propeller turned and pushed the ship forward.

Stefan was amazed and he wondered, "Why cannot this be adapted to farm machinery or land vehicles?"

The mate answered, "Trains are already using this, but it was too large and cumbersome to be used on smaller vehicles. Those were powered by an internal combustible engine. You will see many of these vehicles in America, especially in Boston where the streets are crowded with them. A man named Ford devised a way to mass produce the vehicles and make them affordable to everyone."

Stefan could not wait to tell his wife and mother what a marvelous country they were going to live in.

The next stop was the crew's quarters. They had their own kitchen, dining room and wash rooms so they did not come in contact with the passengers. They did their work like invisible men and Stefan could not remember seeing them except for the waiters, maids and officers. The officers had their own quarters but they ate with the passengers and stayed among them. They were supposed to mingle with the passengers and help them whenever they could. They went through the kitchen where men in white hats and jackets prepared food for the day's consumption.

He said, "Americans eat three times a day, breakfast, lunch and dinner."

Stefan said, "In my country, people eat twice a day. They have the morning meal of bread rolls and coffee and their main meal at night. Life was going to be different in America; there will be much to learn."

The next stop on the tour was the bridge. The first mate showed Stefan what the navigator did, what the officer in charge of the bridge did and how the bridge talks with the engine room. He showed how the ship keeps in contact with the port that they have just left and the one that they will be going to. Stefan was fascinated with the work that had to be done to make sure that the ship was going to arrive at the correct port at the correct time. The docking was all reserved and if a ship was late, a dock would be vacant while a ship that was on time would have to wait to dock. The people on that ship would have to feed the passengers for an extra time, costing money. Ships had to be on time to keep the shipping lanes open.

He said, "The S.S. Mongolia would dock in Boston on March 22 at nine o'clock in the morning and the tugboats will be waiting to push her in past Provincetown on Cape Cod at midnight on that day."

When Stefan returned to his wife and mother, he had many stories to tell and he told them of his tour from beginning to end. He told them what the first mate had told him about America and the motor cars for this was truly a wonderful place. He could not wait to dock in Boston so he could get started living in this country. They had arranged to have Marta and Josef meet them when they got off the ship and they would take them to Cohoes, New York where the rest of the family will be waiting. He looked at Kada and she appeared to be a little pale and it looked like she was having a bout with sea sickness. She did not tell Stefan because she did not want to worry him but he suggested that she visit the doctor. Perhaps he could give her something to help her and the three of them went to the infirmary. There were fifteen people waiting to see the doctor so she waited her turn and finally a young lady in a white dress with a white cap motioned for her to enter the doctor's office. The doctor was pleased to see her but he asked

Stefan to step out while he examined Kada. Olga, of course, did not leave.

He said, "The baby had moved down a little since the last time I had seen you and at the first pain in the abdomen, you must call me at once. Here are some pills to take once a day to help with the sea sickness, but it will make you drowsy and you will want to sleep all the time. That was normal."

Olga stuck to her daughter-in-law like a fly on sticky paper. She even went to the bathroom with her and when she took a nap, Olga sat right there to watch her. She noted every facial expression that came across Kada's face for she was waiting for a grimace showing pain. Kada did not eat the evening meal since she said that the sight of food made her ill. She went to bed early and slept the entire night while Olga made Stefan watch her while she went to the bathroom and the washroom. They did not leave her alone for a moment and finally, they all went to bed. Stefan did not sleep much that night because he was thinking of what the first mate had said about America and he worried about his wife. If something happened to her on this journey, he would never forgive himself for making this trip. Olga could only remember the story of how she was born, the loss of her mother making the journey through the High Tatras with her father pushing her and the guilt that he felt for the rest of his life. It was like the same thing was happening again.

They awoke the next morning to the swaying of the ship. Kada looked pale. She had been in the toilet most of the night and was ready to go back in. Stefan got her a cup of water and made her take a pill. She put her head on the pillow and closed her eyes. He had hoped that she would get used to the swaying of the ship, especially with the pills, but she was looking no better. They must be somewhere in the Atlantic by now where there were storms in March and he looked over at Olga who did not look all that well either. He thought that Kada being sick had made Olga feel bad and he knew that Olga needed some air. He told Olga to go up on deck for a few hours, he would stay with Kada. When she came back to relieve him, he would get some rolls and coffee. Olga said she wanted nothing to eat and she doubted that Kada would eat anything but she got dressed and went to the washroom; luckily it was unoccupied.

When Olga got to the deck floor, she noticed part of the crew with rain gear on. She looked out and saw the heavy rain. Olga sat in the lounge and looked around her. She was alone except for some of the crew that were cleaning up. The waves were high and the ship was crashing into them sending spray to both sides. She wondered why the navigator did not go around the storm. He may not have known it was out there. She prayed to God that she would survive the journey and she promised God that if He allowed her to set foot on solid land, she would never again go out on the sea. There was nothing to do and nothing to see except for the waves, wind and rain, so she went back to the cabin. Stefan would be able to get out and stretch his legs since he was the only one who was not ill. If things got worse, Olga thought, the women would need him to take care of them.

When she returned to the cabin, she found Kada sound asleep and was relieved that the pill was doing its work. Stefan was sitting on the bed trying to remember how much they had spent on the trip so far for he wanted to keep track of the expenses. He wanted to show Marta and Josef that they did not spend the money foolishly. Stefan knew that he would pay them back, but he wanted them to know that he was using it wisely. He was almost finished and asked Olga to go over it with him so he would be sure that he had not forgotten anything. Olga told him that there was heavy wind and rain outside and it was a storm from the northeast bringing cold wind and rain. Stefan decided to go up and see for himself.

When he got up to the main deck, he realized that Olga was not exaggerating because this was a fearsome storm. Everyone topside appears to be busy and the crew members were tying down everything. All of the awnings were taken down or they would have been ripped to pieces. A cook brought in a pot of coffee for the crew and offered Stefan a cup. He accepted it with thanks. The coffee was hot, fresh and looked strong. He put more milk and sugar into it and it tasted fine.

He asked the cook if this was a common occurrence in the Atlantic. "Yes, we usually get one or two storms in March, but this one appeared to be rather strong. The ship's weather forecasting equipment was not very good and we have to rely on visual signs but we should be out of the storm soon. The nice part of the storm is that no one came up from their cabins and there was less work to do. If you follow me to the kitchen, I will give you some rolls, butter and coffee to take to your cabin. They would go to waste anyway since no one was going to come up to eat and I have to make the food."

Stefan took the rolls and hot coffee back to the cabin where Olga was feeling better but Kada was still asleep. They both ate and saved some for Kada. Stefan took out the instructions from Marta so he would be sure that he understood what it was that he was supposed to do. Olga found some paper and a pen and decided to write a letter to Andrej. She wanted to let him know that they were doing fine except for Kada's seasickness. Stefan wondered how Andrej was doing with the notary and he wondered what the notary's reaction was when he found out that the Janek family was gone. He was sure that Andrej would not run the farm as well as he and Olga had and would not keep the records as well. The Republic of Czechoslovakia was losing some fine people because of the inept government and although there were fewer mouths to feed, its more experienced people were leaving. The people remaining would survive, they always survive.

Toward the middle of the afternoon, the storm subsided and the ship did not rock back and forth as much. Kada woke up and ate a roll and Stefan took her for a walk, as she needed the exercise at this time in her pregnancy. Olga came along in case that she became dizzy again. The rain had stopped when they reached the main deck and there were a few people milling around talking. They saw Pani Dubchek, sitting with her two older children, and went to talk to her. She had the two children that suffered seasickness with her because they needed air. The other children were fine and were in the cabin alone. Stefan could not understand how she had fit seven people into one cabin but Pani Dubchek told him that she had a suite. There were two rooms with four beds. The children slept two in a bed, while she had her own bed. They had a private toilet and washroom so with a little bit of scheduling, they managed very well.

The midwife could not take her eyes off of Kada. "The baby has dropped a little more since the last time I have saw you. Your time is coming and I am ready to help. Would it be all right if one of my children stopped in, once in a while, to see if that everything is all right?"

Stefan was happy to have some help and he was impressed with the midwife's concern. She must know something that he was unaware of, he thought, and it was a good thing that they had met her. She excused herself and said that she wanted to check on the younger children and left the two older girls with them.

The older girl's name was Sophie. She was sixteen years old and was happy to be going to America. She wanted to meet boys in America and get married. They came from a little town of Zatec on the German border and their father was killed on the eastern front fighting the French. His name was Alexy and he worked for a large landowner. He ran the farm for the wealthy man who did not spend much time at his estate for he had business dealings all over the world. When Pani Dubchek was younger, before the children were born, she went to the hospital in Prague and trained as a midwife. She was known all over the area and she had delivered countless children. After Alexy was killed, his employer gave her a small interest in one of his enterprises and suggested that she go to America because he wanted the house for his new manager. He gave Anna Dubchek the money for the fare and arranged for her to settle in Boston. She received a dividend from the investment which was enough to live on in Czechoslovakia, but not enough to get by in Boston.

Sophie was talkative and they learned much from her as they

spoke. Anna was going to get a job as a midwife in a clinic in Boston to make enough to supplement her dividend so they can be self-supporting, Anna was a proud woman and she would not accept charity. Her employer had arranged for them to rent a house near the clinic where they could all walk to schools, shopping and church. Sophie did not want to go to school any longer, but her mother insisted that she complete as much schooling as possible. She told Sophie that the more schooling she had, the higher quality husband she would attract. Stefan looked at the girl. She was not pretty, but she did well with the attributes that she had. She was well groomed, well dressed, spoke very well and had a wholesome quality about her. She would attract a fine husband and he knew a dozen men in Ruzbachy who would have married her.

Anna came back with the rest of the children and announced, "It is almost time to eat but we will walk around the deck a few times before we go to the dining room. The meals were part of our fare and we eat three times a day, whether we are hungry or not."

Stefan thought that a walk around the deck was a good idea so they left the lounge also. He told Kada that when she felt tired, they would go down to the cabin. He saw that color was returning to Kada's face because the clean salt air was making her feel better. She even mentioned that she could take some food so they decided to go to the dining room for the meal. They would not get the whole large meal, but something smaller, for they must have food other than large meals.

When they entered the dining room, they saw that many other people had the same idea. They were led to a table for three, next to a large noisy table with twelve people. The men were dressed in formal suits while the ladies had floor length gowns. There were bottles of wine on the table and they were laughing and telling stories. There was also an abundance of food on the table, but they were not eating much and Stefan thought that he would like to have the left overs. They ordered sausages, boiled potatoes, bread and coffee. As they were eating, Stefan looked up and saw the cook that he had met that morning in the lounge. The cook was walking around the dining room asking everyone how they liked the food when he saw Stefan and recognized him. He came over and shook his hand and Stefan introduced Kada and Olga to him.

He took a look at Kada and said, "You need milk, much milk."

He snapped his fingers and a waiter appeared out of nowhere. He told the waiter, "Bring a pitcher of milk for the mother-to-be."

A pitcher of milk appeared on the table. The cook said to Stefan, "If she could not drink it all, you are to take the rest to your cabin and bring the pitcher back when you can. She looks as if she is going to deliver any day now and I would like to be told when she did. It would be St. Josef's day on the 19th and that would be a good name for him, if he was born on that day. My first name is Josef."

He excused himself and resumed his walk around the dining room. The bill was presented and it was one mark but there was no change for the milk. The cook must be an important man, thought Stefan.

When they left the dining room, all eyes at the large table, followed them out the door and Kada felt important carrying her milk. They walked the deck for a while until Kada yawned and they went down the stairs toward the cabin. Stefan was tired and he knew that Olga must be exhausted for she had not left Kada's side except for the time she went to the lounge. The wind, blowing so hard against the bulkhead, had the effect of making them tired and they all felt the need for sleep. They took turns going to the washroom. Stefan gave Kada another pill even though she did not admit to any dizziness. It would at least make her sleep until morning. They went to bed and fell asleep at once.

Stefan got up early and as he looked at the two women sleeping peaceably, he let himself out into the hallway and waited to get into the washroom. He went upstairs to watch the sun rise and the only other person on deck was the first mate with the same idea. The first mate nodded to him and said that watching the sunrise was the best part of the trip. Stefan agreed and they both stood in silence to watch the sun come up over the horizon. Too soon it was over, and they went to the dining room for a cup of coffee. Stefan liked this young man because one always knew where one stood with him. If there was a problem, he came right out and said what he thought and he would be master of his own ship very shortly. Stefan felt a kinship with first mate Kirchoff for he spoke Slovak and they could communicate. Stefan spoke only to the cook and the Dubchek family because he did not know if anyone else could speak with him in Slovak. Most of the people spoke German and he had formed an impression of them as arrogant. He had gotten this impression from the war and it had not changed since. He spent two hours talking to the first mate about the farm, his homeland, the government which did not represent the Slovaks, the poverty created by the war and the Magyars.

It was good to talk to someone other than the two ladies that he traveled with so he felt much better after talking to Kirchoff. The first mate did not reveal much information about himself. He had been in the war on the side of the Tsar, but it had only been for a short time and he did not elaborate. Finally, the loud speaker called him to the bridge so he excused himself and went to work. Stefan went down to the cabin where he found that the women were up, washed and ready to go on deck. Kada wanted help in getting into a deck chair. Once she got down into it, she would stay there for quite a while because it was just too much trouble to get up again. The only reason she would move would be to go to the toilet and then she would wait until the last minute. Stefan did not dare leave her alone because he and Olga had to get her up together.

The sea was calm, the ship appeared to be cutting through the water and it was making good time. He hoped that the storm had not used up too much extra fuel for he knew that the coal was calculated to bring the ship to Boston. If more fuel was taken on, that added to the weight that could be used for paying cargo. As he looked out, he saw that they were going by a large white object in the middle of the ocean. He had no idea what it was when he pointed it out to Kada. A man in the next chair spoke to him in

German. Stefan shook his head, he did not want to speak German even though he could understand a little. The man spoke French, then Russian and finally Polish and Stefan decided that he would answer to that.

The man said, "It is an iceberg. Up north, the sea is frozen and large pieces break off and float south until they melt. Many ships had sunk after striking an iceberg and one that comes to mind was "H M S Titanic" where many people lost their lives. The icebergs are dangerous because, most of it is under water and the only part that can be seen is the tip of the iceberg. If the ship comes too close, then it might hit the part that was submerged and that was the reason that the ship went around it at some distance."

Stefan was fascinated with the explanation. He asked many questions and the man answered all of them. The man seemed pleased to be able to satisfy Stefan's curiosity.

When there was a lull in the conversation, Kada said that she was hungry, so Stefan went off to get some food. He found a small station on the deck where they sold hot buns and rolls. Stefan bought three rolls and three mugs of coffee to take back to the women. The man was gone so Stefan took his chair and settled back. After they ate, Kada fell asleep and she did not appear to have any more signs of the seasickness. It must have been the storm that caused it. Kada slept until the middle of the afternoon and Stefan dozed on and off while Olga did not leave her daughter-in-law's side at all. Things settled down so that they were actually enjoying the quiet of the sea and the drone of the steam engines. It was the calm before the storm.

As he was dozing off, Sophie appeared before him and said, "My mother sent me to find you to see if Kada was all right."

Stefan pointed to her as she slept like a baby so the girl left to report to her mother. When it was time to go to the toilet, Kada asked Stefan to help her up. He took her legs and swung them around until they were on the deck then he and Olga pushed her up so that she was sitting. Olga took one arm, Stefan took the other and they started to pull her as she screamed; for her time had come. They let her down and Stefan ran to the bridge to tell the officer in charge. He asked where they were and told him to go back there and wait for help. As Stefan got back, there were four rather husky men already there. They put Kada's feet up on the chair, folded it all the way back and lifted Kada, chair and all and carried her right to the infirmary where the doctor was waiting. He directed them to the back where they lifted her off the chair and placed her on a bed with clean white sheets. Olga had gone to Anna's cabin and told her what happened and she arrived a few minutes later, along with the nurse. The doctor said that he had plenty of help and sent Olga and Stefan out the door. All they could do now was to wait.

As Stefan was waiting, he remembered Sophie asking if Kada was all right. He was impressed with Sophie's mother. She had known that the baby would be coming soon and now she was in the doctor's office assisting. The matter that concerned him the most was the fact that his child was being born on the high seas. He did not know where the child could claim citizenship for it might be the country to whom the ship was registered, or it might follow the parent's nationality. As he was sitting there, the first mate opened the door and came in. He had just heard that Kada was having her baby and he wanted to check on her. Stefan told him what had happened and that he was soon to be a father.

While he had him there, he asked, "What country might my child claim citizenship when he is born on the high seas?"

The first mate smiled and answered, "Do not worry. The child will be a citizen of the first port of call, which is Boston, so your child will be a citizen of the United States."

Stefan could not have been happier. His child would be a citizen of the United States of America before his parents. He waited and waited but there was nothing for him to do but to sit there and think. He thought of how his life had progressed so far and he thought of all the assets or good things that had happened. Even his four years in the Army were assets since he learned so much of the world in those four years. Now that it was over, he did not remember all the bad things that had happened to him because those memories had receded into the back of his mind. Stefan was a positive person and this would carry through to the children that followed him. Once in a while, he would hear a muffled scream coming from the inner room and he wanted to go in there to help, but there were already three people in there and besides, he was not allowed. He wished that Olga would come in so that he would at least have someone to talk to.

There was a knock on the door. He got up to open it, but before he got there, a distinguished officer stepped into the room.

He told Stefan, "I am Captain Gustov and I had heard that a woman is giving birth on my ship."

Stefan explained what had happened and said, "I am sorry that the baby was early."

The captain laughed and said, "The birth of a baby on a ship going to America is a joyous event. It means that the newspapers will want to write a story about it and my ship would be mentioned. I am very happy about having a baby born on my ship so if your wife and mother are able before we docked, I want to invite all of you to have dinner at my table as guests of honor. The nurse will take care of the baby while we are eating and your wife could stay in the infirmary with the baby until we dock in Boston. The meals for the rest of the trip, are complimentary."

He shook Stefan's hand and said, "If there is anything that you need, all you have to do is mention it to one of the officers and it will be done. If you have any problems, to come to the bridge and speak to me personally." He left the room smiling.

Stefan left the room to look for Olga and found her in their cabin, lying on her bed.

She said, "I do not want to meddle into the birth of my grandson so I kept out of the way."

Stefan took her hand, "As a member of the family, I am sure that Kada wants you close to her."

They went to the doctor's office and waited and Stefan asked her, "How do you know that it will a boy?"

She just smiled and said, "I just know and that is all that I am going to tell you."

Stefan knew that when his mother spoke in those tones, he should not press the issue. They were all under stress so it would not do any good to question her.

It was now six o'clock and Kada had been in the infirmary for three and a half hours. They had not heard how things were progressing because no one had come in or out and Stefan was worried. He told Olga his concern when the outside door opened and two waiters came in with two tables that were on wheels. They pushed the tables into the room; one table was set for two and the other was set with three place settings. One of the waiters went to a box on the wall, pressed a button and spoke into the box and the nurse appeared to take the table of food into the infirmary. Stefan jumped to ask the nurse how things were going and she assured him that the birth was preceding on schedule and closed the door. Stefan and Olga ate their meal in silence. They each had a slice of beef and pork loaf baked with spices. Along side was a potato baked in its skin and a green vegetable that they did not recognize. It had a cheese sauce on it. There were slices of bread with butter and the same kind of pie that they had before. Also on the cart was a pot of coffee with cream and sugar and Stefan said that he hoped that they did not eat this well in America or they would get fat.

About an hour after the men came to serve the meal, they reappeared to take away the dishes. The waiter went to the box on the wall again and soon the nurse came out pushing the cart. Again Stefan jumped to his feet, but the nurse put her finger up to her lips, smiled and said that everything was going fine. Kada was doing her job and it would take a little more time. Olga thought that if they had all this medical help when she was born, her mother might have lived and she might have had brothers and sisters. She felt secure that Kada was getting the best medical care and she was happy for Stefan, but wished that her husband was alive to see his grandson. He would have been proud, but he was probably watching the scene from up above. She looked up to Heaven and knew he was pleased. She looked at Stefan and he had a frown on his face. She tried to persuade him to get some rest and she would be here to awaken him if there was any activity from the other room.

Stefan pulled up another chair so he could rest his feet, his eyelids became heavy and he fell asleep. He woke up at eleven o'clock and for a second, did not know where he was. He thought that he must be back in the army because he was not in his own bed, but he saw his mother and that seemed to bring him up to date. His mother saw that he was awake and spoke to him.

She said, "I have not heard from anyone in the other room. I have heard of mothers going through eighteen hours of labor and this is usual."

Stefan was still worried. He needed a bath and a shave, but he did not dare leave the room. The door might open any minute with the news. He thought that this would be a good time to pray and he promised God that he would go to church every week for the rest of his life if only the birth went well with Kada and the baby was well and healthy. He promised to raise the child in the Christian faith and not to harm Kada or the children EVER!!! He would be a good father all the days of his life.

At midnight, the cook came into the room with a fresh pot of coffee and some sweet rolls, and asked if there was any word. Stefan felt his temper rise, he had been waiting for the last nine hours and he still did not know what was going on. Everyone asked the same questions and he could not give them an answer. The cook told him that it was now St. Josef's day and when the baby was born, it should be named Josef or Josefine. This was a good omen for the child and it should be named after the Saint on whose day it was born. Stefan said that he would consider it, but he felt that Kada had a name all picked out. He could not believe that he was negotiating the name for his unborn child with a cook on an ocean liner five hundred miles from land. He would have to remember this so he could tell Kada later.

The cook stayed and helped them eat the sweet rolls and drink the coffee. He took the empty tray and pot with him when he left.

Stefan looked at Olga who was nodding off and he pulled a chair over so she could put her feet up. He found a blanket in a closet to cover her while she slept. With nothing else to do, he just stared straight ahead and talked to God because he just wanted this night to be over. He even contemplated opening the door and rushing into the room, but each time he thought of it something held him back. Finally, he just settled back in his chair with his head back and waited— he felt so helpless. He just wished that someone would come out and tell him that everything was all right.

It was almost three o'clock in the morning when he heard a baby crying! He thought, at first, that he had fallen asleep and was dreaming, but he was wide awake and he heard it again. He woke up Olga and told her that something was happening and she listened as the crying came once again. She smiled and said that it was over, his son was born.

The nurse came through the door all covered with perspiration and announced, "You have a son. Your wife has given birth to a healthy boy. Mother and son are doing fine and you should be able to see them as soon as the doctor cleans up the baby. Pani Dubchek is cleaning up your wife so it would be a few minutes more."

Olga asked, "How much did her grandson weigh and how long we he?"

The nurse said, "The baby was nineteen inches long and weighed eleven pounds and six ounces. The reason the birth took so long was that this was a very large baby for such a little woman."

She went back into the infirmary while Stefan embraced his mother, who said, "I am happy to see at least one of my grandchildren before I die."

Stefan said, "Before long, you will be seeing all of your grandchildren and I do not want to hear talk of dying at this time of birth. You should be happy that a new life was brought into the world."

They both sat and waited for the door to open again. The doctor came out with his son a few minutes later to show Stefan and his mother the little boy with the red skin and dark hair. He looked beautiful and when Pani Dubchek came out and took the baby's leg in her hand, she said, "Look at how fat the baby is and how healthy. I have to go check on my own children. I will wager that you have forgotten all about them. They are used to staying alone for long periods of time and they can take care of themselves."

The doctor gave the baby to Olga and told her to go in to see Kada. He took Stefan aside to talk to him. The doctor said, "The baby was so large that I had to cut Kada to get the baby and if that had not worked, then I would have had to do a Caesarian. It was a procedure where I would have had to cut open the abdomen and take the baby out. It was named Caesarian because that was the way Julius Caesar was born. It was a good thing that she was near medical attention or there would have been a problem. This was one birth that needed a doctor and not just a midwife. The next time Kada got pregnant, she should see a doctor as soon as possible. He will control the weight of the mother and baby so the next birth should not be so difficult. The cut needed stitches to close the wound and they will have to come out in a week or so. I will take them out before we dock so she will not have to see a doctor in Boston. When you reached your final destination, she should be checked over."

The baby was healthy, and they decided to name him Stefan Josef Janek. Stefan wanted the boy to have his name while Olga wanted him to be named Josef since he was born on St. Josef's day. She said that it was a good omen to name the boy for the Saint. Stefan surmised that she had been talking with Josef, the cook, because those were the words that he used. Kada was just happy that the ordeal was over and she had a son. The doctor told Stefan that he could occupy one of the other beds since they had no other patients but if someone had to use one of the beds, then he would have to go back to his cabin. At about five in the morning, Stefan fell asleep in the bed next to Kada. He had waited until his son was fed and Kada could sleep also. The nurse had a little crib where the baby was put down to sleep and the Janek family slept until noon on St. Josef's day.

The cook came in at noon with two trays of food. They were both hungry, but they could not finish the amount of food on the trays. When they had eaten all that they could, the captain's voice came over a loud speaker. He talked in English, but Kada and Stefan recognized their names and that of their son, Stefan Josef. When the cook came by to see if they enjoyed the food, Stefan asked him what the captain had said. He told them that the captain announced the birth of Stefan Josef Janek on the ship. The parent's names were Kada and Stefan Janek and they were in the infirmary. He also asked for a Catholic priest to stop by so he could baptize the baby; Stefan had forgotten about having the baby baptized.

They were still discussing it with the cook when a young priest came into the room and the nurse followed him with the baby. He brought in some water and salt and he also had a baptismal paper which he filled out. The cook became the godfather and Pani Dubchek was the godmother. Stefan and Kada would ask their relatives in Cohoes, New York to be godparents, but they needed godparents, on board ship, to act as witnesses. There was a brief ceremony when Pani Dubchek arrived and the priest gave the baptismal certificate to Stefan so he could file it in Boston. This was to insure that the baby would be a citizen of the United States of America. Things could not have gone better.

The next few days flew by rapidly. Some of the passengers sent flowers to celebrate the event and some stopped in to see the baby. Stefan and Kada received all the visitors and thanked them for their concern. The passengers spoke of nothing else for the next few days and the Janek family enjoyed their brief stay in the limelight for they were celebrities on board the "S.S. Mongolia."

On the second day after Stefan Josef was born, the doctor allowed Kada to get out of bed and go for a walk and Pani Dubchek went with them in case anything happened. All the passengers that they met stopped them and congratulated them on the birth of their son. They had been at sea for six days and were due to land in Boston within three days. They were on schedule and should be docking on March 24, but no one in Cohoes knew of the birth of the baby. Stefan would tell them when he saw them because he knew that Marta and Josef would meet them once they docked. The immigration department of their new country would take two days to process them and then they would be on their way to Cohoes, New York.

The baby was now staying with Stefan and Kada full time while the nurse was handling her other duties. There were people coming in for seasickness, cut hands, colds, and various other illnesses; the infirmary was a busy place. On the last night on board the ship, the doctor took Kada's stitches out and pronounced her well enough to leave the ship. The captain had arranged for Olga, Stefan and Kada to have dinner with him and a few guests at his private table in the dining room. He had asked them to come in with the baby at seven o'clock in the evening. From the dinner, they would go to their cabin to pack so that they would be ready to leave the ship in the morning. The captain had assigned the first mate to stay with them to insure that everything went smoothly.

At six-thirty on the day before they reached Boston, the first mate came to the infirmary to escort them to the dining room. They dressed in their finest clothes, although they were not as elegant as some of the clothes that they had seen. They had packed everything that they owned in the infirmary and the first mate had arranged to have it delivered to their cabin. Kada held her son tightly as they walked through the decks toward the dining room at seven o'clock. Kada was nervous. She had never been through anything like this for she was just a peasant wife from a small country town.

The first mate held the door open for them and they entered the well lighted dining room. It seemed that all of the passengers were there and an orchestra, at the far end of the room, started to play music. All of the people in the room stood up and clapped as the four of them wound themselves around the tables. People strained to get a look at the baby and there were a few "ahs" as some people saw the child. The nurse was standing by the captain's table and she took the baby and placed him into the crib next to the table. She stood watch in the event that she was needed. A waiter pulled out a chair for each of them and once they were seated, he placed a cloth napkin across their laps. The people sat and waiters sprang from every corner to start serving the meal. There were twelve people seated at their table and the captain had made sure that everyone spoke Slovak. He did not want his guests to be ill at ease because they did not understand the conversations. The first course was a cup of cut fruit and Stefan watched the first mate and did exactly as he did, while the two women watched Stefan and did exactly as he—they were all learning.

The conversation was lively. Seated at the table was the first mate and a couple from Prague, a man and a woman with their teenaged daughter who said that they came from Bratislava and went to St. Martin's cathedral for Mass every week. There were two other couples who lived in America. They were returning from a visit with relatives and they seemed to know some of the other people at the table. They were born in America, were living in New York City and were very well dressed. The men had formal wear while the women had floor length gowns. They apparently had a great deal of money and Stefan vowed that someday his children would have money and live like these people.

The waiter took the empty fruit cups away and brought a salad of lettuce, tomatoes, onions with a white sweet dressing. It had been a long time since they ate raw vegetables and they enjoyed the salad. They did not know which forks to use and waited until someone else started to eat. The waiter brought a basket covered with a cloth and inside were small round warm rolls. He placed a dish of yellow butter on each end of the table. They ate butter in Ruzbachy, but it was more white than yellow. They must put something in it to perserve it, thought Stefan. Everyone took a roll and placed it on a dish in front of them. The dish was smaller than the dinner plate and it had a knife on it that was broad and very dull. The people took some butter on the knife and placed it on their dish. They put butter on the roll, took a bite and then put the roll back on the little dish. When Stefan took a bite, he did not put the food down, but he finished it. Once the salad was finished, the waiter again took the dish away. Kada bent over and whispered to Stefan that they use quite a few dishes and she would hate to be the one who washed all of them.

The waiters came out of the kitchen carrying two bottles of wine each. They filled the glasses at the head table first and then filled every glass in the room. When they were filled, the captain stood up and said that he wanted to propose a toast. Everyone stood up and the first mate motioned for the Janeks to stay seated. The captain raised his glass and everyone in the room did the same.

The captain said in a loud voice, "May God grant this family a happy and prosperous life in their adopted country for it is people like this who will make America strong. They are willing to take chances to have a better life for themselves and their children and may God be kind to you and grant you all your wishes and desires."

Stefan looked up and everyone was raising their glasses toward them and saying, "Here, here."

Stefan felt goose bumps forming on his arms and Olga and Kada were close to tears. They sat there for a few moments and the first mate motioned for Stefan to get up and say something.

Stefan rose as everyone else sat. He looked over the sea of faces and the only words that came to him were "Pombok Zaplotz" (God thanks you).

Everyone clapped and Stefan sat and the waiters came out with the main course. They worked in pairs as one carried a pan and the other served prime rib beef with tongs. The waiter placed a huge piece of meat on their plates and other waiters came by with small red baked potatoes, green and yellow vegetables and something in a red sauce. They asked for a little of each. Stefan figured that the food must be different in America and they would have to get used to it eventually, so they might as well get started now. Also, on the table was a deep dish with a white sauce in it. Everyone spooned a small amount on their plate, cut a piece of meat and dipped it in the sauce and put it in their mouth. Olga tried it first and her eyes lit up and she quickly took a sip of the wine. Kada tried it next and she liked it. Stefan dipped his meat into the sauce and put it into his mouth but tears came to his eyes. It was made from fresh ground horseradish which none of them had ever heard of. It was hot, and they did not put much on the meat the second time around. No one noticed this except the first mate, who just smiled.

The potatoes were cut into little pieces and butter was put on them to melt. The Janeks did not put spices on their food but when Kada or Olga cooked, they put a small amount of salt and ground black pepper for seasoning. The spices cost money and they used them sparingly so they used no spices on their food once it got to the table. The people at the table were liberal with the salt and pepper, but the guests of honor did not use any. The people talked freely while they ate and one of the couples from New York was explaining how the city was laid out. It was the largest city in America and had, what they called "boroughs" which were smaller cities within the large city. They lived in the borough of Queens which, according to them, was the best.

The captain spoke up and said, "The nicest place to live was the one that you are living in at the time." Everyone agreed with the captain, mainly because he was the captain.

When the main course was finished and the dishes taken away, the lights dimmed and the waiters came out of the kitchen with a tray of flaming food over their heads. They wound around the tables in a long line and everyone clapped. The lights went on and they saw that it was a flaming cake. It was cut into the same size pieces and each person got a piece on a small dish, since there was only one fork left, they knew which one that they had to use. Stefan wanted to know what it was, but he did not want to appear ignorant so he did not ask. He looked at the first mate who saw the question in his eyes and he asked Stefan how he liked the "baked Alaska?" Stefan said it was good, but the question was still in his eyes. The first mate then told him that it was very difficult to make it on board ship because it was difficult to perserve the cream and make it cold enough to freeze. The brandy on top also had to be special because all brandies do not flame up as this one did. The questions disappeared from Stefan's eyes and he nodded a thank you to the first mate.

The waiters next came out with coffee and chocolate mints and everyone lingered over the coffee and talked. There was no activity in the lounge that evening because everyone was expected to go to their cabins and pack for the disembarkment the next morning. Stefan was really full. He felt like he would not have to eat for at least three days. Kada was another story, she would eat everything that was put before her and maybe some more. She was tiny, but she loved to eat and before she reached old age in America, she would be double her size.

The following morning, the four Janeks came on deck to watch the ship dock. It would be another two hours before docking so they watched the landscape slide by. They passed the most easterly point of Cape Cod and saw the settlement of Provincetown. There was a couple who were familiar with the area and they were explaining the various landmarks to some newcomers. The area of Cape Cod was a summer tourist area and it did not appear to be many people there at this time of year. The couple pointed out Plymouth rock where the settlers from England landed in November of 1620, a little over three hundred years before. The winds and the rains have reduced the size of the rock, for when the pilgrims arrived, it was much larger. Two small tug boats came out to meet the ship and to guide it into the pier. By now there were many people on the deck and the crew was running from one place to another. Stefan thought that there must be a better method of using the crew to avoid this mass confusion. Everyone seemed to be in the wrong place and they had to hurry to get into the right place. He could not understand why they could not start in the right place in the beginning.

The ship finally came to the correct pier. A crowd of people waited to meet the passengers. Stefan looked out to see the city. Instead, he saw some large buildings and rows of black cars and trucks; he had never seen so many cars and trucks in one place at one time. Before the gang plank was in place they all tried to see Marta and Josef, but with the crowd of people, they could not pick them out. The cargo doors opened as soon as the huge ropes were fastened to the pier and luggage and other cargo was being passed out on a long silver slide. Men, on the pier were catching the material and placing it to one side. There were heavy cranes there, but they would not be put to use until the passengers had left. Kada was holding Joe, as he was now called, very tightly. His name had been Americanized by the captain and the crew so they could follow the customs of the new land.

A message came over the loud speaker summoning the Janeks to the bridge. They left the deck and made the climb up the stairwells to the bridge. The captain was there with his first mate and they said their good-byes.

The captain told them, "Since Joe was born on the ship, you will have to have a special clearing process before you will be allowed to enter the country. You will all have to be examined by a doctor but this is routine and you will have to subject Kada and Joe to more medical tests since there was reason to believe that Joe was born early and that would take an additional day."

He asked, "Who is meeting you at the pier?"

Stefan said, "My brother and sister."

"The immigration department will try to find them and tell them of the delay. Go back to the gang plank and there will be an agent from the American Immigration Department there to meet you and escort you off the ship first. All crippled and older people will be let off the ship before the crowd comes pushing down the gang plank."

Stefan went to their cabin to get their luggage with Olga. One of the crew members was there to help them carry it off. They really needed him as they had three more bundles than they had when they boarded the ship in Hamburg. People had stopped by the infirmary and dropped off little gifts such as little cups, spoons, clothes, toys and bonnets. Stefan hoped that he could afford to be as generous as these Americans were when he had been in his new country for a while. Kada went back to the deck, but she realized that she would not be able to recognize Josef and Marta even if she saw them. She had only seen them a few times and they were much younger then. Josef left Ruzbachy when he was seventeen and he was now close to thirty years old. Marta was thirteen when she left with Josef and she was now twenty-four. She stopped looking for them and began following the events going on around her.

The docking crew had the gang plank secured in a very short time and a man in a business suit came up the gang plank. He spoke to the officer on board. The man had a clipboard and was looking for someone. Stefan, Olga and their helper arrived at the gangplank just as the man saw Kada standing there, holding Joe. He went to her and asked where the rest of her relatives were and Stefan spoke up and said that his brother and sister were to meet them. He gave them their names. The man introduced himself and escorted them down the gang plank until they finally stepped off the ship. They were finally in America.

20

Once they were on land, the agent took them to a large building. One end of the building was open with desks arranged around the outside wall of the room. Next to each desk was a small enclosure that had curtains which could be pulled on each side so that one could insure privacy. This was the area that the doctors used to examine people that the interrogator suspected of having an illness of any kind. It would take two days for the immigration people to process all of the people who were on board the ship and most of them were allowed to enter the country. Some would be rejected and sent back to their country of origin.

Stefan, Kada and Olga were asked to be seated in front of one of the desks. A man, who spoke Slovak, asked them many questions.

"Do you have work waiting for you? Do you have relatives in the country? How much money do you have?"

He did not ask them anything about their health since they would be examined by a doctor at a later time.

Stefan answered his questions and wondered what would come next. The man went on, "Since your son was born on the high seas, he will be examined by a doctor that specializes in babies and he will decide if you are allowed to stay in the country. The examination would be conducted after everyone else has been processed and has left the area."

Another man led them through a door that contained a long hall where they went through a door half way down. The door led into a room that had three beds, a dresser and no windows. They were told to wait for the doctor to arrive. It will be between one and three days, depending on how busy he was. They were shown where the toilet was and where they could wash. Someone would bring them food and they were told that they could leave the room but the doors on the ends of the hall were locked. At five o'clock in the afternoon, a knock came at the door and Stefan opened it to find a small cart filled with trays of food. The man gave him three trays of food, coffee and milk. He said that he would pick up the empty trays later. Their first night in America was spent in a small room, with locked doors.

Olga said, "We might as well be in jail."

The next morning, they woke to another knock on their door, and more food was delivered. They took turns going to the washroom and Kada was the last to go because she had to stay and feed Joe. When she did manage to go, there was a long line. As she came out of the washroom, she smelled food cooking and it smelled good. The smell was coming from a door, down the hall, opposite the door that they used when they came in. Kada went to the door, for a better smell, pushed against it and, to her surprise, the door opened. She looked around and not seeing anyone, she stepped outside to smell the delicious odor of cooking food when a gust of wind came and slammed the door shut. She tried to open it but it locked when it slammed shut and she found herself outside, not knowing the language and not knowing how to get back in. She was on a sidewalk, on what looked like a main street. The sidewalk came up against the brick building that looked like a solid brick wall with one doorway to break the line of the wall. She felt that the best way to solve her problem was to walk around the building and find another entrance.

Kada walked to the corner of the building and found that the building was not square. There was another building attached to this one and it looked exactly the same as the first one. There were windows, but they were frosted so no one could look inside. She walked around the second building only to find a third and now, she was losing her sense of direction. Looking across the street, she saw a store with the door open and that was where the smell was coming from. The smell was from frying bacon or sausage and there were people sitting at tables eating the food. Although she had just eaten, the smell made her hungry but she had no money to buy anything, anyway. She thought, how fortunate she was, that she had just fed Joe before she went to the washroom. She was now lost in the city and, as she walked along, she saw stores that baked bread and stores that sold meat and vegetables. She forgot that she was lost, and just walked up and down the streets looking at all the food, clothes, shoes, tools and everything imaginable. This was truly paradise for she had never seen anything like this before.

She spent hours roaming the streets looking for the front end of the building. Olga and Stefan must be worried, she thought, but there was no way to talk to anyone, even if she wanted to. She stopped a few people but they just shrugged their shoulders and walked on. She was now getting hungry, as it was three o'clock in the afternoon and Joe had not eaten for over seven hours. She had heard that Americans were a rough people, especially in the cities, but no one tried to harm her. It was getting dusk, when a uniformed policeman stopped her and spoke in English, but she could not understand him. She pointed to herself and said "Slovak."

The policeman nodded his head and guided her along the sidewalk until they came to a building marked "Police Station." She recognized the word "Police" and went in with him as she realized that she needed help.

The policeman motioned for her to sit while he went to another part of the building and returned a few minutes later with another policeman who spoke to Kada in Polish. A look of relief crossed her face and she started to talk in a steady stream until he told her to slow down. She explained her problem and he said that he would take her back to the immigration department. He told her not to worry as this happens all the time and he would straighten it out. He led her out the door and walked the way that she had come. They walked by the store that had the wonderful smell and she stopped to look in and the officer, realizing that she was hungry, took her in. He had a cup of coffee and made her eat some fried chicken, mashed potatoes, gravy, corn and white bread with butter. He also got her a large glass of milk when she told him about Joe. She told him that she had no money but he smiled and told her that the department would pay for it. He said, "welcome to America"

*   *   *

Stefan and Olga waited for about an hour for Kada to return and when she did not come, Stefan went to the washroom to look for her. He went to the door to the outside but that was locked so he thought that she must have gone to the wrong room as they all looked alike. He tried all the doors but they were locked and when there was no answer from beyond the doors, he went to the door through which they arrived and knocked on that. He stood there and knocked on the door for a full fifteen minutes before someone opened it and he told the man that he wanted to speak to someone who spoke Slovak. He knew a little English from the days in the prison camp but this was too important to trust to his limited knowledge of the language. When the man came, he explained his problem and they walked around the large hall to see if Kada was there. It did not take long since three-quarters of the people were processed and had left the building or were rejected and were in the area where Stefan and his family were housed. The man could not understand how she could have gotten out and wondered if she were abducted and was being held in one of the rooms

When it came time to deliver lunch, Stefan went with the man and entered each room but Kada was not found. He was worried and someone called the hospital and the police, but they knew nothing. Stefan went back to his room to wait while he and Olga prayed that Kada would be found and not harmed in any way. Joe had not eaten since that morning and he was starting to get impatient. If Kada was not found by supper, he would ask the man for food for him. The man came by to deliver the food at five o'clock and Stefan asked if he could help. An hour later, he came back with a bottle of milk that had a nipple on the end. He showed

Olga how to use it and how to "burp" the baby afterward. That seemed to solve that problem, but Kada was still missing.

*   *   *

Darkness fell on the City of Boston and still they had no news about Kada. At seven o'clock, they heard a knock on the door and Stefan, expecting the worst, opened it to find a red faced Kada with an embarrassed grin on her face. He rushed out to hug her, while Olga just broke down in tears. Stefan was so happy to see her, alive and well, that he did not ask her where she had been. She could tell him later, for tears of joy were streaming down his cheeks. He said that he had feared that he had lost her. Kada went to Olga, hugged her and then picked up Joe for, with her long absence, she knew that he must be hungry. Stefan showed her the bottle which had only a half of an inch of milk left the bottom. He had drunk the rest of it and burped up all the air so he was content to just stay where he was and sleep. The tray of food was still there but she was not hungry, she was just happy to be with her family.

Kada spent the night telling her husband and mother-in-law about her adventure. She said, "Boston is such a large city, with large buildings that all look alike and I became confused. There are shops and stores everywhere, full of food, clothing and other things. There was not a shortage of anything and you could get all that you wanted. Since people were buying, they must be making money. I met a policeman who took me to the station, where another spoke Polish and he brought me back. We even stopped at a store that sold food and he bought me supper. He said that the city would pay for it and welcome to America. America is truly a great country and I am happy that we came."

The next morning, after the meal, a doctor came into the room. He sent Stefan and Olga out of the room to wait in the hall while he examined Kada and the baby. He then sent Kada out of the room while he examined Olga. Stefan was the last to be examined. When he finished, he told them to pack their belongings; they were going to leave the hospitality of the United States Government. They were to go into the great room and wait for someone to talk to them.

As they were sitting on a long bench, a man at a desk motioned for them to come to him. Stefan looked up to see two people standing in a doorway. He recognized his brother Josef whom he had not seen in all these years. The small woman standing next to him must be his sister, Marta. The couple saw them at the same time and ran across the room. There were many tears and Marta took the baby away from his mother so she could look at it closely. No one remembered what was said that day when the family met but it was Olga, with tears in her eyes who said between sobs, "Children we are finally home and together again."

"Welcome to the United States of America," Josef exclaimed.

The entire Janek family was together again.

BVG